Mi ... c, columnist,
jok ... f *Come Dine
Wi* ...

... ewine, shopping
for ... and having her hair
do ... and sandpaper. Her
no ... ...riendship, family, betrayal,
bab ... little bit of that magic in life that
sor ... ...suspecting.

... is her ninth book.

... e at www.millyjohnson.com or follow her on
tw ... ...yjohnson.

It's Raining Men

milly johnson

**SIMON &
SCHUSTER**

London · New York · Sydney · Toronto · New Delhi

A CBS COMPANY

First published by Simon & Schuster UK Ltd 2013
A CBS COMPANY

Copyright © Millytheink Ltd., 2013

5 7 9 10 8 6

Simon & Schuster UK Ltd
1st Floor
222 Gray's Inn Road
London WC1X 8HB

www.simonandschuster.co.uk

Simon & Schuster Australia, Sydney
Simon & Schuster India, New Delhi

A CIP catalogue record for this book
is available from the British Library

Australia TPB ISBN: 978-1-47111-460-1
PB ISBN: 978-1-47111-461-8
EBOOK ISBN: 978-1-47111-462-5

Typeset by M Rules
Printed and bound by CPI Group (UK) Ltd, Croydon, CR0 4YY

As this book has the fortune to be officially launched on Yorkshire Day, I just have to dedicate it to all the wonderful lovely kind friends I have in God's Own County. Too many to name, but I hope you know who are you (blows kiss).

It's
Raining Men

Into each life some rain must fall.

HENRY WADSWORTH LONGFELLOW

May

Chapter 1

Lara Rickman took a large gulp of coffee and then swallowed hard and fast before she could spit it out. It was as cold as a tub of ice cream in a polar bear's freezer. How had it cooled so quickly? Surely her PA had only just brought it in for her and the first sip had been piping hot. She checked the clock in the corner of her monitor to find that, in fact, an hour had gone by – sped by at warp speed, as the hours seemed to these days. And not just hours, but days and weeks and months. Had she really been seeing her darling James for three whole months? Had it really been five months since she'd been up to Yorkshire to see her parents, arriving late Christmas Eve, driving back to London early Boxing Day morning on what could only be described as a whistle-stop trip? Had it been nearly two months since she'd last spent proper face-to-face time with her work friends May and Clare? Even then it had been only for a rushed sandwich in the staff restaurant when their three schedules made a rare crossover, like planets happening to align. They'd eaten so fast it was a wonder that the Benny Hill theme tune hadn't been playing in the background.

Even though they had all worked for the same company for years, Lara, May and Clare had not met before they gravitated towards each other at a conference a year and a half ago, after ending up in the same discussion group. But then again, Cole and Craw Finance was a massive organization which employed over three thousand people and operated from four adjacent buildings in the City; still in the process of being united into one. The three women were amazed to find that they were all from Yorkshire – Clare from York, May from Leeds and Lara from Barnsley – had all been involved with setting up or trying to rescue businesses, and were all born within six months of each other. Enough common ground to kick-start a fledgling friendship between them. They arranged to meet for lunch occasionally when their busy diaries allowed it. All three of them were hard-working and driven career women, who hadn't had close female friendships for years. In each other they found a little of what they had been missing.

Lara was in charge of rescuing ailing businesses or sending them to the brokers' yard. May was a business advisor who helped set up new companies from scratch and Clare was an accountant for the subsidiary firm Blackwoods and Margoyles, which benefited from being part of the Cole and Craw group yet had an independent set of ruling partners. Blackwoods and Margoyles were renowned experts at trying to turn around businesses teetering on the edge of bankruptcy – the last-chance saloon.

At their last sandwich-sharing, the topic of holidays had arisen and all of them confessed they hadn't had a proper break for years. So they made a mad and impulsive decision to book time off together and escape to a spa. And there and then, they'd whipped out their diaries, blocked in the time and Lara had volunteered to find them somewhere wonderful, luxurious, relaxing and indulgently expensive. To her shame, she still hadn't booked it. She had been too busy with either work or her new mad passionate relationship, which was also speeding along at a rate of knots. She was moving in with James that coming week-end. She realized that was fast, but he had been so seductively keen to rush things to the next stage that she hadn't resisted.

She clapped her hands together. She had ten minutes until she went into her next meeting with a trio of ancient accountants; it promised to be an afternoon of total and utter boredom. Lara had lost her work mojo. She was very good at what she did, in fact too good, and promotion after promotion had elevated her into a career of meetings, conferences and supervising other people doing the nitty-gritty parts of the job that she loved to do herself. Lara was fabulously well-paid for what she did, but she was extremely fed up and overworked.

She checked her make-up in the small magnified mirror she kept in her drawer and wished she hadn't. Her make-up was fine but the face underneath it looked tired, her once bright hazel eyes were dull with no hint of a sparkle. Oh boy, did she need a holiday. She gave her short blonde wavy hair a primp with her fingers – it didn't obey combs, never had – and put the mirror away.

She pulled up Google on her screen, whilst taking her Visa card out of her purse, then in the search bar she typed *Superior Cottages*, praying that they still had vacancies. She knew the exact place she wanted to book – she'd seen it recommended in the *Escape From It All* section of a glossy mag she'd read on the train weeks ago. Before the meeting with the Three Stooges she would book the holiday.

First hurdle: the site was down. But at least there was a message informing any would-be customers that one of their operators would be happy to handle their query over the phone. Lara rang the booking line. As luck would have it, a Miss Becky Whiteley answered.

'Superior Cottages,' Becky drawled in her automaton greeting. 'Becky Whiteley speaking. How may I help you?'

'I want to book a cottage but your website appears to be down,' said Lara.

'Yeah, we're having problems at the moment,' said Becky. 'Sorry about that. Can I take your name, please?'

'Lara. Lara Rickman.'

'And which of our cottages were you interested in booking and when?'

'Wren Cottage in Wellem, from August the tenth to August the twentieth.' A beautiful olde worlde log cabin in the grounds of a manor house which had been converted into a spa and advertised every sort of massage under the sun – foot, neck, elbow, Swedish, Thai, Turkish, Bognor Regian, bamboo, hot stone, salt scrubs, hopi candles, being slapped on the back with a cold salmon . . . This place did everything. It had an inside swimming pool the size of Wales, bubbling Jacuzzis, a Michelin-starred restaurant. It was heaven on earth if the hype was to be believed.

It was going to cost them a bomb but they'd all done well for themselves and had earned nice impressive job titles and financial packages to match. They deserved a bit of pamper time. Ten glorious wonderful days of it, to be exact.

'And please include the luxury welcome hamper,' requested Lara. 'It's one hundred and fifty pounds, I do believe.'

Becky's concentration levels were middling at the best of times but today – her very last day in this shitty Watford-based holiday agency – they were at rock bottom. She pressed the wrong key and lost the screen. She frantically stabbed at a few more keys, which only made the situation worse and so she reached for a pen and her reporter's notepad to take down details which she would type up after the call had finished. Visa number, email, address, contact telephone number, holiday dates.

'Yep, I'll get this confirmed for you and email you the details,' she said after Lara had supplied her with all the info. 'Thank you for calling Superior Cottages,' she added and cut off the call.

Becky pulled up the booking screen again. Bugger – what was the name of the bloody cottage? She hadn't written it down but merely committed it to memory, which was a bad mistake as all her thought space was taken up with things Greek. Ren something? She typed the three letters into the search box, and bingo. Well Cottage, Ren Dullem. That was it – she remembered the 'well' bit now too. Thank God for that. She processed the payment whilst thinking how blinking expensive it was. Some people really did have more money than sense. She couldn't find anything about any luxury hamper so she typed the request into the box labelled 'Message for cottage owner': *Luxury £150 hamper needed on arrival*. Job done. She rewarded herself with a drawn-out coffee break and a Twix from the machine.

She would have been flattered to realize that Miss Rickman, who was pressed for time, trusted her efficiency enough to assume the booking was all correct and didn't bother to give the confirmation email more than a passing glance at the dates before saving it to a folder on her smartphone.

Chapter 2

As Clare sat drinking coffee in a French café in St Pancras, she subtly eavesdropped on the conversation taking place beside her between a pretty young blonde woman, and her boyfriend, a man in the mould of Russell Brand – wild hair, trendy facial hair growth, tight skinny trousers, long tapered leather shoes and black leather waistcoat – oozing cockiness and charm in equal measures.

'Mum's at home all weekend,' the girl was saying. 'So that rules out you coming to mine.'

The boy shrugged. 'Looks like my back seat is going to see some action again, then.'

'Ooh, yeah. I'm liking the sound of that.'

'I'll drive you somewhere dark and isolated and then make you scream your head off.'

The girl giggled. 'I liked it when you did that thing with your ...' She turned to the side to check she wasn't being overheard, spotted Clare looking in her direction and then, maddeningly, lowered her voice. Whatever 'that thing' he did to her was, it certainly must have hit the spot. Clare tried not to watch them as they started snogging but her eyes kept wandering over in their direction. The boy wasn't her type at all but there was something dangerous and sexy about him. Clare had never had sex in a car, and had never had a boyfriend who suggested it, either. She had a sudden yearning to drag Ludwig off in his plush Audi and shag him on the moors. She grinned to herself thinking how horrified he would be if she did. They had never had sex out of bed. They had never had rip-your-clothes-off passion *in* bed either, come to think of it. Lud was a love-maker: slow and gentle, considerate and satisfying. But recently, she had been thinking that just once in a while, it might be nice to be grabbed and seduced on the staircase, or ravaged in the back seat of a car. It was the sort of thing she imagined her friend Lara got up to. Lara was spirited and curvy, like a short modern-day Marilyn Monroe, and she had the most drop-dead gorgeous partner who was an up-and-coming big noise in the City. And it was no secret that that type of man had a passionate sex-drive and a wild side.

Clare had met Lara eighteen months ago at a work conference and had immediately liked the sassy, small blonde who'd been wearing the red shade of lipstick she wished she was brave enough to sport. They appeared to be the shortest people in the room, which was the initial ice-breaker. They then found themselves in the same discussion group, along with a tall, slim woman with beautiful long brown hair and large brown doe eyes who looked totally uncomfortable in the crowds of people forming themselves into huddles. She introduced herself to them as May Earnshaw

'That's a good Yorkshire surname,' said Lara. 'I'm from Barnsley.'

'I'm from just outside Leeds,' replied May.

'I'm from York,' Clare had added to the mix. And a friendship was born.

Clare felt a kiss on her cheek from someone behind her.

'Sorry I'm late,' said Ludwig, squeezing her shoulder before taking the seat opposite. He stripped off his smart black Crombie to reveal a drop-dead gorgeous dark-grey suit. He was always so beautifully dressed. The first time she had ever seen him in a suit, three years ago at her birthday party, he had taken her breath away. They had kissed then and been together as a couple ever since.

'Espresso, please,' he said, waving at the approaching waiter. 'Would you like another coffee, darling?'

'Yes, please. Cappuccino.'

'And a cappuccino, please,' he added to his order, his German accent still thickly present although he had lived in England since he was ten years old.

Clare looked over at her solid, reliable Ludwig and tried to imagine him bonking her in a car. She couldn't. She wondered what he would say were she to suggest it. Knowing Ludwig, he would give it a go for her sake, whatever he thought about it.

'You look happy,' Clare said with a smile.

'I am. I've just acquired a very important client,' Ludwig replied, reaching over the table and taking her small hand in his large square one.

'Ah.' Clare wasn't surprised to hear the thrill was work-related.

'Yes, very exciting.' He beamed, pushing his glasses in their thick black frames back up his nose. With those and the flop of hair over his eyes he looked just like Clark Kent when Christopher Reeve played him.

'Lovely,' said Clare and sighed as Lud's phone went off and he picked it up and pressed it to his ear. She transferred her attention to the menu and wished that Lud would rip it out of her hands, seize her arm and pull her passionately towards him. Recently he hadn't given her half as much attention as he had his bloody BlackBerry. Luckily, this time it was a short call.

'Would you like to eat here, my love?' he asked, putting the phone down on the table in front of him. Once upon a time he would have turned it off and put it out of sight.

'Here is fine.' Clare was too tired to go looking for anywhere else and it was convenient as Lud was catching the train to

Brussels in two hours. He was an investment banker, a genius whizz-kid who had flown to the top of his career tree. He was constantly being head-hunted by firms aching to recruit him. He was addicted to work and his ear was constantly attached to his phone, but he was a dear man and she loved him. He was kind, funny, generous ... but lately she had been wondering whether Ludwig Wolke was *the one*. Ever since going to see a stage production of *Wuthering Heights* two months ago she had been having racy dreams about bedding a wild man on some heather-cushioned moors. Heathcliff had stirred her all up inside and made her yearn for something outside her comfort zone – and someone who would make her the epicentre of his world. There were three of them in this relationship – him, her and his sodding mobile.

'Oh, I bought you something,' said Ludwig, suddenly remembering. He reached behind him into his coat pocket. 'It's to keep you company while I'm away.'

He handed over a bag. Grinning, Clare peered inside.

'Paul's chocolate macaroons!' she yelped with delight. He knew they were her favourites. 'I promise not to eat them all at once.'

Lud smiled. 'If you want to eat them all at once, you go ahead and just do it.'

'I'll get fat and you'll leave me.'

'I would never leave you,' said Lud, picking up the menu. 'Not unless you wanted me to. Now, pick something to eat. I want to have enough time for dessert.'

Lovely, kind Lud, thought Clare. Then his BlackBerry went off and she was forgotten as he was plunged, yet again, into his demanding world of high finance.

Chapter 3

May grated cheese on top of the bacon, which was on top of the barbecue sauce on top of the chicken breast. Hunter's Chicken – Michael loved it and she so wanted to pamper him because he was very depressed at the moment.

It was a recipe emailed over by her friend Clare. It was impossible to think of Clare without smiling: The Domestic Accountant. Clare was so clever with numbers but to look at her, one would never have put her in that profession. She was an earth goddess: petite with a large bust, a Cleopatra black bob and strangely coloured eyes that lit up when she started talking about Dyson's latest innovation or her new vegetable steamer. She was so funny. May felt as if she had known her for much longer than the eighteen months they'd been friends. Same with Lara, whom she had met on the same day at a conference at work. Lara had messy short naturally golden hair, wore bright red lipstick and was ballsy with a presence far bigger than her height of five foot two. Really it should have been Lara who was five foot ten and May eight inches shorter. May hated being so tall and conspicuous. She would have been much more comfortable being small and easily hidden away.

Michael was on his way to her from The Pines. She ached to throw her arms around him and let him rest his head on her shoulder. She would give him a long oily massage tonight and soothe away his worries, she decided as she lifted the tray into the oven and then started piping out some whirls of potatoes. Also a favourite.

She wiped a tear from her eye before it rolled down her cheek. She wished she had someone to talk to about the situation, other than Michael of course. As nice as Lara and Clare were, she hadn't quite told them the truth about her boyfriend of six months. Yes, they knew that she was seeing a man occasionally but she had intimated that it was only a casual affair and had underplayed her feelings for him. Her friends didn't know that she was madly in love with him or that he stayed over much more often than she had said. Or that he was married. They surely wouldn't have approved. They hadn't talked at any length or depth about their lives but from the little that May did know, Lara's ex-husband had been carrying on with his first wife behind her back and Clare's sister's first husband had been sleeping with every girl in Sheffield except the one he was married to. May didn't approve of her behaviour herself, although it wasn't exactly a straightforward case of wife versus scarlet woman.

Michael arrived in record time. He strode in through the door and straight over to May, his arms open wide to enclose her. May was taller than him but had mastered 'a bend' when they hugged so that as they embraced his lips were on a level with her forehead, making her feel a little more girly and enfolded. She savoured his lovely manly smell and the warmth of his body and didn't mind that his coat was sopping wet.

'Hello, my love,' he grinned. 'God, am I happy to see you.'

'Likewise,' May said and smiled.

'It feels like three weeks since I saw you, not three days.' He traced the back of his finger down her left cheek, tenderly following the line of the scar that had faded to a dull silver over the years but, to May, was still as glaringly deep, garish and

obvious as the day twenty-two years ago when the neighbour
dog had clamped its teeth onto her cheek.

'I know,' said May. She wished she could see him ever
single night. She wished he would come from his stationery
salesman job straight to her house without having to do
detour to The Pines. But he could only do that when Susa
had passed away – and May didn't want to think about tha
however much she wanted her lover to be hers and hers alone

'How is she?' asked May, pulling off Michael's damp coat an
hanging it over the door near the radiator to dry off.

'Same old, same old.' He sighed. 'Have you any wine, m
love?'

'Yes, yes, of course.' May scurried over to the rack and pulle
out a bottle of Shiraz, uncorking it as she crossed the kitchen t
the cupboard where the glasses were stored. She poured ou
only one glass, for Michael. She thought that if she had an
wine this evening, the floodgates might open in her eyes. Sh
felt exhausted – physically and emotionally. She should hav
ordered a takeaway instead of attempting all this home-cookin
after work.

'It's so bloody sad,' said Michael, taking a long gulp an
savouring the spicy hit on the back of his throat. 'She's just
shell of her former self. There's nothing left of Susan any more
And yet, physically, she keeps going. She seems to get stronge
in body as she gets weaker in her head. There's the cruel iron
of it all.'

As May put her arms around him, she was weighed dow
with guilt that she could be feeling so sorry for herself when
Michael was worn into the ground with the torture of havin
a wife struck down with dementia in her thirties. Michael car
ried a pre-wedding photograph of them in his wallet. His hai
was thicker and longer then, without any grey streaks. He like
to keep it very short now. And he was plumper in the face, hi
cheeks round and pink as he smiled into the lens. Snuggled u

under his arm Susan was pretty, with cropped red hair that suited her heart-shaped face, and a turned-up pixie nose. In that photo they had everything to look forward to; there was not a hint of what was to hit them.

'Take a seat,' said May, and after he did so she started to knead her thumbs into his shoulders. She heard him sigh and she smiled. Tonight was all about him. She would pull out all the stops to make sure that her house was a little taste of heaven for him after the hell of seeing his poor, deteriorating wife at The Pines.

Chapter 4

As Gladys Coffey showed the slim, dark-haired woman into the lounge, her calm and friendly smile belied all the activity going on in her brain. Gladys might have had the title 'Housekeeper' but she was so much more than that: protector, guard dog and, if it came to it, bouncer. Her brain was fast-screening the woman in the plain black suit for any signs of artifice, any hidden agenda. She could usually sniff out an interloper at one hundred paces, but, for once, her radar was circling smoothly without encountering the slightest blip.

'Please sit down, Mrs Hawk,' said Gladys. 'Can I get you a cup of tea?'

'Thank you, but don't go to any trouble on my account. I'm fine.'

Joan Hawk smiled and Gladys saw how generous and full her lips were. Coupled with those nice dark-brown eyes and sharp cheekbones, they meant Mrs Hawk would be a very attractive woman if she applied some make-up and unloosened her long hair from that tight, frumpy ponytail. Luckily Mrs Hawk seemed as far removed from her predatory namesake as could possibly be, if this introduction to her was any guide. She was as dull as a beige bungalow. Absolutely perfect. Lord Edwin Carlton was a very rich old man and was getting more doddery by the day. And he was lonely. Gladys didn't want him falling prey to a flattering line of banter and a pretty face.

'Lord Carlton will be with you shortly,' said Gladys as she left the room. She could tell him to go in now that Mrs Hawk had passed the first stage of the interview – i.e. she had got past Gladys.

As the door closed behind the housekeeper, Joan Hawk looked around her at the opulent lounge with its plush sofas and huge picture windows framing a view of the sea in the distance. It was beautiful here; she had a good feeling about the place. It was what just she, a poor impoverished young widow, needed: solitude, space and in such a splendid setting. She looked up at the portraits on the wall. Mostly they were of old men in powdered wigs, their faces preserved in oil. But taking centre stage, above the great fireplace, was a stunning depiction of a woman in a navy-blue dress. A woman with long dark hair, brown eyes and full red lips. A woman with shapely legs, full breasts and a tiny nipped-in waist. She was the woman Joan could so easily be with a little powder and paint and the right clothes.

Joan had seen the advertisement for a clerical assistant in *The Countess* and couldn't get on the Internet fast enough to look up more details. She could hardly believe her luck: Carlton Hall was huge and inhabited by one solitary old man with no heir. Joan could smell the rich pickings from a mile away. Not only would there be treasures around the house to palm but the possibility of becoming Lady Carlton was in the bag if she played her cards right – and play them right she would because lonely, rich, older men were her speciality.

Joan did her homework thoroughly. There were hardly any details about the immediate area but the nearest towns, Wellem and Whitby, had lots of information about them. Joan decided that she would say she came from Wellem, presuming, quite rightly, that it might be advantageous to say she was a fairly local girl. These old village types were more likely to trust someone who came from the area.

Her thoughts were interrupted by the door swinging open and in walked a slight, wiry man. Joan knew he was seventy but he looked much older, his back stooping with age, his ghost-white hair as thin as gossamer at the sides but much thicker on top, thanks to an obvious toupee. He was dressed immaculately in a brown suit, with a folded blue handkerchief in his top pocket and a matching cravat at his neck. Lord Edwin Carlton himself.

'Good morning, good morning,' he said with a surprisingly strong voice for someone who looked as if a breath of wind might be able to lift him off his feet. 'Delighted to meet you, Mrs Hawk.' He extended a small, soft hand.

'Joan, please,' she said, standing to shake it. Her firm grip echoed his.

'Well, delighted to meet you, Joan,' he said, and as he sat down he trilled a little laugh that told Joan Hawk he instantly felt at ease in her company. 'Do sit down. Would you like some tea or coffee?'

Joan saw his pupils dilate ever so slightly as his eyes rested fully on her. She was very good at spotting such things.

'Your housekeeper very kindly asked me but I didn't want to put her to any trouble.' She gave a regretful little shrug which sent a clear message that she did want some refreshments really.

Edwin rose dutifully from the ornate French sofa and skipped almost skittishly across the room and out of the door, returning a couple of minutes later.

'Gladys is on the case. We shall have tea,' he announced. 'Now where were we?'

Joan saw him glance quickly at the portrait above the fireplace. She knew he was thinking that there was much more than a passing similarity between them.

'My last secretary, alas, left things in rather a mess,' said

Edwin, sitting down again. He sighed heavily. 'Then again, she was seventy-nine and very forgetful.'

Joan nodded sympathetically, hoping that the smirk of early victory which was threatening to lift up the corners of her mouth didn't show. Did anyone say 'secretary' any more? She would have been forgiven for thinking she had just zipped back in time to the fifties.

'I'm an expert at organization,' said Joan, imbuing her voice with an equal balance of softness and self-confidence. 'As you have no doubt ascertained from my CV, I come highly recommended.'

'None better, none better.' Edwin nodded. 'This is the first time I've actually advertised for anyone. I've always used local ladies as secretaries before but . . .'

The door opened and in came the burly figure of Gladys pushing a tea trolley with a very old and delicate china tea service on it. She must have either had it all ready or zoomed around like a Tasmanian devil getting it together, thought Joan. She saw Edwin's face light up at the sight of the tiered plates of cakes. This man has a sweet tooth, she immediately deduced. He was almost clapping his hands together at the sight of the Victoria sponge. All the better for a heart attack.

As Gladys poured the tea, Joan could tell that her ear was cocked towards the conversation.

'So you were saying you've always used local ladies before,' said Joan. Edwin opened his mouth to speak, but Gladys butted in.

'There's no one suitable in the village,' she said.

'At least no one under seventy,' added Edwin.

'I was born not far from here,' said Joan. 'At the other side of Wellem.'

Edwin smiled broadly. 'Were you really?' he said, as pleased as if she had just told him she was from Camelot and had a huge lottery-winner's cheque for him. He turned to Gladys for approval. 'Isn't that encouraging, Gladys? A local girl.'

Joan saw Gladys's eyebrows lift. She only 'hmm'ed' but Joan could tell she was impressed. The old bag was clearly softening. It was another good call; they did prefer local folk working for them. She had been right. Gladys might have been an expert at reading people but Joan was a grand master.

'Milk, sugar?' asked Gladys.

'Milk and one sugar, please,' Joan answered. Women like Gladys trusted women who had sugar. They weren't as self-obsessed, preoccupied by their weight. For the same reason, Joan leaned over and took a Victoria sponge slice. Women trusted women who ate cake. Especially women who complimented the women who had made the cake.

'Oh, this is so light,' flattered Joan. 'Is the baker local?'

'I made it myself, actually,' said Gladys. Joan could see she was trying not to beam.

'Oh.' Joan showed the right amount of surprise. The sort of delighted shock that was tempered with admiration without sliding into sycophancy. 'It's lovely.' And there was no better way to say that it was lovely than to wolf it down and reach for another slice. 'I love home-baked stuff. It goes straight to my hips but I can't resist it.'

She saw Mrs Coffey smile a smile that reached up to her eyes and totally engulfed them. The woman was defrosted and it had taken only two little pieces of sponge and a cube of sugar to do it. There was no need for any more to be eaten now. Joan hated anything that could affect her perfect figure.

'So,' said Edwin, the word heralding that the interview was to be resumed and Mrs Coffey could go. He waited until she had. 'There's a cottage in the grounds that comes with the job. Gladys has had it cleaned and repainted. It's small but comfortable.'

I've got the job, said Joan to herself, but she contained her delight and nodded at his words as if hooked on every one of them.

'To recap, then,' continued Edwin. 'You're a local girl with a flair for organization. And my housekeeper likes you.'

'Well,' began Joan, making a girlishly extravagant gesture of wiping crumbs from her face with delicate dabbings of fingertips, 'I like to think I'm as organized as anyone can be and if your housekeeper likes me then that's great because I hate not getting on with anyone I work with.'

Lord Edwin Carlton held his hand out. 'Then that's good enough for me. Welcome to Carlton Hall, Mrs Hawk. You're hired.'

Everyone wants happiness,
no one wants pain,
but you can't make a rainbow
without a little rain.

ANON

August

Chapter 5

Lara tried to chop the red pepper like Delia Smith – the knife tip never leaving the board and the heel doing the cutting, in an action apparently reminiscent of rowing a boat – but Keely's laser gaze was putting her off any rhythm and the knife was going all over the place.

Really, she didn't know why she was bothering to make her speciality pasta dish. Keely and Garth would both sit at the table, poking at it with their forks as if it were a dead animal, and then, when it had gone completely cold, push their plates into the middle of the table and announce that they didn't like it and were off to see what else was available.

Lara prided herself on being quite a good cook – not as good as the domestic goddess that was her friend Clare, of course, but then Clare could have given Nigella a run for her money. She was always sending Lara recipes on email which she had tried and tested. Even so, in the three months that she had been living with James and his children, nothing she had put in front of his eleven-year-old son, Garth, the Olympic nose-picking champion, and his fourteen-going-on-forty-five-year-old daughter, Keely, had hit the button. Home-made fish and chips, pasta, rice, chicken, steak, lamb, fajitas – you name it, she'd tried it all. And yet everything had been greeted with pairs of curled-up Elvis lips.

'What's that supposed to be?' said Keely at last, upping her silent staring treatment to something more active. She stood leaning against the worktop, arms folded, her whole body oozing teenage attitude.

'Beef pasta,' Lara answered, forcing a jolly Doris Day smile.

'What sort of pasta?'

'Cavatappi. The curly stuff.'

'So it's spag bol with curly pasta instead of the long thin variety?'

Lara blew her cheeks out.

'Well, it is and it isn't. This one has got a few more ingredients in it than a spag bol,' replied Lara, feeling her face begin to heat up and begging it not to. It would only give Keely the satisfaction that once again she had 'got' to her.

'Like what?'

'Courgettes.'

'I hate courgettes.'

'And mushrooms.'

'I hate mushrooms.'

Lara knew it wasn't really the food, it was her – Lara – that was the problem. And not only because she was Lara, Keely's father's live-in lover, but because she wasn't *her*: the one whose name haunted her. The one whose name was on the edge of Keely's tongue, just waiting to run free into the air at every available opportunity. And sure enough, when Keely opened her mouth again *that* name sprang like Tom Daly off the top diving board.

'When Tianne used to stay over, she made the best spag bol in the world.'

'Oh, did she?' Lara tried to look and sound composed, but she didn't quite bring it off. That bloody name. Tianne (a compound of Tina-Anne) Lee. *Tianne used to make us laugh like drains. Tianne used to be an absolute riot. Tianne's farts smelled of Chanel Number Five.* Bloody Tianne. More and more Lara felt like the unnamed heroine in *Rebecca*, but in her case it wasn't

James's ex-wife, Miriam, that was ruffling up the waves, but bloody Tianne Lee, James's ex-girlfriend: the equivalent of the first Mrs de Winter. Except she wasn't dead. She was alive and well and living in a trendy flat in Notting Hill with her swishy dark-brown hair, spray-tanned skin and incapable-of-being-closed legs.

Lara glanced up at the clock to see it was ten past eight. She stirred the sauce with annoyance. Why was James getting back in from work later and later? Especially when she told him that tonight she was leaving the office early in order to make everyone a family meal. Even more especially because it was Friday night and who didn't want to rush home at the weekend? She had never realized that children could cause such stress – especially ones who so obviously resented her. She badly needed James at home to smooth the way and support her because the situation wasn't getting better however much she'd hoped it would. He was the bridge between them and without him around, the two sides would never unite in an arc of cordiality.

Before she'd moved in she'd taken the time to try to get to know Keely and Garth, and even though they were quiet when she used to visit, she had presumed that they might grow to like her, because she was keen to like them. Lara had had a happy childhood, despite her family not having much money. She certainly didn't have the privileges that James's children had, but she was always loved and well fed and felt safe. The last thing she'd ever wanted to do was make the children feel threatened by her, and she'd been prepared to do anything to make them get on with her. She had tried everything and had even looked up on the Internet how to win over a partner's offspring. None of it had worked. It was as if they knew she was pulling out all the stops to befriend them and the aim of their game was to block all attempts. Lara had cried to herself in the bath a few times but James merely said they would 'come around eventually'. The twelfth of never would happen before 'eventually' did, she thought.

Lara had been so excited about bringing her belongings into James's beautiful large house and becoming part of his family, but lovely Manor Gardens in Dorking had turned out to be anything but a sanctuary. James had dismissed his children's inability to warm to his new lover as a mere teething problem. Yet although he knew that she wasn't comfortable in the house without him, his getting-home time seemed to be delayed by a further twenty minutes with every passing week. At this rate, it wouldn't be long before he would be arriving home at the time he should be setting back off for work.

'Where are you, for God's sake, James?' she said under her breath. 'Help.'

'Dad's late, isn't he?' said Keely, still doing her best staring, but this time she added an annoying sneer to her face. 'Again.'

'Yes, he is.' Lara sighed.

'He was never late home when he was going out with Tianne. He used to race in so he could get ready to pick her up early.'

That damned name. Dropped like a tiny stone into a pond and yet it sent out three miles worth of ripples from its centre.

Lara didn't bite, however much she wanted to shout out that she didn't give a toss about Tianne – even if she did. She reminded herself again that she was the first woman James had lived with since he had divorced Miriam. She alone had received the privilege, although with Keely's eyes boring holes into her, it didn't feel much like a privilege.

As if Keely was reading her thoughts, she opened her mouth, gave a little sigh and said: 'Funny how you moved in just after Kristina said she was working too many hours and threatened to leave.'

Lara didn't gratify that with a comment either. *Don't react,* she told herself and tried not to sever an artery as she cleaned the knife.

'Yep. I heard her telling Dad that she would walk out if he made her work more than two evenings a week. Obviously that would mean there was no one to feed Garth and me unless he got another doormat in.'

Don't bite. She knows just what to say to bug you, Lara.

What if that were true, though? What if the au pair had put her foot down and James had grasped the opportunity to draft in some extra child cover from his lover?

The first voice countered the second doubting one: *Lara, not all men are total users. There's no point being with James if you don't trust him. So do you trust him or not?*

Of course she did. He worked too hard to be seeing someone else anyway. He was head of consultancy at Harrison IT, or HIT as it was more commonly known, and determined to reach even greater heights within the company. Plus, he loved her. He had told her he did, so it must be true.

Lara had met James at the Ritz at the very prestigious celebrity launch of a book by Harrison Harris the self-made billionaire founder of HIT. Her immediate boss was a personal friend of Harrison Harris but couldn't attend and asked if she would do so on his behalf. The first person she saw on walking into the foyer had been James Galsworthy and she had instantly been drawn to his confident stance, as well as his beautifully cut Savile Row suit. People were hovering around, keener to speak to him than to the author. She didn't think she would have a cat in hell's chance of catching his eye, but someone nudged her, the glasses perched on her nose fell onto the floor and James trod on them en route to catching up with one of his colleagues. He bent to pick them up, apologized and handed them back with a deftly produced business card and a promise that he would buy her some new specs. He took her out to dinner the next night and she cooked him breakfast the morning after in her Islington flat. It was the first time in Lara's life that she had ever slept with someone on a first date, but it felt right. Plus, it helped blast out the memory of her recent rat of a boyfriend, who had dumped her the previous month for a blonde bimbo with knocker implants the size of barrage balloons. And her ex-husband, who had been carrying on with his ex-wife within a month of their wedding. Oh, Lara was so good at picking faithful men.

Keely made a disgruntled sniff and then turned her biggest gun on Lara.

'You do know, don't you,' she began, quietly enough, 'that Dad saw Tianne behind Rachel's back and Chloe's back? He'll see her behind yours. She's like a drug to him.'

Bull's-eye.

Lara stopped stirring and saw the twelve-inch-long sideways smirk on Keely's face that recognized she had wounded her. But before Lara could say or do anything the back door opened and in came James, bringing a blast of showery air with him.

'Hello, princesses,' he said with his big smile. 'My goodness, where is the summer? I thought this was supposed to be August.'

Lara's heart lifted to see him. Keely didn't usually stand around pouting and grimacing when he was present. She would disappear up to her room to talk to her friends on Skype or listen to music or sit in the middle of a Pentagram.

'Smells good. What's for tea? I am absolutely starving.'

'Pasta,' said Lara. 'And there's plenty of it.'

'Great. We all love pasta in this house. I'm just going up to get out of these things and I'll be back quick as a flash.' He put down his briefcase and stripped off his big overcoat. His short fair hair was shiny with raindrops. 'God, I need a warm shower.'

And he was gone, taking with him the warmth his presence had brought. Keely reached for a packet of gum on the worktop and popped a piece into her mouth.

'What we were talking about?' she said, with as much innocence as a serial killer caught by the police whilst holding a severed head dripping with blood.

'I am Mrs de Winter now,' said Lara, far louder than she intended.

'What?' said Keely.

'Er ... nothing,' said Lara, transferring her wonderful-smelling dish to the oven. Not that she was that proud of it any more. She'd lost her appetite. James would wolf it down not even noticing what it tasted of, and Keely and Garth would look at it as if a stray dog had just climbed on the table and deposited it from its bum.

Lara pulled a bottle of white wine from the fridge and screwed off the top. She poured out two big glasses and took a sip from one, trying not to throw her head back and drink the whole lot.

'Tianne would never drink wine from a screw-top. She said it was common,' said Keely, tossing her long brown and caramel extensions back over her shoulder. 'Just saying.'

Lara was about to take another sip of wine but she lifted the glass too high and the liquid cascaded all down her face. Keely burst into exaggerated laughter. Then – thank God – she moved forwards and out of the kitchen. Lara was left dabbing herself with some kitchen roll and trying not to explode with embarrassment. Keely had tortured the new family pet long enough for today.

Chapter 6

Clare looked at Ludwig across the dining table and thought, as always, how handsome he was by candlelight. He really didn't know it either because inside he was still the class gawky kid with the funny German name and no confidence in himself. She understood this because inside she was still the class female odd-bod with one eye that was ice-blue and one that was bright green. No wonder they had been drawn together from the moment he was introduced as the new boy, aged ten, to the rest of an amused class at primary school. His parents had moved from the Black Forest to York for work reasons and she and Lud gravitated towards each other from the very first minute of meeting. They had been good friends for years, even though, at eleven, Lud went to the local boys' school and Clare went to the local private girls' school. After getting a degree from Cambridge he moved to London to take up a fabulous job on Threadneedle Street and they saw each other about once a month for a catch-up. Everything remained on a close but platonic level until her thirtieth birthday, when he had got a bit tiddly at her party and snogged her. And she had found herself snogging him back and rather enjoying it.

She couldn't wait to tell him her exciting news. The partners at her company moved as slowly as God's millstone, but they'd got there in the end. She knew Lud would be delighted for her – nearly as pleased as her parents would be. He obviously had news of his own, though, because he was extra smiley tonight, as if he was trying to hold in a grin that was too big for his mouth. He was reading the menu and his blue, blue eyes were twinkling.

After the waiter had taken their order they both began speaking at once. Ludwig, being the consummate gentleman, waved at her to go first.

'Guess what happened to me today, finally,' Clare said, beaming.

'I don't know. You found the secret of eternal life? You checked your lottery ticket and found you had won?'

Oh, it was much better than that.

'I was pulled into the boardroom . . .'

'Yes?' Lud leaned forward in his seat and reached for her hand.

'And I was offered a partnership. The first woman in the history of the firm. Me!' She squealed and Lud stood up and came to her side of the table to hug her, full of congratulations.

'My darling, that is brilliant,' he said, but she picked up something in his voice. For some reason it wasn't as wonderful to him as she'd hoped it would be.

'I'm so excited. It's the stuff of dreams. I've wanted it for ever but I never thought they'd offer it to me.'

'Is it what you want?' asked Lud, returning to his seat.

'Yes, yes, of course it is,' said Clare, now slightly confused, her eyebrows dipping in the middle of her forehead. Why would he ask that?

'So that is good,' he said. 'I'm very proud of you. You deserve it, Clare. You've worked very hard all your life for this moment.' He paused. 'I also have news.'

'Well, come on, let's have a news day. What have you got to tell me?'

'I have been offered a promotion.'

Nothing that Clare didn't expect, then. She grinned.

'There's a shocker, smartypants.'

'It's in Dubai,' he went on, subdued.

'Dubai?' Clare gulped. She didn't expect that. 'Why Dubai? You won't take it though, will you, if it's there, surely?'

'It's a new position.'

He didn't say that he wasn't taking it.

'You've accepted it?' Clare felt slightly faint as if all the blood had been diverted from her head.

'Not yet.'

Not yet was the same as yes, wasn't it?

'You're going to live in Dubai?' Clare's mouth formed the words but her brain was refusing to accept them. Lud wouldn't have taken a position in Dubai without talking to her about it. At least her old, dear, familiar Lud wouldn't have. The one who wasn't ruled by his smartphone. 'When . . . when . . .?' Her lips felt as if they were losing their power to obey her.

'Monday. I go on Monday.'

'Monday?' She sounded like a deranged echo.

'Well, I am flying to Dubai on Monday to meet with people, to decide if I want to take the position but they want someone quickly and they've made me an offer I would be an idiot to refuse. If I say yes, there will be a little toing and froing for a couple of weeks then I start a two-year contract.'

'I can't believe you didn't say anything until now.' Clare bit her lip to combat the tears of hurt which were rising to her eyes.

'I didn't want to say anything until I had been offered the position for sure. Now I have and am here talking to you about it, but suddenly everything is rush rush rush.' He coughed. 'Clare, I was hoping you would come with me.'

Oh no, this couldn't be happening, thought Clare. There had to be a god of timing who was seriously pissed off with the world and had decided to wreak vengeance. Of all the places in the world where Clare would have loved to live, Dubai was right up there in the top three. The endless sandy beaches, those beautiful seas on her doorstep, the sun, the shopping. She pictured herself diving beneath warm water that was as blue as Ludwig's eyes.

Lud's hand squeezing hers popped the bubble of her reverie.

'It's all right, I know how much the partnership means to you,' he said. 'I can't believe we both have such great news, but . . .' She knew what that 'but' meant: great news that wasn't great news if you zoomed out and looked at the whole picture.

Clare swallowed hard and tried to block out all images of going to Dubai with Lud.

The wine waiter arrived at their side with a bottle of iced champagne.

'I took the liberty of ordering some for us when I made the booking,' said Lud. 'To celebrate.' He dropped her hand and her fingers seemed to grow cold in a second.

The waiter twisted out the cork and poured the Cristal into two long flutes. Then Lud's phone rang and he immediately he picked it up to answer it.

Maybe if he had ignored it, things would have been different, but even now, in this most intimate of moments when he was asking her to give up everything that she had worked for to follow him thousands of miles around the other side of the world, she was less important than whoever was at the end of the phone. The significance of him taking the call was massive to her.

Over dinner they talked more about Dubai and the partnership. The position in the land of blue skies and opulence sounded wonderful, although Lud said that he didn't want to pressure Clare into making any rash decision. But Clare knew that however much she wanted to be seduced into going with him, when the time came for her to tell him her answer, it would be no. And all because he had picked up his phone just after the champagne had arrived.

Chapter 7

Lara laid her head on James's chest and listened to his heartbeat: still racing after sex. He liked her to be on top, which she hated because she didn't like all her flesh on show. He relished the sight of her generous breasts bouncing up and down. Lara worried about her stomach jumping up and down as well, banging on his and making slapping sounds, although he – in the throes of passion – never seemed to mention it. Tonight, he was too tired for much foreplay; he had just enough energy to conjure up an erection for her to work her magic on, with her on-top bouncy dance, then he came and whispered how much he had needed that. Lara, unsated, was glad to climb off at the end and snuggle up to his side. He lay, his arm around her, in such a post-orgasmic glow one would have been forgiven for thinking he had just eaten a huge portion of Ready-brek and acquired a neon orange aura.

She knew she had tried extra hard just then, haunted by pictures of him in bed with Tianne. Had the sex with his ex been so good that he couldn't stay away? Was she some sort of siren, luring him in to crash against her rocks?

Lara didn't like to acknowledge to herself that she was envious of Tianne's and James's history. Especially as she noticed that sex had become much more perfunctory since she had moved into his house. She hated to admit that it would slide very quickly into bored middle-aged, old-married-couple sex if they didn't take care to address it. In the early days, at her old Islington flat, their lovemaking had been much more mutually satisfying. And when she moved into his gorgeous boudoir of a bedroom and they became a co-habiting couple, she'd hoped their sexual repertoire would only increase, but it had worked the other way. Okay, so they both worked long hours and were tired, but she was always ready to put her heart and soul into sex when things were heading that way. She couldn't remember him giving her an orgasm since she moved in, though, and somehow doubted the hedonistic minx that was Tianne would have stood for that. *Tianne Tianne Tianne* – all roads seemed to lead back to bloody Tianne. Lara needed to know whether what Keely had said had been the truth. It was the elephant in Lara's room. She started off by bringing up the subject casually.

'Was that okay for you? That's your favourite position, isn't it?' she said, stroking the few fine greying hairs on his chest.

'Oh, boy, yes,' he replied with breathy pleasure. 'And you're so good at it.'

'Have . . . have all your exes done that for you?'

'Erm,' he said, thinking. 'Yes, at one time or another. Some enjoyed it more than others.'

'Like who?'

'What do you want to know for?'

'It's interesting,' she replied, still stroking, still trying to sound light.

'Well, if you must know, Rachel didn't like it – said it made her feel fat. Chloe liked it, but then she had a great figure.'

Too much info, thought Lara. On top was bound to be okay if you had no wobbly bits and also the cocky confidence of the very pretty Chloe, who stripped off to her bra and very tiny pants to model for catalogues.

'Not that you haven't got a nice figure,' added James quickly. 'Chloe was actually a bit too skinny for my liking. And I don't like fake breasts. Plus, she was the most boring woman I've ever met. She had a brain the size of an undergrown pea.'

That cheered Lara a little. Even if she wasn't exactly thrilled about such a grey word as 'nice' to describe her attributes.

'What about . . . Tianne?' pressed Lara. The name was like a sour sweet in her mouth and came out almost in a spit.

'Oh, well, her, she . . . she loved it. Then again, the sex we had was always on the spicy side.'

Spicy? What did that mean? Did he rub cayenne pepper over his willy? Did she shove a chilli up his arse at the crucial moment? She felt a green-eyed monster rear inside her at a sudden vision of Tianne and her long, flowing dark hair bouncing wantonly on top of James, both of them screaming in joint ecstasy. She swallowed hard.

'Do you ever see her?'

'Who?'

'Tianne?'

'No,' said James. 'Can't remember the last time I saw her. Why all the questions?' He pulled himself away from Lara and propped himself up on the pillow. 'What's the matter, darling?'

It would be very bad form to quote his daughter, thought Lara. But then again – bugger it.

'It was just something Keely said.' She tried to make it sound as if she hadn't been chewing it over in her mind for hours. 'That you found Tianne irresistible.'

She felt James tighten for a second, then his muscles suddenly relaxed and he laughed.

'She's winding you up,' he said. 'Tianne was a little tart. I was the older man with a wallet. That was my attraction to her. She even—' He snapped his mouth shut.

'What?'

'Nothing.'

'Go on.'

'No, it's nothing – really.'

But Lara knew that was a big fat lie. He had been about to tell her something intimate, and she had to know what it was now. 'You have to tell me. What? What did she do?'

James groaned with equal measures of resignation and impatience. 'Okay, okay, she used to pretend to be a prostitute in bed. She wanted me to tuck money into her knickers before we had sex. She was a mercenary little cow. I had to fight with her to get the notes back. Satisfied?' His head fell back forcibly onto the pillow.

Did that turn you on? Did you love her doing it? Do you want me to do that? Do I need to spice myself up? Rub my nipples with Tabasco sauce? Lara's brain filled up with ludicrous questions. They were queuing at her mouth to jump out.

'Did you like her doing that?' *Please say no.*

'I can't remember,' James replied, the impatience rising in his voice now. 'I suppose at the time, in the moment, it was ... exciting.'

Lara felt him shrug. He was obviously lying and did remember. How could you forget that? She wished she could rip what she had just heard out of her head because now, in the dark, she saw an XXX-certificate sex scene that even Ron Jeremy would blush at. Not only was there the right amount of sweat and groaning, a couple lost in the throes of erotic sex resulting in a mutual orgasm of tsunamic proportions, but now there was the added element of a pair of knickers stuffed with twenty-pound notes.

'Did you ever sleep with her again after you'd finished?'

'Oh God.' She heard James slap his head but she carried on relentlessly. She *had* to know.

'Behind Rachel's or Chloe's back?'

There was a telling pause before he answered, 'No, of course not.' And he must have known that she noticed because he amended that to: 'I slept with her once. Behind Rachel's back, okay?'

'Why?'

'I don't know. We bumped into each other in a pub one night after work and, well, things weren't going that well with Rachel. They were bloody awful, actually. I ended up going back to hers for a chat and a coffee . . .'

He tailed off but he didn't need to say any more, Lara could guess the rest. *She was like a drug. Heroin. Once he'd had her, he was hooked.*

'Oh,' she said again.

'The evil cow went straight round to Rachel's to tell her what I'd done. That's what sort of person she was. I hope I never see her again,' James went on, with such venom that Lara's shoulders were instantly unburdened of half their tension and she felt the air escape from her lungs. Tianne Lee might have been a drug, but it appeared that James had managed to wean himself off her after realizing what destruction she left in her wake.

'Did—' she began to ask, but James patted her arm.

'No more. Go to sleep, darling,' he said. 'I don't want to talk about her. Suffice to say that I wouldn't touch anyone like her ever again, not even with a ten-foot barge pole.'

Lara bit down on the stream of questions lined up waiting to be asked, but she knew they wouldn't go away. They'd infiltrate her dreams and torture her through the night – if she ever managed to get to sleep.

James had no such problem. Within minutes he was snoring gently. He had the ability to drop off immediately after an orgasm. His tensions were relieved; Lara only wished hers were.

She nestled close to James's trim body and tried to force herself into sleep whilst wrestling dark-haired demons with money falling out of their pants. She wondered why women felt the need to know details about a man's other lovers when all it did was torture them.

Chapter 8

Clare braced herself before ringing the number. It was ridiculous how nervous she became when phoning her own father. She was thirty-three, not three, for God's sake.

It rang four times before a woman's firm voice recited her number down the phone and asked who was speaking please.

'It's me, Mum. How are you?'

'Alice. How lovely to hear from you, darling. How's Martin?'

'No, Mum, it's me – Clare.'

'Oh, Clare, how are you?' Was it Clare's imagination or had the temperature dropped a degree in her mother's voice?

'Fine, Mum. Are you okay?' Damn. Her parents hated the word 'okay'. How could she forget? 'Good, I mean. Both of you?'

'Daddy's in the garden. I presume you're ringing to say "Happy Birthday" to him. Your card hasn't arrived.' Dorothy Salter's voice had the merest nip of annoyance in it.

'Oh, no.' Clare's heart sank. She had posted it days ago. 'Has the postman been today?'

'Not yet,' said her mother. 'Alice and Martin's card arrived on Tuesday. Toby and Polly's card arrived last weekend.'

Great. She bet her clever-clogs IT genius sister Alice had had the card biked over at enormous expense. And perfect bloody Polly would have posted Toby's card for him. Her brother was useless but her sister-in-law was an obsessive diary keeper. Mind you, she didn't have much else to do except clean their eight-bedroomed mini manor in Harrogate and do a Zumba class when she got super bored waiting for her QC husband to come home in his swanky suit from an exhausting day counting his fees. Well, today was the day when Clare would make her parents' eyebrows rise to the ceiling and beyond. She had wanted to tell them as soon as she found out, but had sat on this secret until now – an extra birthday present for Daddy.

'I do hope the card comes today,' said Clare. 'I posted it ages ago so he would get it in time. Can I speak to Dad?'

'Of course.' She heard Dorothy turn away from the phone to call her husband. 'Lionel.' A rap on the window. 'It's Ali— Clare for you.'

Clare bit down on her lip to offset the twinge of pain she felt at hearing her mother almost get her name wrong. In a moment she was going to deliver *the* line that might have her mother calling Alice by Clare's name for once, the next time they spoke. It was her Shirley Valentine moment, the moment after golden-knickers Marjorie Majors gets the answer wrong and Shirley, who knows what man's greatest invention was, is waiting to say the words that will revolutionize the way she is thought of: 'The wheel, miss.'

'Hello, Clare,' came the brisk voice of her father, taking the phone from his wife's hand.

'Happy Birthday, Dad. I can't believe my card hasn't arrived.'

'Yes, well, we haven't had today's post ... Ah, apparently we just have ... I think your card is here. Is it in a blue envelope?'

'Yes,' said Clare, with relief, because tucked inside the card was a voucher for them to go to Rockley Hall, a beautiful restaurant not far from where they lived and which they frequented at least once a month.

'How's work?' asked Lionel Salter. He always asked that early in a conversation.

This is it, Clare, your Shirley Valentine moment.

'Well ...' Oh God, it was just too delicious to keep in her mouth any longer. She wanted to lead up to it slowly but her gob had other ideas. 'I've been made a partner.' In her head she raised two fingers to her supremely snobby cow of a sister and arrogant arse of a brother. *Sit on that and swivel, Alice Salter-Frampton, and you as well, Toby.*

'A partner?' said her father, gruffly. As if she had just told him a joke that wasn't very funny.

'Yes, Dad, I've been made a partner.' Oh, those words felt like the best flavour in her mouth. Better even than her speciality peanut-butter cheesecake on an Oreo base.

There was a momentary silence then Lionel Salter relayed the information to his wife in a voice that didn't quite believe the words it was saying. 'Dorothy, Clare has been made a partner.'

There was some twittering in the background, probably her mother fainting and her dad banging his hearing aid against the wall in fear that it was broken.

'Dad, Dad, are you still there?'

'Yes, I'm still here.' Her dad actually sounded as if he were smiling now. 'That's very well done, Clare. Very well done. We're delighted. I suppose your chap must be thrilled too?'

Clare raised her eyebrows in surprise. Her father rarely referred to Ludwig. Ironic, then, that he did so now when Lud would be going to Dubai in two days to possibly start the ball rolling on a new life without her.

'Yes, he's thrilled.' It wasn't a lie. Ludwig was thrilled for her. The chance of a lifetime that she couldn't possibly pass up.

Ludwig ticked all the boxes on her parents' list of essential qualities for prospective partners: successful, grand job title, drove a top-of-the-range Audi. It was just a shame he 'wasn't British', as her dad put it. Clare opened her mouth to tell her dad that they weren't together any more and then shut it again. Today was not the day for any news that would take away the shine.

'Wonderful news.' She could hear the elation in her father's voice and it made her spirits soar so high they needed oxygen to breathe. 'We'll tell Toby and Alice straightaway.'

As Clare put the phone down after the conversation her eyes flooded with happy tears. Despite the fact that a hard weekend of working in the office loomed, she was ecstatic. She couldn't remember the last time she had heard her father say he was going to brag about her to her siblings, instead of the other way round. Then she realized she couldn't remember, because he never had before.

Chapter 9

Lara had a rotten weekend. James was in the office all day Saturday and 'popped in' on Sunday too, for an hour that turned out to be four. At least Keely was out shopping with her one and only friend Paris for most of Saturday and stayed over at hers that night. Garth was on his Xbox playing some game that involved a lot of shooting and shouting to his friends down his headphone mike. Lara felt more lonely rattling around in the house than she ever had when she was living alone in her cosy Islington flat.

She also had too much time to think. What Keely said about Tianne played over and over again in her head. She knew she was being stupid and immature. Tianne was an ex for a reason and James was with Lara now. He couldn't change the past any more than she could change the mistakes she had made with men. And, boy, had she picked some beauties. James had been honest with her and admitted to sleeping with Tianne behind Rachel's back. What more did she want? Mrs de Winter was dead and gone, long live Mrs De Winter. Then came the counter argument: he'd kept it quiet about doing the dirty behind Rachel's back until last night. She remembered him telling her in the past that he had never been unfaithful to anyone. However badly his relationship was going with Rachel, bonking Tianne behind her back was cheating – full stop.

James was too tired for sex on Saturday night, and it was never even mentioned on Sunday. He kissed her, wished her goodnight and then turned over. He was snoring within minutes. They'd had sex every time he visited her old flat; he'd been mad for her, even when he'd come over from working very late. He was going off her. That was the obvious conclusion.

Eventually Lara dropped off and the dream world continued to torture her. Tianne appeared as a tiny-waisted naked being with gravity-defying tits and an arse like two perfectly shaped apples. Sitting astride James, Tianne turned around to her without breaking her rhythm, her long curly hair bouncing. Lara didn't sleep very well and awoke feeling drained and on edge. She got up and made a jug of coffee with the old-fashioned percolator she had brought with her. She loved its bad-tempered hissing and spitting and the homely aromas it produced that filled the kitchen. Even though it was a dark Monday morning, she perked up at the prospect of sharing breakfast alone with James. She longed for more of these wonderful early mornings with James and Colombian Roast and the comfortable quiet.

Miriam had rung the previous night to say that she was picking up the children on Tuesday afternoon and taking them over to France for a week. Miriam didn't ask, she dictated. It was no wonder the children had been brought up to think the world revolved around their family. But wonderful timing it wasn't, as Lara would have had a whole week alone with James if she wasn't going on holiday with her friends. She watched him sipping from his World's Greatest Dad mug and looking through his emails on his iPhone and her heart leapt in her chest as if it were trying to break out of her body and pounce on him. She wished this holiday were at any other time, because right now she needed to stay here with him and recover what they had when they first met.

James had a really powerful aura surrounding him, as men in high positions usually did, even the ones who had major belly paunches and jowls. But James was blessed by being sickeningly handsome with it. In fact, it was as if he had been created according to her own personal checklist: angel-fair hair, baby-blue eyes, soft kissable lips, strong jaw always showing just the right amount of designer stubble. Tall, but not too tall that she looked like a midget at the side of him when they walked anywhere together, because she was only five foot two. And he dressed exquisitely. His shirts were expensive, his suits handmade, his shoes shone. Sometimes she didn't know what such a successful, handsome man as James Galsworthy saw in her. She wasn't his usual type. She had sneaked a few looks on Facebook at his exes and they were very much from the same mould with their curtains of dark hair, dark soulful eyes, oval faces and long legs, whereas Lara kept her blonde hair short and she was much curvier than his past girl-friends. She might not have their attributes, but she had some special ones of her own: her eyes were a beautiful shade of hazel, fringed with long thick black lashes; she also had a magnificent chest and James was definitely a boob man. She puffed up after reminding herself that she had at least that advantage over his exes.

'I'm going to be really late home tonight,' James announced as he carried on checking his messages. Lara's heart sank. This was their last evening together before her holiday and she'd planned a romantic dinner. Plus, Keely was having Paris over to stay the night so there would be not one but two teenaged females making evil eyes at her.

'Oh,' she said, unable to keep the disappointment from her voice. 'Can't you get out of it? Keely and Garth go away to France tomorrow and it's our last—'

'I only wish I could, darling,' he interrupted her. 'It's going to be a very late, very boring meeting with bankers, who will probably drone on for hours because they love the sound of their own voices. Sorry.'

'Oh, well, can't be helped,' said Lara. Unfortunately men working in lofty positions, men such as James, had to put in long unsociable hours. She thought about staying behind at the office herself but she remembered that she had promised Kristina an extra night off to go to the West End with her new boyfriend and someone needed to be at home with Keely and Garth, however uncomfortable they made her feel.

James picked up his briefcase and leaned over her. She raised her lips to his but he kissed her on the forehead and she felt a little sting of rejection. They had been together for only six months and he was kissing her on the forehead. She felt as drained as if she had been living with him for years, having birthed and brought up his children.

'Don't wait up,' said James.

'Surely you're not going to be that late, are you?' gasped Lara with some horror.

'I hope not, but you never know,' replied James with a loaded sigh. 'See you later, darling. I'll grab something at Waterloo so don't bother to make any dinner for me.'

And with that he was off, with his rubbish kiss and his 'Don't wait up'. Did he really have a meeting with boring bankers? That was her first thought as the door closed.

Oh God, Lara, a voice strangled with impatience said inside her head. *Stop with this paranoia. You're being ridiculous. James is living with YOU. He didn't live with Chloe, he didn't live with Rachel, he most certainly didn't live with Tianne – but he HAS chosen to live with you. Get over yourself.*

Oi, you, said a countering rough Yorkshire voice. *You can't blame her for being a bit of a fruit loop. Not after the luck she's had with blokes. Give her a break.*

Fair point, said the first voice. *But let's try to keep things in perspective, shall we? We don't want to encourage any self-fulfilling prophecies now, do we?*

Lara heard Keely's door creak open upstairs. Time to go to

work, she decided, before she came face to face with the world's biggest spoon and heard even more words to torture herself with.

Her mood was glum as she caught the train to work. Her department was having a refit so she and her team were temporarily crammed into the grotty windowless basement of the massive Cole and Craw Financial Institute building which was chilly and had rubbish overhead lighting. This just added to the increasing hatred she felt for the job she had once loved. She should never have taken the lucrative promotion that had been dangled in front of her face. Without the promotion she would have stayed happy in her old position and wouldn't have had to work directly for Giles Billingley, the three-chinned chauvinistic pig who thought women should be paid less, fetch the tea and not object when he stroked their bottom. It was going to be good to be away from the dirty old bastard creep for a fortnight. She couldn't even find some respite at work from her less-than-perfect home life because, as atmospheres go, they were each as bad as the other. A weekend at home being continually on edge wore her down as much as two days in the office. Recently Kristina had been in a worse mood than usual, complaining about how many dried bogeys she'd had to remove from underneath any surface in the house to which they would adhere. Not forgetting the walls, where the charming Garth would flick them.

The black cloud above Lara's head followed her into the lift and down to her make-do office and stayed stubbornly with her as she sat at her desk and logged onto her computer. She'd had such high hopes for this relationship and yet she saw James less now they were living together than when they had separate houses. Something was happening to them. Or was it *someone*?

Against her own better judgement, Lara logged onto her Facebook account. She had set it up years ago when a friend had emigrated, as a way of keeping in touch, but they never really had so it had lain dormant, until she logged on to look up Tianne after having that name shoved down her throat by Keely on a regular basis. Tianne's timeline was full of exciting singles' events worthy of a chick-lit book: theatre trips, festivals, holidays in hot climes, cocktails in a variety of European venues. In every one of her photos, Tianne was posed smiling at the camera with her white teeth, wild dark curls and a practised pout of a mouth. It was very evident that no one could ever find Tianne Lee as wonderful as she found herself.

Tianne was a newly fledged solicitor working for a very prestigious firm in the City. She was, it seemed, the woman with everything: flashy job, flashy car, flashy wage – everything except a boyfriend. Her status was still showing her as single. There had been quite a few entries since the last time Lara had spied on her, and some more photos added. Again that Simon Cowell-type, white-toothed smiling pose against backdrops of the Eiffel Tower, the Moulin Rouge, a casino in Las Vegas and even some of her standing outside the Old Bailey in a pin-striped suit.

Thanks for all my birthday cards and messages.

That was the last entry on the timeline – yesterday. Small lettering said there were comments about that post, and Lara scrolled down to read the conversation between a friend called Aleisha and Tianne.

Did you do anything nice for your birthday at the weekend, darling?

That would be telling.

Tell me then.

Met a friend for dinner and cocktails ;).

Cocktails or COCKtails?

Both. More when I see you.

Lara forced herself to log out and stop her lurid imaginings.
Two working days to go until her holiday. Maybe a good blast
of sea air would blow all those ridiculous, head-rotting pictures
of Tianne out to sea where they could get eaten by a passing
shark.

Chapter 10

May's lovely dream was pierced by the sound of her alarm clock. She and Michael had been alone on a deserted beach. They were cuddled up on a double sunbed, the sun warm on her back, the only sound the swishing of waves ebbing and flowing. Suddenly it was five twenty in the morning and Michael's heavy arm draped over her made it doubly hard to get up. She pressed the snooze button, then snuggled close to him for five more delicious minutes. Michael started to stroke the small of her back, then his hand dipped to her buttocks. She knew he wanted to make love. He was always ready for sex in the mornings. His appetite must have been enormous when he was much younger and newly married to Susan, May suddenly mused. That thought of him in bed with Susan brought a big wave of jealousy splashing over her even though she knew she had a cheek, seeing as that woman was still his wife.

Grudgingly she lifted his arm and slid from underneath it just as the alarm went off again.

'Michael,' she said as she kissed him. 'Michael, I can't. I've got an early meeting.'

'Spoilsport.'

May chuckled. 'I know.'

'Morning, darling,' he said. 'Wow.'

May was standing there naked, looking for her underwear in the drawer.

'Come back to bed and let's make love.'

Thousands of fizzy beads of excitement bubbled inside May at the thought of that. If she weren't so conscientious she might have been tempted to take a day off sick, for the first time ever. Monday morning had never felt more like a Monday morning. Having sex with the man she loved was a much more exciting prospect than having a meeting in Clapham and then doing a presentation to a boss who would be hell-bent on finding holes in her plans because he was the envious, talentless little shit of a nephew of the MD.

'I know, I know,' said Michael. 'A nice idea, but we have work to do.'

'Where do you have to go today?'

'Derby,' said Michael.

'Derby? Again? You were there on Saturday and most of yesterday, weren't you?'

'Big client – needs lots of attention, darling.'

'Do these people not realize that you might have a life at weekends?' May huffed angrily on his behalf. 'Who wants to talk paper on a Sunday?'

'You'd be surprised how many workaholics like to do exactly that. Thank goodness it's just the one customer, then I can come home and . . .' His voice tailed off sadly.

May slipped her knickers on quickly then rushed to put her arms around Michael. It was Susan's birthday today. He would take her flowers and sit by her side and talk to her about what they should have been doing: having a meal in a nice restaurant, watching a show, staying in a plush hotel afterwards. May wished she had never agreed to go on holiday with her friends. Michael needed her far more than they did. She should be with him. But when push came to shove, she just couldn't bring herself to let them down.

Michael's hands moved to fondle her breasts. 'Oh, May, you are lovely,' he said. 'I'm so glad I found you. I'm so happy you're in my life. I think I'd have topped myself if I didn't have you.'

May kissed his head and wished she could tumble back into bed with this sexy, tortured man. Michael started stroking her nipple and she had to pull away, even though she really didn't want to. She was already going to be hot and bothered on the Tube thinking about what might have ensued had she given in.

His smile said he knew exactly what effect he was having on her.

'I love you so much,' she said.

'I know you do,' he said. 'I'm a very lucky man.'

Chapter 11

Clare closed the box of cleaning materials that sat beside her suitcase. She had two full days left to work, then she had ten wonderful days at the spa, and after that she would hit the ground running with her new job. Longer hours – as if she could do many more; greater responsibility – as if she hadn't enough already. But it would all be worth it for that note she had heard in her parents' voices on Saturday morning. She had replayed that conversation back to herself so many times over the weekend. It had made up her mind for her. She knew what she had to do and she would be doing it in her lunch hour today. She was meeting Ludwig in Covent Garden at twelve. He would be flying to Dubai that evening.

As she was thinking this, a tinkle on her phone heralded a text from him.

Can't wait to see you for lunch xxx

Oh God, that wasn't helping. He didn't know what he was in for. She wished it were one o'clock now and she was back in the office with the lunch behind her.

The morning at work dragged, as she knew it would. The clock hands crawled around to lunchtime. Ludwig was waiting for her in the restaurant with two glasses of champagne already ordered and on the table. He stood up and kissed her, not noticing that she turned her head slightly so his mouth landed more on her cheek than on her lips. He handed her a glass of champagne, lifted his own and chinked it against hers.

'I've got some pictures of the apartment,' said Lud, digging in his jacket pocket. He straightened out the sheets of paper and handed them over to Clare. 'I thought they might tempt you, even though I promised myself that I wouldn't pressurize you,' and he winked.

'Wow,' she said, meaning it. Spacious and cream-coloured, big bouncy sofas and an open-plan arrangement with, since it was a corner apartment, two full walls of windows letting in the light. There was a view of the sun-sparkled Dubai sea in the near distance. The sight of those blue waters nearly had her throwing away her life as she knew it and promising to go with Lud. Clare loved the sea; she loved the smell of it, the feel of the cold salty water against her skin, the sensation of slipping underneath it and disappearing into another world. Dubai and that sea could be her home for two years. Everything she loved – space, sun, sea . . . Was she mad turning it down?

'That's the apartment right there to the le—'

Then Lud's phone rang again and his attention shifted away from her.

Oh Lud, it looks gorgeous, it really does and half of me wants to go with you so badly, but the other half knows I can't. I can't miss this opportunity to be the angel at the top of the family tree for once. I can't be second best any more. To you or anyone.

'I shall be back home on the day you return from the holiday with your friends,' he said. 'Let's toast that the time until then will fly.' He drank, she didn't. Clare replaced her glass on the table.

'Lud, I think we should split up.'

His lips paused on the glass.

'We can't have a long-distance relationship; we'd just be delaying the inevitable. We wouldn't survive it.'

'Other people manage,' said Ludwig, putting his glass down. He looked calm, but she had totally knocked him off balance, she knew.

'I've been thinking . . . your change of job happening at the same time as my promotion is fate, Lud,' said Clare, pushing down on those feelings of protest which were trying to rise within her. 'You need someone who will support you and give you a family, someone to work for and look after. I'm not that woman.'

'Are you sure, Clare? Can you put your hand on your heart and say that you are taking this position because *you* want it?' His words were gentle, almost a whisper, and yet they plunged into her chest and straight through the centre of her heart.

'Yes,' she said. 'I can say that. I am sure.'

'We can make this work, *Liebling*.'

Clare took a deep breath.

'I don't want to.'

She watched him gulp hard.

'I see.'

'I love you but I'd never forgive myself if I didn't give my job everything I had. I have to. And, let's face it, your work is your priority too.'

'You're my priority,' he said firmly.

'No, I'm not,' replied Clare. 'I can't remember the last time we had a conversation for longer than five minutes without your phone coming between us.' Lud opened up his mouth to answer and Clare held up her hand to stop him. 'You don't have to apologize or explain, Lud. I know how it is. This is your golden moment and you must take it and this is my golden moment and I must take it. You can go to Dubai this evening as a free man. And concentrate on your job without the distraction of me.'

'There is more to my life than work, Clare,' he said, shock evident in his voice that she could think otherwise.

'Is there?' she replied. 'I don't feel there is any more.' She didn't say that she felt ever-so-slightly bored too. She didn't say that she heard girls in the office talking about saucy encounters and wishing she had some to report of her own. She could let him go kindly without grinding his face into the dirt.

'It's okay,' he said, reaching over and closing his warm hand over hers. 'I understand. It's you who needs to focus on your job without the distraction of me.'

Clare sighed guiltily. This was horrible. She sounded like a right hard cow.

The waiter arrived at their side to take their order.

'Do you want to eat?' asked Lud. Clare's lowered head moved slowly from side to side.

'Just the champagne,' Lud told the waiter. 'If you could bring me the bill, thank you.'

'I'm sorry,' said Clare.

'Don't be,' replied Lud. 'You've worked hard. You deserve your moment in the spotlight. I know how important it is to you.'

And he did. Over the years Lud had witnessed the many achievements of Toby and Alice Salter eclipsing everything that Clare did. How could he deny her the fifteen minutes of family fame?

The waiter brought over the bill. Lud gave it a cursory glance and then replaced it on the plate with some notes from his wallet.

'I hope you're really happy in Dubai,' said Clare, fighting back the emotion that had lodged like a hard lump in her gullet. 'I hope you find what you're looking for.'

'I had found it,' he said. 'Can I get you a taxi back to work?'

'No, I'll sit here for a bit and then take the Tube.'

Lud leaned over her and kissed her head, his hand curving tenderly around her arm.

'Goodbye,' he said. 'It's been fun.'

'I hope we can still stay friends,' said Clare, almost desperately, not wanting to let go now that she had separated them, but feeling that she had pushed him too far away to reach for again.

He nodded gallantly, like an old-fashioned soldier, then she watched his broad back cut through the crowd of café customers until it had disappeared totally from sight. As she followed him with her eyes, she did not realize that in his pocket lay the Tiffany engagement ring which he was going to present to her over lunch.

Finished, gone, just like that. All those years of togetherness ended with just a few words. Now she was free to concentrate on being the family superstar for the first time in her life. The Salter runt who was clever but never managed the genius heights of her smart-arse siblings had finally managed to outshine their achievements. And Ludwig could go and conquer the world and find himself a woman that he would ignore his phone for. The thought that he might sent the tears tumbling down her cheeks and onto the pristine white tablecloth.

Chapter 12

May's meeting in Clapham at nine that morning was with a man trying to set up a wholefood restaurant. She arrived at half-past eight to find Mr Terry waiting for her, an enthusiastic smile plastered all over his face. She reckoned he would be onto a winner too. He was so keen to get started, the property was ideal, the plans he had to renovate it were simple, cheap but effective ones, and his menu looked fantastic. She envied his passion for his work and his self-employed status, answering to no one but himself. May loved her job; she just hated all the rubbish that came with it: namely reporting to a man who didn't seem to have a clue what he was doing. He had all the management skills of a dead squirrel. Thank God he escaped to a golf course as often as he did and left everyone to get on with it.

May had allowed the full morning for the meeting but was done and dusted by just after half-past ten. She didn't want to get back to the office too early so took herself off to a café near the park. The waitress brought over a frothy cappuccino and a millionaire's shortbread which, disappointingly, had a very unbuttery base and not enough chocolate topping. As she was staring out of the window, May's eyes zoomed in on the building opposite, a grand old house almost hidden behind a high brick wall and tall trees. There was a sign at the side of the gate which she could just make out: The Pines. Her heart started to thump faster. Was it *The* Pines, the one in which Susan Hammerton resided? It had to be. Michael had said it was in the Clapham area and surely there couldn't be two establishments around here with the same name.

She drank the last of her coffee and wondered if this was a sign that she should do what she had intended to do for ages now: volunteer some money towards Susan's care. There must be luxuries that weren't on the basic bill that would make her life easier. She had broached the subject with Michael but he waved it away, too proud to accept. He didn't need to know, though – she was sure that she and The Pines could have a secret arrangement.

May crossed the road and walked down the path that led to the front door of the magnificent Georgian building with a large and established front garden. It must be costing poor Michael a fortune, thought May.

The reception area had large, square, black and white floor tiles and as May walked over them towards the main desk, she felt as if she were a piece on a chessboard.

'Morning, my love. Can I help you?' asked a white-uniformed woman manning the desk. She had a thick and friendly West Country accent and a welcoming smile.

May opened her mouth but didn't really know how to start. So she plunged in.

'Hello, I wonder if I could speak to someone about one of your residents.'

'Well, would you give me a few more details, please?'

'I'd like to see if there is anything I could contribute to make her stay here a little easier?'

'I'll get the matron for you,' said the receptionist. 'Would you take a seat over there for a few minutes? There's a coffee machine if you'd like a drink.'

'Thank you.' May took a seat and waited, though she didn't

use the machine as she was all coffee-ed out. Anyway, she wouldn't have had enough time as the woman returned almost immediately with someone who was just like a matron from a *Carry On* film – flat shoes, wide girth, short curly hair under a white starched cap, and oozing efficiency.

'Hello, there,' she boomed. 'I'm Marian Plaistow, Matron of The Pines. Would you like to come into my office?'

'Certainly.' May followed her through the door to the left of reception and took a seat at the other side of Matron's neat and tidy desk in her large, square and very sunlit office.

Matron settled her bulk into her big leather chair, threaded her fingers together and asked, 'So how can we help you?'

'I hope I've got the right place,' began May. 'It's about Susan Hammerton.'

'Ah, yes. Susan. Are you a relative?'

No, I'm shagging her husband.

May settled for: 'A friend of the family. I understand that she is unlikely to improve.'

Matron gave a slight nod, clearly used to not divulging any confidential information.

'I wondered if there was anything she might need that isn't standard issue. Any medicines or treatments that might make things easier for her, luxuries, anything at all?'

Matron shook her head slowly from side to side.

'Not really,' she said. 'I can't think of anything we could do that we aren't already doing. She is a very old lady. We can only make her comfortable.'

May shrugged her shoulders. 'Ah, I just thought I'd ask. No worr—'

Then her brain caught up with her ears. Crikey – if thirty-five was very old, what the heck was eighty?

'Very old? You said "very old".'

'That's right.'

'She's thirty-five.'

Matron looked confused. 'I think we might not be talking about the same ...'

'Susan Hammerton?' Surely there couldn't be two Susan Hammertons living in two The Pines in the area? May felt a tightness in her throat as if cold bony fingers were closing around it. She lifted up her handbag from the floor and foraged inside it for the passport-sized picture of Michael that she kept in her purse. When she found it, she handed it over the desk for Matron to take from her.

'This is her husband. He's thirty-four.'

Matron looked at the photograph, back at May and then back at the photo.

'I'm sorry, but this isn't Mrs Hammerton's husband. She's a widow in her nineties.'

The grip squeezed tighter. May felt her head grow light with confusion as thoughts zapped madly around it, trying to work out what was going on.

'This man comes here to visit her,' said May. 'Michael Hammerton.'

'Ye-es, that's him,' said Matron. 'But he ...' She answered slowly and carefully. 'He's a relative of Mrs Hammerton. Not her husband, though.'

'I don't understand.'

Matron handed back the photograph. She had an inkling of what might be happening in front of her eyes – she was a woman, after all. She leaned over the desk and said in a low voice, 'I shouldn't be saying this, but that man is Mrs Hammerton's great-nephew Michael. He doesn't visit that often. But when he does,' she coughed, embarrassed, 'I believe he usually comes with someone. A blonde.'

'A woman?' asked May, the grip so tight now that she could barely get out her words. It was a ridiculous question. Of course it had to be a blonde woman.

Matron nodded.

'His own age? Thereabouts?'

Again a nod.

'Could it be his sister? He has a sister?' May tried not to sound as hysterical as she felt.

Matron shook her head this time. 'I don't think the woman is his sister.'

May wanted to ask why. What were they doing to make you think it wasn't his sister? What have you seen? Her imagination was going bonkers. Were they snogging, holding hands, bonking over the reception desk?

Matron's face was creased sympathetically. 'I'm sorry,' she said. 'I don't think I can help you.'

May sniffed and wiped at the escaping tears with the edge of her index fingers. 'No, don't worry. It's not your fault. Thank you.'

'Would you like me to get you a cup of tea?' asked Matron kindly, pushing over the box of tissues which she kept at her side of the desk.

'I'll just go,' replied May. 'Please don't say I was here.'

Matron pushed back her chair so that she could stand and show her out but, by the time she was on her feet, May was striding down the chequered hallway and running back to the Tube station.

Questions began to stockpile in May's head as she waited for the train but there was no one to give her any answers. *I don't think the woman is his sister.* What did that mean? Of course she knew what it meant; the tone of Matron's voice implied an intimacy that brother and sister wouldn't have. May wanted to double-back to The Pines and interrogate Matron further, but she would come across as a deranged nutter. She felt a nutter as well. She felt as if she were standing in the middle of a world where all the safe walls around her and the ground beneath her were crumbling and falling. It hurt.

Chapter 13

At two o'clock Lara received a call from Clare. 'Hellooooo there,' came Clare's trill down the phone. 'Are you all packed, then, missus?'

'Not yet,' replied Lara, snatching a look at the clock. She would have to make this a quick call because she had a meeting in ten minutes and needed to get a sandwich as she had sugar-shakes. 'But it won't take me long. I'm only taking the three ball-gowns.'

'No worries, you can always borrow one of mine if you run short,' chuckled Clare. 'I can't believe we are actually going, can you? I can't remember the last time I had a holiday.'

I can't believe I left the booking so late and risked there being no rooms left, Lara didn't say.

'Are you still intent on driving, Lars?'

'Yes, I'm fine driving. The place is a bit off the beaten track so at least if I drive we can go directly there instead of faffing about with taxis when we get off the train at Whitby.'

'It's a long way, Lars. I feel guilty.'

'Don't. I'll drink a lot of coffee. Plus I like driving at night. I find it relaxing.'

'I hate driving at night,' said Clare. 'I hate driving full stop, to be honest.'

'Well there you go then. We'll both be happy if I take the wheel.'

Clare needed to get away to a fresh space so much. She hadn't had a holiday with girlfriends since she was in her early twenties – over ten years ago. She didn't even know where those friends were now. Careers and husbands and babies had had too much of a divisive effect on their lives. Some uncomplicated female company was just what she needed – and a glorious pool, lots of fluffy white bathrobes and air heavy with aromatherapy scents.

'How will you manage to tear yourself away from your handsome James for ten days?' asked Clare. 'And the children.'

Lara almost laughed. She had let her friends think that she had the perfect life in Dorking in that gorgeous big house. When she had shown them pictures of James, they had wolf-whistled. So this was the man who had whisked her off her feet and into his home like a whirlwind, they had grinned. Lara had also showed them photos of her 'step-children' and she hadn't put them right when they cooed and said how lucky she was to have such a sweet-looking ready-made family. They presumed the children loved her and she loved them and all was hunky-dory in her world. And because Lara wanted it to be that way and was sure that it would be, because she was pulling out all the stops to make it be like that, she had smiled and nodded and agreed that she was very lucky indeed. The lie just got too big to own up to.

'Well, I'll be all the better for a battery recharge,' said Lara. 'The children are staying with their mum for the week anyway.'

Clare tried not to think too much about children – she couldn't have the career which had been carved out for her and be a mother as well.

'I am so looking forward to this holiday. It's well overdue,' said Clare. She needed someone to reach into her head and massage everything away so it was just a big empty shell with no thoughts of work or family or Ludwig.

'Yes, it will be great,' replied Lara, hoping she sounded convincing.

'I can't even remember the last time I saw you face to face. Five years ago, wasn't it?'

'Ha ha.'

It was ridiculous that they all worked for the same company and yet saw each other so rarely. Lara couldn't remember when she had last spent any quality time with Clare either.

'Things okay with you, then, Lara?'

'Absolutely,' said Lara, injecting a positivity into her voice that she didn't feel. Her paranoia was ridiculous. How the hell did teenage girls have such a handle on psychology? And why? Lara had fallen over backwards to join the family home without putting anyone's nose out of joint in the process. She had never tried to take the main motherly role although, from what she had learned of Miriam's maternal skills, she didn't have a great deal to worry about. Miriam was a barrister; that her nickname was 'Barracuda Barrett' was an indication of her warmth and gentleness. Not. She had left James for a High Court judge who lived in France and they commuted weekly into London on the train, staying at their very swanky pied à terre in Knightsbridge. Miriam, luckily, had no interest in wasting her time picking fights with her ex-husband's new partner. Lara suspected she didn't ever appear in Miriam's conscious thoughts. But it wasn't the brilliant glacial ex-wife that Lara was worried about; no, it was young, 'spicily sexy' Tianne. She would try her best not to think that, as soon as she was out of the house, Tianne would move in. That was a ridiculous notion. She had to trust James – not all men were the same. Even if all the ones she had been out with seemed to be of a very similar design.

'Lud okay?' Lara asked. Now he sounded like a nice man. She liked the look of the big square-shouldered Ludwig on Clare's photos so much. It was clear from what Clare had told them that he adored her.

'He's good, yeah,' said Clare, with a forced lightness to her voice. She flicked her eyes to the clock. 'I'll tell you about him when I see you. Have to flee – got a meeting in ten.'

'Ha, me too,' said Lara. They said: *Have to flee – got a meeting in ten* to each other so much, it was almost a stock catchphrase.

Lara had a lot to do before she left for her holiday, especially as her second in command, Elise, wasn't as competent as she would have liked her to be – probably because her heart wasn't in it at all. Mind you, Lara could hardly blame her. Working here was like appearing in a seventies sitcom: the men were sleazy and gropey and the women were second-class citizens, even those as high up in managaement as she was. Giles Billingley saw anything in a skirt as fair game.

'I'll pick May up first then we'll drive around for you.'

'Lovely,' said Clare, her mouth now full of a bacon and Brie sandwich. The canteen was too far up itself for her liking. Everything had to be complicated: boiled egg and caramelized onion, beef, Stilton and walnuts, quiche slices with leek and cranberry. It was just wrong; someone was trying far too hard to fuse together ingredients that didn't want to be mixed and totally cocking up the tastes. They should have got their fundamentals right and concentrated on the bread first, she thought. She could show them how to make a proper loaf, given half the chance. She wished she had more time to bake. Although there was no one in her life to do any baking for now. 'See you tomorrow evening. Time?'

'I'm picking May up at about eight so we'll ring when we set off from hers.'

Lara then pressed the speed dial for May, but she had to ask if it was May when she picked up because her voice sounded drier than a sand pit.

'May?'

'Yes. Hi, Lars.'

'You okay? You sound rough.'

'Me? I'm totally fine,' May lied. She had just had to take two tablets because she had the stirrings of a migraine from holding in all that stress, and she hadn't had one of those for a long time. She wanted to run away from the paperwork on her desk, search out Michael and face him head on with the thousands of questions which were fermenting in her brain. She didn't want to phone him or text him. She needed to look into his eyes when she spoke to him. She needed to see him chuckle and say, 'What the fuck was that matron talking about? If you don't believe me, I'll take you to see Susan and then you can find out for yourself which one of us is telling the truth.'

'I've just been speaking to Clare. She's getting quite giddy about tomorrow,' said Lara, hoping that May wasn't coming down with something. She sounded very croaky.

'Me too,' May answered, forcing enthusiasm into her voice. 'I'm packed and ready. Have been for days.'

'That's good,' nodded Lara, then she chuckled. 'I have the sneaking suspicion that Clare will be taking a few bottles of bleach with her. And her slow-cooker. And her stain removers.'

'I wouldn't be at all surprised,' smiled May. 'Bless her. Mind you, if Clare can't get ketchup out of a shirt, no one can.'

Clare made them both laugh with her obsession with all things cleaning and cooking. But not unkindly so. Lara was convinced there was a TV programme in it – the Domestic Accountant. Clare didn't mind them taking the mick out of her in the slightest. Especially when she could chalk points up in the air for things like successfully advising Lara on the best way to get chewing gum out of her step-son's favourite shorts.

'Anyway, this is just a quick one,' Lara went on. 'I'll be at yours for about eight tomorrow evening. Okay with you? It'll be nice to have a catch-up.'

'Yes, lovely,' said May, battling the tremor in her voice. 'I can't wait.'

But she could wait. The last thing on her mind at the moment was going away on this trip. And a catch-up would be very one-sided because, if her worst fears were realized, there was no way she was going to tell her friends all about this mess.

'Me neither,' said Lara.

'Great,' said May. 'Have to flee – got a meeting in ten.'

'Yep, me too. See ya tomorrow.'

Lara stuffed her own sandwich into her mouth and washed it down with a coffee that had gone lukewarm. Everything in her day went at eighty miles an hour. Would she be able to handle a slow pace for a week and a half? She had an inkling that the holiday would be cut short after two days as all three of them were too addicted to their desks. And, feeling as insecure as she did at the moment, maybe that wouldn't be too much of a bad thing.

Chapter 14

May didn't have a meeting in ten, but she wasn't in the mood for small talk. She forced numbers and calculations of gross and net margins into her head in an effort to stop the questions and theories which were demanding to be heard. She batted them away with all her might, and added up, filled in spreadsheets and let plans of setting up Mr Terry's wholefood restaurant in Clapham take over her brain.

Her PA knocked on her office door and then bobbed her head in.

'Night, May.'

May glanced at the clock. It had somehow become seven o'clock. The last time she had looked at it, it had been three. Michael would be on his way over to her flat, expecting to share the Marks & Spencer's meal for two which awaited them in her fridge.

'Night, Berenice. See you tomorrow, lovely.'

'You work too hard,' said Berenice, a bright and pretty girl in her early twenties – ambitious but good-hearted with it.

'It's seven o'clock and you're still here too,' countered May.

'Yeah, but I've been sitting reading a magazine since six. I'm meeting friends for a meal. It wasn't worth me going home and I don't feel like shopping – have you seen the weather?'

May looked through the window and saw the rain lashing

the glass. She had a sudden urge to open the window and let it fall on her face, saturate her, flood her mind and wash away every last memory of that man.

'Have a nice time,' said May. 'Where are you going?'

'Some Malaysian place,' said Berenice. 'Seventeen of us for my friend's twenty-first. See you in the morning. I'll be early, but not so sure about bright.' And with that she gave a little wave and closed the door.

Twenty-one seemed a million years behind her yet it was only twelve. Twelve years ago she finished her Business, Management and Leadership degree at Exeter and it had felt as though the world was her oyster. Too bad she'd harvested an oyster in a month with no R in it.

May gulped down the massive lump of emotion clogging up her throat as she put on her coat and switched off the office light. For the five-minute walk to the Tube she played a game with herself, working down the alphabet and naming a film star for every letter, anything to avoid thinking about the scene that would soon be played out at home. On the Tube she tried not to look at the couple opposite her who were holding hands and whispering to each other. The woman had shiny brown hair and love was making her chestnut-coloured eyes shine. Just as May's had been shining until that morning's trip to Clapham. It was her own fault. She should never have let herself fall for a married man – it was hubris, karma, kismet.

She wished she had never struggled to put up her stupid umbrella in the flash storm last November. She wished she had told the man who stopped to help her put it up to piss off and leave her alone. She wished she hadn't accepted his offer of a coffee and shelter from the rain in a nearby tea shop in Covent Garden. She wished she hadn't let him open the door for her, pull the chair out for her, work his charm on her. She wished she had walked out there and then when he told her he was married to a dying woman. She wished she hadn't let him convince her he was lonely and tortured and stumbling through life not knowing where he was or what he was doing any more. She wished she hadn't been a stupid idiotic soft touch with a scar on her face who was so sodding grateful to be loved and found attractive that she believed all the rubbish that tumbled out of his lying gob.

It was impossible to stop the tears from falling by the time she reached her street. She tried to push them back into her eyes, but they wouldn't go. She deserved them. She let them drip steadily down her pale cheeks and then had to stand at the corner in the rain and steady herself before she approached her front door. Michael's company Mondeo was parked outside her house.

As she put her key in the lock, May realized she didn't have a plan of action. Even if she had, she would have ignored it, though. Her head went into a spin as she heard his cheery call.

'Hiya. I thought I'd make a start on dinner. Found everything in the fridge.'

May took off her coat and hung it on the newel post at the bottom of the stairs, on top of Michael's. Then she doubled back, removed her coat from touching his and hung it on a peg on the wall instead.

May walked down the hallway towards the kitchen. Every step taking her closer to a confrontation she didn't want to have – but knew she must. *Oh, please, please make him have a plausible explanation. I'll never put another foot wrong in my life, God, but please do this one little thing for me.*

Michael looked so carefree and happy as she stepped into the kitchen. He was wearing her apron and taking the top off the potato dauphinoise carton. She didn't know where to start, what words to use.

'What's up, darling?' He noticed the expression on her face and hurried around the table to embrace her.

When her hand shot out to stop him and her voice delivered a fierce 'Don't!' he looked at her as hurt as if she had slapped him across the face.

'May?'

'How old did you say Susan was?' She hadn't known what she was going to say until she said it. Her words were as much a surprise to her as they were to him.

'Thirty-five,' he said, without a quiver in his voice or a nervous blink of the eyes. 'What makes you ask that?'

'She isn't in her nineties, then?'

'What?' He angled his head, like dogs do when they are trying to understand what is going on.

'I said, *Auntie* Susan isn't in her nineties, then?' Her voice was trembling.

Michael's eyebrows arranged themselves into an arc of confusion but a flickering tic under his eye had appeared. He was holding his composure, but only from the nose down. He had been well and truly rumbled and he knew it.

'I know,' said May, sounding a lot stronger than she felt. 'I know that Susan Hammerton is in her nineties and that you are her great-nephew. I know that you go and visit her with a blonde – your real wife, I presume?'

God, this sounded like an episode of *Jeremy Kyle*. All that was missing was a three-toothed best friend brandishing the results of a DNA test.

'You can't know that because it isn't true,' Michael blurted out.

'I do know it because I went to The Pines this morning. To see if there was anything I could do for your wife.'

He gasped. 'Why did you do that? Don't you trust me?'

'What?' May's jaw dropped so low that it was in danger of hitting the floor.

'I'm not married,' he chipped in quickly. 'I've never been married.'

May stood there in the sort of shock that follows a bucket of iced water being tipped over the head. He had admitted one lie. How many more would come tumbling out behind it?

'Who was the red-haired woman in the photo you showed me, the one you told me was Susan?'

'Just an ex. An old ex. I'm sorry.' Michael sank to the chair and his head dropped into his hands. He began to sob and May's upper body instinctively lurched forward to hold him – a habit established over the last nine months of emotionally propping him up – but her more sensible legs remained rooted to the spot. 'Oh God, what a mess. I'm so sorry, May. Everything got out of hand.'

Got out of hand? What the heck did that mean?

Michael rubbed his eyes but May couldn't see any moisture on his cheeks or fingers. Were his tears false as well?

'Okay, okay, here's the whole truth. Oh, May ... I ... love you so much.'

Instead of making her insides as soft and squidgy as a newly baked cookie, those words now made May's heart freeze. They were like getting a cheap, wilted garage bouquet by way of an apology.

'Promise me you'll listen and not leave.'

May didn't speak. She couldn't have moved even if she tried. Plus, where would she go? This was her house. Eventually she nodded slowly. 'I'll listen.'

'Okay ... okay,' began Michael with a pronounced shake in his voice. He was pressing his hands down as if he was trying to tell someone to shush, but the only person speaking was him. 'When we first got together, I was scared of getting too involved too quickly, do you remember?'

May nodded again slowly but she couldn't clearly recall it because her thoughts were wrapped up in thick fog that sense couldn't penetrate.

'I didn't mean to say that I was married,' he blurted. 'But

once the words were out, I couldn't take them back. I thought if I said something like that to you, you wouldn't get involved with me. I didn't intend to fall in love with you and for this to be such a big mess.'

Once again his head dropped like a lump of lead into his hands and then he sniffled, wiped his nose on the back of his hand, raised his head and smiled. 'I'm so glad it's out in the open now. Come and give me a hug.'

May's emotions were in a tailspin. She looked at Michael with his arms opening like the petals of a big tropical flower, and a sensible voice inside her reacted to the scene and asked, *Is that it, May? Is that all you're going to get? Is that all you deserve?* When she didn't leap instantly into his arms, his expression changed from relief to confusion.

'May, what's wrong?'

If May's heart hadn't been in lockdown, she would have laughed at this point. Was he serious?

'Are you for real?' she asked.

'May. I've told you the truth now. And it's better for you because I know you didn't like the idea of me being a married man . . .'

Now she did laugh. One humourless, confounded hoot of laughter.

'And how long was Susan going to stay alive? Were you going to have her die and then go to the funeral?'

'May.' He actually had the nerve to appear shocked that she could suggest such a thing. May looked at him but didn't recognize him. It was as if someone had taken her lovely Michael, stripped out his insides, put something dark and nasty back instead and then re-presented him to her. How could he even hope to shovel such a big putrid heap under the carpet as if it were a crumb that he couldn't be bothered to pick up? This was like one of those Internet romances where people fell in love but it was all a hoax and the person they thought they'd met didn't really exist. Susan Hammerton had become a real person to her. May had felt truly guilty about her, sad for her, angry for her; she had even wanted to give some money to the home to make her last days as comfortable as possible. She had no doubt now that Michael would have invented a funeral and had her cry buckets over a woman who had never inhaled one single breath. He would have walked into her house with a black suit on and a sad basset hound face and let May cook for him, massage him, comfort him and then take him to bed. Whatever he said in protest, she knew that's what would have happened.

'I . . . I didn't think that far ahead. I was getting more and more tangled as the days went on . . .'

'Oh, what a tangled web we weave,' said May to herself. And *boy* was Michael one trussed-up spider.

A rush of anger swept through her like a forest fire raging over dry twigs. 'And *who* was the woman you took to see your wi— aunt?'

He waved his hand in the air. 'Ah, that was someone I had a couple of dates with. Ages ago.'

'At the same time as me?'

'No.' His eyes flickered left. He was lying.

'Why did you tell her the truth and not me?'

'I didn't like Kim as much as I liked you.'

That made sense. Not. Her name was Kim, then. That detail hurt.

'Is it really over with her?'

'Yes, of course.'

'Michael, were you really in Derby for most of the weekend, or were you with her?'

There was a definite pause before he answered: 'Don't be silly.' It was a very telling pause. It wasn't over with Kim at all.

May's fingers raked through her long brown hair. Was she in a bad dream? Was she Alice in some kind of horrible Wonderland? If she stepped backwards, would she fall down a pissing rabbit hole into a pack of living, breathing playing cards who wanted to chop her head off? Her brain was dizzy with so many questions; she truly believed that even if she did have her head chopped off, that wouldn't stop them coming.

'So . . . let me recap,' said May, spinning her finger around in the air, because she needed to summarize the situation for herself more than for Michael. 'When we got together, you were scared of commitment, so you said you were married to a dying woman.'

He nodded vigorously, before saying, 'Correct.'

'At the same time you were also seeing another woman but you didn't like her as much as me so you were able to take her to visit your ill aunt in The Pines.'

Now he was smiling – *actually smiling* –as if this analysis was a big step towards all this silliness being over and done with. 'That's it.'

'Then when you realized that it was me that you wanted to be with, you dropped the other woman.'

Again that pause. 'Yes.'

'The woman you were with this weekend.'

'Yes. I mean, no.'

But they both knew that he was leading a double life. Kim wasn't part of his past, he was two-timing them both with each other.

'If I hadn't gone to The Pines this morning, I wouldn't have known any of this.'

'You shouldn't have,' said Michael, with an admonishing finger-wagging tone in his voice.

'So it's my fault?' May pressed her hand against her chest.

'No . . . I didn't say that. But . . .' He sighed. 'It's obviously my fault. I've been an idiot. Although, if you think about it I haven't actually done that much wrong . . .'

May countered through gritted teeth: 'Except two-time me. Or is it three-time me?'

'Well, my wife doesn't actually exist so I wasn't being unfaithful to her. And Kim and I aren't married either. And you and I aren't married . . .' His argument petered out, so weak that it died on his lips.

May considered all the energy she had wasted thinking about his predicament, the heaviness of guilt. She was saturated with it, weighed down with it, exhausted by it. Maybe she deserved it all – for taking another woman's husband. Even if, technically, she hadn't, she had believed he had a wife, and so, although he had nothing more than an invented wife, she had slept with a married man.

But she loved him. She couldn't just cut off nine months of real affection like that. And he was telling her that he wasn't married to anyone after all. And maybe she was imagining those pauses and Kim was in the past, as he said. If she could draw a line under what had happened and forget it they could carry on as normal. Better than normal . . . because it would be on an honest footing.

May Elizabeth Earnshaw – where is your pride? Where are you from? The voice which stabbed the idealistic bubble in her brain and burst it sounded like a mixture of her mum, her dad, her granddad and two nannas. All good people, proud people, decent people.

May looked at Michael and his eager face. She looked at his kissable lips and those big soulful eyes. But with every pleasant thought came a large black stamp that flattened it. He came forward, enclosed his big arms around her and smothered her face with kisses, but they felt cold against her cheek because the man who was holding her was no longer that dutiful, needy Michael. This Michael was a bare-faced, two-timing bastard of a liar. She knew what she had to do; she had no option. He would cheat on her again because no man could respect a woman who put up with crap like that.

May extricated herself slowly, because there was still a big part of her that wanted to stay against this man who had shared her bed so many times, who told her he loved her and wanted to spend the rest of his life with her. But she had been out with a liar before, she had experienced the dread of having her trust betrayed over and over again, and it had made her ill. Michael had mended the heart that had been battered by that liar, only to smash it up even more. She had a pain in her chest as if something had split inside her, something which hadn't quite healed from the last time the two sides of it were wrenched apart.

'You have to go,' she said. 'I don't want to see you again.'

Michael just laughed as if she had told a joke, as if she didn't mean what she said.

'Look, I made a mistake. A huge one, I grant you, but come on, love.' He held his hands out in supplication. 'I didn't kill anyone.'

May wasn't sure about that. She felt dead inside. Her surprisingly composed exterior belied an interior chaotic mess.

'Just go, Michael,' she said wearily, raising her cold brown eyes to his hope-filled ones.

Still he didn't believe she was serious and advanced towards her.

'JUST FUCKING GO.'

That stopped him. He stepped backwards as if her words had physically winded him. He had never heard May use the F-word. She couldn't remember ever using it herself. She was as shocked as he was that she could sound so incensed.

He recalibrated his thoughts. She could almost see the machinations going on in his head: *I'll leave her to cool down and think things through, then I'll come at her with another offensive.*

Sure enough, when he opened his mouth to speak, he proved her right.

'I know this has all been awful for you, May. And you're going to need some time. Okay, okay. Here's what I'm going to do. I'll leave, go home and let you sleep on things. I'll come back tomorrow ... Oh, hang on, I can't. I'm on an overnight in Der— Durham. Wednesday, I'll definitely come back on Wednesday and we'll talk it all through. Just, please, hear me out, darling May. I love you. I never meant to hurt you – I trapped myself and didn't know where to run to. I'm an idiot but it's you I love. We can recover this. I'm going to make sure we do.'

She remained impassive – at least on the outside; inside was a maelstrom of chaos.

Michael smiled nervously, picked up his keys and then hovered for a few seconds, deciding whether or not to brave kissing her on the cheek. Looking at her furious face, he thought not.

'So I'll come around on Wednesday night?' he recapped. 'I'll drive round straight after I get back from work. Sevenish. I'll take you out for dinner – no, I'll cook something here and we can talk. I'll bring a bottle of that wine you like.'

She opened her mouth to tell him that she wouldn't be here, that she would be in a spa in Yorkshire, then she shut it again. She needed to book herself in for a treatment where he was battered out of her system with a rolling pin. Oh God, she hoped he wouldn't follow her up to Wellem

'I want your key for this house back,' she said.

He looked surprised, but eventually said, 'Okay,' and struggled to unhook it from the ring of others in his hand. May wondered if one of those keys fitted the door to Kim's house. He seemed to be taking for ever to work it loose, and she knew he was playing for time. Eventually, he had it and placed it gently down onto the table as if it were glass and in danger of breaking.

May didn't move as she heard his footsteps on the oak flooring in the hallway. She stood rigid as the door opened and stayed open for ages, as if he was standing there waiting for her to run after him and declare that she had changed her mind and wanted to invite him back to scoff the Marks & Spencer's dinner for two. But eventually it closed and within the minute she heard a car fire up. Then and only then did May's shoulders slump forward and she didn't so much cry as howl.

She reached for the phone to ring Lara or Clare, desperate to hear a kind, friendly voice, but then pulled her hand back. What would she say to them? What sort of a fool would she look? She didn't know them well enough to expose herself as a married man's slut to them, even if he wasn't actually married. Instead she sat at her table and soaked her hands with tears. She was an idiot of the highest order and as such she deserved the heartbreak she was feeling.

Chapter 15

Clare's flat felt extra lonely when she walked into it that night. Lud's things were dotted around the place and she took a long breath and began gathering them up, either for him to collect or for her to forward: his thick woolly scarf hanging behind the door, his big blue trainers next to her smaller pink ones in the hallway, his spare watch next to her phone, the book on the floor at his side of her bed, his razor and toothbrush, his bottle of cologne, which she opened, inhaling the scent and feeling, just for a moment, that he was in front of her. Devoid of his homely clutter, the flat looked instantly emptier. It was as if their presence was so much bigger than their volume.

There was no cheery text from Lud that night to say that he was missing her. She felt its absence greatly. He would be in the airport now, waiting for his flight. As she packed the last bits for tomorrow's trip, she wondered how her parents would receive the news that she and Ludwig were no longer an item. Probably be quite delighted that she was now free to meet a good old English chap.

Maybe it would have been better if she had started the new job immediately: going away would give her time to think and she wasn't sure that would be a good thing. On the other hand she did need a break, because she was so very tired and she wouldn't have the chance to relax and recharge her batteries once she began her new position. The partners lived and breathed the place. Sometimes she was convinced they stretched time so that they could be there even longer than twenty-four hours a day. At least she wouldn't have time to miss Ludwig after her name joined the list of partners' names on the stationery − that would help matters. And the sooner she moved into the big office on the holy second floor, the more warmth would rush into her parents' voices when she spoke to them. The more love they would allot her. The more time they would give to her. Success equals attention. That's how it had always been in the Salter family.

Chapter 16

The sound of giggling greeted Lara as she pushed open the door to Manor Gardens. It was the laughter of two teenage girls and, mixed as it was with covert whispering, it was not a pleasant sound.

A head with swishy blonde hair appeared over the galleried landing and then quickly withdrew at being spotted. More chuckling ensued. Lara sensed she was the subject of the hilarity. She was obviously being hailed as the wicked stepmother. She forced a smile to her face as she took off her coat and prepared to be nice-lady.

'Hi, girls, have you eaten?'

She heard a loudly whispered imitation of what she had just said, but delivered in the sort of northern accent associated with the depths of a working pit, and then more giggles. Lara suddenly felt like crying. Was this typical? She didn't know anyone who had gone through the stepchildren experience to ask. She couldn't find any common ground with Keely because Keely wouldn't let her find it. As for Garth – well, he hated everything that wasn't an Xbox or something he could stick his finger into and pull a bogey out of.

'We've eaten, thanks.' Paris's voice floated down. 'Kristina made us something.'

Lara hoped they would stay upstairs and do whatever teenage

girls did – swoon over Justin Bieber or One Direction/Take That/David Cassidy – whoever was 'in' at the moment. She would rather they remained out of her way and snickered about her, than watched every move she made with permanently mocking eyes.

Lara went into the kitchen and opened the fridge door, pulling out a can of diet cherry Coke and the box containing the small crustless quiche that she had earmarked for tea, seeing as she wasn't going to be sharing a candlelit supper with James. The box felt very light. She opened it to find that it was empty but had been sealed up again and replaced on the shelf. She knew Kristina wouldn't have done such a thing, and Garth wouldn't have wasted precious Xbox time inventing ways to annoy her. This had all the hallmarks of a Keely prank, which is why she always kept her toothbrush in her make-up bag and a 'dummy' in the glass in their en-suite bathroom. She didn't trust Keely not to do something gross with it behind her back.

Lara was totally fed up with the constant attempts to provoke her. She fought hard to push down the rising tears when Keely came into the kitchen wearing her perma-smirk, which widened even more when she saw Lara holding the empty quiche box. It was ridiculous – at work Lara could reduce grown men to rubble, at home a spotty grotty teenager with delusions of becoming the next Kate Moss was doing the very same to her.

'Having quiche for tea, I see?' she said, her face a perfect arrangement of innocence.

'I was going to, but it seems someone beat me to it.' Lara tried to laugh it off but didn't really manage it.

'Shame. What time is Dad coming home?'

'Late,' replied Lara. 'That's all I know.'

Keely sauntered over to the fridge and opened the door.

'He's always late these days,' she huffed.

'Well, he's very busy at the moment,' said Lara as breezily as she could.

'Yeah, I noticed.' Keely sounded genuinely annoyed – with her father, for a change.

Lara saw her chance to shine and dived in. 'Would you like any help packing?'

'No, thank you. Kristina's done it.' Keely pulled out two Pepsi bottles and closed the fridge door.

'Okay,' said Lara. 'As long as you're sorted.'

'I am, thanks.' This was said almost pleasantly. God – was this a breakthrough?

'I hope you have a really nice time in France,' said Lara with a sudden determination to win Keely over. It happened in films. Eventually the kind-hearted would-be parent broke through all the defences the child had erected and friendship flowered.

'Of course I shall. I'll be with my mum.'

'Bring me back some rock,' joked Lara with a light laugh that resulted only in Keely giving her a sideways frown.

'I do mean it,' said Lara. 'I want you both to have a lovely holiday. I only ever see the insides of offices when I go to France, no time for sightseeing or shopping.'

'Well, I'm sure you'll have some shopping time in *Yorkshire*,' returned Keely, her voice giving the county the status of a dog turd.

'I'm sure we shall.'

Keely took one step out of the door and then doubled back.

'I feel sorry for you, Lara,' she said, an alien softness in her voice.

'For me? Why?'

'Because you think that Dad could really fall for someone like you.'

'Like me? What do you mean?'

'Where do I start? High-street clothes, inferior cooking,

inferior face, funny northern accent ... is that enough to be going on with?'

No, it wasn't a breakthrough, obviously.

Lara didn't want the tears to appear in her eyes, but it seemed she had no choice – they sprang there in one leap and shimmered. Keely had just reduced her to as low as she could possibly get.

'Keely, why do you feel the need to hate me so much?'

Keely's head swung back round to her step-mother-in-training and, just for a second, she saw Lara as she really was – a good-hearted woman pushed to the brink, a kind woman who had never done her any harm. But Keely was a spoiled brat, raised by parents with primarily their own interests at heart, and that behaviour had become ingrained in her. To admit she had been a complete bitch to someone who was trying to be nice to her would be to admit that she – Keely – was wrong, and she didn't do apologies. Besides, she enjoyed sticking the knife in Lara and twisting it. It gave her the power she felt was missing from the rest of her life: Keely didn't have the power to get any mark at school above average, the power to be popular with her peers, the power to hold her parents' attention and the mirror told her that she would never reach the supermodel status to which she aspired. But still, she did feel just a tad rotten then and the only way to combat the feeling was to be even more rotten. She wafted past Lara with the bottles of pop and the word 'Loser' thrown over her shoulder.

In her wake, Lara could smell her own perfume on Keely. So she had been in her room, going through her things. Her gorgeously expensive perfume – Rain – wasn't too lower class or northern for the snobby Keely, then? And what was an 'inferior face'? It would be funny if it didn't hurt so much. And did it make her such a bad person not to be obsessed with designer labels, as the rest of the Galsworthy family were? Lara liked shopping on the high street and she had put together a beautifully smart capsule wardrobe, even if the labels littering it were more likely to be from Next and Dorothy Perkins than Stella McCartney and Chanel.

Lara couldn't wait for the moment Miriam took Keely – and Garth – out of her life for seven whole days. She had been craving some time alone with James, and the chance to be his girlfriend again rather than being the despised not-quite-step-mother. She resented having his children dumped on her and being extra worn out when she saw him. The thought of seven whole da— And then she remembered that of course her holiday was booked at the same time as the children's. God forgive her, but she was on the brink of praying for an illness to pay her a visit – one that was not too big, just serious enough to give her the excuse not to go to the spa. She needed to stay with James and get them back on track. She could feel him slipping away from her a little more with every passing hour.

Chapter 17

Lara came in from work the next day to find the note she had left for Keely and Garth, a few lines to wish them a lovely week away, still couched in bags of sweets, untouched. She put it in the bin where last night she had found her missing quiche, squashed down at the bottom.

Without the hostile children there the house already felt like a different place: lighter and less threatening. Even Kristina was singing, which was something Lara had never heard her do before. James had come home early from work for once and was now all showered, scented and shaved and looking handsome in a Fred Perry blue polo shirt and jeans. Lara really didn't want to drive up to Yorkshire that night. She wanted to stay here for the week and mosey around the house during the day, making Clare-standard dishes for James's tea, which she would bring to the table wearing something skimpy and revealing. But her case was packed and in the hallway. She would be setting off in less than an hour to pick up her friends and travel the motorways through the night to avoid the traffic.

James poured a glass of wine, instinctively offering it to Lara first.

'Driving,' she said, holding up her hand against it.

'Of course, sorry. I forgot. That's a shame, darling.'

'I wish I weren't going,' she said.

James sighed. 'It'll do you good to be with your friends. And it's not as if it's for ever. You'll be back in the blink of an eye.'

Lara nodded, trying not to look upset that he didn't say that he didn't want her to go either.

'I know,' she said. 'I just wish I'd known that you were going to be alone in the house. It seems such a missed opportunity.'

James took a long sip of the Chenin Blanc and nodded slowly. 'Well, can't be helped. And you're hardly going to Timbuktu. I do believe they have mobile signals in Yorkshire.' He winked, polishing off that first glass of wine in double-quick time. Lara wished she could abandon all her plans, pull a glass out of the cupboard and join him.

'Are you going to be okay in the house by yourself?' she teased. 'Not too lonely without me?'

'Possibly,' mused James. 'I think I know the way to the kitchen and to the clean underpants in the drawer. Kristina will point me in the right direction if I get lost, I'm sure.'

'Will you miss me?'

'Of course I'm going to miss you.' He replied. 'But I'm very busy at work, as you know. At least with you gone I won't have to feel guilty about being late home. I do feel awful that I'm leaving you alone so much with the children and their teenage hormones. It won't be for long, I promise you. I'll make more time for us when you come back. I'll be counting the days and, selfish as this sounds, I hope every one speeds by.'

Lara beamed. At last – an admission that he was going to miss her and wanted the time when she was away to go fast and an acknowledgement that he knew things weren't easy for her in the house.

'You'd better go soon, hadn't you?' said James, checking his Rolex. 'By now the roads should be much clearer of traffic and the sooner you get there and are safe, the better.'

Lara moved forwards and placed her head on his chest. She

loved him so much. She wished Miriam would have an epiph-
any and decide she wanted the children to live permanently
with her in France. She felt James's lips kiss her hair. She lifted
her head and let him kiss her lips, which he did – slowly and
deliciously. That felt so much better. He wasn't going off her
after all. What a stupid cow she was.

'You take care and ring me when you get there,' he said.
'Drive carefully and not like a loony in that fast car of yours.
Promise?'

'Promise,' she said.

He picked up her suitcase and carried it to the car for her.

'I won't ask you if you have everything, because you're Lara
and so you will have,' he said. He always said she was the most
capable, organized woman he had ever met. Then he kissed her
softly on the mouth again and stood on the doorstep, waving to
her until she was finally out of sight.

But in fact Lara's brain hadn't been functioning to full capacity recently and all the needles that Keely had been using
against her had punctured her self-belief. Half an hour into her
journey she realized she had forgotten her glasses. It really was
too far to turn back and get them, but at the same time she
needed them. She intended to do a lot of reading on holiday
and she couldn't even read a menu with big lettering very com-
fortably without them. Bugger. There was nothing else for it.
She pulled into the side of the road, texted May that she was
going to be slightly late, and turned back.

Someone had taken her space so she had to park further up
the road than usual. The front door was locked. She slid in her
key and breezed inside, then straight up the stairs to get them
from her side of the bed where she remembered she had taken
them off after making her packing list.

''S only m—' she called, her words dying in her throat when
she heard the small excited pants.

A female voice.

'Yes, yes, oh God, don't stop.'

Lara's footsteps slowed and she took the remaining eight of
them with the stealth of a Siamese cat with slippers on. Was
James watching porn? But she knew he wasn't. That voice
wasn't coming out of a TV.

'Do you like this?' she heard James say, followed by a
crescendo of delighted female yelps. Lara pushed open the bedroom door, then froze. Secured to the bed with a selection of
his best Austin Reed silk ties was a naked woman, and an
equally naked James was just lifting his head from between her
legs.

'Shit, oh shit, oh shit,' said James, attempting to scramble from
the bed and reach something to cover himself up with, whilst the
woman made no effort to struggle from her restraints. Her long
dark hair fanned out around her head.

Tianne.

It couldn't be anyone else.

'Lara, it's not what you think,' said James, who had quickly
wrapped himself in his blue robe. The one she had bought him
for his birthday.

Lara didn't know what she thought. She felt as if a bomb had
been put under her world and it had just blown up and none of
the pieces falling around her could be put back in any order
that made sense. She viewed the carnage in front of her
strangely objectively. So this was younger, smoother Tianne.
Tianne who didn't want commitment, just 'spicy sex', fun with
no strings. She had small pointy breasts, rather pudgy thighs, a
waist far from the trim one of Lara's imaginings, and she was
sporting a Brazilian. She seemed quite content to lie there,
tethered to the bed – *their bed*.

Lara picked up her glasses from the bedside table, brushing
past James, who was stuttering, holding out his hands as if he
wanted to touch her but found there was an invisible force-field
holding him back.

Lara turned on her heel and marched out of the door on automatic pilot. James followed her, pleading for an audience, beseeching her to listen.

'Please just hear me out. Listen, darling.'

With her hand stretching out to open the front door, Lara twisted back round to face him. He's only given me oral sex once – ever – thought Lara, unable to take her eyes away. Tianne got foreplay. That hurt. She hated him. She wanted to slap him and she wanted to throw herself against him and cry and feel his arms around her.

'Okay, then. I'm bloody listening.' Keely would have loved the way she said that – pure South Yorkshire.

Given the platform to speak, James now found he couldn't say anything. He stammered and stroked his forehead a bit and then paced up and down in front of Lara until eventually he halted, shook his head and said, 'I'm sorry.'

'Oh, that's all right, then,' Lara said, and smiled.

'Is it?' James looked delighted.

'Is it fuck!'

'Oh.'

'Bitch, you said. Evil cow. I wouldn't touch her again even with a barge pole, you said.' Lara was shouting and hoped the podgy-thighed, fat-waisted, pointy-titted naked cow upstairs heard.

'I know, I know,' said James, looking very much as if he was in pain.

'I haven't been out of the house an hour. My, you had this well planned, didn't you?'

'I . . . I just . . . I just wanted . . .'

'Don't tell me, let me guess – a shag. A spicy shag?' suggested Lara. 'I think that's obvious.'

'I thought we were going a bit stale,' James explained, advancing a step towards her. 'But it was a mistake. I see that now.'

Lara's head jerked up. She rotated her finger in the air as. 'Er, rewind that a moment. What did you say – *stale?*'

'It's the house situation, too much work, the kids being around – it's not the same as it was in the beginning.' He did have the cheek to look guilty as he dropped that one, thought Lara.

'It's not the same as it was in the beginning?' she echoed back at him. Calmly, even slightly amused. He'd rushed her into his house, thrown at her the child-care and the domestic duties which his au pair refused to do, gave her rubbish sex and then had the gall to say they'd gone stale. He had intimacy and attention on tap but he had still returned to Miss Spicy Sex. 'James. It's YOU who is at work all the time. It's YOU who isn't putting any effort in. And, in case you have forgotten, they're YOUR bloody kids!'

God, if only her friends could see her now. May and Clare thought she had such a perfect set-up. They probably imagined she was passionately ravaged by a besotted James from the moment she walked in through the door at night whilst the children made 'I love you, Lara' cards in their bedrooms and Kristina busied herself in the kitchen cooking lobster. What would they say if they only knew the truth?

Lara's adrenaline-fuelled composure crumbled just as surely as if it had been hammered with a wrecking ball. She turned back towards the front door and her fingers closed around the door handle to open it.

'Ti— Oh God, I mean Lara, don't go like this.'

He couldn't even get her name right first time.

Lara opened the door then slammed it behind her so hard, she wouldn't have been surprised if they'd felt the reverberations in Glasgow.

Chapter 18

Lara concentrated fiercely on the driving, occasionally wiping the unwanted tears leaking from her eyes. She didn't want to cry. James didn't deserve her tears. He had probably gone straight back upstairs and carried on where he had left off giving Tianne bloody Lee a good time. The whole Galsworthy family didn't give a toss who they stood on to get what they wanted. James hadn't got as far as he had in his career by having a selfless conscience, she should have known that. Top management had to have spare hearts of brick for when they needed to call on them.

'Stop it, now,' she told herself. 'No tears. No more.' She pressed her side where there was a real throbbing ache as if her heart were bruised from banging itself in frustration against her ribcage.

Pictures of Tianne writhing in ecstasy from James's oral attentions tried to force their way into her head, but she drove them back. She could hear her phone ringing in her handbag and she knew it was him because she had assigned the tune 'My Guy' as his ringtone. She wondered if Tianne was still tied to the bed whilst he was dialling her number. She didn't even contemplate answering it.

She parked around the corner from May's house to reapply some make-up and check that her eyes weren't even more bloodshot than she suspected them to be. Her phone rang again as she was putting her mirror back into her bag. She both didn't want to hear his voice – and she did, very badly. He had bought her that phone. Stored in its memory were so many of his loving texts and photos of them together in her flat – before they got 'stale'. She opened the car door, threw the phone on the ground and stamped on it hard with her heel until the damned ringtone stopped. Every stamp was accompanied by a primal grunt of anger. May's elderly neighbour, Mr Wilkinson, walked his Labrador hurriedly across the road to avoid her. Then Lara took a deep breath, pushed down the rest of the tears that were threatening to spill out of her, and strode purposefully to May's door.

At the sound of the doorbell, May checked her reflection, hoping she didn't look as tired and drawn as she felt. Alas, she did. She opened the door and forced a big smile, throwing her arms around Lara. May didn't want to let her go. Lara was the same build as May's late mother: warm and small, and just for a moment May let herself believe that her mother was holding her, comforting her, telling her everything was going to be all right. She pushed Lara to arm's length before the tears started falling again.

Lara needed that hug from May. She had been seconds away from crying on her tall friend's shoulder when May pulled away. Both thought the other looked tired. Both thought there was no need to mention it – after all, they *were* tired, that's why they were going on a battery-charging holiday

'I can't believe I am actually doing this,' said May. 'After all these years of not having a proper break.'

'Well, you are,' said Lara, picking up May's case for her. 'We all are.'

'Are you okay to drive all that way during the night?'

'Course I am. I prefer to drive at night anyway.'

'Well, don't blame me if I nod off,' said May. 'I'm absolutely knackered. I look it as well, don't I?' She forced lots of bubbly cheer into her voice.

'You look fine to me,' said Lara, but it wasn't true, because May appeared to have aged five years since Lara saw her last. She looked as if she needed a much longer holiday than one of ten days.

The traffic was ridiculous across the city to Clare's flat. They crawled along, never finding a cause for the hold-up even when they turned on the radio to check the travel news. May checked her mobile. Forty-eight missed calls from Michael had been registered but her phone had been on silent so she hadn't heard a single one of them. She needed to think but everything was crowding her brain at the moment. She didn't want to give him any opportunity to talk his way out of anything.

Clare was waiting for them on the doorstep of her flat, which was one of six stylishly converted from a beautiful old Georgian city villa two years ago. The façade said grand and stately, inside said hip and trendy. Clare had the bottom one in the right-hand corner which had a small courtyard garden that Clare, being Clare, had filled with brightly coloured pots of flowers.

'I've been ringing you both but I couldn't get a reply,' she said, leaping forward to hug her before moving on to do the same to May.

'I've broken my phone,' said Lara, wondering how many more times James had rung and wishing now that she hadn't crushed it. She wanted to hear what he had to say for himself. She wanted him to tell her she had been hallucinating, and she wanted to believe whatever crap he was going to tell her.

'I'm not sure I could live without my phone,' said Clare.

'Mine is off and is going to stay off,' said May, flicking the battery out of the back of hers. 'At least, I'm going to have a damned good try this holiday.'

'I've made us all coffees,' said Clare, handing out plastic-topped containers. 'Extra strong. I'm determined to stay awake and keep you company, Lara.'

'Yeah, dream on,' Lara said with a smile. 'You'll be asleep first, I bet you anything.' On the doorstep she noticed a big square tin with a carrying handle next to Clare's suitcase. 'Is that cleaning stuff?'

'Just a few bits,' said Clare.

Lara and May both shook their heads whilst grinning.

'Have you packed a lawnmower as well?' said May.

'No, otherwise I wouldn't have had enough room for my steam cleaner,' parried Clare, picking up her tin.

'I don't know why Lud hasn't made an honest woman of you yet,' Lara said as she wheeled Clare's case to her boot. 'I'll marry you.'

'Get to the end of the queue, love,' said Clare.

'I presume you've got your swimming costume?' Lara closed the boot and they all climbed into the car. As well as her love of all things domestic, Clare was passionate about swimming. The gorgeous pool in Wellem spa had been the deciding factor when Lara was checking out its credentials on the net. She knew her friend would go nuts about the large crescent-shaped pool with the Grecian pillars and feature waterfall.

'I would forget my own legs before I'd forget my cossie,' replied Clare, clicking on her seat belt.

Lara took a long drink of coffee before putting the car into gear.

'And we're off,' she announced.

'Good riddance, London – at least for ten days,' cheered Clare from the back.

May and Lara could have said goodbye to it for so much longer.

*

Despite all their plans to gabble their way through a catch-up in the car, Clare, as Lara predicted, was the first to drop off to sleep – within twenty minutes of setting off from her house. Then May followed, although she fought it because she did want to stay awake and chat to Lara so the journey wasn't so boring for her. But her head was weary, exhausted from thinking about, and then from trying not to think about, Michael. She drifted off to sleep wondering what he would do when he turned up at her house tomorrow and found her gone.

Considering the late hour there was a surprising amount of traffic on the roads. That was good for Lara because it made her concentrate on the job in hand and kept her thoughts from drifting back to the scene in the bedroom. Ridiculously her brain seemed fixated on trivia: that the tie at Tianne's left leg was the one James wore when he met the prime minister. And how very skinny and white James's bum had looked from the back. She hadn't realized how small his buttocks were.

The aftermath of an accident on the M1 added another half-hour to their journey, not that the others would notice. Clare was snoring softly in the back and May was fast asleep in the passenger seat, her head resting on the window. Lara was glad to be going away now. She would flush James sodding Galsworthy out of her system with lots of cool, clear water and fresh fruit. She would run from his image on treadmills and imagine Tianne's face on a punchbag as she pummelled it. She would emerge from the spa holiday a fully purged and stronger person. Thank GOD she hadn't sold her flat in Islington. Too bad it would be another three months before her tenants left it, though.

The satnav was telling her that she was on the home straight at last. Less than half an hour away from the postcode that she had typed in. However, the satnav was also telling her there were no named streets pertaining to the postcode, so she hoped she'd keyed in the right one. She was getting tired now. She wanted a hot shower and a hard scrub-down with a loofah and to fall into bed too tired to think – and hopefully too weary to dream.

She left the A64, as instructed by Brian Blessed's voice, and headed down and up a twisty country lane which seemed to go on for ever. It was a good job there was a bright full moon ahead because there was absolutely no street lighting here and the roads were muddy and full of unfriendly hairpin bends. Her headlights picked up an old signpost and she slowed down to read it.

'Useful,' she commented to herself, seeing that all the letters seemed to have been scratched out. Only the last 'em' remained. She carried on until the satnav told her to take a right. This must be wrong, Lara thought to herself, driving down a road that seemed to be a fly-tippers' paradise. Old mattresses and sofas lined the verges. This did not herald the drive up to a swanky – and very expensive – spa complex.

'What the f—' A finishing post showed up on the satnav and then Brian boomed a congratulations to her for reaching her destination – a destination which looked absolutely nothing like the Internet picture she remembered. This holiday cottage was made of old stone, whitewashed long ago, and now, with the aid of lots of honeysuckle clinging to it, had acquired a shabby-chic charm. It was a one-storey build with a neat grey slate roof and lots of tiny windows set in two-foot-thick walls. To the left was a small terraced garden with a bench affording a view of what she supposed, in the daylight, would be a cove. It might have had an old charm of sorts, but it was hardly the newly built log cabin she was expecting. And where were the surrounding cabins: Robin, Lark, Swift and Finch Cottages, not to mention the main manor house? She reached in her handbag for her phone to check the email confirmation, then remembered she didn't have a phone any more.

She pulled on the handbrake and killed the engine. There appeared to be a note pinned on the door.

Miss Lara Rickman - key under mat.

It was too much to think there was another Lara Rickman expected in the area. This had to be the place, then. She was too weary to go looking around for the main complex.

Clare stirred in the back. 'Are we here?'

'Well, there's the question. I think so.'

Clare leaned forwards and shook May's shoulder. 'May. We're here.'

May stretched a crick out of her neck. 'Thank goodness.' Her eyes focused on the building to her right. 'Ooh, that's different to what I was expecting.'

They all made a stiff exit from the car.

'I think they've given us the wrong cottage, but we'll sort it in the morning,' said Lara, picking up the key from under the mat. Nice security measure, she thought. This wasn't looking good. Was God having a laugh with her life today?

'What a lovely smell,' said May.

'Honeysuckle,' replied Clare with a yawn. 'Gorgeous, isn't it?'

The door creaked open and Lara felt on the wall for a light switch. It was an old-fashioned type – like a nipple. Like Tianne's sticky-out nipple. The light revealed a large square room with a monster-sized oxblood leather sofa and chair in front of a huge stone inglenook fireplace. To the right of the room was a chunky pine dining table with a square wooden crate on it. The note attached to it read: *Hamper.* Lara unpacked the crate whilst May lumbered in with two suitcases and Clare went on a brief exploration of the bedrooms. Inside there was a waxed packet of bacon, a paper bag full of eggs, two large triangles of cheese, a home-made loaf, some soup, jam, butter, milk . . . There was nothing luxury about it. No champagne, no cocktail chocolates, no little jars with exotic-sounding French names. Lara huffed and knew that as soon as the morning sun was up, she was going to be having serious words with this spa hotel.

The kitchen and the lounge were one big room and formed the heart of the cottage. There was no upper floor so all doors led off from this main room – six in total: a front and a side door, a bathroom and three small bedrooms.

'Any preference as to sleeping quarters?' asked Clare. 'They're just about all the same.'

'Nope,' said May. 'Take your pick.'

'I'll see you in the morning,' said Clare, picking the corner bedroom; it looked slightly smaller than the other two – and seeing as she was the smallest of them all, that seemed fitting. 'I'm beat. Lara, what are you doing? Rest, woman.'

'I'm putting these luxury items in the fridge then I'm off to bed myself,' she replied, adding more than a splash of sarcasm to the words 'luxury items'.

'Come on,' said May. 'You must be knackered. Get to bed, Lara.'

A wave of tiredness suddenly hit Lara and she knew she needed to put her head down on a soft pillow.

May pushed her into the first bedroom. 'Go to sleep,' she said. 'We can't sort anything out now, it's nearly two o'clock. '

Everything would have to wait until the morning.

The best thing one can do when
it's raining is to let it rain.

HENRY WADSWORTH LONGFELLOW

Chapter 19

Lara slept surprisingly well in the single bed with a very fat quilt tucked around her, until the sunlight peeping through the cream-coloured curtains woke her up at seven a.m. And though she hoped to drift off to sleep again, there were too many images from the night before waiting to torture her. She wondered what had happened after she had gone. Had James and Tianne carried on where they had left off after it was clear she wasn't going to pick up the phone? Did Miss Brazilian stay the night in their bed? Did Tianne try to ring her to deliver all the delicious details of their illicit union, as she had with Rachel when she sought her out especially to brag to her that her James had been a naughty boy? That thought really hurt – because surely James would have known she would try to get in touch with Lara and make things even worse. Lara's heart was clearly not as important as his knob. He hadn't given a toss about her in all this, had he? Actually he had been giving less and less of a toss about her since she moved in. More and more it looked as if Keely's observation was true: Kristina's cut hours had indeed coincided with James's rush to move her in. Lara had jumped through hoops for him out of affection and a genuine desire to help, and her reward was to be labelled 'stale'.

Once again she heard in her head those delighted little whimpers of pleasure coming from Tianne tarty Lee's lips and she felt hot tears of envy and pain rising to her eyes. She slapped her face to shock the tears into retreat then bounced out of bed and over to the shabby, cream-framed oval mirror on the wall to give herself a good talking-to.

'Lara Rickman. You are not going to spend this holiday moping around after James tossing Galsworthy. You are going to have a good time with your friends as soon as this booking mistake is sorted out. Now do you hear me?'

The face that stared back at her seemed to have lost weight overnight. She hunted in her case for her make-up bag. It was time to brush the life back into her bouncy blonde hair, put on a façade and get ready to kick ass with the spa managers.

May had had a fitful sleep. She hadn't had much problem drifting off in the squashy cosy bed, but then the dreams had started. She couldn't remember much about the first one, other than that she had woken up crying because she had discovered that Michael was married to a very old woman with bright red hair and he idolized her. It had felt like hours before she got back to sleep, only to dream then that she had gone round to Michael's house and found him happily married to a very pretty blonde. He opened the door, saw it was May, then his whole expression changed into something cold and hateful as he told her to go away and leave them alone. May saw them kissing just as the door closed. She had spent a lot of the night crying silently into her pillow. What he had done to her was beyond cruel. She would never let another man into her heart again.

She emerged from the bedroom hoping to slip unseen into the bathroom, but bumped straight into Lara instead.

'Blimey, May, are you okay?' said Lara.

May wanted to fall onto her friend's shoulder and sob. Instead she half-lied. She wouldn't get away with trying to pretend she hadn't been crying.

'I've had the worst dream,' she said. 'I ran over a dog. Awful.

This is what happens when you give your brain some time off the leash.'

'Poor May.' Lara smiled. 'I'm going to find the manor house and get this mess sorted. We need healing treatments and plenty of 'em.'

'I'll come with you,' said May. She could do with some fresh air and company. Anything to keep her thoughts snaking towards Michael.

A loud snore came from behind the closed door to the third bedroom. It made them both smile.

'I think we can safely assume that Clare won't be coming with us,' said Lara, making May grin. And that surprised May, because she didn't think she ever would again.

After dressing quickly they left Clare a note saying that they'd be back soon, then they set off to find the spa. In the daylight they could see that the cottage was in a beautiful spot. To their left the view was of the rooftops of the main town of Wellem and its small harbour. Down below them was a tiny horseshoe cove, although they couldn't see much of it from this angle. If you looked at it from directly above, the cove would probably appear to have the shape of a lopsided heart. Across to the right was another small cottage, perilously close to the edge of the cliff. It looked as if the rocks had worn away over time and the house would crumble into the sea within the next couple of years. For that reason, it was easy to deduce that no one lived there. Or, if they did, they were daft.

It was warmer outside the cottage than in it, yet the sky was full of clouds. Clouds that didn't look right, thought Lara. May was clearly thinking the same because she glanced up and said, 'What a strange-looking sky.' The clouds were doughy and low and a faint sweetness hung in the air, a scent that Lara associated with dry ice.

'Shall we walk?' she asked, pointing to the path that wound down presumably to Wellem. 'Or shall we drive?'

'Let's walk,' said May, leading the way. 'It doesn't look that far.'

Lara looked behind her again. There was definitely no manor house or other 'exceptional log cabins' as the advert put it. She followed May down the path which met with a crude road after two hundred yards. There was a lone cottage on the other side of the junction, but no more houses until just after a sign pointing to Spice Wood on the right. Every dwelling was made of thick rough stone, with not a new build to be seen.

'There's a shop,' said Lara, pointing across the road. Above the door read: Hubbard's Cupboard. A strange name for a shop, she thought, considering how bare its namesake was in the nursery rhyme.

'I'll wait outside. It doesn't look big enough to fit two people in,' said May, calculating how far she would have to bend down to get through the tiny door. She sat on the wall and looked down at the sea. It was a pretty little place, despite those grey clouds which seemed to float, then fall and dissipate, before a puff of other grey ones replaced them.

Lara pushed the door open and a loud bell on a spiral of wire heralded her entrance into the shop. As she walked in, silence fell and the male shopkeeper and a very eccentrically dressed old man with a pipe clamped between his teeth both turned to stare at Lara as if she had two heads – and neither of them attractive. It was like a scene from an old horror film, where the villagers make it clear that strangers are not welcome in these parts.

'Hi,' said Lara, feeling heat rising to her cheeks as the two men continued to stare at her. The older one was dressed like Sherlock Holmes in a long cape and deerstalker. Below his knees the resemblance ended: he was sporting pink pumps. His gaze never shifted from Lara, not even to blink. It was as if his eyelids were glued up. 'Er, can you tell me where the manor house is, please?'

At least her question made them tear their eyes away from her and towards each other for a moment of collusion.

'The manor house?' said the shopkeeper. 'Carlton Hall, you mean?'

'Is that the spa?'

'No Spar here. The nearest big supermarkets are in Wellem. Spar and Tesco.'

'Ah, not Spar with an "r",' Lara clarified. 'I mean the health spa. The big building?'

They were looking blankly at her. Hang on; Lara's brain caught up with her ears.

'Sorry, did you say the nearest supermarket is in Wellem?'

'Yes. It's about five miles away.'

'Isn't this Wellem?' Now she really was confused.

'This is Dullem,' said Sherlock. 'Ren Dullem.'

Lara scratched her forehead in confusion. This was odd. But if they were in the wrong village, how come there was a note for her pinned on the door. 'There's obviously been a huge mistake,' she muttered to herself. 'Erm, we're in the cottage up there,' she said, and pointed over her shoulder. 'It's the white one, with the honeysuckle, at the top of the path.'

'Well Cottage,' said the shopkeeper. 'Staying there, are you?' He and Sherlock exchanged disgruntled looks, their eyebrows raised.

'Do you happen to know who owns it? I think there's been an error in our booking and we shouldn't be here.'

'Oh, yes, I know who owns it,' said the shopkeeper. 'I know only too well.'

If the sun was shining this would be an incredibly pretty spot, thought May. She had forgotten what quiet in the daytime sounded like; she was so used to traffic outside her house, city noises, bustling rush. She felt naughty, as if it were illegal to be doing nothing. It was such a lovely warm day too; it didn't make any sense for those strange clouds to be in the air. They only seemed to rest over the bay; there were none in the distance at all.

She didn't want her thoughts to wander over to Michael again but they did. She wondered how many times he had tried to ring her now. What was he doing? Was he thinking everything through, trying to unpick the knots and find a way they could make this all right? He was wasting his time. He couldn't make that amount of deception go away. It was all spoiled beyond any salvage operation. She felt tears start to rise as memories of all the lovely times they'd shared together pushed through the shit of the past few days: sex, snuggled up in front of the TV, cooking together. They hadn't gone out much in their 'courtship'. May had insisted on that. It would have been wrong, when Susan was hospitalized, to gallivant to the pictures or to fancy restaurants. And she hadn't ever been to Michael's house because she didn't think it right to invade the space he shared with Susan. How could she have been so blind and stupid? She hadn't spotted a rat in the whole nine months; she had given him all her trust and he had abused it. That was it. She would never ever go out with another man, ever. Michael was the last and worst of a list of useless tosser boyfriends. She was going to become a nun and glue up her genitals.

'Morning.'

She looked up at the word to see a man striding past on his way down the hill. An incredibly tall man with untidy black waves of hair skimming the back of his neck. He had wide shoulders and long legs, big thighs and a fine chunk of bum pushing at the material of his faded blue jeans. May's brown eyes locked with the man's even darker brown ones and something rather odd happened. The world melted away around them. For a second, the dark-eyed stranger appeared as if through a distorting photo lens that faded the background and brought him rushing towards her. Her hands went tingly and she felt ever-so-slightly faint. It was like a blast had occurred inside her and the fallout had rushed down to her nerve endings. And the effect wasn't just one way. The man stopped suddenly as if he had run into an invisible wall. May saw the Adam's apple in his throat rise and fall as he swallowed. For one long moment there was just May and this man on the planet. Then he quickly ripped his eyes away and carried on walking. Luckily for May he had gone round the corner just before she leaned backwards too far over the wall and fell into the shrubbery.

When Lara emerged from the shop, she couldn't see May anywhere. Then her friend's head popped up from behind the wall, covered in heather.

'I fell,' May explained. It was the only thing she could explain. She certainly couldn't explain why the sight of that man sent her into a tailspin. He wasn't exactly George Clooney and his jeans and checked lumberjack shirt weren't off a Paul Smith hanger, but whatever chemicals he was kicking out, boy oh boy. She'd fallen all right. It was just as well they were leaving and going to the spa, then. Her brain really did need recalibrating. This wasn't normal behaviour. Especially not mere seconds after declaring to herself that she wouldn't let another man near her in a million years.

Lara lent her an arm to lean on so she could lever herself up.

'They don't seem to like strangers around here,' she whispered when May had righted herself. 'I'll be glad when we can leave and get to the spa. Turns out we're in the wrong village. This isn't Wellem – it's Dullem, and can't you just tell?' She stole a glance upwards at those lumpy clouds. 'Dull by name, dull by nature.'

'But that doesn't make any sense ...' began May, checking her trousers for rips.

'Stupid flaming holiday agency sent us to the wrong place.

Stupid flaming me obviously didn't check the booking confirmation properly. I am really sorry about this – I promise I'll sort it.'

'So who owns the cottage we're staying in, then? Did you find out?'

'Val, Jean or Frances Hathersage. The guy at the shop didn't know if they all still own it jointly or if one or other has sold out to the rest. I'm gathering they are three sisters. They didn't know where Val was based, Frances lives on a farm at the other side of the bay and Jean, who seems to be our best bet, lives up at the cottage we passed on the way down. Apparently there's no love lost between them.'

'They sound like three dotty old ladies, don't they?' Smiling, May rolled their names around in her mouth and conjured up a picture of old maids knitting by a fireside.

'I hope they're not dotty enough not to give me a refund,' said Lara, pushing up her sleeves, literally and metaphorically. God, she'd need a massage after all this stress. The tension was settled in her neck and needed battering out with a big bamboo stick.

Lara plodded up the hill, which seemed a lot steeper on the way up than it had on the way down. She wiped her forehead clear of perspiration. The skies should have been pure and blue with this heat, not full of stodgy clouds.

May's thoughts were a long way from focusing on the gradient of the hill. What the hell had just happened to her with Mr Nice-bum? It must be shock, she reasoned. After all that had happened with Michael and her resolve to become a born-again virgin, her body had temporarily revolted and made a reverse thrust. There was no other explanation for it. God, she really did need a holiday. At least the perfidious Michael had slipped into the dark recesses of her head for a while – that alone was worth a moment's insanity.

They turned right onto the path that led to the cottage. There was a painted notice hanging on the gate:

La Mer
Trespassers will be shot.
Strangers will be shot twice.

May pulled a 'yikes' face at Lara. Not so much a sweet little old lady as Ma Baker, then.

Lara heard a dog barking inside the house as she knocked; it was a weird strangled sound as if it came from a very old dog with an instinct to make a warding-off noise but finding the effort too much. There was a beautiful bench made from twisted tree branches outside the door which appeared to have been painted recently – turquoise. Blue window boxes stood on the stone sills full of compost but no plants. Actually there were no flowers anywhere in sight. Unusual for an old lady's garden, Lara thought.

There was no answer so she knocked again, but before she could pull her hand away the door was flung open, and impatiently so. Facing her, and the complete opposite of what she expected to find, was a hulking great man with long, straggly black hair and a face full of equally black beard. He looked like either a descendant of Rasputin or a man who plays as the number eight at rugby for France. At first glance she judged him older than she was; at second glance she realized they were roughly the same age since, under all that hair, there was definitely a thirty-something face – but it wasn't a friendly one.

'What?' he snapped.

'Is Jean Hathersage in?' said Lara, cowed for a second but then recovering in defiance of his rudeness.

'Yes. What do you want?'

Lara huffed. 'Can I see her, please?'

'I'm Gene Hathersage.'

'You're Jean?' Then Lara twigged. She almost said, I thought you were a woman, but that wouldn't have been very wise, she realized. There was nothing about this hairy beast of a man that resembled a woman.

'Gene with a "G". It's a man's name as well, you know,' he said, as if he had read her thoughts.

'Yes, yes, I know,' Lara replied nervously. 'Gene Wilder. Gene Hackman. Gene ... er ... Alexander ... Oh, hang on, that was Hilda Ogden, I think.'

'What do you want?' he barked, waiting for her to explain why she was trespassing on his property.

'Well, there's been some mistake,' Lara began, and she smiled, hoping to encourage his sympathetic nature to the fore. 'We should have been booked in at the spa in Wellem. It appears that we've landed up at your cottage instead. So we just need a refund, then we can get on our way.'

'Not my problem,' said Gene Hathersage, shrugging his great shoulders. He looked from Lara to the stunned-into-silence May behind her, then back to the smaller, curvier woman with the messy blonde hair, who was standing stubbornly in front of him, but there was no hint of approval coming from his night-black eyes, only cold annoyance.

Lara was incensed but she kept her temper under wraps and pushed out her smile again. 'Well, it's not ours either.' Why the hell hadn't she checked the booking confirmation properly? It wasn't like her to be off the ball like that.

'You booked it, you paid for it. Like I say, not my problem.'

And with that Gene Hathersage closed the door in Lara's face just as she was about to continue her argument.

'Well, I . . .' She plonked her hands on her hips and opened and closed her mouth like a gasping fish. She turned to May. 'Did you hear that? How bloody rude.'

May chewed on her lip. She might have worked in an aggressive male environment, but she had never met anyone who gave off as much belligerent testosterone as the man she had just seen.

'We'll have to ring the holiday agency,' she said.

'Yes, we certainly will,' said Lara, marching away from *that man's house*. The sooner she never saw him again, the better. She hoped, when she traced them, that his sisters would be more affable.

Chapter 20

Joan Hawk was changing. She had been working at Carlton Hall for nearly three months now and, though the changes had been subtle ones, they hadn't escaped Gladys Coffey's notice. First it was the introduction of heels replacing the flat ballet shoes she had worn in the early days. Then it was longer lashes, false or mascara – Gladys wasn't sure, but they were definitely longer. Then it was the presence of glossy lipstick – pink after week three, now the shade was veering towards red. Then the shapeless dresses were replaced by skirts and blouses, open to three buttons at the neck. Today, Joan's hair was hanging free in two dark curtains framing her face, no longer secured by a hoop of elastic.

'Good morning, Gladys,' said Joan with her usual wide smile.

'Morning, Joan,' returned Gladys.

She's started to disapprove of me, thought Joan sauntering past her. It amused her.

There was something not quite right about Joan Hawk, Gladys thought, watching her hips sashay down the hallway and into the study where Lord Carlton was waiting for her. She wondered where Joan had been because she had no business to be up that end of the house. Gladys knew Joan had been regularly snooping because she had laid little traps for her. Hairs

Gladys had stuck across cupboard doors had disappeared; deliberate sprinklings of dust had been unsettled. Most annoyingly of all to Gladys, Joan had slipped under her radar. Enquiries to people she knew in Wellem had brought no information about her. Gladys was convinced that, despite Joan's supposed knowledge of the area – which could easily have been gleaned from books –Mrs Hawk had no more been brought up in Wellem, than she herself had had an affair with the Shah of Persia.

She had tried to broach the subject with Lord Carlton only yesterday but had been surprised at his reaction.

'What is it you're trying to tell me, Gladys?' he had snapped – and he had never snapped at her in the forty years she had been working at the house.

'I don't think Joan is a local girl,' said Gladys.

'If she says she is, then she is. Why would you question her?'

Gladys had been reduced to stuttering something in her defence, but it sounded childish and ridiculous.

'Badly done, Gladys. After having to suffer working with Flora and Doris, women of the highest incompetence whom you engaged to "help", it's a blessed relief to have the enormous burden of running the estate and all that entails taken from me. It's been a living nightmare, these past years. Do-able when I was younger, but not now, Gladys.' Then he had delivered a mighty hammer blow. 'And if I hear you have been stirring up trouble behind Joan's back, I'm afraid we shall have to think about parting company. Even after all these years, Gladys. I'm too old for politics and back-biting.'

He had walked off from her shaking his head and she had felt wounded by his coldness. She couldn't leave Carlton Hall. It was as much her home as her cottage near the village square was – probably more so, because she had spent more of her life here than there. Her mother had been the housekeeper here before her, and Gladys would come here often as a small child to help her mum dust or sweep the floors. Looking after the present Lord Carlton was Gladys's life. She would be lost if he let her go.

But Gladys Coffey could no more have stopped her instincts buzzing when her radar picked up a threat than she could have controlled the tide. She knew that Joan Hawk was not who she claimed to be; something was up. And there was too much at stake for her to do nothing about it. Gladys had been hard-wired into doing what she had always had to do: her job was to protect Edwin Carlton and his interests, as she and her family had protected his father before him. She would risk all she had to do that. So she would just have to be more subtle in her detective work in future.

The trouble was, times were changing fast. For a start there was that Internet thing that could spread information and rumours around the world in seconds. The world was shrinking and their peaceful, isolated life was under threat. People were even starting to come to Ren Dullem. That hadn't happened for many years. Gladys knew that yesterday the first lot of offcumdens had arrived in the cottage Gene Hathersage had decided to rent out.

From now on Gladys was going to have to be very watchful and very careful.

Chapter 21

Clare was still in bed when Lara and May returned to Well Cottage. May put the battery back in her phone to find there was another missed call from Michael from the previous evening. Just seeing his name on the screen pierced her below the rib. She should go into Contacts and edit his name to 'lying dickhead' because that's what he was. So why was she suddenly having a rush of missing-him feelings? How long would it take her stupid heart to catch up with her more sensible and dignified brain?

She handed the phone over to Lara, who was eager to get them out of this mess. Lara fiddled with the phone then growled to the heavens.

'I can't believe it. There's no signal. What a godforsaken hole.' She thought for a moment, tapping the phone against her lips. 'Okay, here's what we do. We'll book in at the spa and just leave the cottage. I'll pay for it.'

'Don't be ridiculous,' said May, squeezing her arm. She didn't want Lara to be upset. It wasn't the end of the world that a mistake had been made. May was just happy to be anywhere but Surbiton expecting Michael to turn up with a charm offensive.

'No, I got us into this mess, I'll get us out.'

'There's a landline phone. I'll ring directory enquiries,' said May, crossing to the table in the corner where an ancient black

Bakelite phone stood. 'I'll see what the spa say. Fingers crossed they'll understand.'

'Bet it doesn't work,' tutted Lara, cross now that she had destroyed her phone and couldn't retrieve the booking confirmation to see what it said.

The old phone did work though. May rang and wrote down the number for the spa at Wellem and then rang it. The half of the conversation Lara was listening to didn't sound too promising.

'They've got no vacancies,' said May, covering up the mouthpiece as she conveyed the message to Lara.

'None at all?' groaned Lara. 'They must have. Speak to the manageress.'

'I am. But she's not being very helpful.'

'Let me have a word,' said Lara, who had a much more authoritative voice than May's gentle tones.

'Be my guest,' replied May, handing over the phone. Lara was so much better at confrontations than she would ever be.

'Good morning,' began Lara in her best I'll-get-my-own-way-so-let's-not-waste-time-twatting-about-shall-we? voice. 'I understand you have no vacancies.'

'That's correct,' said the voice at the other end, immediately summoning up in Lara's head a picture of a woman whose mouth was stuffed with Krug-soaked plums.

'My friend has, of course, explained to you—'

'I'm afraid there are no vacancies however much you want to dress up the facts. Not until the seventeenth of October,' said plum-filled-gob woman with an exasperated little laugh. Was everyone in the area determined to be impolite and unhelpful?

'I'm sure if I were Kylie Minogue arriving with an entourage you'd find us a vacancy,' Lara snapped.

'Probably, but you aren't, are you?' And with that the phone went down before Lara could answer her, which was just as well because Lara's face was turning puce.

Lara put the receiver back on the cradle and tried not to scream. It was only then she saw the writing on a piece of paper tucked underneath the phone: *All phone calls will be billed separately.*

As if the man wasn't getting enough of their money.

Lara's next call was to the Superior Cottages Holiday Agency but apparently the girl who had made the original booking had left, and though the manageress made a lot of sympathetic noises, she did point out that if the booking was incorrect the error should have been pointed out at the time. She pulled up the confirmation email at her end and the booking read: *Well Cottage, Dullem.* So no, they couldn't have a refund. Lara, for once, found herself beaten.

'What the hell are we going to do?' she said. She felt like crying, which wasn't like her at all. She was Miss Super Efficient, who never made mistakes and never took no for an answer. 'Shall we go home?'

May was horrified at the idea. Home was the last place she wanted to go. She wanted to be as far away from Michael as possible, and the bonus for her was that if they weren't in Wellem, as he thought, there was no chance that he would turn up out of the blue. 'Why don't we stay?' she suggested.

'Here? In this . . . this . . .' Lara was going to say dump, but it wasn't really. A little shabby in a chic kind of way, but clean and cosy and so very peaceful. And the terrace was lovely. The thought of going back to Surrey and picking up the pieces of her relationship, sifting through them for any hope, turned her cold. That was if any of that relationship still existed. She couldn't be sure that Tianne hadn't bagged all her clothes up and left them out for the Monday bin men. And as her flat was being rented out, she didn't have a home of her own to go back to. She was between the devil and the deep blue sea. And, at this moment, the deep blue sea was marginally closer.

'Morning,' said a voice, interrupting her thoughts. Into the lounge walked Clare, in very baggy pink pyjamas, rubbing her hands together. 'What's happening? Are we heading up to the spa, then? I want to check out the super-duper pool with the Grecian pillars.'

'Do you want the bad news first,' replied Lara, 'or the really bad news?'

'And how does he get off charging one hundred and fifty pounds for a bit of bacon and cheese?' Lara snapped, looking in the fridge at the contents of the far-from-luxury hamper. She heard a snap behind her and turned to see Clare putting on some rubber gloves.

'You're not serious,' she said, guessing exactly what was going to happen next.

'If I'm going to be staying in this cottage, it's getting a fettle,' Clare said. Her words came back at her as a faint echo – she couldn't remember the last time she had used the word 'fettle'. The first time she had used it in front of Ludwig he had said, 'I have lived in England since I was ten years old and I have never heard this word. What on earth does it mean?' Then he had tried the word in his mouth and laughed like a drain for no real reason, which set her off laughing and they fell onto the sofa and the laughter gave way to some serious snogging. She stole a look at her watch and wondered what time it was in Dubai. And what Lud would be doing. And with whom.

'Well, I don't know about you two, but I'm starving,' said May. Her stomach was making all sorts of feed-me noises. 'Shall we go and find somewhere to eat and do a bit of exploring before you whisk out your bleach?'

On cue, Lara's stomach grumbled. She'd been so cross she'd forgotten they hadn't had breakfast. And she didn't fancy cooking up what *that man* had left on the table. Luxury hamper indeed. She'd get her money back for that as well or die in the process.

They walked down the hill again and Lara showed Clare where the rude Hathersage bloke lived and the shop of staring people.

'What the heck are those?' Clare asked, pointing upwards. 'I've never seen such pathetic clouds in my life.'

'God knows. This place is weird with a capital "W". The people are even weirder.' As Lara said this, they passed a row of houses and in every one of the five a curtain drew back and a male head was seen, candidly staring out. 'See? I'll have a complex by the time we get back home. If we get back home. We might have been imprisoned in a new *Wicker Man* and burned by next week.'

'Can you smell the sea?' said Clare, pulling the salt air up into her lungs. She could live without the promise of a gorgeous spa pool if she was able to swim in the sea, which she would much prefer, if she were honest. She was a bit concerned about the hygiene of pools but not at all about the sea, even though Lara had once teased her about whales weeing in it. Clare loved the sea. She had always wanted to live by it, but had never had the chance — work kept her away. And being near to the great expanse of water now brought all those longings flooding back. She could have been living in Dubai, she thought, with the ocean on her doorstep. Lud was a strong swimmer too. They loved to swim together . . .

She shook the thought of Lud away. There was no point thinking of him now; she had made her bed and would have to lie in it, and it was a bed without the once-loving German man who had ranked her above his work. She couldn't have Dubai and him if she wanted the job of a lifetime and her parents' approval and there was no point in choosing a man for whom she was obviously losing her value. There had only been one decision she could have made in the end.

Coming up the hill was a crocodile of ten small children all waving home-made flags with lettering on them: *Dullem Summer School*. They were led by a very good-looking male teacher with curly blond hair and Paul Newman baby-blue eyes. As they passed, he and the children – all male – stared at the women in the way that May and Lara were fast becoming used to.

'What the heck is wrong with us?' hissed Clare. 'Have they never seen a stranger before?'

'Tell you what I haven't seen yet – any women,' said May.

They carried on wending their way down the hill, passing a cute little school on the right with a tiny square of playground. The building looked as old as the rest. A row of houses on the left looked abandoned, the roof crumbling in on three of them. Ribbon-thin cobbled streets, far too narrow for cars, spidered off on both sides of the road and looked ripe for exploring.

May sighed. 'This would be so beautiful if it weren't for those damned clouds casting a grey gloom over everything.' She visualized the sun lighting up the white-painted buildings and shining down on the pocket-sized beer garden of the pub they were just about to pass, the Crab and Bucket. It had a chalkboard sign outside which read: *Today's special, fisherman's pie*.

'Nice name. Are we going in, then?' said May.

'What, and have the whole pub stop drinking and stare at us? No, thanks,' said Lara.

'I'm not going into the bar with my eyes,' added Clare.

'Well you can't go in without them, lovely,' laughed May. 'Anyway, you have beautiful eyes.'

'Which just happen to be different colours. Why couldn't they both be green or blue? Why did I have to have one of each?'

'Vive la différence,' grinned Lara.

But May knew where Clare was coming from. Like her friend, May wanted to blend in and not stand out. If there had been an operation to shrink her and totally erase that silver line of scar from her face, she would have had it immediately.

'They'll burn me for being a witch,' Clare went on.

'Well, let's carry on a bit further and see if we can find a nice café,' May suggested, noticing another curtain twitch in another house. Jesus. It was like being in a John Wyndham novel. She'd bet anything that when they got to the heart of the village they would encounter a load of white-blond kids and some walking man-eating plants that turned everyone blind.

They passed a butcher's shop, a greengrocer and an equally small bakery, all of them with just enough room for the counter and two customers. The shopkeepers – no surprise – stopped serving to look at the three strangers passing by the windows.

'Still no women,' said May, out of the corner of her mouth. 'That's bizarre.'

There was a pretty post office covered in ivy and next door to it a shop that, if the bay-windowed display was anything to go by, sold an assortment of sweets, gifts, pipes and wrapping paper. They passed some more rundown cottages that looked on the verge of crumbling like shortbread biscuits, a shop with a window display full of blue school uniforms, then – at last – they were at the sea front and there they found a café called, not very imaginatively, the Front Café.

'Hallelujah,' said Lara. 'Now we're talking. Get ready for more stares.'

Seeing customers inside, she paused before pushing open the door. It wasn't pleasant being the focus of this sort of attention; in fact it was downright creepy.

'Let's just go in and get it over with,' said Clare. 'They'll take one look at my eyes and I'll be the one up for sacrifice, so you shouldn't worry.'

Lara opened the door and, sure enough, everyone's conversation cut off. Those in chairs with their backs facing them turned round to see the newcomers. Lara, May and Clare sat down at the nearest table and each picked up a menu, keeping their heads down until the novelty value wore off. Lara fished her glasses out of her handbag, grateful that whilst the words on the sheet were clear through them, the rest of the room was blurred. Ah, the joy of being long-sighted. It seemed ages until a general hum of conversation started up again and people returned their attention to their coffees.

'The waitress is a woman,' whispered Lara. 'They do exist in Ren Dullem after—' She bit off the rest of the sentence as a young, generously built woman with a very bonny face waddled over, taking a notepad out of her pink stripy apron pocket.

'What can I get you ... ladies?' she said briskly, but pleasantly. She looked quickly from one to the other, her eyes reaching Clare last. And then a curious thing happened: her mouth rounded into a silent gasp and her whole face softened into a smile. Her eyes were locked on Clare's as if they couldn't believe what they were seeing. 'Oh, my.' Clare was used to people taking a second glance at her different-coloured eyes but she'd never had someone stare at them so brazenly.

'Erm ...' Lara traced her finger down the page. 'Could I have a cheese and ham toastie, please?' It was a bit early for chips but she ordered them anyway.

'Same for me, but onion instead of ham,' said May.

'Quiche, please,' said Clare, avoiding the waitress's intense stare. 'And chips too – why not? I'm on holiday. And three filter coffees?' She looked to the others for approval, and they nodded.

'Holiday? Here? Where are you staying?' The waitress's pen stilled on the paper.

'Well Cottage. It's—' began Lara.

'I know where it is. The Hathersage place.' The lady in the striped apron sniffed before turning her back. It's very likely that she has the same opinion of the wild man of Borneo as I do, thought Lara. She was rather glad that she wasn't the only one who found him boorish.

'Well, isn't this nice?' said May. 'Here we are at last. All together.'

Lara stifled a giggle then apologized. 'Oh, I'm sorry, May. It isn't nice at all. Have I totally bollocksed up everything beyond repair?'

'No,' said Clare. 'I'm looking forward to going in that sea and Well Cottage is very sweet. I had a lovely sleep – I don't know about you two. I haven't slept through till nearly lunchtime in yonks. I was convinced I'd wake up at five as usual.'

'I bet you wished you'd known me better when you entrusted me with booking this holiday,' sighed Lara.

'Ah shush,' admonished Clare. 'I've got the sea to swim in and a cottage to clean. I'm more than happy.' She nudged Lara affectionately. 'You would be really sickening if you were perfect all the time.'

God, if they only knew, thought Lara.

'Well, you can add me to the happy list,' said May, combing her hair forwards with her fingers in an attempt to cover the scar on her cheek, a habit she'd had since childhood. Poor May, thought Lara. She was so self-conscious over that scar yet she guessed that others – such as herself – barely noticed it. May had told them that the neighbours' dog had jumped up at her when she was a little girl and sank its teeth into her cheek. Neither she nor Clare had been surprised to learn that May had been distraught to hear that the dog had been put down. Despite being so much taller and imposing than either Lara or Clare, May carried the most vulnerable air of them all. Lara, especially, felt very protective over her delicate soft-hearted friend.

May continued: 'I don't care where I am, I just want to be away from London.' *Away from Michael, away from my house that is full of memories of him.*

'Really?' Lara's eyes looked distinctly watery. She really did want them to convince her she hadn't made a total mess of things.

'YES. So let's forget about chasing up the Hathersages and just enjoy ourselves. Things sometimes happen for a reason,' Clare insisted. '*Que sera sera . . .*'

'Okay. I believe you,' smiled Lara.

'At flaming last.' Clare punched the air in a gesture of victory.

'Your funny eyes seem to have bought us a way in with the café owner or the waitress or whoever she is,' said Lara.

'Well, it was about time they came in useful.' Clare smiled.

Her eyes had brought Lud into her life. The two odd-bods who had bonded. He had accepted her and loved her for her differences, whereas her mother had once taken her to hospital to see if she could have one of the colours changed.

The café door opened with a pronounced bang. When they turned round it was to see a young woman in a wheelchair impatiently ramming her way in before the tall man behind her could hold the door open. May's heart rate doubled. It was the man from earlier, the one in the checked shirt, the one who was zapping out sexy chemicals in her direction.

The woman in the wheelchair stopped rolling for a moment to take in the three strangers. She noticed that the one with the brown eyes and the long brown hair was looking at something higher than her eye level. She tracked the stranger's gaze to somewhere behind her, and when she turned and found the man she'd come in with was returning the attention she rolled backwards into his legs to break the contact. She had a scowl on her face which looked like the wind had changed and left it permanently etched there. She then started whispering something to him; it seemed very aggressive, if the strange staccato dance which her head was doing was anything to go by. May, Lara and Clare all exchanged raised eyebrows.

'Well, that was interesting,' said Clare. 'Did you see the way that man was looking at you, May?'

'No,' lied May, who was willing her cheeks to stop going red. She could feel them burning up.

'Frank, Daisy, what can I get you?' said the woman in the apron, approaching the newly arrived couple.

Frank offered Daisy a menu, which she snatched from his hand. She gave the menu a look-over, while casting overtly hostile glances at May.

'Jesus, if looks could kill,' said Lara watching the one-sided eyeball attack. 'Have you met her before or something? In a past life, when you were a witch-finder general?'

'Nope,' said May, pressing down on her chest where her heart was leaping about like a small child on Christmas morning. It had no right to dance about like that – especially not for someone she now assumed was in a relationship with this Daisy. She'd done that once before and the key words were 'never again'.

'I don't think I ever saw anyone less likely to have the name Daisy,' whispered Clare, fighting a giggle in her voice. 'Wheelchair or no wheelchair, that is one grumpy cow.'

If first impressions were anything to go by, thought Lara, removing her glasses and taking a crafty stare, Daisy was as far from being a sweet little flower as she was from being Darcey Bussell. In fact the woman looked more triffid than daisy. Her brown hair, scraped back into a harsh ponytail, did nothing to soften features that really did need softening: eyes like chips of grey ice, a long thin nose and a mouth like a cat's arse at the prospect of a rectal examination. Frank, however, had a kind face, with large brown eyes and a generous mouth that looked capable of delivering smiles, which Daisy's did not. He had

black wavy hair with flecks of grey just above the ears, and sun-
tanned skin as if he worked outdoors a lot. Lara aged him at late
thirties. The hands holding the menu were large and square, no
ring on the third finger of the left hand. If this was his woman,
there was still time to escape. He reminded Lara of someone,
though she couldn't quite place the memory.

Their order was taken, but Daisy must have changed her
mind about something because Frank rose from his seat to go
to the counter.

'Francis,' she called. 'Just leave it. Tell Jenny that ham will be
fine.'

Francis.

Immediately Lara knew who the man reminded her of: that
idiot with the long hair and beard, albeit this was a less hostile,
much gentler version. More Jesus than Charles Manson. Lara
bent her head low to share her theory. 'I think that may be
Francis Hathersage – another one of them with an androgynous
name. He looks easier to deal with – shall I ask him for a
refund?'

'What's the point, Lars?' said May. 'We're here now. Let's just
stay instead of hunting around. It's high season – everywhere
will be booked solid.'

Lara noticed that as Frank came back to his seat he glanced
over at May again. And she noticed that May kept stealing the
odd sneaky peek at him.

The coffees arrived. The café owner – Jenny – brought them
over on a tray, giving a friendly smile, a smile that was directed
more at Clare than at the other two, it had to be said.

'Ah, this is nice,' said Clare, stirring in a sugar. She felt her
shoulders loosening – albeit by a minute degree. Her muscles
were so full of knots these days, it was as if someone had been
coming into her bedroom at night and doing macramé with
them. Even Lud's strong thumbs couldn't circle them into sub-
mission. She'd miss his massages – he was always willing to try

to help her de-stress. She sipped at the coffee and tried to dismiss thoughts of him.

'Are you sure you don't want me to have a word?' Lara cocked her head towards the next table.

'No, Lara,' said Clare. 'Leave it. Let's just forget the weird start and enjoy it. I want to get into that sea.'

The food arrived: thick toasties with golden chips and a cress-sprinkled salad on the side, and a more than generous portion of home-made quiche for Clare with red cheese bubbling away on top. May's stomach howled such a welcome to the food that the others couldn't fail to comment upon it.

'Someone let a wolf in?' said Lara, which made them all giggle and heads twisted in their direction again.

It was quite obvious from the body language that as Jenny visited each table she was imparting some knowledge about the three women in the corner. And whatever that information was, it was raising the temperature throughout the café rather than pulling it down, apart from at the table next to theirs, where hostile vibes continued to be missiled from Daisy's direction. Lara wondered if Daisy would be able to unpucker her mouth enough to get in the ham sandwich which had just arrived for her.

'So, come on, then ... let's begin. What's happened since we last sat down and talked properly? Clare – you first,' said Lara, picking up a chip, trying it between her teeth and putting it back down again before it burned a hole through her lip.

'Well, I just made partner, as I told you. I'll hit the ground running when I get back. As I speak, all my stuff is being moved into the grand corner office I've had my eye on since day one. Yeah – life's good. Oh, and I treated myself to a new kitchen. I stole some space from the spare bedroom that I never use.'

'And Lud?' pressed May. 'How is he?'

'He's good too,' Clare said, nodding.

'Smashing,' replied May and Lara in unison, both silently wishing they had a Lud in their lives, instead of a dud.

'Bet your mum and dad are happy about your partnership,' put in May, trying not to sound snidey.

'My parents are delighted,' said Clare with a genuinely puffed-up smile.

They would be, thought May and Lara simultaneously. Neither of them had met Clare's family but from what she had said about them they had gathered that they were rather a snooty lot. Clare's elder brother, Toby, apparently walked about as if he had a permanent eggy fart smell under his nose and as for her sister, Alice, well, she came across as someone who would make old Daisy on the next table look like Bonnie Langford. It was obvious that Clare never quite cut the mustard for her parents.

May had felt sad when Clare dropped that into a conversation one day because her own mum and dad had always been so loving and supportive. May missed her lovely warm parents so much. They were gentle, kind people who'd had her – their only child – in their mid-forties. Her mum had worked in a care home; her dad had been a car mechanic. He'd got May tinkering on engines as soon as she was old enough to hold a spanner.

She had lost her father to a cardiac arrest six years ago, her mother to a brain haemorrhage eight months later and the pain of them leaving her had hardly dulled.

'Come on, then, Lara – how's life with the kids? Are you being a nice or a wicked stepmother to them?'

'Oh, it all takes a bit of getting used to,' trilled Lara, ripping at her toastie. Really she wanted to say that if Cinderella had been anything like Keely Galsworthy then maybe the old step-mother had a point.

'We want more detail than that,' pressed May.

For a split second, Lara wanted to open her mouth and let it all out: how disappointing moving in with James had been, how his kids hated her, how he seemed to want another au pair rather than a lover ... and the carnage she'd witnessed the night before. These women were her friends – they'd be there for her. She opened her mouth, but what came out was:

'Oh, we're just all finding our feet. The children are friendly, the house is gorgeous. James is ...'

a lying, using, two-faced bastard.

' ... top dog at work. Sexy as ever.'

'Isn't he just,' cooed Clare, imagining how very different to Lud James Galsworthy would be in bed: masterful and dominant.

'Your job okay?' This from May, biting down on her toastie and finding it very tasty.

'Yeah, it's good,' said Lara, thinking that if she were Pinocchio at this moment, she would have been able to hang a whole line of washing on her nose. But dumping the details of her crap life on them was hardly fair when they'd all come on holiday to have a laugh.

'Okay, May – you now,' said Clare, and Lara breathed a sigh of grateful relief that the spotlight was off her.

May shrugged. 'Ah, not much to tell.' *There is, May – spill every bean to your friends and lance the boil that is Michael Hammerton*, said a voice inside. But May knew she wouldn't. She was too ashamed of falling for a married man – who wasn't married in the end. The other two were happy and all was going so well for them and she had no intention of dragging their spirits down on their holiday. 'Everything good in my world. Job great.'

At least the last part wasn't a lie. She loved what she did, helping enthusiastic people make their business dreams come true – she just didn't like where she did it. She hated commuting, and hated the Tube and the overcrowded train that she had to stand up in every morning. 'Boss is a bit of a prat,' she added, putting it mildly, 'but apart from that it's okay.'

'How's your lovely house?' asked Clare. May's house was very 'May': warm and cosy and the right side of chintzy.

'Great,' May replied. She needed a cat – a big black lazy cat to make the house feel less empty when she came in from work in the evenings, but the road outside was too busy. She dreaded to think what it would be like going back to that house with all its tainted memories of being with Michael in it.

'How's your chap?' asked Lara, through a mouthful of sand- wich.

'Oh, he's good. Working hard, lots of driving hours.'

'Happy?' asked Clare.

'Absolutely.' May nodded, her eyes on her toastie. Happy? She wasn't sure she would ever be happy again. Then again, she didn't deserve to be.

'Well, all this time we've been waiting for a major catch-up and we've done it in five minutes,' Lara said with a laugh. 'We could have saved ourselves a bomb and done this over coffee in the canteen.'

'Except we never see each other,' put in Clare. 'Ridiculous that three people who work on the same street have to travel a couple of hundred miles in order to have a natter.'

'Yes, isn't it,' said May. 'It's so good to be with you both for longer than a snatched coffee. Even if we aren't staying in the super snobby spa.'

Lara and Clare knew what she meant. As strange as Ren Dullem was, it was preferable to going back with their three empty hearts to three empty houses.

Chapter 22

'That was a nice lunch,' Clare remarked. After their savouries had been devoured they had been extra indulgent and had a sweet – a delicious home-made ginger and lemon torte for herself and Lara, while May had chosen a summer-fruit trifle.

Frank and grumpy Daisy had left the café halfway through their desserts. Daisy was clearly unhappy about something because she left her apple pie – and she didn't look like a woman who abandoned puddings easily. Lara wondered if it had anything to do with the frequency with which Frank's eyes wandered over to May, as if his were full of iron filings and May's were made of magnetized metal. He clearly found her attractive, something May would have found hard to believe – but not Lara. May was as warm and sunny as the month after which she was named. She had the biggest, kindest heart of anyone Lara knew, and she hadn't a clue about how lovely she was, with her long swishy hair and big brown eyes. Lara would have loved to be as tall and willowy as May. May didn't have a lot of confidence in how she looked, though. She wore cardigans and coats that were too big for her as if she wanted to hide herself away in them and often stooped as if she was trying to make herself shorter.

They all had more coffees, enjoying the novelty of not having to stuff a sandwich down whilst on the run between meetings. Time felt as delicious as the desserts. Plus, it was quite fun to see the gossip machine at work as new people came into the café, spotted the three female strangers and immediately bowed their heads to each other and began whispering.

May bought some good vibes by giving Jenny a large tip. They left the café to a flurry of hushed tittle-tattle, from which the odd coherent word could be picked out: *rain, Well Cottage, that Hathersage, contact lenses.*

'Your eyeballs have caused quite a stir, it seems,' May said, nudging Clare when they were out of hearing distance of the café.

'So I gather. They're going to come for me at midnight and burn me as a witch.' Clare laughed, then stopped abruptly. 'Actually, that's not really funny. What if they do?'

'Just don't adopt any black cats whilst you're here,' said Lara, elbowing her from the other side.

'Such a shame there's all that cloud,' said May as they walked back up the hill to Well Cottage. It felt as if someone had hiked up the gradient a few degrees – she was knackered by the time they reached the school. 'Am I going through an early menopause or is it really hot?'

'It's hot,' replied Clare, lifting up her black fringe and wiping her moist forehead. 'Talking of hot, that bloke at the next table was really staring at you, wasn't he, Miss May?'

'Was he?' May shrugged.

'You were looking over at him quite a lot as well.' Lara winked at Clare.

'I was looking at him to see what he was looking at,' said May.

'He was quite handsome in a farmer sort of way,' said Clare. She liked men with kind faces. Lud had a lovely kind face and the man in the café carried with him the same air as her ex, as if he took life's stresses in his stride. Although if first appearances were anything to go by, Frank Hathersage had drawn the short straw with Daisy. Clare imagined Daisy would give him quite a few grey hairs over the years.

As if Lara was reading Clare's thoughts she then said, 'His girlfriend was a bit of a grump, wasn't she?'

'Can't be any fun being a young woman in a wheelchair,' replied May. 'Maybe her accident is very recent.'

'Yeah, maybe,' said Clare, shamed into temporary silence. She didn't like to think of what life would be like without being able to move her legs. She didn't think it would be worth much if she couldn't kick them underneath the water when she was swimming.

Lara cast a scowl at Gene Hathersage's cottage as it came into view. Robbing bastard. How could he justify renting out a cottage at the same price as a luxury spa? She was going to go into that holiday agency in person when she got home and give them what-for. They might have been brave on the phone, but when she turned up, all guns blazing, that snotty manageress was in for a verbal kicking of the highest order. Then she reached into her pocket for her phone because she had forgotten to tell Kristina to pick up the dry-cleaning. Her hand stilled in mid-air, like a gunfighter poised to take a shot. She couldn't ring, seeing as her phone was in three million bits on the ground somewhere. But at the same time she did feel duty-bound to hunt out a phone and ring Kristina anyway.

Are you joking, Lara? cried an exasperated voice in her head. *Have you actually turned into the doormat that Keely accused you of being?*

But I've got the dry-cleaning ticket in my purse. They can't get it back without the serial number, replied the wimpy side of her brain.

Sod his flaming shirts and suit. If you ring Kristina with that number I'll kick you with Gene Hathersage's leg, roared a much stronger voice.

She felt the wimpy side's lip wobbling at not being part of the Galsworthy household any more. There was a prick of tears behind her eyes and she was relieved when they turned the corner and Well Cottage stood in front of them.

'I might have a nap,' said May, stretching out her long arms and yawning. She blamed the sea air. 'Anyone mind?'

'I'm going to scrub. I'll mind you sleeping if you mind me cleaning,' said Clare, reaching for the key.

Lara followed the other two into the cottage. 'I fancy sitting outside with my book. I never have the time to read more than a page these days.' Lara loved reading. She couldn't actually remember the last time she'd had time to indulge her love of a good gritty crime novel. She'd downloaded the latest John North thriller to her Kindle months ago and only managed to read the first chapter. She put the kettle on and made herself and Clare a coffee as May disappeared into her bedroom. Then, as Clare pulled on her rubber gloves and dipped into her cleaning box, Lara took her Kindle outside to sit on the terrace with the view of the sea and the little cottage on the far side of the headland. She had dropped off after a chapter, lulled by the sound of the seagulls breaking the gentle silence.

Clare hummed softly as she worked so as not to wake May. She thought she heard May sniffling in her room but when she gently called her name there was no reply.

She rubbed down the skirting boards and brushed hard at the fluff at the carpet edges. She loved to clean and cook and make cushions and would dispute that she was borderline OCD because it was a pleasure for her to do such things, not a chore. Any psychiatrist would only have told her what she already knew: that her actions came from an overwhelming desire to have the cosy home her hungry heart craved. She had grown up in a large, dark, cold house with an equally cold family. 'Nesting' was her way of creating a world where she felt secure and safe, warm and protected. In her space, she wasn't constantly

compared to her gifted siblings or feeling like the world's biggest
disappointment because she had straight A grades and not A
pluses; she was in control and doing what she enjoyed, not what
she felt she had to.

Whoever had cleaned the cottage hadn't done a bad job
really, but not to her exacting standards. She dusted everything
that was wooden and sprayed it with polish, rubbing it in until
the surfaces shone. Then she moved into the kitchen area and
took all the plates and pans out of the cupboards to give them
a good wash. Then she wiped down the insides of the cupboards themselves.

Ludwig would have loved this cottage, she thought. They
had been talking about buying themselves a fisherman's house
by the sea one day: somewhere to escape the rat race and live
the simple life for a few weekends a year. Clare scrubbed extra
hard at the draining board as if she were trying to rub away
another unbidden memory of Lud. He was gone from her life
and there was no point in pulling back the retreating memories
of him and polishing them till they shone too. He had a wonderful job in a fabulous place – the sunshine and opulence
would drive her from his thoughts. She had begun to slip from
them anyway. She would have only prolonged the agony by
agreeing to a long-distance relationship. He was affording more
and more priority to his work and less and less to her. And
once she was in her fancy new office, with her name on the
company letterhead, she would also forget him so much more
easily because she wouldn't have time to think about him.
They'd finally be nothing more to each other than just someone the other used to know. Clare carried on scrubbing hard
until her knuckles went white.

After she had cleaned the bathroom she decided to tackle her
tiny bedroom. As she was polishing the mirror, she noticed that
her left earring was missing: one of a pair of pearl studs which
Ludwig had bought for her last birthday. She had to find it. She

shook her T-shirt and the back butterfly fell to the carpet. She picked it up and then got down on her stomach and searched around for the pearl. It must have only just become detached, she thought, if the butterfly was still on her person.

It wasn't under the bed or the chest of drawers. She shuffled commando-style over to the weighty oak wardrobe in the corner of the room and saw a flash of white in the pile of the carpet but she couldn't reach it. She got back up and looked around for something long to nudge the earring towards her. She tried a wooden spoon and the poker but the earring was too happily lodged in the thick unworn pile of the carpet to respond to any cajoling by them. Her only option was to slide the wardrobe away from the wall, exposing the corner.

There was no way Clare was going to let a stupid thing like a massive heavy wardrobe beat her. It would have been sensible to wait for May and Lara to wake up and help her but patience was not among Clare's best qualities. The wardrobe had short stubby bow legs and she jerked on the front right one, but absolutely nothing happened except that her back gave a warning that if she did that again she might end up saying, 'Ouch!' at a very high volume.

She took a scarf from her drawer and wrapped it around both legs on the right-hand side. If she could just nudge the wardrobe out of its groove in the carpet and manoeuvre it far enough along she could make some space between it and the wall, and then she would be able to wriggle inside the gap and push with her feet. She pulled as hard as she could, and again, until she felt the wardrobe shift from the position it had occupied for God knows how long. It took ten minutes of stop–start pulling for there to be enough pushing space at the left-hand side. At last Clare was able to place her back against the wall and lift her feet against the side of the wardrobe. She was crunched up so much that she barely had room to breathe. When the wardrobe had moved another six inches, Clare saw the earring beneath her feet. But she kept on pushing because she had seen something behind the wardrobe – a small arched door that had been papered over in a half-hearted attempt to hide it. After everything that had happened so far, Clare wouldn't have been at all surprised to open it and find Mr Tumnus there.

Chapter 23

Joan took the sandwich that Gladys had grudgingly made for her lunch into the garden. She sat on the bench outside the grand dining room, which was one of the many rooms never used in Carlton Hall because the cleaning would have been far too much for one person. The furniture had been covered in sheets for years. If she ever became Lady Carlton, she would invite all the local dignitaries to dinner and make use of that beautiful room with the huge table and mirrored walls. Imagining Gladys running around making seven-course meals for a hundred people, she tittered to herself.

She had been nothing but pleasant to Gladys, but she knew that her shine had worn off as far as the old woman was concerned. Gladys suspected she was up to something, and she was right, of course. But Gladys's days of being alpha-female at Carlton Hall were numbered. Joan had already overheard Edwin telling the interfering old bag to stop bitching about her. All it would take was for Joan to become terribly upset about 'Gladys's attitude' and the housekeeper would be out on her ear. For the time being, though, Gladys was useful. Joan didn't want to end up lumbered with cooking and general skivvying as part of her duties. And Gladys did make a very nice sandwich, she thought, as she bit into the Wensleydale and red-onion marmalade on home-made granary bread.

There was no real rush. For now, Joan was happy to earn a generous wage for doing very little work. She had plenty of time off to catch the bus into Wellem and occasionally book herself for a treatment in the very nice spa there, or idle around the shops in Whitby, or sit in one of the wine bars practising her pout. There was no need to hurry; this job needed a slow hand. And every day she came a step nearer to having her name on Edwin Carlton's will.

Chapter 24

Clare started gently teasing off the torn tissue-like wallpaper then her impatience stepped in and her actions turned to rips until the old door was fully exposed. From the shape of it, Clare expected that behind the door lay a priest hole or a small chapel. There was a keyhole above an iron hoop for a handle. She pushed and pushed but the door wouldn't budge. It was as if it were cemented shut. So that seemed to be that, then. But Clare didn't want to give up. She tried again, harder, and felt the door give. It was sticky but she was determined and after ramming it a couple of times with her shoulder it opened, with a Hammer-horror creak, onto stone steps that twirled and plunged into darkness.

There was no light fitting or switch and it was black as midnight down there. Clare climbed over the bed for her phone and turned on the torch application, and with the aid of its light she trod down the steps, but carefully because they were narrow and there was no consistency of depth between them, plus there was no rail to hang onto. The air in the twisty staircase was getting cooler by the second and her journey seemed to go on for ever. She couldn't imagine what she would find when she reached the bottom of the stairs. It was too deep for it to be an ordinary cellar. It had to be something far more exciting than that. Then she noticed that the steps were getting broader and shallower and much easier to negotiate, also there was a hint of light coming from somewhere below which was getting stronger as she stepped down what was to be the last turn. It had to be some sort of smugglers' cave, surely. Maybe she'd find forgotten treasure down here – in one of those chests they always showed on pirate films, spilling gold coins and jewellery. Maybe it was a dungeon full of skeletons. She hoped it wasn't going to be something boring and disappointing after all those steps – like a room full of old sewage pipes which once pumped their filth out into the sea. Without warning, the closed-in turret opened out into a water-filled cave and straight ahead was an archway in the rock leading out to the sea. The water in the cave was clear and a bright blue-green as if it were lit from beneath, though that wasn't possible. When she bent to dip her hand into it, the water was warm to the touch. Clare sat on the step and studied the scene that lay in front of her. The underground pool was beautiful, like something out of a recurring dream she'd had. She'd read somewhere that dreams about swimming in blue water meant she was desperate to explore her emotions, which sounded right. She wanted to dive there and then into that lagoon with its amazing blue-green water.

Tomorrow she would put on her costume and swim here. If Lara insisted they go and stay somewhere else now, after this find, she would refuse whole-heartedly to budge.

Lara was awoken by a sizzling sound followed quickly by the smell of frying bacon. She yawned, stretched, picked up her Kindle which had dropped to the ground, and went inside, unable to resist the challenge to her senses.

'Hi.' Clare turned round and greeted her. She was standing by a pan with a spatula in her hand. 'I'm making bacon butties.'

The smell of baking bread was almost overwhelming that of the bacon.

'You haven't made a loaf as well, have you?' Lara wouldn't have put it past her.

'No, that loaf in the "luxury hamper" was a fresh baker's one and they go stale really quickly so I covered it in milk and popped it in the oven for fifteen minutes to soften up. The bacon is lovely and thick and smoked. I've done all the cleaning and thought I'd do a bit of cooking. And guess what I've found?'

Lara went to put the kettle on, only to find it was already full and newly boiled. She got on with the business of brewing a pot of tea. The teapot was a huge brown one with a fat belly: a proper cottage teapot.

'Go on, surprise me. A family of meerkats nesting in your skirting board?'

'Not even close.' Clare's eyes were full of excitement. 'A secret door, a spiral staircase and a lagoon.'

'What?'

'Honest. I lost my earring, nearly broke my back trying to shift the big wardrobe in my room to retrieve it and found a doorway behind it.'

'No way. Show me.'

Lara followed Clare into her room and saw the ripped wallpaper before she noticed the door.

'You'd better put that wardrobe back before the nutter down the road sees the damage,' she gulped. 'He'll have your guts for garters.'

Undeterred, Clare opened the door and stood aside so that Lara could descend if she wanted to.

'How far does it go down?' asked Lara, looking down into the inky darkness.

'Miles. Lara, the water is beautiful. You have to see it.'

'Let me get some shoes on.'

'Wotcher,' greeted a yawning voice from the living room. They turned to see May now standing in the doorway, the last vestiges of sleep shocked out of her by the sight of the damage. 'What the hell have you done, Clare? Don't tell me you're stripping off the wallpaper and are redecorating as well.'

'I've found a staircase that goes straight down to the sea.' She smiled proudly. 'Have a bacon sandwich first then I'll show you.'

'Ooh that sounds very exciting,' said May. 'Both the stair thing and the bacon sarnie.'

'Come on then,' urged Clare. 'You'll need some carbs inside you to manage all the stairs.'

Minutes later they were all munching away. 'This tastes so good,' said May, savouring the delicious smoked bacon. 'All the better for someone having made it for me.'

'That luxury hamper had some lovely stuff in it. The cheese is gorgeous and the butter isn't from a supermarket. I wonder if it's from Frank Hathersage's farm.'

'Still not worth one hundred and fifty pounds, though,' grunted Lara. 'I shall be having words with Gene the Mean about that. There's no way he is charging us that amount of money for basic foodstuffs.'

'Shall we brave the local pub tonight?' asked May, licking her fingers as she popped the last of the bread into her mouth.

'Yeah, why not?' said Lara. '*He* might be in there and I can shame him into giving us a refund. Right – where are my shoes?'

Clare was very giddy, hardly able to wait to show off the cave to the others. She led the way slowly, holding her torch down so they could see each step.

'Blimey,' said Lara. 'This must have taken years to carve out.'

'And why would you? Unless it was for something very important,' added May.

'Precisely,' nodded Clare. 'It has to be a smugglers' cave, don't you think? Careful.' She steadied Lara who nearly missed her footing.

'I'm going stair blind,' chuckled Lara, patting her heart.

'Nearly there,' replied Clare, reaching the wider steps.

'Oh wow. Oh wowdy wow wow,' gasped Lara at the first sight of the lagoon. 'Oh Clare, no wonder you wanted to show it off.'

May was almost dumbstruck. 'God, how gorgeous,' she said, as breathless as if she had been winded.

'Isn't it? No way am I staying anywhere else now, Lara Rickman. Not even if Wellem Spa begged me.'

'Where's the light coming from?' asked May, bending down. 'And the water's warm. That's crazy.'

'Wonderfully crazy,' said Lara, checking for herself. They could add it to the list of crazy things that had happened already so far. Although this was probably the first one that merited the title 'wonderful'.

Chapter 25

'What a lovely evening,' said Lara as they strolled down the hill. She couldn't remember the last time she had spent a full day in jeans and trainers and hardly any make-up. She had eased into holiday mode far more quickly than she had expected to. Or was she forcing herself to, so she wouldn't have to think about the James and Tianne chaos back home? She wasn't sure.

'Those funny clouds have gone.' May pointed to the sky. 'Maybe they don't come out at night.'

As they passed Gene Hathersage's cottage, Lara glanced sideways at it, wondering if she should ask him about the hamper now. She decided against it. She was too relaxed to get wound up this evening; she'd collar him sometime over the next couple of days and say her piece then.

They all expected that as they walked into the Crab and Bucket the locals would freeze their activity in order to start staring – and they weren't disappointed. For a good five seconds after the three women entered, there was a pin-drop silence and a halting of action as if someone had hit a pause button, then that same someone pressed play and normality resumed.

The pub lounge was low-roofed and heavily beamed. The walls were decorated with cases of stuffed fish and nets, models of lobsters, crabs and basket catching pots, giving it a typical seaside feel. There were ten people sitting at three tables, all men. The funny Sherlock Holmes man with the pink pumps was sitting in a high-backed Chesterfield seat in the corner and sucking on a calabash pipe that wasn't lit.

Surprisingly there was a woman behind the short, but well-stocked, bar. She looked no older than twenty and had a pierced lip and dyed black hair fastened into two high pigtails interwoven with blue hair extensions.

'What can I get for you ladies?' she asked cheerfully, her eyes mainly on Clare. It seemed that their reputation had preceded them.

'Gin and tonic for me, please,' replied Lara.

'Same for me.' This from May.

'And me,' added Clare, looking around the pub.

'How are you finding Well Cottage, then? Sweet little place, now, isn't it?' said the barmaid as she lifted the first glass to the optic of gin. 'Gene's had it all done up. You're the first visitors.'

'And the last,' called one of the locals, although it was unclear whether this was a response to the barmaid, or part of his own conversation.

'Yes, it's lovely,' replied May.

'Two pints when you're ready, Shirley.' An elderly man appeared at the bar with two empty tankards. Having given in his order, he turned to Lara. 'It would be better if we got the sun. It's always cloudy here. Bet you won't be back in a hurry.'

I bet we won't as well, thought Lara.

'It's a pretty place,' put in May. 'We had a walk around earlier.'

'Hathersage had no right to—' the man at the bar snapped before the barmaid interrupted.

'Shhh, Uncle Morris,' she said, levering the tops off three small bottles of tonic whilst she gently admonished her elderly relative. 'No village politics, if you please. Same again for Milton as well?'

'Oh, I dunno.'

Shirley shouted over to the strange old man with the pink pumps. 'Old Peculier or Sea Brew?'

The old man held up an affirmative thumb.

'Milton, is that thumb for Old Peculier?'

Again the thumb went up.

Old Peculier, there's a shocker, thought Lara.

May handed over a twenty-pound note and Shirley slid it into an ancient till before handing over the change, which wasn't much.

'Blimey, it's not cheap to drink here,' whispered May, returning to the table.

'I bet they've got one price for us and one price for locals,' said Lara, in an equally low voice. 'No one seems very happy to have holidaymakers around. Don't you get the feeling people are trying to put us off staying here?'

'Well, I'm not going anywhere,' put in Clare adamantly, thinking of that lovely lagoon underneath the cottage. If anything could empty her mind of all the rubbish that was heaped up in it, it would be swimming in that clear, warm seawater.

'You mean you're going to stop cleaning and take some time to swim?' joked Lara.

'The house is lovely and tidy now,' sniffed Clare. 'I can relax.'

'You haven't done my bedroom,' teased May.

'Don't set her off.' Lara slapped May playfully on the arm. 'Actually you haven't done mine either.'

Clare laughed. 'You can stuff off, the pair of you. Anyone fancy some crisps? There are no calories in crisps when you eat them on holiday.'

Shirley arrived at their side with a cloth to wipe the table after they'd ordered another round and eaten two bags of cheese and onion crisps between them.

'Sorry about my Uncle Morris earlier,' she said. 'Miserable old bugger.'

The place is full of them, thought Lara, as Gene Hathersage and his scowling face took centre stage in her mind.

'They're not used to holidaymakers here,' Shirley went on. 'And they don't want to get used to them.'

'We sort of noticed,' said May.

'Can't see why anyone would want to holiday here, though, I have to say,' Shirley said with a shrug. 'I'm ticking off the days till I go to Cambridge uni next month.' She puffed up proudly as she said it.

'Congratulations,' said May, a sentiment which was echoed by the others.

'Yeah, there will actually be some other girls to talk to.'

'Women seem a bit thin on the ground here,' said May.

Shirley nodded. 'You're telling me.'

'Shirley,' called Uncle Morris from across the room. There was a subtle warning in the way he said her name. Shirley flapped her hand at him and turned head-on to face Clare.

'Do you mind me asking . . . are they contact lenses?'

'No,' said Clare, dropping her eyes from Shirley's intense stare. 'Quite natural.'

'Amazing,' said Shirley. 'Everybody is talking about them.'

Clare raised her eyebrows and puffed out her cheeks. She didn't ask why; she was afraid of what the answer might be.

Just then the door to the pub bounced open and Daisy wheeled herself in, followed by Frank.

'The choice of females in this area is very limited for men, poor sods, as you might gather,' said Shirley, leaning low over the table. It sounded very much as if she wasn't a fan of Daisy's either.

Daisy's wheels spun in their direction then stopped dead. She noticed the three women, cast them one of her evil stares, then turned to Frank and started gesticulating like a very angry

Italian. He tried to calm her down but obviously didn't manage it as Daisy sped away from him and barged straight into May's chair as if she was in a dodgem car and not a wheelchair.

'This is my table,' she said, her eyes narrowed.

May stood up to move. If this was the only table that gave enough space for her wheelchair, she would quite happily go to another – despite Daisy's rudeness. However, when she looked around she saw there were at least two other tables that would give her more room to manoeuvre.

'I'm sorry,' said Frank, his rich bass voice fighting embarrassment.

'Don't you apologize for me, Francis Hathersage. We always sit here,' screeched Daisy.

She couldn't have been older than thirty, thought Clare, but Daisy was already showing signs of being a fully fledged battle-axe. Those scowls made her look much older than she was and they'd give her a healthy serving of deep wrinkles within the next ten years, she bet.

'It's fine, we'll move,' said Lara, more because she didn't want to give the holidaymaker haters any ammunition, plus it gave them brownie points for being so gracious in the face of such immature behaviour. She didn't actually feel gracious, though; she felt like slapping the little madam.

'Please don't move,' said Frank, his eyes on May. 'We'll sit—'

'We're sitting here,' insisted Daisy, speaking over him and then calling triumphantly to Shirley: 'Usual, Shirley.'

No please to that request, noted Lara, who hated bad manners. Keely and Garth hadn't been taught any manners at all by their parents. They scoffed at her whenever she waited for 'the magic word' and never delivered it.

Lara, May and Clare moved over to the table near the window.

'I thought you were going to lamp her, Lara,' said Clare quietly.

'I did think about it,' she replied with a sweet smile, holding up her hand to stop May speaking. 'And before you say being so rude and angry is part and parcel of being in a wheelchair, no, it isn't, May.'

'Let's go back to the cottage after this round,' said May. She was going to find herself in trouble if they didn't. Her eyes were constantly drifting over to Frank and, when Daisy wasn't watching, his were doing the same to her. There was something about the man that was making her heart hungry in her chest. But, as she had already proved to herself, she was absolutely rubbish at judging character. He was bound to be yet another knobhead.

'I don't know about you two but I'm ready for bed,' said Clare. 'And I want to be up early to go swimming in that lovely water.'

'Yeah, well, an early one won't do me any harm either,' said Lara. Despite having napped that afternoon, she knew she wouldn't take any rocking to sleep that night.

They simultaneously drained their glasses and stood to go. They didn't know whether to mark their leaving with a 'goodnight' but it felt rude not to, so they did. Only Shirley replied verbally. But Frank smiled, May noticed. Daisy ignored them, but then Lara was used to being invisible – it was like being back in the company of Keely.

As they were going up the hill, a truck trundled into the drive to La Mer.

'It's him,' said Lara, emboldened by the two gins. 'I'm going to collar him.'

She slipped through May's hands as they tried to hold her back.

'Er, Mr Hathersage, can I have a word?' said Lara, striding towards him just as he climbed out of the driver's side. He looked even bigger than he had standing in the doorway, not that Lara was cowed by that.

'What is it now?' he said with faux patience.

'That luxury hamper you charged us one hundred and fifty pounds for. It's not worth a quarter of that.'

Gene Hathersage crossed his arms as if he meant business.

'From what I remember, the note from the agent was that you would pay one hundred and fifty pounds for a luxury hamper. In my opinion that is indeed a luxury hamper but there was no indication that you wanted your money's worth. I don't *do* hampers, Miss Rickman. You should have been grateful that I cobbled something together for you.'

And with that he turned to go, but he was arrested by Lara's voice again.

'A refund would be decent, Mr Hathersage.'

'It would,' said Gene over his shoulder. 'But I'm not decent and you're not getting one.' And with that his long legs strode into his cottage and they heard the door slam so hard it seemed to rattle the whole village.

'Bloody cheek of the man,' exclaimed Lara.

'So that's who you were talking about,' said Clare.

'He scares me a bit,' said May.

'Well, he doesn't scare me,' said Lara. 'You wait and see. I'll have a refund from him for that hamper before this holiday is over. Or die in the process.'

'That is what I'm worried about,' said May.

Chapter 26

The next morning Lara swam into consciousness as if she had been gently lifted up from the depths of sleep on a magic carpet. James had his arm looped around her; she could feel his presence at her back. Something inside her swooped upwards with joy and she turned over to cuddle him, smacking her head into the wall in the process. The rude awakening confirmed that she was alone in a single bed, the 'presence' was the wall itself and there was no arm around her, just a fold of quilt. Tears sprang to her eyes and wouldn't be pushed down. They were raining so fast onto the pillow that she thought she must have grown another hundred ducts to channel them.

She wondered what James was doing now. Was he alone? Was Tianne looking through her underwear and laughing at the absence of 'spicy' G-strings? She twisted around again to look at her watch on the small shelf on the wall and saw that it was eight o'clock. James would be at work. She – if he had thought about her at all – would be in a compartment in his head, to be dealt with at a later hour.

Men could do that, stuff problems away in boxes. Women bore their heartache like scabs and worried at them constantly, making them bleed, whereas men could shelve their feelings away until it was a more convenient time to deal with them, if at all. Well, she had lived in a man's world for too long and some of their techniques had rubbed off on her. Emotion might have blindsided her when she was half asleep, but she wasn't going to let it take over her holiday. She visualized scooping up her sad feelings in a cloth and knotting it, then consigning it to a bin in her head labelled 'Wanker'. Then she locked it and stepped away from it to see if the fastening would hold. The wanker bin jumped around as if whatever was inside was desperate to get out. She knew it would eventually work the lock and spring out to torture her, but for now she was okay.

She didn't want to spoil a holiday that had cost her this much money. They could have gone abroad for this. She supplanted any residual thoughts of James with pictures of the ridiculously hairy Gene Hathersage and confirmed her resolve to get some of their money back. Anger dried up her tears like a blowtorch. She pictured the cranky, horrible man counting out twenty-pound notes and handing them over, apologizing profusely as she hovered over him in the air, like Xena Warrior Princess. Then Lara did what she hadn't done for years because she was usually bright and awake by five o'clock – she nestled her head down into the fat feathery pillow and dropped back into a deep and indulgent sleep.

Clare awoke at nine, much later than she'd thought she would. She remembered that she'd had the nicest dream about the lagoon, except in her dream it was a thin strip of fluorescent water that ran on for miles. She was in her bathing costume and carrying a towel and her phone-torch down the winding stone staircase within five minutes of rising, after leaving a note on the kitchen table to tell the others where she had gone.

Once at the bottom of the steps, she switched off her phone for artificial light was no longer needed, and took a moment just to look at the lovely water. Where it left the cover of rock to join the sea, the water was dull grey, but in the lagoon it was bright blue, or was it green? It seemed to drift between the two colours and back again. She dipped her toe into the warm water and wondered what was heating it. It had to be something in the rock below, a natural phenomenon like the hot springs in Iceland. Just yards away, at the mouth of the cave, the water would be much cooler, she knew. Giddy with excitement, she sat at the edge of the rock, then slipped into the water. She gasped with delight at the feeling of it on her skin and then dived down to find the lagoon even more clear and blue that it looked from above. When she reached the other side she surfaced and saw another set of steps winding upwards. She wondered if they led to a door behind another person's wardrobe – and did they even know it existed?

She kicked off the side and headed out of the lagoon for the open sea. As she anticipated, the waters were cooler here, but the view was worth it for she found herself in the tiniest of horseshoe bays. To the left was the main harbour of Ren Dullem, but it was completely unreachable by land from here. Above her head, those mad grey clouds were swirling again as if puffed out from a giant machine.

Clare let the water soothe her soul and her mind and thought of nothing but swimming and disappearing beneath the surface to look at the rocks and surprise little fish, totally losing count of time. Oh, how she had needed a swim like this in the sea to take her away from all the bearing-down pressures in her life that she wouldn't admit to anyone but herself. She hardly ever went swimming any more; she had no time. Then when she did, it was only to an overcrowded baths stinking of chlorine – and that wasn't a *swim*. Not like this, gliding and slipping like a fish under the gently buffeted waves.

'Hello. Hello.'

She heard the call as she lifted her head out of the water and spun round to trace where it was coming from. She couldn't see anyone.

'Hello.'

Clare looked up and saw a figure, seated, and waving from the small cottage that looked perilously close to the cliff edge.

Clare waved back for no other reason than that it seemed rude not to.

The figure now appeared to be beckoning her.

'Come, please.' The voice was deep but it was a woman's, she thought. And was it a wheelchair she was sitting in? Oh God, it wasn't Daisy, was it? She wasn't so impressed by Clare's swimming that she wanted her to be her new bezzy mate, surely? But as the figure carried on beckoning, Clare knew it wasn't Daisy. This woman was a lot older.

'Er, yeah,' Clare shouted back. 'I'll come up.' If I can find your house, she added to herself. She wished she'd pretended she hadn't heard the old lady, really. She didn't particularly want to go visiting people she didn't know. *Silly Clare*, said a voice in her head. *Never thinking before you open your mouth*. The voice sounded like her mother's.

May and Lara weren't up when Clare got back into her room. She had a quick shower, dressed, grabbed her handbag and thought she'd take a walk and buy some more bacon and bread, leaving a second note for her lazy friends. As she went down the road she was busy musing about the waving woman on the cliff when Gene Hathersage almost ran her over, pulling too fast out of his drive. He braked hard and wound down his window.

'Watch it,' he barked.

'Sorry,' said Clare. 'I was miles away.'

'I wish,' said Gene, raking the hair away from his face.

'Er ... can you help me, please?' asked Clare. 'Where did

you get that lovely bacon that was in the, er . . . hamper? Was it from your brother's farm?'

Gene Hathersage looked at her with eyes that were almost black. 'No,' he said flatly, though she got the idea he could have said a lot more. 'There's a butcher's to the left down the hill. Him.'

'Also, how do I get up to that cottage on the headland, please?' Clare pointed behind her in the direction of the waving woman's residence.

'Why do you want to get up there?' His eyes were narrow slits now.

'The lady in the wheelchair there invited me up. When she saw me swimming,' replied Clare, feeling the need to add more detail as Gene Hathersage was just staring at her eyes. His attention was going from one to the other but he was saying nothing and it was really disconcerting. 'She waved at me and asked if I'd go and see her.'

'Swimming where?'

'In the lagoon underneath . . .' *Oh, shit.*

His head tilted to one side. If his eyes got any blacker they'd start to smell of coal. 'How did you find that?'

'I . . . er . . .' She couldn't exactly say that she'd wrecked his house and discovered the door that led down there, even though he knew she must have.

To her great relief and total shock, he didn't ask any more questions but gave her the directions she had asked for.

'Go through the woods, take the small path right up the hill,' he said, before crashing the gearstick forward and setting off at G-force before Clare could thank him.

Clare carried on walking, aware that the four men and one elderly lady she passed had turned to watch her. By the time she got to the butcher's, her cheeks felt red and hot enough to cook a barbecue on.

'It's lovely bacon,' she said, complimenting the butcher after ordering nine rashers of it.

'Comes from Frank Hathersage's farm,' he replied, wrapping it in waxed paper and then placing it in a paper bag. 'He runs a good farm, does Frank.'

'Thank you,' said Clare, a wry smile on her face as she handed over her money. She wondered if Gene knew that the bacon was from his brother's place – she thought not. He hadn't looked very happy to hear his name mentioned.

Clare bought a basket hanging outside a gift shop and put her bacon into it. It felt like proper village shopping with a basket to carry and food wrapped in paper. The gift shop was full of lovely things handmade by the locals, she read on the labels. Jams and relishes, wiry bronze figures, embroidered cushions, driftwood mirrors and cabinets, wooden cats, pottery. There was no tat normally associated with the usual commercialized gift shops: the ubiquitous clotted-cream fudge and rubbishy ornaments. She bought some blackberry jam. It would be lovely on toast with that salty farm butter.

She found the village square and the church, a small but sturdy Gothic build with a high bell tower. It was set in a beautiful churchyard and exuded an air of quiet tranquillity. Clare wandered between the higgledy-piggledy gravestones, reading the names and testing herself on translating the Latin wording.

The dates on the graves went from as far back as the 1700s to as recently as three months ago. The gravestones were all shapes and sizes – angels, crosses, flat slabs. Some stood erect, some leaned to the side as if they were having a snooze. But, strangely, amongst the disorganization, eleven graves stood together in a perfectly straight line, their stones a uniform arch, each bearing the expression *Fratres A Mare* at the top and a single male name below. Their wives and children lay in graves nearby, but not with them.

Brothers from the sea, mused Clare. What the heck did that mean? At first she thought they might have all died in a boat accident together, but no, the death dates were different. She noticed that the eleventh grave, which was next to the fence, had a neighbour. A twelfth grave, with the same arched stone, had been dug in land outside the original border of the church-yard but the fence had been replaced around the back of it, as if it were once shut out and had been welcomed back in again. Odd, thought Clare. It very much looked to her as if one of the 'brothers' had initially been buried on uncon-secrated ground. Below the familiar words *Fratres A Mare*, the carved words announced that Seymour Elias Acaster lay here after dying in 1969 and that he was the beloved husband of R. Below that was a small Latin inscription: *Illis quos amo deserviam*. She racked her brains trying to work out what the Latin meant but only got as far as recalling that *amo* meant I love. Maybe something about deserving love? The words on the grave weren't as intriguing as its position. Had Mr Acaster been a criminal? Didn't they used to bury criminals on land that hadn't been blessed? Clare loved a good mystery.

She pottered back up the hill, calling in at the bakery to buy a cheese pastry twist to nibble on. As she walked out of the shop she crashed straight into a man who extended his arms to stop her falling.

'Careful,' he said. She looked up to see a handsome face with cat-green eyes. Then he smiled. 'So you're the witch everyone is talking about.'

'Excuse me?' said Clare, flustered for a whole number of rea-sons.

The man dropped his hands from her arms and a little part of her was sorry about that.

'In the nicest possible way,' he said.

Clare made a small embarrassed laugh and stepped shyly past him. She didn't expect the stranger to catch her up.

'You're staying at my brother's place, I hear,' he said, holding out his hand to be shaken. 'I'm Val. The younger, good-looking brother. Don't tell Gene you met me or he'll charge you double.'

Clare shook his hand out of courtesy. His fingers were long and cool and soft. They weren't the hands of a man who worked hard with them.

'You're Val? We thought you were three sisters,' said Clare, scrabbling around for something to say. 'Frances, Jean and Val.'

'Blame my mother – she was a great fan of the movies,' said Val. 'Gene Kelly, Francis Sinatra – and Rudolph Valentino. Plus, I was born on the fourteenth of February. It was destiny I would be called Valentino. All the best lovers are born then. '

'I see,' said Clare. 'Well, have a nice day,' and she carried on walking.

'Where are you off to?' He fell into step with her.

She contemplated telling him that she was exploring the village, but feared this latest addition to the Hathersage clan might tag along. The people in Ren Dullem were unreadable.

'I'm going to meet a . . . a friend.' That seemed to be the easiest explanation.

'And does this friend live in Ren Dullem?'

She turned to him to see him smiling again and felt a shameless shiver of pleasure at the way he was looking at her: like an eagle might view a mouse. It disturbed her and yet strangely thrilled her at the same time. Val Hathersage was super handsome and she suspected he knew that. And he'd reminded her of how flattering it was to make someone's pupils dilate, as Val Hathersage's had.

'Yes, she does,' replied Clare.

'You're very secretive,' laughed Val. 'I'd like to know more about you.'

Clare felt a tremble of excitement trip down her spine. Was he coming on to her? She couldn't remember the last time a stranger had made a move on her.

'Oh, there's not that much to know,' replied Clare, realizing how out of practice she was at being chatted up.

'Your eyes are amazing,' said Val. 'Magical.'

'Weird, you mean.'

Val's hand touched her arm and she stopped walking.

'Not used to compliments, are you?' he said.

No, I'm not, replied Clare in her head. Ludwig used to compliment her all the time. Somehow along the way he'd started presuming that she knew how he felt about her and stopped saying the actual words that her hair looked nice or she smelt beautiful.

'Okay, I have to leave you now,' said Val. 'I know you'll be heartbroken but I don't particularly want to risk running into my brother.'

They were almost at the woods. Clare pointed beyond them in the general direction of the house on the cliff.

'I'm going up there.'

'Ah, that's where you're heading,' said Val Hathersage. There was a passing resemblance to his older brothers in the shape of the face and the generously curved lips, but this Hathersage had a much slighter frame and lighter eyes, and those eyes were twinkling with mischief. 'That makes sense. You've been summoned.'

Clare didn't ask him what that meant. She had the feeling that Val might be the sort of person who said things just to get a reaction. Or gave cryptic teasing answers which inspired even more questions.

'Well, I'll leave you to see *your friend*,' he said. 'Nice speaking to you, witch lady.'

'Nice—' But that was as far as Clare got, for Val Hathersage encircled her waist with his hands and spun her into the woods, pressing her against the wide trunk of the nearest tree.

'I want to kiss you,' he said softly, gazing into her eyes. 'But I won't. We've only just met and I'm a gentleman. But beware, beautiful eyes, this place isn't for the faint-hearted. Even witches aren't safe here.' And as suddenly as he had grabbed her, he released her and she found that all sorts of fireworks started pinging off in her head. 'We'll have a picnic lunch in these woods tomorrow,' he said. 'Meet me here at twelve. That's noon, not the witching hour.'

And with that Val Hathersage turned and casually strolled off, leaving Clare with cheeks as flushed as an Aunt Sally's. He looked behind him once, grinned, saw that he'd had the desired effect on her, and then carried on up the hill, his hands in his pockets, taking a right before his brother's cottage.

Despite the height and breadth of his older brothers – and Gene's rudeness – this brother, with his line of patter and self-confidence, might be the most dangerous of the three, thought Clare, as she willed her racing heartbeat to calm down and behave before heading into Spice Wood.

Chapter 27

May woke up and had a coffee by herself as Lara was still sleeping, despite it getting on for lunchtime. She decided to head into the village and look for Clare after finding her note on the table.

There was no sign of Clare in the shops. May bought a newspaper and then wished she hadn't. The front-page article was about the stabbing of a teenage boy in Birmingham and featured his heartbroken parents. May dropped the paper in the bin outside Ward's Chemist, which was wearing a covering of honeysuckle as thick as a winter jacket. Real life wasn't something she wanted to be part of at the moment. The world outside Ren Dullem had her idiot of a boss in it and an unmarried-married man who had smashed up her heart. She didn't know how many other lies were waiting for her in that particular story but she was sure there were more. One part of her was telling her to cover her ears and not listen to any more; the other part wanted to hear every single detail. The trouble was that men like Michael were always hoping to get away with damage limitation and told the truth on a need-to-know basis. May had been there before. Liars were always the worst. They were so good at saying what you wanted to hear when they'd been uncovered. That was the problem – May knew that she had been weakened by heartbreak and was scared of how seductive Michael could be. She was lonely and vulnerable – perfect prey for a manipulator. Being in a place where he couldn't find her was the best thing that could have happened. She wished she could have confided in Lara and Clare but she felt ashamed. She didn't want them to think of her as the slut she felt she had been.

She zoned out, thinking about Michael, and was staring at a display of gifts in a shop window, but seeing none of them, when she felt a gentle tap on her shoulder. She turned round to see the big figure of Frank Hathersage, with his gentle eyes, and the dark hair that she wanted to drag her fingers through.

Stop that, May Earnshaw.

'Hi,' said Frank, a nervous smile playing on his lips. 'I'm so glad I've seen you again. I wanted to apologize for yesterday. Daisy was out of order . . . I . . .'

'It's fine,' said May, her voice coming out in a tremor. God, this man really was handsome. He had an effect on her knees that was positively illegal. 'It must be very frustrating for her being in a chair.'

'Nevertheless,' said Frank, his pupils as dilated as hers, 'rude is rude and that was . . . she was . . .' He was having an equal amount of trouble in articulating himself as May was.

'She . . . er . . . the wheelchair . . . must be awful sat, I mean sitting . . . in a chair . . .'

'No, yes, I mean . . .'

Frank broke eye contact and pinched the top of his nose with a finger and thumb.

'I'm really sorry,' he said and laughed softly to himself. 'We don't see many new people in this village. We get a bit tongue-tied with strangers.'

'Oh, don't worry,' said May, feeling her cheeks getting warmer with every passing nanosecond. She was hardly Miss Coherent herself. She needed to get a grip. Was her brain so desperate to eject Michael that it was seizing on the first available man to act as a lever? That was dangerous. A potential frying pan and fire situation.

'Anyway, like I say, I apologize. For Daisy, and for not stepping in at the time. I didn't know what to say for the best. She's very easily inflamed.'

'It's fine. Really.'

He touched her arm and it was as if someone somewhere had pressed a button and released twelve million volts of electricity. May's eyes sprang open to their widest and she knew he had felt it too.

'Static,' he said with a laugh. They both knew it wasn't.

Chapter 28

Clare walked through the woods with her basket – or rather she stumbled because the terrain was as unfriendly as the rest of the village – with the possible exceptions of Shirley in the Crab and Bucket and cocky Val Hathersage. There were potholes and mounds and sharp stones jutting out of the ground. In fact it felt more like an assault course than a walk.

She had just nearly gone arse over tit for the third time when she leaned against a gnarled old tree and asked herself what the bloody hell she was doing, heading up to a total stranger's house when she was supposed to be on holiday. Still, this morning had been a weird one: swimming in a lagoon in the cellar, and being pinned to a tree by a man who said he wanted to kiss her ... It was in keeping that she now tried not to break her neck in order to visit someone she didn't know or care about.

You know why you're going, said a voice in her head. *It's the same reason you will turn up tomorrow for a picnic with Valentino Hathersage. You've been moaning about a life devoid of excitement and now you have corners to peep around, the unknown to encounter. This is the adventure your spirit has been crying out for.*

Whether the conscious Clare agreed with that or not, her feet carried on picking their way through the sticky-out roots and rabbit holes until the trees cleared and she was facing the one-storey cliff-top cottage that she had seen from the bay.

Approaching the dwelling with her basket in her hand, Clare was all too aware that from a low-flying helicopter, with her crimson top on and carrying the basket, she would look a dead ringer for Red Riding Hood. She paused by the door and wondered again why on earth she was here.

'Ah, well, in for a penny,' she said to herself and rapped on the weather-worn wooden door.

'Come in,' said a quiet but gravelly voice.

Clare lifted the handle and pushed, half-wondering if she was going to walk in on a wolf dressed in granny clothes. Then she stepped into the dark interior of a beamed cottage. It had a scent that she couldn't quite pin down: sea air, salty, fresh, old, musky. It wasn't unpleasant but she doubted she'd find it in Boots.

Wheeling towards her was a very old lady, her lower half wrapped in a blanket made up of crocheted squares, which had seen better days. As had the old lady, if Clare were honest. She was squat, with wrinkled leathery skin as if she had enjoyed too much sun over the years, and fine white hair that was not quite all tamed into the long plait which hung over one shoulder. The old lady arrived at her side and smiled with full pale lips that were cracked and looked sore. Her teeth weren't in the best state but she appeared to have most of them. But what caught Clare's attention and drove all those other features into obscurity were the woman's eyes: the left one was a faded blue, the right bright green. The old lady's hands stilled on her wheels as she looked into Clare's face and a gasp caught in her throat.

'Please sit down,' she said, grasping Clare's hands greedily with her own. Clare noticed she had strange short fingers, the joints swollen with knots. And they were so chilled that she had to fight the urge to rub them vigorously for her until they were warm.

The weird thing was that Clare didn't feel in the slightest bit awkward in the midst of this strange situation. There was the faintest buzz inside her as if something were being transmitted down her nerve endings. Thinking rationally, it must have been the fact that the wheelchair-bound lady was gripping her so tightly that it was cutting the circulation off and giving her pins and needles. What other explanation could there be – really?

The lady's smile appeared to be draining slowly from her lips as she released her grip on Clare's hand.

'You're not from . . . from around here, are you?'

'Er, no,' said Clare. 'From North Yorkshire though. York to be exact.'

'Land-born?'

What else? But Clare answered with a polite, 'Yes.'

The lady's head dropped wearily. 'It would have been too much to hope.'

Clare was unsure what to do now. Obviously this poor old dear had mistaken her for someone else. Awk-ward. She stood to go.

'Please don't. I thought I might know you. But it isn't to be, I see.'

Clare made a stab in the dark. 'You've heard about my eyes. You thought I might be a long-lost relation?'

'Something like that.' The poor old dear looked quite distressed. Clare could see her hands shaking.

'Can I get you a drink?' asked Clare. 'Cup of tea? To warm you up?'

'Thank you, that's kind. Just water, please.'

Clare got up and walked towards where she supposed the kitchen was. It was a mess, by her standards. The lacy white curtains could have done with a soak and the grout between the tiles would have benefited from a scrub with a toothbrush. She found a cup in the stone sink and washed it. Then filled it with water from the tap and brought it back into the sitting room, setting it on a small square table in front of the old lady. 'There you go.'

'Thank you.' She lifted the cup and sipped at it. 'I heard that you arrived at full moon.'

'Was it? I didn't know that.'

'It doesn't matter. Clare, isn't it?'

'Er . . . yes.' Obviously the village-drum system of communication worked efficiently then.

'My name is Raine.'

She had the voice of someone who had been smoking fifty cigarettes a day for the same number of years, but her pronunciation was almost genteel, like BBC announcers from long ago.

'Nice to meet you, Raine,' said Clare. 'Do you live alone up here?' She wondered how long Raine had been cooped up in the house. There was no road to speak of and no way of negotiating those woods in a wheelchair.

'Since my husband died, yes, I live alone.' Raine sipped at her water again with surprising delicacy.

'Do people bring you shopping and things?'

'Yes, the villagers are very kind. I did have a girl who came to clean for me – Colleen – but she left to go to work in a city. Who can blame her? The ladies who come to help me are nearly as old as I am. And it takes them an age to get here through Spice Wood because the terrain is treacherous. They try to help, bless them, but they can't do much of the heavy housework.' She sighed. 'I'm too old to care much about that, though.'

'Are you from around here?' asked Clare, suspecting old Raine might be lonely and in need of a natter, and she could spare five minutes to do that with her, at least.

'No,' said Raine. 'I'm an offcumden too. But my husband was a local man.'

'It's a very pretty village,' said Clare.

'It is,' said Raine. 'So tell me, my dear. What brought you to Ren Dullem?'

'A mistake,' said Clare.

'A mistake?' repeated Raine.

'Yes, we should have been at Wren Cottage in Wellem, not Well Cottage in Dullem. A stupid holiday agency mixed it up.' She had wanted to curse them when they first arrived, but then she had found the lagoon.

'You found the lagoon,' said Raine, as if dipping into her thoughts. She smiled.

'Yes,' said Clare. 'I'm going to be in trouble with the landlord. I ripped off quite a bit of wallpaper to open the door. I hope I can slide the wardrobe back to hide it when we leave.'

Raine patted Clare's hand, and despite the leathery skin and the yellowing teeth and strangely coloured eyes, Clare felt a very sweet vibe coming from her. Poor old thing. She must be very lonely and a bit batty.

A pure white cat leapt up onto Raine's lap and scared the living daylights out of Clare. The cat had a green eye and a blue eye, except they weren't very bright in colour, being clouded with cataracts.

'Poor old Albert,' said Raine, giving him a long stroke down his back. 'He's been deaf since day one and now he can't see much either. And he's as arthritic as they come. It would be a kindness to let him go but the time isn't quite here yet.'

Clare thought of how she'd never met anyone with eyes like hers, and suddenly there was a room full of them.

'Where did you find him?' she asked, leaning over to give him a tickle behind the ear.

'He found me,' said Raine. 'He turned up at the door one day, twenty years ago, miaowing, thin as a reed. No one in the village knew anything about him. They wouldn't have abandoned a cat like him.'

'You mean with his eye colour?'

'People have old ways in Ren Dullem,' said Raine. 'Superstitions.'

'Someone in the village called me a witch today,' Clare confided. She recalled the crush of Val Hathersage's body against her own and a naughty thrill tripped down her spine.

Raine threw her head back and laughed. 'Yes, well, we're rare and wonderful creatures. Aren't we, Albert? Us *two-colours*.' The old cat was purring like an engine.

Clare glanced at her watch. The message she had left for the others said she was just popping out for some shopping. She ought to get back in case they were waiting for her.

Just as she was about to say that it had been very nice to meet Raine, and that she was going now, a huge wave of sympathy for the old lady with the old blind cat engulfed her. Especially one living in a house that could have done with a really good clean

'Look, the day after tomorrow,' she began, hardly even believing herself what she was about to promise, 'can I come back up and give your house a once-over for you?'

'Oh, no. That's very kind of you but—'

'Really.' Clare held her palms out as if pushing the denial back. 'Anyone who knows me knows that, if I'm not swimming, I'm at my happiest with a cloth in my hand. I would really love to do it for you.'

And because Raine wanted to see Clare again, because she couldn't quite believe that a woman who had arrived at full moon, and had eyes like the shifting colours of her lagoon and swam like a ribbon in the sea could just be an ordinary holidaymaker, she relented.

'That would be wonderful,' she said.

Chapter 29

Lara awoke to find an empty house. There was a note from Clare to say that she had nipped out for some shopping and a note from May to say that she had nipped out to find Clare. Lara got dressed with the intention of nipping out to look for them both and hopefully finding them in Jenny's café. In the bathroom, she pulled on the string to turn on the light and a loud bang ensued. The bulb had blown and taken all the electricity in the house down with it, as Lara discovered when she tried to switch on various other lights. And where the hell was the fuse box?

'This is all I need,' she huffed to herself, knowing that if she didn't find it she would once again have to go down to misery guts's house and ask for some help. After looking in all the obvious places she still hadn't found it and so instead of searching out her friends, she would have to pay the unjolly giant Gene Hathersage a visit.

When she knocked on his door there was no answer, nor did the old dog bark, but his scrappy old truck was there, suggesting that he was in and ignoring her.

'Hello,' Lara called, walking around to the back of the house. There was a beautiful walled garden there and more furniture made from twisted pieces of wood: a table and two chairs and various arches covered in roses and possibly peaches. It was overgrown but probably only by one summer. Maybe Mr Hathersage had been too busy hiding from people to come out and do some gardening, Lara mused as she knocked on the back door. No answer. She knocked twice more with hard knuckles, but no success. Bloody man. She looked in his truck just to make sure that he wasn't lying down behind the seats trying not to be spotted; he wasn't there either.

There were various outbuildings near the house and Lara picked her way through the long grasses running riot over the path and looked through the cobwebby window of the first one – a small shed-like structure full of logs. There was a larger, newer building behind it, with a large metal door slightly ajar. Bingo, thought Lara. She pulled it open, walked inside and whistled. Facing her was the most beautiful carved horse. To one side of it the crude shape of a dog lying down, its head resting on its front paws, was emerging from the wood. This must have been the piece currently being worked on as there were fresh cuts of wood around it. Behind the horse was an enormous high-backed seat made to the same twisted-wood design as the furniture in the walled garden. There were more carvings – large and small – dotted around the space, exquisitely detailed pieces sitting beside the expertly crafted rustic furniture. Surely these couldn't be from the hands of Gene Hathersage? He didn't look the type to have the patience to create such beautiful things.

There was a sudden rumble to her side, followed by the revving rasp of a chainsaw. She spun around to see *him*, clad in an industrial apron, holding the saw.

Jesus H. Christ, she said to herself. It's Leatherface. I've had it.

She was sure he must have been able to hear her heart thumping over the sound of the machine. He turned it off when he realized he had given her enough of a scare – and a little bit extra.

'What are you doing in here?' he barked.

'Looking for you,' Lara replied. 'Did you make all these?'

'This is private property and that's my business.'

'I'm not exactly asking you what size underpants you wear,' growled Lara.

'Yes, I did make them. Hopefully that answers your question sufficiently.'

'Are you always so rude to lodgers?'

'You're the first I've had,' he replied, his brown-black eyes challenging hers to maintain contact.

Lucky you're not asking me for repeat custom, thought Lara. She smiled her sweetest smile and said, 'All our lights have blown and I can't find the fuse box. I knocked on the door to your house but you weren't there and I didn't know if you were in because I didn't hear your dog . . .'

Gene dropped the chainsaw noisily on the table behind him.

'I'll get my toolbox,' he said. 'I'll meet you at the cottage in five minutes.'

He turned from her, stripping off his apron, and Lara was left to go back up to Well Cottage on her own, presumably because he didn't want to walk with her. Well, that was fine, because she didn't want to walk with him either.

Chapter 30

He must have taken one stride for every two of hers because she arrived at the cottage only seconds before him.

'Would you like a cup of tea?' she asked politely.

'Going to be a bit hard boiling a kettle with no electricity,' grumped Gene. 'What are you going to do to the water, breathe on it?' He didn't wait for an answer. He lifted a chair, took it into Clare's room, surveyed the displaced wardrobe and all the paper torn from the wall, and then climbed up to reach a box high on the wall. Lara winced. If Clare's efforts to expose the doorway didn't give Gene Hathersage a legal right to keep their extortionate bond then nothing would.

As if reading her thoughts he said, 'I'll be charging for the damage to that wall. Unless you put it right.'

'Whatever you have to do,' drawled Lara, and then under her breath she added, 'another three million quid won't matter.'

'Why would you want to go moving the wardrobe?' Gene threw over his shoulder.

'My friend lost an earring.'

'Oh, I see.' He didn't turn around but she watched him nod whilst he did something with pliers. 'I always start moving wardrobes and ripping off wallpaper when I've lost jewellery.'

Lara didn't dignify his sarcasm with an answer but she felt duty bound to be polite.

'Can I get you a cold drink in the absence of house electricity?' she offered, forcing politeness. 'Milk, water?'

'Nope, I'm fine thanks. I'll only be a couple of minutes and I need to get back. Not all of us are on holiday.'

'I would have thought that as your first customers you might have been a little more courteous to us,' said Lara, her temper breaking free of its leash. She had to have a lot of patience in her job and she was only glad that she didn't have to deal with Gene Hathersages every day. They'd be worse than gropey Giles Billingleys.

'I should never have opened up Well Cottage,' he muttered.

'Why? Because – God forbid – tenants might complain that you've charged them a hundred and fifty pounds for a lump of cheese and the ingredients for three bacon butties? Or because they just might want to find the fuse box to put a light on because your electrics haven't been serviced properly?'

Gene Hathersage twisted to face her. He looked extra enormous standing on the chair, half electrician, half giant. His legs looked eight foot long in those faded, distressed jeans.

'No one wants strangers here. It's caused all sorts of bad feeling.'

'Trust me, Mr Hathersage, I would never have willingly booked this cottage. Not in a million years.' Lara's voice began its crescendo as her temper not only slipped its lead but ran straight past the huskies, fell down a mountain and started gathering snow to itself, like a massive destructive snowball. 'We thought we were heading for a fortnight of R & R in a luxury spa with massages and pools and first-class cuisine, not a cottage in the back of beyond, luxury hampers that are about as luxury as a toilet seat made out of broken glass, a sky full of clouds, no mobile reception, no Internet, no civilization and a village full of people that look at us as if we're from the planet Arse.'

Planet Arse? This from a woman named Best Industry

Speech Maker the year before last. Clearly her standards were slipping.

Gene Hathersage speedily turned back to the fuse box. She thought she saw his shoulders shaking. He actually had the cheek to be sniggering at her. She flounced out of the room, picked up her Kindle and threw herself on the sofa. Twice she reached the bottom of the screen and realized she hadn't absorbed a word so she gave up. She had just turned it off when Gene came through the door carrying the chair.

'All sorted,' he said.

'Thank you,' Lara replied, with the world's worst impression of a genuine smile of gratitude. Oh, she couldn't wait to fill in the feedback report.

'Please do call again, Miss Rickman, if you encounter any other difficulties.' Gene's faux sweetness matched her own insincerity exactly. She noticed how straight and white his teeth were as he gave his parody of a smile.

'Thank you, Mr Hathersage. I do hope I won't be troubling you again.'

'Not half as much as I wish it,' she heard him mumble as he left the cottage, closing the door ever so softly behind him.

When Clare walked in and saw Lara's expression, she hardly needed to ask what was up.

'Gene bloody Hathersage, that's what's up. Had to go and fetch him to mend the fuse . . . God, the cheeky git. How dare he?' *What are you going to do to the water, breathe on it?* Lara had just worked out what he meant.

Then May made a breathless entrance. 'Saw you coming up the hill, Clare, but I couldn't catch you . . . What's up?'

'Lara's had to go down to see Gene Hathersage again. About the fuse box, this time,' Clare filled her in.

'He called me a dragon,' said Lara, and she relayed the insult to the others.

Lara expected a modicum of sympathy; what she got were her two friends laughing so much they had to lean on each other for support.

'I'll make us something to eat,' said Lara, taking Clare's shopping basket from her. 'Seeing as you two are too busy wetting yourselves at my expense.'

They had cheese and bacon toasties with home-made minted pea soup. There was a plastic container full of the soup in the 'luxury hamper' and though Lara would never have admitted this to Gene Hathersage, even under extreme torture, it tasted like manna from heaven.

'So where did you get to this morning?' asked Lara, spooning out the last of the soup and wishing there were more.

'Just wandering around,' said May. She didn't mention meeting Frank Hathersage. She was trying her best to forget him and the electric effect he had had on her – literally.

'Clare?'

'I had the most gorgeous swim downstairs. You'll have to come with me and try it out,' raved Clare. 'As I was swimming the old lady who lived in the cottage on the headland waved at me and invited me up.'

'You didn't go, did you?' asked May.

'Yeah, I did,' replied Clare. 'Sweet old thing. I think she thought I was someone else, though. The villagers have obviously been talking about us. And you'll never guess what: she has the same eyes as me.'

'Poor beggar.' Lara nudged her.

'Oi. Oh, and you know what else I discovered? The third Hathersage – Val – isn't a Valerie, it's a Valentino.'

'Oh, no,' said Lara. 'Not another brother.'

'And there's us thinking that they were three sweet little old ladies crocheting in rocking chairs.' May smiled, also wishing there were more of that soup.

'Whereas, in reality, one is an unsociable git, one is saddled with the world's rudest girlfriend . . . and do tell what *Valentino* is like. Did you meet him? And are you leaving that?' Lara swiped Clare's abandoned burned crust from her plate.

'Definitely got the family looks, but lighter-coloured hair, green eyes. Leaner and shorter. He's friendly enough. I'd say he's slightly younger than us, by a year or so. Very handsome and knows it.' Clare kept it to herself that she had arranged to meet him. He was her secret for now.

'Who do you reckon is the eldest?' said Lara. 'Nice Frank or horrible Gene?'

'Frank, I reckon,' May said and Clare nodded her agreement. 'I'd put him at about thirty-six, thirty-seven, Gene a couple of years younger.'

'I'd put Gene at about twelve,' Lara said sniffily. 'No wonder he lives with a dog, a load of wooden tree trunks and no Mrs Hathersage.'

Clare gathered up the plates. 'What shall we do this after-noon, then?'

'Shall we have a drive around the area?' suggested Lara.

'If you don't mind,' said May.

'Don't mind at all,' said Lara. Physical distance between her-self and the landlord from hell would be very welcome.

Chapter 31

They decided to torture themselves by going to look at the spa in Wellem – and wished they hadn't. The manor house was absolutely stunning; it was like a smaller version of Downton Abbey. The female staff in their pristine, white, Chinese-style tunics were more than slightly snooty. 'No, you can't go that way,' shouted one from behind the reception desk when they tried to have a nosey at the Greek Pool area.

'Can't we just pop our heads round and see what it looks like?' asked May.

'It's not an open day,' twittered the woman, before immediately metamorphosing into a sycophantic pool of drool as a large woman wrapped in a cloud-like robe emerged from the door marked 'Salon'. 'Oh, good afternoon, Mrs Palmerly. And how are we today? How was the chocolate wrap?'

Lara felt like saying that it was a shame the woman had dismissed her so easily because she was the Sultan of Brunei's niece and thinking of booking herself and her entourage of two hundred people in for a month, but in the end she couldn't be bothered. She'd do battle with them for their lack of customer-service skills when she got home. It would give her something to keep her mind off everything else that would be waiting for her back in Surrey.

They couldn't get to see the log cabin they should have been staying in because it was behind gates closed to the general public. Lara felt slightly sick and very, very guilty again.

'I'm not just saying this,' said Clare, linking her arm on the way back to the car, 'but I couldn't be happier than having that lagoon at my disposal.' She didn't add that part of her enthusiasm for staying was her rendezvous with Val Hathersage in the woods tomorrow. No – she wouldn't have swapped the swirl of excitement he was causing in her gut for a fleecy dressing gown and a low-calorie salad. She couldn't get their little interchange out of her head. She thought of his soft lips and knew he would be the most amazing kisser.

'I'm happy enough too,' added May with a gentle smile. 'I feel as if I'm relaxing for the first time in ages.' And she didn't want to be at the spa, where Michael might contact her. The greater the distance between them, the bigger the deception seemed. Unbidden, snatches of conversation kept coming to her, lies she had no reason to doubt were truths at the time: highly detailed updates on Susan's condition and his apology for smelling of perfume when he arrived at her house. She'd imagined him dabbing it on Susan's neck and wrists in a tender attempt to make her feel like an able sentient woman or in a vain hope that the scent might drift to a part of her brain and awaken it. Thinking about it now in the cold light of realization, he had probably come straight from Kim's house and it was her that he smelt of.

'Okay,' said Lara. She didn't really believe them, but she knew that if the shoe were on another foot, she would have said the same.

They walked around Wellem, which was a much more commercialized seaside town than Ren Dullem. It was spread out and hilly, and it even had roads that two cars could fit on, side by side. There were tacky souvenirs in the many shops and at least three fish-and-chip shops claiming to be the best in North Yorkshire. May wasn't sure about that as she watched a delivery of fish fillets coming out of a van emblazoned with a sign that read: Dock & Tanner Fisheries, Leeds. *They had their fish shipped in from Leeds?*

But at least Wellem didn't have those weird clouds floating above it. The day was bright and warm and the beach was crowded with deckchairs and sunloungers. Children were making sandcastles and racing into the sea, only to retreat quickly, screaming that the water was freezing, then laughing and charging back yet again to fling themselves into the waves.

Clare bought two wind-up torches – buy one get one free – in a hardware shop so she could have some reliable light in the cavern. Then the three of them sat on a bench eating mediocre ice creams, staring out to sea. There were big chips of ice in Lara's chocolate one – she was less than impressed and abandoned it after a few licks. That ice cream seemed to sum up the whole town: full of promise but not delivering at all. There were the usual amusements supervised by bored-looking individuals and a funfair that looked about as much of a thrill as having cystitis. There was no energy about the place at all despite being full of holidaymakers. Wellem was as tired as a blown flower, whereas Dullem was an unopened bud. It was a far prettier place with much more potential. Lara wished a letter would drop out of the sky inviting her to sort the place out.

They found a restaurant before heading back but it was far more welcoming outside than it was within, where it was borderline grubby. At least the locals carried on drinking when they walked in and didn't down tools to stare at the newcomers. The menu looked okay so they ordered food but May found a hair in her chilli and that put her and the others totally off their food. Lara complained and got a refund, but that didn't stop May throwing up in the grimy toilet.

May wanted to get home and into bed. Her head was pounding. Clare helped her into the car and Lara drove to Well

Cottage as quickly as she could on the ridiculously winding roads.

'Poor May,' said Clare, stroking her sleeping friend's forehead. 'She's so hot. I hope she's not coming down with anything.'

The way this holiday was going, Lara wouldn't have been surprised.

Back in Well Cottage they helped May to bed with a bucket at her side and a cold cloth on her head. She hadn't thrown up since the restaurant, thank goodness. Lara could be sick herself if she thought about those hairs in the meal.

'Nightcap?' asked Clare, closing the door softly on the sleeping May. 'I have a bottle of wine in my suitcase.'

'I'd love one. I'll get the glasses,' replied Lara, making a half-hearted attempt to rise from the fat comfy sofa.

'Stay there, I'll get them.'

As Lara waited, she glanced around her at the room. It wasn't exactly equipped with the newest of items: the TV was old, with a small screen and an enormous depth to the back, and the coffee table and bookcase had seen better days. But it was homely and not once since she arrived had Lara wished she had brought her laptop. She'd thought doing nothing would drive her up the wall after a few hours – she couldn't remember the last time she had *done nothing* and not felt that it was a complete waste of time. But, sitting there, she thought she could pick up her Kindle, snuggle back into the plump cushions and read into the small hours of the night, ignoring the dictates of the clock that she should go to bed/get up/eat lunch.

'Here you go,' said Clare, proffering a full glass of red wine.

'Thanks, love.'

'Don't get excited, it's not exactly a Château Petrus.'

'I couldn't care less if it was Château Um Bongo, just let me at it,' said Lara, as her hands closed greedily around it.

Clare plonked herself in the big armchair, which seemed to mould to her shape.

'God, this is nice. Wish May were okay and having a glass with us.'

'I'm expecting us all to fall down with some dreaded lurgy. That's what usually happens when people stop working and relax. Allegedly.' Lara, of course, wouldn't know about that at first hand, because she never took the time to stop working and relax.

'Don't say that, Lars.' Though Clare knew it was true. Still, being full of bugs in bed would be miles better than being behind her desk at Blackwoods and Margoyles. It wasn't that she didn't enjoy what she did – and she was more than honoured to be asked to join the partners – but she would have even less time for other things she *really* enjoyed doing. She barely had space in her diary to see her friends or a man, if she ever found another one. She wished she could split herself in two and one half of her could do justice to her promotion, make her parents proud, be at the office number-crunching twenty-four-seven. And the other half could stay at home, buy a cat, a dog and a house rabbit, cook, write a recipe book, make cushions, have babies. Tomorrow's secret adventure would do her good and take away from all the turmoil that was going on in her head.

'Have you managed to find a signal to ring Ludwig to say you're having a disastrous time?'

'I'm not having a disastrous time and, yes, of course I have,' said Clare, lying about the phone call. 'If you want to borrow my phone to ring James . . .'

'Oh, it's fine.' Lara flapped her hand. 'He's abroad on business until Tuesday and so I said I wouldn't get in touch with him before then.' Then she took a long sip of wine to douse any tail fumes of the untruth that might be still lingering in her throat.

'Has he gone anywhere fabulous?'

'Spain.' Uncomfortable with lying to her friend, Lara changed the subject. 'So, going for another swim in your cave tomorrow now you've bought a torch?'

Clare smiled back. 'I most certainly am. If you and May don't mind.'

'I don't mind at all. This is a holiday to unwind. I never thought we'd be glued to each other all day every day. It's just great to be near you, if that doesn't sound too soppy.' And it was true. She was certainly glad she hadn't cancelled this holiday to stay with James.

'I don't know where all my friends have disappeared to over the years,' sighed Clare. 'I remember being best buddies with Beth Lofthouse and Fi Ballatyne at school and *knowing* that we'd always be in each other's lives. Then they met men. Fi had a baby and moved to Canada and Beth went all weird and converted to tree worshipping. I haven't heard from either of them in ten years and yet once we were as close as sisters. We went to Ibiza together when we were twenty-one and had the maddest time.'

Lara nodded. 'Carol Brady and Hannah Craddock were my bezzies. Carol started messing about at school, got dropped from the top set and ended up palling about with the girls in her new class who hung around with bad lads and smoked. She dropped me like a hot brick – I was gutted. She ended up getting pregnant at fifteen. I saw her a couple of years ago and she walked past me in the street, even though I knew that she knew who I was. I was quite upset about it actually. She looked old and rough and a bit scruffy.'

'And your friend Hannah?' Clare prompted.

'I was her bridesmaid ten years ago. She was a solicitor but jacked in her job as soon as she got married, had three babies in quick succession and ended up with a new set of friends who had time to go to coffee mornings and push prams around the park. We just drifted apart. Our friendship obviously wasn't as strong as we thought; it couldn't survive all the changes.'

Clare took a long sip of wine. 'I miss having lots of female company, you know, just sitting with a glass of wine, like this; not rushing, just talking is lovely. I miss taking time to smell the roses, don't you, Lars? I've forgotten what it's like to *stop*.'

'Yep, I know what you mean exactly.'

'And on that note, Lars, I'm off to bed.' Clare stood up to go.

'Well, I'm going to sit here and read,' said Lara. 'You're not throwing that half glass away, are you? G'is it here.'

Clare laughed. 'Your Barnsley accent's come right back.' She put her glass down next to Lara's on the coffee table. 'Fill yer boots, lass. Nighty night.'

'Night, Salty,' said Lara, taking the throw from the back of the chair and wrapping it around her so she was extra snug. She settled down to read and took a long glug of the wine. A little bubble of bliss pinged in her head. She could get too used to this if she weren't careful.

In bed, Clare switched off her bedside light, closed her eyes and visualized herself in a floaty dress walking through a wood, the sun picking out motes flying in the air, the ground smooth underfoot and full of violet bluebells. In the distance was Val Hathersage spreading a blanket on the ground, setting two champagne glasses on it, pulling plates out of a basket. Then he saw her and came running towards her and she didn't have enough time to say hello because he pushed her against a tree and began kissing her, furiously, hungrily. His hands, at first gallantly on her waist, strayed upwards to her breasts and she gasped as he fondled her and his lips sank to her neck nipping it with exquisite force. Then she felt his fingers pulling up her dress, stroking her thighs, slipping into her silk knickers, tantalizingly soft as they found what they were looking for and circled, tickled, rubbed until the feeling shuddered through her body and she screamed out his name wantonly, whoreishly, as she asked him to do all manner of things to her, on the blanket, in the bluebells, risking discovery.

She felt as if, tomorrow, she would be diving into life at last and it would be the same feeling as diving into the lagoon.

Chapter 32

Gladys walked into the study, immediately saw Joan seated at the desk reading the huge familiar ledgers, and, with a heaving bosom and a pinched mouth, she retreated and marched up the stairs to find Edwin Carlton. She discovered him in the upper corridor where he was straightening a picture of his father Gilbert – the one who had started it all. The picture had tipped itself to the side overnight. Gladys was one hundred per cent convinced it was an omen.

'Sir, I need you to come immediately and see what's happening downstairs.' She wouldn't have dared, even after all these years, but she was itching to grab his sleeve and pull him at a rate of knots into the study.

'What is it, Gladys? Have we been invaded by aliens?' He seemed amused. He was wearing that stupid smile again, the one he had acquired of late. It was part of that spring-in-the-step lightness that usually accompanied a spring in the heart. Gladys wasn't daft – she'd been in love a few times herself and wasn't too old to recognize the signs of someone in the early stages of being besotted.

'Joan is looking through the ledgers,' whispered Gladys through clenched teeth, after a cursory check behind her that no one was eavesdropping.

'I know,' said Edwin. 'I asked her to.'

Gladys's eyes sprang open so far her eyeballs were in danger of pinging out of their sockets.

'You can't let her see those,' she said, concentrating a shout into a hiss.

'I don't see why not,' said Edwin, displaying impatience in his voice. 'I need help. The accounts are a mess and the succession of little old ladies you've brought in to assist me over the years, Gladys, have given me many a sleepless night.'

'But what about Lawrence?' Gladys's anger was changing now to desperation.

'He's eighty-two now, Gladys. Blind in one eye and the other isn't much better. As an accountant his sight is a required commodity, I would have thought.'

'His junior—'

'Has left,' Edwin interrupted. 'Who can blame him? We can't keep the young men here any more. It's not fair to try, Gladys. It's just a matter of time. The world is shrinking as we breathe. There are no women here, the village is dying.'

Gladys opened her mouth to speak but nothing came out. What Edwin was saying was true. The end was nigh. Gladys dropped her head into her hands. She hadn't sobbed since she became a widow twenty years ago, but she was dangerously close to it now. She felt Edwin's arm slide around her shoulder. It was the first time he had comforted her, the first time he had needed to.

'There's nothing in the books but names and lots of numbers, Gladys. The estate is in trouble, my dear. A fresh pair of eyes on things can't do any more harm than Lawrence has done in the past few years. I'm afraid he made some bad decisions for us, investment-wise. Poor chap, not as on the ball as he was in his younger days. He's struggled on too long, as we all have.'

Taking advantage of the drop in his guard, Gladys turned her mouth as near as she could to Edwin's ear.

'I don't trust Mrs Hawk, it has to be said. No one knows of her in Wellem.'

'Wellem is much bigger and far more spread out than Ren Dullem so the residents wouldn't all know each other,' said Edwin, dropping his arm away from Gladys. 'And, as she herself said, Mrs Hawk was only a small child when she left.'

Gladys knew that whatever she said, Edwin would have a stronger counter-argument, but she couldn't stop the warning slipping from her lips: 'Be careful. All those years will mean nothing if it comes out.'

'I know, Gladys, but you don't have to worry,' he replied stiffly. 'Enough now. Remember our recent conversation? I won't have discord in this house.'

Edwin turned from her and back to nudging the painting into its proper place.

Gladys wiped her eyes and returned to her duties downstairs whilst thinking that any warning Gilbert Carlton might have been giving out by tilting his portrait on the wall was long overdue. If he'd only stuck to dry land that day, none of it would ever have happened.

Chapter 33

Clare didn't get up until half-past ten. She found Lara fast asleep on the sofa wrapped up in the throw and looking snugger than the proverbial bug. She checked on May, who wanted to stay in bed and sleep. Her headache was gone but she felt washed out. Clare brought her some fresh iced water and then went into the bathroom to prepare herself for her picnic with Val. She couldn't have been more excited had she been sixteen and on her first date with the school sports hero. She bathed, shaved her legs and underarms, washed her hair, put on her best push-up bra and nice knickers. She applied just enough make-up to look fresh and understated.

She didn't have a floaty dress as she had worn in her fantasy, but she had a nice summery cream skirt with small blue flowers on it and a matching blue T-shirt which showed off her generous bust very nicely. She hadn't brought any perfume with her so she nipped into Lara's room to steal a squirt or two of her Rain, giving herself a light spray on her hair, behind her ears and up her T-shirt, but not on her neck in case Val Hathersage gave it any attention with his lips.

Clare studied herself in the huge mirror in Lara's room. This was the most reckless she had been ever. Then again, what was she doing wrong? She was single and merely going for an innocent picnic in the woods. But if everything was so innocent, why were there butterflies leaping about in her stomach and flittering their wings around her nether regions?

At ten to twelve she slipped quietly out of the house and took a very, very slow walk down the hill. She didn't want to appear too keen. She practised looking casual and laid-back even though her heart was thundering in her chest. When she checked her watch she saw that it was now eight minutes to twelve – had her watch stopped? She idled outside Gene Hathersage's drive for a moment and studied the view that he had from the windows in his gable end. Ren Dullem, despite having a totally rubbish name, was a beautiful spot. At least it would have been had the sun been able to cut through those weird clouds that looked as solid as dumplings. She imagined how the whole sea might sparkle if the skies cleared, like the water in the lagoon. She intended to swim in there later and climb the second staircase to see where it led.

There was no sign of anyone coming up or down the road at twelve. She walked further down the hill, looking in the windows of the row of abandoned cottages, wiling away another five minutes. Then she strolled slowly up the hill again, checked in the woods – no one was there. She walked down the hill again, her excitement segueing into annoyance. Ludwig would have cut off his own legs rather than be late for a date.

Ah, but this isn't Ludwig and that's why you are here, said her subconscious, wagging its finger at her. *You are now playing a different ball game, lady.*

After the fourth time of wandering up and down the hill, Clare huffed loudly and her stride picked up pace. She was going back to Well Cottage. Val Hathersage could go to hell. She walked past the woods without even a glance.

'Hey, you, witch lady,' called a voice from behind her. She twisted round to see a man with fair waves of hair and a lop-sided grin. He was holding a Tesco carrier bag in one hand. He made no apology for his lateness as he fell into stride with Clare and together they silently walked into the heart of the wood.

Chapter 34

Joan cross-referenced the rough notes she had made so far with the mighty ledger on the desk. However many times she looked at the figures, they didn't tell her what could be going on. The Carlton estate had apparently been financially supporting the whole of the village like some private benefits office since 1928. At first glance it appeared that everyone in Ren Dullem had been blackmailing the Carltons and extorting money from them. It had started with Gilbert Carlton and was still going on with his son, Edwin. Some ridiculous financial investments had whittled away at the estate capital, causing it to be only a small fraction of what it once was, and yet payments were still haemorrhaging out of bank accounts.

The door creaked open and Edwin made a smiling appearance with a china cup of tea which he set down beside Joan, on its saucer.

'Just as you like it, my dear,' he said.

She could smell the infatuation on him, mingled with a heavy application of old-man cologne. Had no one told him that stuff stank?

'You smell nice,' she said, giving him her best practised smile.

'Oh, do I? Thank you. Alas I'll never be as fragrant as you, dear lady.'

Joan released her best tinkly laugh. Edwin's wife looked

down on them from the artwork on the wall and Joan could have sworn she looked more disapproving than usual. Joan now wore her hair in soft curls and tucked behind her right ear, in the same style as Mary Carlton.

'Edwin, I don't understand what all these costs to the estate are.' Joan tapped the pile of ledgers with her pen.

'Oh, they aren't important,' he said, dismissing them with one wave of his hand. 'I just need you to double-check that they are all still being paid by the bank and the balance sheets are correct.'

'But what are they for?'

'Just costs.' Edwin nodded. 'Nothing to worry about.'

'Why would you pay—'

There was a knock on the door followed swiftly by the entry of Gladys. It was she who should have been called Hawk, thought Joan. She hovered constantly around her these days. And gone was the smiling trust; she knew that Gladys detested her presence in Carlton Hall.

Tough.

'Patrick has arrived to cut your hair, sir.'

'Has he? It doesn't need doing, does it? You shouldn't have booked him so soon after the last cut, Gladys.'

'I didn't. You did.' Gladys felt a twinge of panic. Edwin was becoming more and more forgetful these days. Senility was a pattern in the Carlton men; but none of the others had a Joan Hawk in their presence to take advantage of it.

'Oh, did I? Just tell him that I'll be along in a moment, Gladys, would you, please?'

Gladys didn't rush to leave and Joan smirked. The house-keeper really didn't like her being alone with Edwin and it seemed to have something to do with these ledgers. Joan's radar began to twitch and flash and she felt a kick of excitement in her veins. If Gladys didn't want her reading those ledgers, there must be a reason.

'Edwin, how would you like me to cook you dinner this evening in the cottage?' said Joan, when the door at last closed behind Gladys. 'To say thank you for being so kind to me.'

'Oh my dear, you don't have to do that,' said Edwin.

'No, I don't have to,' said Joan, 'but I'd like to. I do an excellent chicken casserole.'

Edwin clapped his hands together. 'My favourite.'

'Really?' But Joan already knew it was his favourite. She had done her homework.

'I'll have it ready for seven o'clock, is that okay with you?' It was Gladys's afternoon off. She usually left Edwin a plated cold supper on Friday.

'What a treat!' Edwin smiled. 'I'll tell Gladys not to make me anything.'

'Yes, you do that.' Joan wished she could be a fly on the wall when Edwin told Gladys. She'd instantly know why and spend the night panicking that Joan just might find out what was going on at Carlton Hall, because sure as hell something was.

Chapter 35

Val brought no blanket to spread on the ground, nor were there any crystal glasses waiting to receive iced champagne, only a can of warm Chardonnay and a bottle of beer to drink, some pre-packed sandwiches that looked like they had come from a garage and an already opened packet of McVities chocolate digestive biscuits.

'Thirsty?' asked Val, pulling on the ring pull of the wine can and handing it to Clare. She took a throatful of it and winced inwardly. She was sure it would strip gloss paint in one application.

Next, Val offered the sandwiches. 'Any preference? Got roast beef or egg mayo? Or shall we have one half of each?'

'I don't mind,' replied Clare, though she was a bit funny about beef. She hated fat on her meat.

'One of each it is, then.' He handed a triangle of each flavour to Clare, who was sitting on a fallen tree trunk, then sat down beside her and gobbled his egg mayonnaise sandwich in two clean bites.

'Just come back from Wellem,' he said. 'Picked these up on the way. Didn't have time to do the proper picnic thing with the basket and sausage rolls. Sorry.'

'What were you doing there?' asked Clare, softened by his apology. 'Work?'

'Work?' He seemed amused by that prospect. 'Well, I suppose you could call it that. Dropping something off for someone. They paid me to do it. Best ask no more questions,' and he touched the side of his nose with his finger.

He made whatever he was doing sound secretive and exciting. She bet it wasn't dropping off hanks of wool for the local knitting shop.

'Sounds illegal,' said Clare, quickly swallowing the piece of beef fat she had just felt in her mouth before she gagged.

'Not that illegal,' replied Val, licking his fingers. 'I'm not stupid. Wouldn't want to embarrass the family by being put in prison.' And he laughed again to himself. Everything seemed to be a private joke to Val Hathersage.

'I'm gathering you don't get on with your brothers.' Clare abandoned the vile beef sandwich and Val was quick to leap on it and polish it off.

'Mr Angry and Mr Stupid? No, I don't. I never have got on with them, really. They're only my half-brothers anyway.'

'You don't live with Frank at the farm then?'

'You must be joking.' Val roared with laughter. 'The very thought! I don't have a house. I don't want to be tied down to property. Where I lay my hat down is my home. And at present, my hat is in a room above a garage.'

He took a mouthful of beer and then leaned over to Clare, seized her behind the neck and placed a kiss on her lips. His breath tasted of alcohol and smoke. Then he released her and reached for the biscuits. 'Sorry, just had to do that. You're beautiful.'

'Why are we here?' asked Clare, her insides vibrating as if they were a washing machine set to spin.

'Why not?' Val grinned. 'You obviously fancy me. I fancy you. Girls on holiday want some fun. You look like a girl who *needs* some fun.'

'What do you mean?' Clare felt herself blush.

Val chewed quickly on his mouthful of biscuit so he could speak again.

'I can tell that you haven't had fun in a long time.' He studied her. 'Let me make some guesses about you: you've only ever had boring boyfriends but you dream about being thrown on the ground and made love to. Your whole life is just one big frustration. I can smell frustration on women; they wear it like a perfume.'

Clare tried not to let her amazement show on her face. 'You're wrong,' she said, but it came out more breathlessly than she intended.

'No, I'm not,' he replied. 'Shall I show you what I mean?'

'Absolutely not,' laughed Clare as he leaned towards her. 'Eat your sandwich.'

'I find you very sexy,' said Val, shrugging his shoulders at her rebuffal. 'You remind me of someone.'

'Let me guess: Gywneth Paltrow? Jessie J? Cheryl Cole?'

'Cleopatra.'

Clare chuckled. 'Bump into her a lot around here, do you?'

'Not recently. Think she's moved to Wellem.' Val grinned. And boy was he working those green eyes. Clare would have bet that those eyes had managed to loosen quite a few sets of knicker elastic.

Clare took a long drink of the wine. It was revolting but at least swilled away the taste of her sandwich. It wasn't exactly one of Lud's picnics. He had taken her to a boating lake last summer and they had feasted on the cutest cucumber, salmon and Caerphilly sandwiches all cut into heart shapes. There had been strawberries dipped in dark chocolate, petite pastry parcels, spiced chicken goujons and ice-cold Prosecco with raspberries.

'Finished then?' Val's voice broke up the memory.

'Yes, I think so,' replied Clare, brushing crumbs from her

skirt. When she lifted her head, Val was at her side. His green, green eyes were staring down into hers.

'You really are lovely,' he said and leaned closer.

'Am I?' Clare swallowed, feeling his breath on her cheek, feeling his hand in her hair, feeling his lips fall onto hers. Oh he really was as good a kisser as she thought he might be. He pushed her backwards so she was lying flat and his soft lips travelled down her face to her neck which he nipped delicately between his teeth. His fingers tripped down her arm, skimming past her breast. She gasped with delight. Then, without warning, he pulled apart from her and sat up.

'That was nice. Want a biscuit?'

'A biscuit?'

'Yes. I don't want you getting too carried away.'

Clare pulled herself up. Of all the things she had been expecting next, a bloody McVities digestive wasn't one of them.

They resumed their seats on the fallen tree trunk again and Clare took a biscuit from the pack, although she didn't really want one. Val lit up a cigarette as if they'd had more than just a snog.

'My ex used to love having sex in these woods,' said Val, exhaling a long breath of smoke. 'She was a wild woman. Always dragging me up here, she was.'

Nice, thought Clare. Just what every woman wants to hear, a good old ex story.

'Is she still in the village?'

'Naw, she was too bored by this place. Packed her bags and went to London. The roads are paved with gold there, as you know.' He took a long, satisfying drag on his cigarette. 'She'd done all the things she wanted to. There were no fresh challenges for her.' His accent on the word 'challenges' made it sound as if he meant 'men'.

'There seem to be a lot more men in the village than

women, why is that?' As she spoke Clare dropped the biscuit to
the grass. It tasted soft and old. 'I've only seen a couple –
Shirley, Daisy . . .'

'Don't get me started on that bitch Daisy,' said Val. 'And
Shirley wasn't born here; she was adopted. Girls don't tend to
be born in Ren Dullem and, if they are, they aren't anything to
write home about. Have you met Jenny yet? Pretty enough
face but she's been twenty stone since the day she was born.
Now Colleen Landers was an exception.' His face softened as
he said her name. 'She was a freak of nature in this village was
Colleen – a real beauty.'

Clare felt slightly peeved that the man she had just been passionately kissing was extolling the virtues of an ex. Still she
couldn't stop herself asking questions.

'Miss her a lot, do you?'

He shrugged casually. 'Not much point. If Colleen had
wanted to be with me she wouldn't have gone. Whatever
Colleen wanted, Colleen got.'

'Do you think she'll ever come back?'

'Not a chance.' Val laughed. 'There's no one to come back
for. She ate everyone up and spat them out.'

'What about coming to see her family?'

'Colleen doesn't do duty.'

Clare decided immediately that she didn't like the sound of
Colleen Landers. She could imagine what a spoiled, self-
obsessed little madam she must be.

'She had hair like sunshine,' said Val, with a nostalgic expression on his face. 'Long, golden silk and eyes the colour of
chocolate.' He seemed lost in his reverie, but Clare noticed that
he threw her the quickest of sly glances so she knew that he was
trying to wind her up and inflame her to envy. Head games.
Not that it should come as much of a surprise. Val Hathersage,
she was realizing, was just one big head game. She imagined
Colleen Landers to be exactly the same.

'Why are no women born in Ren Dullem, then?' asked Clare, moving the conversation away from the paragon of beauty that was Colleen Landers.

Val grinned. 'Has no one explained the legend of Ren Dullem to you?'

'No,' said Clare, leaning forward with interest.

'As if there's really a legend. I'm joking!' said Val. 'Just one of those things. Must be something in the air. We're cursed. We must be if the best-looking woman born in the village is Daisy Unwin ...' He shook his head. 'Frank is a fool if he marries her. He doesn't love her. He just feels sorry for her because—' He pulled his words up short.

'Because she's in a wheelchair?' suggested Clare.

'No, because he put her there. They'd only been going out a short while, and he crashed the car they were in. She's made him suffer ever since and the stupid bastard puts up with her. Feels guilty and that he has to *atone*.'

'Oh, no! That's terrible,' said Clare. 'How awful for them both.'

'More awful for him,' said Val. 'She's the biggest cow you could ever meet. Don't make eye contact with her or the snakes on her head will come out and get you.' He curled his fingers over and wiggled them.

Clare giggled. Well, he certainly was very different from Lud. He might not have put a lot of effort into the picnic, but she had never met anyone like him before. He was a free spirit who obviously didn't give a toss what anyone thought about him.

'I have to make a move,' he said suddenly, killing the cigarette and placing it behind his ear. 'Same time tomorrow?'

'I can't. I'm busy,' said Clare. Damn. Still, it wouldn't do him any harm to hear that she wasn't going to jump to attention whenever he clicked his fingers.

'Are you now?' There was a challenge in his green eyes. 'I might be busy the day after. We'll have to see, then, won't we?'

'Yes, we shall,' said Clare, lifting her eyebrow ever so saucily and hoping she didn't look like Roger Moore.

Val Hathersage leaned towards her but his lips merely butterflied past hers, then he stood up to go.

'I bet you're fantastic in bed,' he said, and left her with a quickened pulse and a Tesco carrier bag full of packaging.

Chapter 36

Lara was up and eating a huge omelette stuffed with melted cheese, a wedge of thickly buttered bread on the side, when Clare arrived back at the house. She had taken a slow walk back to Well Cottage, her brain busily picking over what had just happened. That Val Hathersage was a tease of the highest order was the one thing to come out of her deliberations.

'Hiya, where have you been?' Lara smiled, shaking Clare out of her in-depth analysis. 'What the hell is that on your neck? A lovebite?'

Clare gasped in horror and checked herself in the mirror. It was. How could she get out of this one?

'It looks like a bruise. Haven't a clue how I got it. Unless it was when I caught myself on a rock in the lagoon yesterday.' She made a mental note to keep dabbing it with some spot cover.

'You must bruise like a peach,' Lara said with a laugh, getting up from the table to put her plate in the sink. 'Fancy a brew?'

'I'd love one,' said Clare, sitting down quickly in case there were grass stains on her skirt. 'How's May?'

'Still asleep. I checked on her about five minutes ago. At least while she's sleeping she's not feeling ill.'

Lara turned on the tap to fill the kettle. No water came out. She tried the other tap – nothing.

'I don't frigging believe it. We don't have any sodding water now.' She raised her eyes heavenward. 'Please God, please tell me that I don't have to go down to that man's house again.'

She counted to three and twisted the cold tap again, to no avail.

'That's it. I've had it. If he thinks he can get away with charging us all this money for a stupid house with no stupid water he's got another think coming.' Lara stomped over to the door to put on her shoes, and then she stopped. 'I can't. I can't go down and see him. I might be tempted to breathe fire on him.'

'I'll go,' said Clare, smiling at the image of Lara incinerating Gene Hathersage with dragon breath.

'Thank you,' said Lara, very happy to be relieved of seeing that damned man again.

Clare set off and shut the door behind her, but the latch didn't catch and it swung open again. Lara didn't bother to shut it. The day was warm and the air was nice and fresh as it drifted into the kitchen. She wished it could blow into her ear, collect up all the rubbish in her head, and blast it out of the other ear.

Lara's spirits were in a dip today. After Clare had woken her up, she had fallen back into another sleep and had the most awful dream about James. In it, he was holding her at arm's length and telling her all the ways in which she was inferior to Tianne. She wasn't as intelligent, her hair wasn't as long and it was the wrong colour, and she was soooo much older. Behind her, Tianne, who in the dream was Keira Knightly, and Keely were laughing hard at everything James was saying to the extent that they were bent double. 'I'm just saying this for your own good,' James kept repeating as he reeled off another list of her inadequacies, and however much Lara tried to get nearer to him, to be held against his chest, his arms wouldn't bend. She had woken up in tears on the sofa, feeling as if she had been run over by a steamroller.

More than anything she wanted to hear his voice. She wanted to make a lie of that dream and hear him say that he missed her and wanted her back. She wanted his arms around her and for it to feel like the first time they wrapped around her. She remembered it exactly: they had just come out of a restaurant on their first date and the cold air of the night had blasted them like a machine gun.

'Come here,' he had said and pulled her close to him. Then, just as her brain started smiling with pleasure, he made it faint with ecstasy by tilting up her chin and kissing her masterfully on the lips.

It was all gone, though, smashed with a big hammer. She would never be able to clear her head of that picture of him and Tianne on the bed.

'Fuck you, James Galsworthy,' she said aloud. It felt good, cathartic, to say his name wrapped in profanities. So she said it louder. 'Fuck you, bastard.' And louder. 'Fuck you, sodding bastard sodding prick-face shithouse tossing wanker knobhead penis.'

'Er, Lara.'

She turned round to see Clare standing there, with the saturnine figure of Gene Hathersage darkening the doorway. From the amused glint in his eye, he appeared to be enjoying the foul-mouthed floor show.

'I met Mr Hathersage outside. He was just coming up to tell us that the water was off for half an hour in the whole village,' said Clare, cringing for her friend.

'I'll be off, then,' said Gene Hathersage, a big fat smirk apparent under his mad beard, Lara noticed. His face wanted to make her swear even louder.

Clare shut the door and walked over to Lara with a look of great concern. 'Are you okay, Lars?'

'The Tourettes, you mean?' *No, Clare, I'm not. I'm hurting, I'm confused, I'm lost.* 'Yeah, course I am. I was just checking out the acoustics in the cottage.'

'I didn't know you could swear like that.'

'Neither did I.'

'Seriously, are you okay?' Clare looked concerned.

'I'm fine. Sort of. Oh, I don't know, Clare,' said Lara, dropping down onto a chair at the thick pine-topped table and letting her shoulders slump as if she were deflating. 'Do you ever feel that you are on a treadmill and daren't get off because if you do you'll realize you've been on the wrong one?'

Clare opened her mouth to answer: *All the time, Lars, all the fucking time.*

'Oh, ignore me.' Lara shook her head as if trying to whip up some sense in it. She was being a miserable cow and Clare didn't deserve to listen to her woes. She put the stopper back in her bottle and clapped her hands. 'How about I come with you and take a swim in your lovely lagoon?'

'Oh, yes,' said Clare, her eyes gleaming with pleasure. 'That would be fabulous.'

'Jesus Christ, Clare,' said Lara, shining one of the BOGOF torches down the steps. 'Are there even more steps than there were before?'

'Oh, stop moaning. We're nearly there.'

'Is there a stairlift?'

Clare laughed. 'Think how much good it's doing your leg muscles.'

'It's killing my heart though.'

Clare stepped down the last turn. 'Look, we're here.'

'Oh, my. It really is lovely, isn't it,' said Lara. She was looking forward to getting into the water. She only wished she could get as much out of swimming as Clare did.

When she slipped into the warm water she sighed with delight. 'Oh, yes, this is definitely worth the ordeal by stairs. It's nearly as nice as the pool at the Wellem Spa.' She winked over at Clare.

'It's far better,' came the answer just before Clare dived down into the lagoon. The water was gin-clear and so very deep.

Lara didn't take up Clare's invitation to swim over to the front of the cave and out into the open sea with her. She wasn't as strong a swimmer as Clare and was happy enough staying in the warm waters of the lagoon. After half an hour, Lara got out and sat on a rock to dry herself off. She was so glad she had ventured down to Clare's secret watery place. She could under-stand why her friend was so delighted with her find.

'I'm going to leave you to it,' she said, taking one of the torches. 'I'll go and check on May.' She held her hand up as Clare opened her mouth. 'You enjoy yourself here. I'm quite happy babysitting. I've got to a good bit in my book anyway.'

'I won't be that long,' said Clare.

'Be as long as you like,' said Lara, looking up the staircase and shaking her head. This place must be like heaven for Clare, she thought. But, the way Lara was feeling that day, she might end up drowning herself in that pool if she stayed any longer.

Chapter 37

Gladys put down the delicate china teacup, opened up her handbag, retrieved a tissue from it and then wiped her eyes.

'I'm frightened, Raine,' she said. 'I'm frightened of that woman. He didn't want me to plate a meal up for his supper. I know they're going to have dinner together and he'll be putty in her hands. He's old and lonely and she's a wily piece.'

Raine's hand came out to touch Gladys's arm, but she knew her skin was cold and wouldn't offer much comfort.

'Gladys, I've only ever seen you cry once before in all the years I've known you.'

'It's since *she* came,' said Gladys, blowing her nose on her tissue and reaching for another. 'How can I have got it so wrong, Raine? She's dangerous. I'm scared for us all. For Edwin, for the village, most of all for—'

'Gladys.' Raine leaned over to pat her friend's shoulder, squashing Albert on her knee, though he didn't seem to mind that much. 'The world is a much smaller place these days. It could only ever have been a matter of time.'

Gladys's great shoulders were shaking as she sobbed, but she went on: 'I bet there isn't a drawer in that house she hasn't looked in. She's out to seduce Lord Carlton. She even wears her hair like Mary did. He's asked her to look at the estate ledgers and I know she's picked up that something is amiss. And she isn't the type to leave a thread unpulled, that one. He thinks he can trust her but I know he can't.'

Raine nodded. Gladys wasn't telling her anything she didn't know already. She had tasted the bitter salt of betrayal in the wind.

Clare reached for her towel, shoes and torch and, carrying them high over her head, she swam around to the other side of the cavern, where the second staircase was. She lifted herself out of the water and dried herself off before slipping on her shoes and draping her towel around her shoulders. She was going to find out where those steps went to. If nothing else, it would burn off some calories.

Her calves were certainly feeling it as she made her ascent. Finally her torch picked out the last of the stairs and a door, but just as her hand reached out for the iron hoop she heard voices. Raine's was one of them. The tower of steps led to her cottage.

Gladys looked around her at Raine's room and she felt more than a twinge of sadness. They were supposed to look after her and yet the place needed bottoming. She deserved better.

'I'm going to come up on my next day off and give this cottage a really good clean for you, Raine. Tell me they're bringing you food?'

'Yes, my dear, they are,' said Raine. 'But the cleaning is too much for them. Dorothy needs a new hip and a new knee. It takes her over half an hour to walk through the woods. And Margaret isn't up to bending or stretching. The others do the best they can too.'

'Someone needs telling about this,' said Gladys, filling up again and dabbing her eyes with her tissue. 'We've all been under the impression that you're being looked after. Properly.'

'I am.' Raine smiled. 'I have everything I need. A bit of dust doesn't bother me.'

'Val Hathersage could come up here and sort this place out for you. He does nothing but sleep and eat, that one. David Hathersage would turn in his grave to see what a waster his son turned out. And to see all the trouble between the brothers.'

'He isn't much like them, it has to be said. Such hard-working, decent boys.'

'That Colleen Landers led the poor boy a merry dance,' said Gladys. 'She smashed his heart to pieces. I bet she was less than useless when she was supposed to be helping you out.'

'Well, cleaning after an old lady wasn't where her passions lay, if that's what you mean.'

'We all know where her passions lay,' huffed Gladys. 'Most of them in Spice Wood. I worried when she left the village. She was such a mercenary creature.'

'She wouldn't have said anything. I never doubted her,' replied Raine. 'For all her faults, she was one of ours. It would never be one of ours.'

'That's my point,' Gladys insisted, her voice rising to a high pitch. 'Mrs Hawk isn't one of ours. And if she's from Wellem, as she claims, I'm Ingrid Bergman. And Gene Hathersage has brought more strangers into the village. He's rented his cottage out. I heard that Daisy Unwin gave Jenny a right blasting in the café for serving them. And not only serving them but serving them good food. Daisy thinks she should have done more to discourage them, not encourage them going in.'

'Jenny has too much pride not to want to give the best on her menu.'

'Agreed. She's a wonderful cook. And Daisy gave Shirley in the pub the rough end of her tongue as well.'

'Shirley can look after herself and Daisy Unwin will have to change her ways,' said Raine softly. 'She's got problems, that young lady. The village has been a closed bud for too long, Gladys. It needs to open up and flower. Everyone is under so much pressure to do the right thing: Edwin, Jenny, the young people . . . And as for poor Milton – he's spent his whole life in this village inventing things. I hear he's working on an invisibility shield now.' Raine laughed. 'He should be resting, taking things easy at his age.'

'He's loved every minute of it, Raine. He's more alive at ninety-three than half of the young men in the village. He's still in love with you, of course. You gave his life meaning. Without you to inspire his projects he wouldn't have found a place for himself in life.'

'Dear Milton,' said Raine. Clare heard the smile in her voice. 'I can still see him as a boy, all lanky arms and legs and his mother's ridiculous haircuts.'

'He would die for you, Raine.'

'I know the sacrifices they've all made, and would still make, Gladys. But it's time to stop. There's nothing here for the youth. Who can blame them for leaving? The village needs an infusion of new blood. Enough is enough. I'm tired, Gladys. I'm tired of being a curse.'

'You've been a blessing to this village. So many of us wouldn't have been born had it not been for you. Myself, for instance, and my five brothers.'

'You might have had sisters had it not been for me.'

'But I might not have done.' Gladys's voice was firm and brooked no nonsense. 'I hate to hear you talking like this. Please think about my offer again. Move in with me, Raine. I'm rattling around in that house since Charles died. There's plenty of room and you'd have company.'

'I'll make one more move in my lifetime,' replied Raine. 'And it won't be to another house.' She smiled. 'You're a good, kind woman, Gladys. Thank you. Let fate take its course. Let the village become part of the rest of the world again.'

'That can't happen whilst—'

Raine finished off the severed sentence. 'Whilst I am here. I know.'

'Raine, I heard something about one of the women staying in Gene Hathersage's cottage . . .'

'I've met her. I saw her swimming in the sea and I waved at her to come up.'

Gladys's mouth fell open. 'Oh, Raine, what were you thinking?'

'Her name is Clare. She's a lovely girl. She's coming to see me tomorrow. She found my lagoon, Gladys. I trust her. We have a connection. When I heard about how she looked I thought she might be like me, but, no, that is just a happy coincidence.'

'Oh, Raine, please be careful.'

'I shall,' said Raine, picking up on that. 'Clare is no Mrs Hawk.'

Clare padded carefully down the steps so she wouldn't be heard through the door. So, Val was underplaying the aftermath of Colleen's departure. Clare found herself guiltily pleased that Miss Perfect Colleen Landers wasn't all that perfect after all. She had left his heart in little pieces. And what was all that about Daisy and Jenny? Who was Milton? Where had she heard that name before? And why did Raine have to be careful of Clare? What were they saying about Gladys not having sisters? Questions were flooding her brain. What the hell was going on in Ren Dullem?

Chapter 38

May was up and drinking tea when Lara arrived back at the cottage. Her legs were knackered from climbing all those stairs. A life in power heels had a detrimental effect on calf muscles, apparently.

'Hello, missus,' May greeted her. 'One has been swimming, I see. How was it?'

'Absolutely beautiful. You must go and have a swim. Anyway, how are you?' Lara flicked her towel over the airer that hung from the kitchen ceiling. She thought that May looked very pale.

'Better for a good sleep, thanks. I need to get the cobwebs blown out of my head so I'm going for a walk. Want to come?'

'As long as it doesn't involve any steps at all,' replied Lara. 'Just give me five to have a quick shower.'

'Is Clare staying down there?' asked May, unlooping her handbag from the chair back.

'Yep. She'll have grown gills by the end of the holiday. If she hasn't already. Oh, and remind me to tell you about my latest embarrassing episode with our landlord. You'll enjoy it lots.'

The air was so beautifully warm outside. Lara cast a looks-could-kill glance at those stupid clouds that weren't real clouds. There must be a chemical plant over the headland, she decided.

They were probably all being poisoned by gas. She'd ask Jenny what caused them if they decided to call in for a coffee.

May winced for Lara when she heard about the Tourette's incident. Then she laughed heartily, picturing it all in her head. Her friend really had got off on the wrong footing with Mr Hathersage.

Coming up the hill towards them was a skinny man in jeans and a muscle top with a Jack & Jones logo on the front. His arms were covered in tattoos, one a picture of Marilyn Monroe. He had bright-pink streaks in his hair and mock-croc shoes with long pointed toes. He was holding a North Yorkshire tourism guide. Behind him, travelling at a much slower pace, was another man, much taller and heavier and sporting a more traditional look: curly brown hair, conservative jeans and a plain white T-shirt.

'Excuse me, girls,' said the skinny man. His voice was light and effeminate. 'Have you any idea where the abbey ruins are?'

'Sorry,' said May, 'we aren't from around here.'

'Hallelujah,' said the man. 'A friendly voice. Gideon, hurry up. I've found some real people who aren't inbred locals.' He clasped his hands together with delight. 'We haven't had a sensible answer since we arrived here. One woman in a wheelchair ran over Gideon's toe. She was like a bloody mad Dalek. Half expected her to start shouting, "Exterminate, exterminate" at us.'

May and Lara exchanged amused glances. They obviously knew who that was.

'Hi,' said Gideon, finally catching up with his friend. 'I'm Coco's husband.'

'Coco?' said Lara.

'That's me.' The pink-haired man showed off a ring on the third finger of his left hand. 'I never get tired of showing it off. We thought we'd have a drive around the area. I've never been here before, and if this place is anything to go by I never will again.' He shuddered. 'I thought that butcher was going to fillet me.'

Behind him Gideon raised his eyes skyward and puffed out his cheeks.

'And we can't get a bloody signal on our phones,' Coco continued. 'Gideon reckons there's a jammer causing that. They obviously don't like anyone having new-fangled ideas here.'

'A jammer?' asked May.

'Oh, the satellite signals are definitely being interfered with somewhere around here,' said Gideon, pushing his glasses back up his nose.

'Why?' said Coco flamboyantly. 'And what the buggery bollocks is going on up there?' He pointed to a puff of grey cloud floating over their heads.

'We think there might be a chemical plant nearby,' said Lara.

'No, there's no plant,' Gideon answered. 'For the want of a better explanation, I'd say they were coming from a crude attempt at a cloud machine.'

'Jesus, has Kate Bush moved here with Donald Sutherland?' Coco snorted, and broke into the first verse of 'Cloudbusting'.

May and Lara exchanged amused glances as Gideon studied the clouds above their heads and murmured, 'Yes, definitely man-made clouds, those. The question is why, of course.'

'Someone with a cloud fetish?' suggested Coco. 'God knows they've got perversions for everyone today: dry-humping buildings, sniffing old slippers, washing in pee. Okay, onwards and upwards, then,' he said. 'We might just skip looking for the old abbey and head off to Beirut. I hear the locals are friendlier there.' He inhaled deeply near Lara. 'Oh, you're wearing Rain. Lovely. Not one of my faves usually, but on you it smells divine.'

Gideon rolled his eyes. 'Ignore him. He's got a perfume shop,' he explained. 'He sniffs at everyone.'

'Emporium, please,' tutted Coco. 'I'll give you "shop".'

Lara laughed as he playfully slapped Gideon's arm.

'Anyway, lovely to have met you,' Coco said, turning back to Lara and May. 'Hope I don't read about you becoming human sacrifices in the *Mirror*. Come on, Gideon.'

And with that, the couple were off, rounding the corner in front of Gene Hathersage's cottage and disappearing from view.

'Ren Dullem is getting a stranger place to be by the second,' said May.

Lara said nothing. If life got any stranger, she thought she might spontaneously combust.

They walked to the far end of the village, passing the church with its highly decorative stone-work, and gargoyles that reminded Lara of her letch of a boss. A cobbled lane at the side of the church curled up the hillside and there was an arrow-shaped sign at the bottom which read: *Hathersage Farm*. As they stood with their backs to the harbour and looked up the hill they could see a large butter-coloured building between the trees. So that was Frank's farm. Nearby they discovered a pretty little park with a conical coffee kiosk next to the empty swings, but the window was abruptly pulled shut when May was three footsteps away from ordering drinks there. She turned to Lara and held her hands up in exasperation.

'Let's go to Jenny's for a coffee,' suggested Lara. She had to laugh. Life in Ren Dullem made less sense than her dream world.

'Fancy an ice cream?' asked May, spotting a darling little shop completely covered in ivy and honeysuckle. 'I'm going to sprint over so they don't have a chance to shut.'

But the shop didn't close in front of them. It was manned by a teenager with huge grey eyes. He looked terrified in their presence, and even dropped the first cornet that Lara ordered onto the floor.

'I don't know whether to be insulted or thrilled that he was so jittery serving us,' whispered May when they left the shop.

She licked her clotted-cream and raspberry ice to find it absolutely delicious. Immediately her brain started ticking on what she would do to improve that little ice-cream business. It needed tables and chairs outside, for a start.

'Let's pretend we are flattered and that he didn't look at us as if we were dirty old predatory cougars,' said Lara. She had chosen rum delight. There were big pieces of truffle chocolate in the mix. She mmm-ed with pleasure as they made their way to one of the seats facing the sea. It was obviously one of Gene Hathersage's creations, with its back made of twisted branches. He had an incredible talent. She wondered if he sold them. He'd be a fool if he didn't. He must do − or how else did he make his money? How did any of the locals make money if no one ever came to Ren Dullem? Did the money just circulate from one business to another?

'Isn't it a strange place, Lars?' said May at last. 'I feel as if I've stumbled into a book.'

'In the horror section?'

Lara knew exactly what May meant. But this weird little place was better than the real life waiting for her back in Surrey. She was content to stay here, even if their holiday was marred by meeting some of the rudest people on the planet.

After they had finished their cornets, and as they set off at a slow walk back to Well Cottage, a brown van came rumbling down the road. The gold lettering on the side read: *Hathersage Farm, Fresh Meats*. Lara noticed that the van had quite an effect on her friend. She could virtually hear May's heart racing from a metre away. Interesting, she thought.

The van pulled to a halt in front of them.

'Hello, ladies!' The jovial, kind face of Frank Hathersage appeared through the driver's window. 'Having a nice day?'

'Yes, thank you,' replied Lara. May appeared to be struck dumb. 'That your farm up there? The creamy-yellow one?'

'Yep, that's mine,' said Frank, pride in his voice.

'It must have a fabulous view of the harbour.'

'It does. Especially when there's a storm. It can be very dramatic. I should open up the farm when the weather is bad and charge for the view. Exploring the village, are you?' He was looking at May but it was Lara who answered again.

'Yes, we are.'

'Well, there's one place you should visit: the ice-cream shop over there,' said Frank. He pointed through the window with a huge square hand – a farmer's hand.

'Just have done,' Lara replied with a smile. 'And we tried to buy a coffee from the kiosk but, strangely, it closed as we were about to order.'

'Old man Unwin is a funny one – don't take any notice,' said Frank in a low voice, as if old man Unwin had bionic hearing and could pick up what he was saying. 'He's Daisy's uncle.'

That figured, thought both May and Lara together.

'His wife is in charge of the school clothes shop,' Frank went on. 'That's likely to shut up too if you try to venture inside.'

'Oh, that's a shame. I'd run out of black plimsolls and was going to call in.' Lara laughed, wondering why May wasn't joining in with the conversation even though she and Frank Hathersage couldn't keep their eyes off each other.

'We've had lots of your bacon since we've been here,' said Lara, scrabbling around for something to say now, seeing as May wasn't helping. 'Absolutely delicious.'

'I'll drop some off to you at the cottage, if you like.'

Lara was going to say not to trouble himself but she thought that May might like that very much.

'That's kind of you. If you're passing.'

'I'll make sure I am. Well, enjoy the rest of your day, Miss Lara, Miss May.'

He knew their names. The whole village probably knew more about them by now than they knew about themselves.

'And you,' said Lara, giving May a nudge.

'Yes, the day, enjoy it all of it,' said May, sounding like a defective talking doll.

Frank drove off with a toot of his horn and Lara raised her eyebrows at May.

'You fancy him,' she said with a grin. 'You'd better keep right out of Daisy's way. It won't be just your foot she runs over with her wheelchair.'

'Oh, shut up, Lara, and let's get a coffee,' said May, marching off. Yes, she fancied Frank Hathersage like mad and was trying not to. She knew they would get on like a house on fire if they were left to it and her thoughts had escaped to him often. But she'd already been with one man with a so-called disabled partner and her heart had been mashed to a pulp in the process. She wasn't going to make that mistake again.

Chapter 39

Jenny was delighted to see their faces, that much was obvious. The café was empty so they could sit at one of the lovely tables in the window. They were only going to order a coffee, but the menu was so tempting that they found themselves requesting afternoon tea as well.

'No one ever orders afternoon tea,' said Jenny with glee thick in her voice. 'It'll be a pleasure to make it.' She wobbled off behind her counter, rubbing her hands as she went.

A three-tier cake stand arrived, the top layer packed with tiny cream scones and pastries stuffed with custard and crème patisserie, and on the other two plates were dinky sandwich triangles: egg, cress and spring onion, cheese and pickle, crisp cucumber, ham, crushed celery and tomato.

'Blimey, I'll never eat all this,' said Lara.

'No, you won't. You'll eat half.' May reached for a cheese and pickle. 'Tuck in.'

'We've just had ice cream.'

'So?'

'You've suddenly found your tongue now that Frank Hathersage isn't around.' Lara winked at her.

May sniffed. 'Don't be ridiculous, Lara.'

'Where's your other friend?' asked Jenny, bringing over a big old pot of tea and two delicate blue and white cups.

'Swimming,' Lara replied through a mouthful of egg sandwich. 'She's part mermaid, that one.'

Jenny dropped the tray of tea. One of the cups smashed and boiling water splashed onto May's leg.

'Oh God, I'm so sorry. Are you okay?'

'I'm fine,' said May, rubbing at her bare leg and trying not to show that it did actually hurt quite a bit.

Lara was on her knees picking up bits of crockery. The teapot had survived, surprisingly. Jenny returned with towels and a sweeping brush.

'You should have left that for me; you might have cut yourself.'

'It's fine, Jenny, really.'

Jenny's soft grey eyes were brimming with tears as she sponged up the water. 'I'm so sorry.'

'No harm done at all.' Lara squeezed her shoulder. 'Why don't you sit down with us and steady yourself?' Lara pulled a chair from another table and patted the seat. She gently pushed the shaking Jenny down onto it.

'Want a sandwich?' asked May, trying not to think about the throbbing spots on her leg. 'They're delicious. I can recommend the chef.'

'No, I'm all right, thank you,' said Jenny, blowing her nose on a napkin and then smiling gratefully at May's kind comment. It was quite obvious that the young woman didn't have a lot of confidence in herself.

'Is this your own café, then?' asked Lara, trying to cheer her up with some conversation.

'Well, the village owns it but I suppose you could say it's mine, yes.'

Lara couldn't help thinking that was a weird way of putting it. 'So you don't own it?'

'No,' said Jenny, having considered her answer before giving it, as if worried she were being trapped by a trick question.

Not something else weird, please, thought Lara.

'It's a grand little business,' said May. 'Lovely food. Did you go to catering college?'

'No!' Jenny laughed as if that was a totally absurd suggestion. 'My mum used to run it. I took it over when she and Dad retired last year. I just picked up how to cook from her.'

'She must have been a very good cook.'

'Yes, she—'

The door to the café opened as if a battering ram had been placed behind it. In a way it had been – it was Daisy's wheelchair. This time she was followed in by a reed-thin woman wearing thick glasses, a sour expression on her very plain face and a knitted top that even Lara's granny wouldn't have been seen dead in. Jenny leapt up from her seat as if she had been caught red-handed fraternizing with the enemy, which she had, really. The air seemed to chill around them.

'Hi, Daisy, Pauline,' called Jenny, with hopeful buoyancy in her voice that they'd play nicely.

If looks could kill, Jenny would have been impaled like a human dartboard.

'Two cappuccinos, sprinkles, and two pieces of chocolate dream cake,' said Daisy, her nose wrinkled up with disdain.

'Please,' added the mousey Pauline, getting out of the way whilst Daisy wheeled herself into position so her legs were underneath a table. She was making a lot of crashing noises as she did so. Lara didn't hold out much hope for the long-term preservation of Jenny's furniture if Daisy Unwin were a regular customer.

Daisy and Pauline immediately started to gossip, their heads close together, the object of the game clearly being to unsettle the other customers. So Lara and May remained steadfastly unsettled by it.

Jenny brought out replacement cups and a fresh pot of tea, setting them on Lara and May's table before she delivered the cappuccinos and cake to the gossips. That didn't go down well. May heard some very disgruntled mumbling coming from Daisy's mouth when Jenny took over the cutlery and serviettes.

The atmosphere in the café had changed with the arrival of Daisy and her crony. The temperature had plunged and there was a perceptible crackle in the air of electric disapproval. May and Lara nibbled on their sandwiches, certain that Daisy wouldn't be able to resist making her feelings audible. They were right.

First the exaggerated sniffing started. This was followed up by:

'Jenny, are your drains okay? There's a funny smell in here.'

Lara did an involuntary snort. She was suddenly catapulted back to her junior school days sharing a class with Cassandra Wath the class bitch and big-mouth. The last time Lara had seen her − at Christmas, when she visited her parents − Cassandra had been stocking up freezers in Iceland − the shop − and had a spot on the side of her nose the size of Iceland − the country. She had grown into the face she deserved: a perma-scowl that said, 'This woman is too mean to be happy.' It was the sort of face Lara thought Daisy would have in a few years' time. She was starting to get it already.

Jenny didn't answer.

'There were some gay boys in town today, apparently, Jenny,' Daisy said loudly. 'One had pink hair. Offcumdens. Lowering the tone of the place.'

'I think she's bracketing us in there.' Lara giggled, setting May off.

At last Daisy made a direct approach. 'I don't know what's so funny. You aren't welcome here. No one wants you here.'

'Maybe not,' said Lara, drying her eyes on a serviette. If Daisy Unwin wanted a battle, then Lara would pick up her gauntlet. 'But Gene Hathersage wants our money. So we're staying.'

'How long for?'

'Three months at least,' replied Lara, as sweet as sugar. 'We may even move in. With our families.'

Pauline started choking on her cappuccino.

'Gene Hathersage is an idiot,' spat Daisy.

Lara wasn't going to argue with her on that. But she did feel like throwing a few mischievous twigs onto the fire.

'His brother is very handsome, though. We like his meat,' she purred.

This time Daisy started choking. Jenny disappeared behind the counter like a bartender in a western.

'You stay away from my Francis, you pair of sluts,' screamed Daisy. 'And you can tell the witch to stay away as well. Fuck off, the lot of you, back where you came from.'

'Calm yourself, Daisy,' Pauline said, as firmly as her thin voice could manage. 'Come on, deep breaths.'

'I'm not well,' Daisy barked, a furious tremor in her voice as she breathed in and out deeply. Enough was enough. Lara wasn't feeling the fun any more. She didn't want to goad Daisy into an asthma attack. She put twenty-five pounds in notes on the counter in front of Jenny, telling her to keep the change. As she and May left the café she heard Daisy's dulcet tones behind her: 'And good riddance. She puts me off eating with the scar on her face.'

Incensed, Lara turned on her heel to go back in but May caught her arm.

'Leave it, Lara.'

'How dare she . . .'

'Don't rise to it. She wants us to react.'

'Ooh, I want to slap her so hard,' growled Lara. How dare the bitch say that about May. It was cruel and unnecessary. Even more so coming from a woman in a chair who must know what it was like to have a stigma.

'Poor Frank. I think he's going to end up more unhappy

than his future wife,' said Lara, letting May lead her away from Jenny's café.

May didn't answer. She merely followed Lara through the village and up the hill, wishing she were worthy enough to deserve someone as gorgeous as Frank Hathersage.

'Guess where the second set of steps downstairs leads to?' said Clare, as soon as May and Lara walked into the cottage. 'I've been dying for you to get back so I could tell you. Only Raine's cottage on the headland.' Clare couldn't wait for them to answer.

'How did you find that out?' asked Lara, kicking off her shoes. 'Don't tell me you climbed up the second set of steps and there was a door at the top?'

'I did indeed. And there was,' Clare replied, with a proud nod of the head. 'I tell you, there's something really strange about this village. I mean, really strange. If you heard the conversation I heard through the door to Raine's cottage, you'd feel the same.'

May crossed the room to put on the kettle. 'Go on, then, Sherlock. Intrigue us.'

'Well,' began Clare, making herself comfortable at the dining table. 'I overheard the old lady – Raine – talking to someone. Raine was saying she was a curse on the village and the other person was saying that she was a blessing actually and that she wouldn't have been born if Raine hadn't done what she'd done.'

'Which was what?' asked Lara.

'I don't know. Raine went on to say that the other woman might have had sisters had it not been for Raine, instead of brothers.'

May and Lara exchanged blatantly amused glances.

'Are you sure they weren't reading out a play script?' suggested May.

'Don't be daft. Of course they weren't.'

'Well, you go and enjoy deciphering all that creepy stuff,' Lara said jokingly. 'Meanwhile, I'll have a life.'

'And talking of creepy . . .' said May. 'We bumped into mad Daisy in Jenny's café.'

'She was foul,' shuddered Lara. She didn't repeat what she had said about May's scar as she knew it would embarrass her but it was still really annoying her. 'We all have to stay away from Frank, she said.'

'Oh, okay. I'll try very hard to resist his advances.' Clare laughed, but there wouldn't be any danger there. She had her eye on the Hathersage brother who was capable of shaking up her staid existence and exorcizing the ghost of nice, safe Lud.

Chapter 40

Lara took a can of Diet Coke from the fridge and went outside to the terrace. In the distance, where there were none of those ridiculous clouds overhead, the sea was dappled with sunlight. There was a light and warm breeze that made her shiver with delight as it touched her skin. Her parents had a lovely south-facing terrace at the back of their house. Her dad had built it because he and her mum liked to sit outside whenever there was a hint of sun. They'd all had many a happy tea sitting at the iron table on the terrace, a fire-pit warming them as the night grew chilly.

Was it really eight months ago when I last visited my parents? Lara retraced the year – but no, she hadn't been up to Yorkshire since Christmas. And even then she had shot off on Boxing Day to get some prep done before she returned to work the following day. She felt a huge wave of shame wash over her. She was an only child and hadn't seen her mum and dad in all that time. Where the hell had the year gone? In fact, where had the last few years gone? Had she done anything except rush from appointment to meeting to appointment? Even her relationship with James was shoehorned into their mad working lives. And when she did free up some rare couple time in the evenings he was still working. Well, she'd thought he had been working. He obviously had enough time to squeeze in Tianne frigging Lee. Literally.

She loved her parents and loved her friends and yet how much real time did she spend with them? She'd seen more of Keely and Garth than she had people she liked. Her priorities were all to cock. A tear dropped on her jeans and she dabbed at her eye to poke back any others with intentions of following. She didn't want May or Clare to see that she had things on her mind.

Her mum and dad would love it here, she thought, listening to the silence broken now and again with the shrill squawk of the seagulls – it sounded as if they were laughing at the offcumdens as they flew overhead. Her parents had never had a lot of money but they had saved to put her through university and were so proud of her every achievement. They'd be gutted to find out that inside their successful, power-suit-wearing daughter was a lonely, unloved woman with nothing in her life but a job that she really didn't want to do any more.

Clare joined her. 'Wotcher,' she whispered. 'I've just heard a van outside so I've come out here to leave May alone in the house to answer the door. I think she has a bit of a soft spot for Frank and, from the way he looks at her, I think it's mutual.'

'Witch,' said Lara, smiling, glad of her company.

'Oh, don't you start. I heard a bit of gossip from . . . from the old lady, Raine.' She lied about the source.

'Go on,' said Lara, shifting round in her seat to face Clare.

'It appears that Frank caused the accident that crippled Daisy. A car accident. They hadn't been going out that long and, well, he's obviously so guilt-ridden that he's decided to do his duty and look after her.'

'Poor Frank,' said Lara. He appeared like an honest, decent man. Maybe if he hadn't been so much of a good man, he could have cut and run from Daisy and been happy. Sometimes, Lara thought, having a conscience could be a right old bummer.

They heard a knock on the outside door and Clare giggled. 'He's here, with his big meaty package.'

'Shhh,' said Lara, giggling too.

'Can you get the door, May?' Clare called. 'We're a bit busy.'

'Er . . . can you get it? I'm busy too.'

'No, we're busier. Sorry.' Lara clamped her hands over her mouth to stop the laughter exploding out.

May started flapping. She shot to the long mirror on the wall to check her face and brush her hair forward on the left over the silvery line of scar. Then, after arranging herself, she took a steadying breath and opened the door to Frank, looking the picture of calm.

'Hi, Frank, come in.'

Frank had to bend to come through the door and even when he was inside, his head wasn't that far off the ceiling beams. He looked like a giant visiting a child's Wendy house. May tried not to think about those big arms closing around her.

He was holding a couple of bags. 'There's some bacon in here for you, some fillet steaks and chicken breasts. I've also put in a couple of my pies – I'm told they would be award-winning if I ever entered any of the butchery competitions.' He put it all down on the table next to the teapot.

'Oh, that's wonderful, Frank, thank you,' said May, aware that she was wiping her hands on her dress, something she always did when she was nervous. 'How much do we owe you?'

He waved away the suggestion that he wanted any money. 'Call it an apology after Daisy's behaviour. Wouldn't mind a cup of tea, though. Haven't had a chance to stop for one all day.'

'No, we can't let you—'

'I insist. My charge is a cup of tea. And that's the end to it.'

'Thank you, then. That's awfully kind of you. Please sit down.' May turned the kettle on, hoping that he wasn't looking at her bum. The kettle seemed to take hours to boil.

'I think it's on a go-slow,' she said, turning to Frank.

'I'm in no rush now. I've nearly finished for the day,' he said.

'There're some biscuits in the cupboard.'

Clare's voice drifted in from outside. 'Hi, Frank.'

'Hello, there,' he replied.

Why are you two sods staying out there? 'Do you want a drink?' May called to them.

'No, we're okay, thanks,' replied Lara.

May was going to slap them both later.

'So . . .' she said eventually, putting the fresh pot of tea on the table and then taking the packet of biscuits and a small plate out of the cupboard. She hadn't a clue what she was going to say next. Being in the presence of Frank made her tongue tie itself in knots.

'So, are you enjoying yourself here, in Ren Dullem?' asked Frank, rescuing her as he spooned one sugar and a small splash of milk into his cup.

'Yes,' said May, sitting down at the table. God, this man and his lovely heavily lashed eyes absorbed all her conscious thought and struck her silent. She forced herself to get a grip and make an effort at conversation. 'We don't have much time off work and we decided on a whim to book a holiday and spend some time with each other. We should have been at the spa at Wellem but there was a coc— an error in the reservation.'

'Some error,' said Frank. 'Though I'm a great believer in things happening for a reason.' He looked straight into her brown eyes with an intensity that had her bones vibrating. She knew he felt the connection between them too, because of the way he quickly turned his head away and scanned the kitchen.

'Gene's done it up well,' he said. 'It wasn't lived in for a lot of years. It was our grandmother's cottage. In fact, it's been in the family for generations. Gene bought our shares, mine and our younger brother's.'

'There's a lagoon downstairs,' blurted May, 'though you'll know about that.'

'You found it?' He looked surprised.

'Clare found it.'

'Your friend with the . . .' He pointed to his eyes, one then the other.

'Clare with the witch eyes,' May said loud enough for her friend outside to hear. 'Yep. That's her.'

Frank smiled as if a private joke was going on in his head. 'Yes, of course.' Then he shook himself out of his reverie. 'How long are you staying?'

'We leave next Friday. We've got a full week left,' said May, tipping the biscuits onto a plate and offering them to Frank. Both of them noticed how much her hand was shaking. He took the plate from her and put it back down on the table.

'I think they were too heavy; you were going to drop them,' he said.

'Thank you.' Her eyes locked onto his again. And they wouldn't unlock.

'I should go,' said Frank, standing up and only just clearing the ceiling. He hadn't even taken a sip of tea.

'Of course,' said May, totally flustered now. She hadn't a clue what chemical reactions were making her insides fizz. 'You'll have things to do.'

'I haven't got anything to do,' said Frank, so quietly that no one else could overhear, 'but if I stay for that tea I'll end up kissing you and that would be wrong. See you later, May.'

'Urggghhh,' was May's strange, unintelligible noise in response to that. She didn't get up to show him out. She wasn't sure her legs would support her.

Clare wasn't certain she had made the right call when she and Lara casually walked back in after hearing Frank's van leave. May looked as if someone had taken out her brain and replaced it with a Bird's Trifle.

'You okay?' said Lara. 'May, talk to me.'

'I'm fine,' May replied. 'I'm just a bit astounded by his generosity. He left us loads of meat and wouldn't take any money for it. Wasn't that nice?'

'Yes, it was,' Clare and Lara chorused, not believing a word of May's explanation as to why she was a whiter shade of white.

Chapter 41

At seven o'clock precisely Lord Carlton knocked on Joan's cottage door. She opened it wearing the dress she had 'borrowed' from Mary's wardrobe. Navy-blue with a white trim, it was fitted around the bust and waist and had a flared skirt. It was far too frumpy for Joan's taste but perfect for the purpose for which she needed it. She had sprayed herself – and the room – liberally with the bottle of perfume that she had found in Mary's dressing-table drawer. It had gone off a bit after all those years, but when Carlton crossed the threshold she saw his nose lift in the air and she watched the effect of the perfume snake to his brain. His face softened and his eyes twinkled as the memories sparkled behind them. Even his snow-white toupee seemed to sigh with delight.

'Come right in and sit down,' said Joan, smiling at him with her red-lipsticked mouth. 'It's nearly ready.'

The lounge, dining room and kitchen were all one room in the *bijou* dwelling place. She had scrubbed at it this afternoon, making it shine. Joan didn't like housework. Upstairs her bedroom was a mess of clothes not hung up and general undusted, uncleaned grime that had built up over the months she had been here. She hadn't bothered to clean it because Edwin would not be going in there. At least not tonight. After old Stanley Hawk she'd had enough of old men fumbling her. She'd let Stanley paw her, fall in love with her and marry her because he had a fortune. He hadn't told her it was tied up in trust funds for his children. Luckily he had died not too long after she learned that. In his will he had left her ten thousand pounds for every completed year they had been married, but his family let her have twelve on the proviso that she buggered off immediately, carrying only the things she came with. She agreed, although the bags she came with ended up being stuffed with treasures from around the house; disappointingly they turned out to be mostly reproductions and nigh-on worthless. At least Edwin Carlton had no children – and he had a title. She quite fancied herself as Lady Joan – or would she be Lady Anne or Lady Jo or Lady Joanna? Maybe she would double-barrel Carlton with her maiden name: Lady Joanna MacLean-Carlton – it had a wonderfully genteel ring to it.

'I know you don't drink,' said Joan, 'so I've made some elderflower cordial. Granny's recipe. There is some fermentation that takes place in the process, but I can assure you it's minimal.'

She poured him a tall glass of cordial – bought from Tesco in Whitby and laced rather heavily with vodka.

'Thank you,' said Edwin, reaching out to take the glass. Joan noticed that on his middle finger he was wearing a ring with the family crest on it. She shivered with delight at having her own coat of arms as well as a title.

For starter she had made a prawn cocktail, the Marie-Rose sauce featuring a hearty splash of vodka too. 'Every little helps,' she had trilled to herself with a chortle because these were Tesco prawns. She was serving them up in some large seashells she had found in the kitchen cupboard. She brought them out and set one in front of Edwin.

'It won't be up to Gladys's standards, I'm afraid, but hopefully I won't poison you. I bought these fresh from the fish market in Wellem.'

'We have a small market on Saturdays in Ren Dullem, you know,' said Edwin. 'Gladys gets ours from there.'

'Ah, I didn't know that,' replied Joan. Not that it would have made any difference if she had known. Who wanted to shop in Dullem? It was a creepy little place, full of staring people who obviously hadn't seen an attractive woman before, if their own were anything to go by. It was like walking through a James Herbert novel, with those odd foggy clouds. Wellem was far more buzzing and no one's eyes bored into her back when she passed them. She still had nightmares about that fat little woman in a wheelchair who scowled at her because she'd dared to stir up the waters and say a very flirty hello to the tall, dark, handsome man who was pushing her. He reminded her of someone she was going to marry once: Adam. A strong, gentle and kind Scottish man from South Yorkshire, with red hair and a heart as soft as a marshmallow. She still thought about him, and regretted that she hadn't managed to hang onto him.

'This is lovely,' said Edwin, tucking in as if he hadn't eaten for a fortnight. 'I've starved all day for this. I didn't even eat the lunch that Gladys prepared for me.'

Just what I want to hear, thought Joan. The alcohol will get into your bloodstream so much more quickly.

'I've been thinking, Joan, maybe you and Gladys ought to go to the pictures or something together. I'm sure she'd appreciate the company. Should I ask her for you?'

God forbid, thought Joan. 'No, don't ask. I'll do it. I wouldn't want her to feel obliged. I'm quite happy with my books in the evenings.'

Joan refilled Edwin's glass. The fire in the grate had been heaped up high so that it would engender a thirst which would be beautifully quenched by her 'granny's iced cordial'.

Next, Joan delivered her chicken casserole to the table, the meat saturated in red wine. She hoped all the alcohol hadn't been boiled off, but she would keep his glass topped up if so.

'Chicken casserole,' she announced. She heard his stomach rumble with pleasure as the aroma of the rich sauce drifted up his nostrils.

'Do excuse me,' Edwin apologized. 'My goodness, I feel like a king.'

'I made the bread myself, on the range,' Joan said with a titter, pushing towards him a plate of Tesco baps just warmed in the oven. 'I'm a proper little housewife, aren't I?'

'Gladys forbids me to eat white,' said Edwin, pulling at his red silk cravat to loosen the top button on his shirt. Beads of sweat were appearing on his forehead. He took a long glug of the cordial.

'But Gladys isn't here, and I shan't tell if you don't,' Joan promised, winking then watching as he tucked into the soft white bread with the eagerness of a child diving into his first Easter egg.

Edwin spooned a heap of potatoes onto his plate. Joan speared a chunk of chicken and thought that it didn't taste half bad for a packet mix and most of a bottle of cheap red wine.

'It's nice to have your company,' said Joan, lifting her glass and holding it aloft in a toast. Edwin hurriedly picked his up and chinked it against hers.

'Cheers, my dear. Although if you're looking to me for good company, I fear you are going to be sadly disappointed.'

'Nonsense,' said Joan. 'My late husband was seventy-eight when we married. I've always found the company of older people much richer than that of people my own age. I think it's because I was brought up by my grandparents.'

'Oh?' asked Edwin. 'Were you? Why was that?'

'I never knew my father. My poor mother, alas, had a lot of problems.' She tapped her temple, indicating that her mother's problems were mental ones. 'It's only in the last few years I've actually gotten to know her properly.'

Sometimes she used this story, sometimes she said that both parents died in a car crash, sometimes in a boating accident. Sometimes they were still alive and living in Australia.

'That's very sad,' said Edwin. 'I hope your mother is well now.'

'Thank you, she's doing brilliantly. It's been a long journey for her though,' Joan sighed.

'I do feel for anyone who doesn't come from a close family. I had the most wonderful parents and grandparents. And great-grandparents. I have very fond memories of them all.'

'Yet you never had your own family, or remarried after Mary died?'

Edwin's hand stilled on his third bap.

'No, try as we might, we were never lucky on the children front, but we had each other. Until she was taken from me so early. Since then, no one has quite filled Mary's shoes. Still, I've had enough to keep me busy all these years. There's more to running this estate than meets the—' He cut the sentence short then continued. 'I mean, I take the duty of looking after the people of Ren Dullem very seriously.'

'Like an old-fashioned lord of the manor?' said Joan.

'Yes, just like that,' replied Edwin.

'Unusual, though, in this day and age.'

'Ren Dullem is an unusual place,' remarked Edwin, spearing another potato on his plate. His eyes were slightly glassy, Joan noticed.

'Very odd name for a place. Doesn't make it sound very attractive.'

'It's from the French *Reines de la Mer*. People couldn't pronounce it properly and it became what was much easier to say: Ren Dullem.'

'Queens of the Sea – isn't that what it means?' Joan pressed.

'Goodness, it's very hot in here,' said Edwin, fanning his face with his hand.

'I'll let the fire die down. More cordial?' Joan plied Edwin with a full glass. 'Sounds like a ship, doesn't it? *Queens of the Sea*,' she repeated.

'Yes, yes, it does.' Edwin nodded as he chewed noisily. 'This is very good. Excellent chicken. As good as Gladys would make any day.'

Joan made light conversation about the general area because Edwin started to get edgy when questions about Ren Dullem were asked. She needed to lull him into a false sense of security, get him chatting until he couldn't stop. Edwin waxed lyrical about geology and rocks and things that Joan couldn't even be bothered remembering five seconds after he had mentioned them; she had to work hard to stop herself dropping off. She cranked up the momentum again with the raspberry trifle. She didn't tell him there was half a pint of sherry in it.

'A pure indulgence,' said Edwin, his words slurring into each other beautifully now. He took a spoonful of the pudding, closed his eyes as if tasting heaven and then swallowed. 'My dear Joan, please do not tell Gladys that I am eating cream.'

'Our secret,' said Joan, giving him her sweetest smile. 'And you do know that I can be trusted with anything you tell me, Lord Carlton.'

'Edwin, please,' he said, lolling from side to side.

'Edwin. I'm an old-fashioned girl. I've always prided myself on being completely trustworthy. I know that Gladys is worried that I might see something in the ledgers that maybe I shouldn't, but even if I did – well, I'm a "secret-ary." And I'm a very good and loyal one at that.'

'You are the best,' said Edwin, dropping his hand heavily onto Joan's and squeezing it. He did not leave it there, though. His gesture was meant to be grateful and affectionate, not sleazy or seductive.

'What are the village secrets I should be aware of now that this is my home?' Joan asked brazenly, taking this up a notch or two now. Edwin was getting drunker by the second and yet he wasn't opening up. If she had been sitting here with Stanley Hawk, she would have leaned over at this point and started stroking his chest. But that would terrify Edwin Carlton, she knew. He was not hungry for sex; he was hungry for company, for gentle affection.

'Oh, there are no secrets to Ren Dullem,' he said.

So he was still hanging onto the lie, despite the fact that he must be wankered by now, thought Joan. He had dropped his spoon in the trifle twice in the last minute. Joan was getting frustrated but she also knew that she couldn't move quickly. Any drunker and he would pass out, and she didn't want his carcass on her sofa all night.

'Let me make some coffee,' she said, touching him on the shoulder.

'Wonderful,' he said, not realizing there were beads of red jelly on his chin as he scraped his spoon in the bowl to retrieve every last bit of trifle.

By the time Joan had brought the coffees to the table, Edwin was asleep, leaning back at an uncomfortable angle in his chair and snoring softly.

Shit, thought Joan, shaking him gently and then more forcibly until he shuddered out of his slumber. His glassy eyes pulled in and out of focus on Joan, and now that drowsiness was coupled with alcohol all sorts of confused messages were being sent to his brain.

'Mary?' he said. 'Is that you?'

Bingo! 'Yes, Edwin,' Joan replied, altering her voice to the sort of thin, reedy posh voice that she thought Lady Mary Carlton might have had.

'Oh, it is good to see you, my love.' His hand rested on Joan's shoulder, touched her face tenderly.

'Edwin,' Joan licked her lips, 'what were you telling me just then? About the secrets in the village.'

Edwin closed his eyes, tired of trying to focus and just content to hear his beloved wife, touch her, take in her scent. 'Oh, Mary, there isn't anything you don't know. Nothing's changed.'

'I've forgotten, Edwin,' said Joan, trying to keep the excitement at bay in her voice. 'What's going on? Why are we paying out so much money from the estate to the villagers?'

'The twelve families, Mary. We shall always look after the twelve families.'

Twelve families? What the frig was he talking about? Why couldn't he give her a straight answer?

'Why, Edwin? Why will we look after the twelve families?'

'You remember, Mary. Gilbert shouldn't have made them go out.'

Gilbert, as in his father? Gilbert Carlton? Had to be.

'Gilbert, my love?' said Joan sweetly.

'They all told him it wasn't safe but he insisted and then the boat sank.'

'Ah, yes, and they all drowned. I remember.' Joan guessed at the most obvious conclusion. So this Gilbert's family paid out guilt money. And were still paying it?

'No, my love.' And he mumbled something.

Joan tried to decipher his words but they were sliding into each other. 'What did you say? *Rain saved them?*'

'Saved them all,' Edwin replied, then he slid into an unconsciousness that he would not be woken from.

Chapter 42

The girls stayed in that evening and cooked one of Frank's pies, which they ate with two tins of mushy peas bought from the shop. It was a delicious supper.

'Don't panic if I'm not around in the morning,' said Clare. 'I might go off for an early swim before I go up and see the old lady.'

'There's a shocker. Bet you can't wait to get up in the morning to go for a dip and then whip out your J cloths – you'll think you've died and gone to heaven,' chuckled Lara, and she yawned. This sea air was a killer. Either that or those funny clouds were full of valium. 'I'm off to bed. Enjoy your scrubbing in the morning, you mad bag.' She was asleep before her head touched the pillow and had a restful dreamless sleep, the type of sleep she rarely had any more.

Clare set her alarm for eight. She wanted to be out of the house early to clean Raine's cottage. She'd have a swim later, she decided.

May lay awake for what felt like hours. What Frank had said to her was playing in her head on a continual loop. She had so much wanted him to kiss her, but if he had kissed her then he wouldn't be the sort of decent man she thought he was. She had to stop thinking about him – he belonged to another woman. She was already being punished enough for falling for a man whom she thought was attached.

*

Clare was awake before her alarm went off, ready and willing to go. Creeping about so she wouldn't wake the others, she left the house with a big bag of her most reliable cleaning materials and set off for Raine's cottage. As she walked through Spice Wood she saw the trunk where she and Val Hathersage had sat and eaten sandwiches, where he had leaned over and kissed her and pressed her against the forest ground. She wondered if they would have mad passionate sex when she saw him next. Would he be as good at it as his kissing suggested he might be?

Raine was up and waiting for her.

'I'm not too early, am I?' Clare asked.

'Not at all.' Raine's old weathered face split into a grin. 'Could you fetch Albert for me? He's having one of his turns.'

Albert was sitting staring at the wall, swinging his tail. Clare picked him up and he made a disgruntled yowl. She put him gently on Raine's lap where he settled immediately and started purring.

'He attacks the wall if you leave him and hurts himself,' Raine explained. 'It's dementia.'

'That's very sad,' said Clare, giving his old head a stroke. She'd always wanted pets but her parents wouldn't have them in the house. When she was little she had dreamed of having a lovely home full of children and cats and a big friendly dog with an extra-waggy tail.

'It's nearly time, isn't it?' Raine's old fingers stroked him under the chin. 'Nearly time to let go. But we won't go without a fight, will we, darling?'

'I've only ever had one pet,' said Clare with a sad smile as she snapped on her Marigolds. 'A goldfish that I won at a fair. I had him for a year and I sobbed for days when he died.'

Raine was curious. 'I thought you'd be the sort of person who had lots of animals.'

'I work too many hours.' Clare sighed. 'Wouldn't be fair.'

'Didn't you have pets as a child?'

'No,' said Clare, imagining a cat sitting on one of her mother's cushions and leaving hairs. She shuddered at the scene that would have followed. 'My parents aren't really animal people. Shall I make you a cup of tea before I start?'

'Just a cup of cold water will be fine, please,' said Raine.

'I should drink more water,' said Clare. 'I'm always telling myself that. Might lose some weight off my bottom if I flushed out my toxins." She fetched the cup for Raine and then rubbed her hands, impatient to get started on making the house spick and span. She didn't mind that Raine watched her. She liked the old lady, felt comfortable in her presence.

'What do you work as? A cleaner?' asked Raine after a while. 'You're very good at it.' She nodded with admiration at the shine Clare had brought up on her brass ornaments.

'Me? I'm an accountant,' replied Clare, squeezing a lemon into a bowl of water. She always had lemons among her cleaning materials. 'I work in London for one of the top-rated financial firms. So I sort out people's messes and try and save them from bankruptcy. And I've just been promoted to partner. I start my new job as soon as I get home.'

'That's very impressive.'

Clare dunked her cloth into the lemon water.

'I've worked long and hard to know what I'm doing.' No one had worked harder or for longer hours than Clare.

'There's no ring on your finger, I notice.'

'It's difficult doing the job I do and being in a relationship.' But as she was saying this Clare realized that the male partners in the firm seemed to manage it somehow.

'So there's no young man in your life.'

'No. But I'm fine with that.' Clare conjured up a smile. She would have to get used to saying that she was single again. 'I'm the first woman to be made a partner in the firm, ever. I don't need a man.'

'What a shame you have no one. You're a beautiful girl. Singular.'

'I'm nothing special.' This was not false modesty. Clare really didn't think she was.

'One day you will meet a man who makes you feel special.' Raine put her head to one side. 'If you haven't already.'

'I doubt it,' said Clare. 'I'm married to the job. I'm like a nun but my husband isn't Christ, it's a double-entry ledger.'

'I gave up everything to be with my husband,' said Raine, a mist in her eyes. 'My home, all that was familiar to me. But I knew from the first moment that I wanted to be with him and I never regretted following him.'

'Love at first sight?' Clare smiled. 'Does it really exist?'

'Those who fall in love at first sight would argue that it does.' Some wispy white strands of hair had broken loose from the long plait she wore and Raine tucked them behind her ear.

'There was someone,' Clare admitted. 'Until recently.' She climbed down from the sink and stepped back to check that the window was smear-free. 'We had known each other since primary school. He'd moved over from Germany and was a class oddity, like me. He had his funny accent; I had my funny eyes. We were friends for many years before we became a couple. He's very clever, handsome, funny, kind . . .'

'And where he is now?'

'Dubai. He is doing the job he loves over there. I'm doing the job I love over here.' She rinsed her cloth in the sink then wrung it hard, twisting it with force. 'We obviously didn't love each other quite enough in the end. Work got in the way.'

'That's a great shame,' said Raine. 'Seymour was a very special man. I would have given up anything for him, and the reverse was true also.'

Seymour. The name on the mysterious gravestone that

she had seen the other day. Clare wondered if she dare mention it and ask why it was that he was originally buried outside the churchyard. She decided that she daren't. Not yet.

Albert yawned and then stretched out his furry legs in an effort to ease out the stiff arthritic pains in them before settling down again in a different position on Raine's knee.

'I heard' − *felt* − 'you yesterday outside the door.' Raine pointed to an old locked door in the wall opposite her chair. 'You should have knocked and come in.'

Clare felt a blush spring to her cheeks.

'I'm sorry,' she said. 'I didn't know where the steps led until I heard your voice. I never thought that the two houses might be connected.'

Raine smiled. 'It's a smugglers' cave. Joshua Hathersage, who built both cottages, was a renowned smuggler of spices.'

'Clever.' Clare nodded, impressed. 'I'm presuming he's an ancestor of Gene Hathersage − the guy we're renting our cottage from.'

'Oh yes. A renowned cad.'

Clare didn't know if Raine meant Joshua or Gene.

'Quite a feat, though − carving those steps.'

'Oh, yes. But spices made men rich so it was all worth it for them.' Raine putt the old bones of Albert down on the floor. 'My dear, would you put some food in Albert's dish for him? He likes the fish type best.'

'Of course,' said Clare, smiling as Albert made a stiff robotic walk into the kitchen and sat by his bowl. She ripped off the top of a pouch of trout-flavoured food and squeezed it out for him. He greedily dived head first into it.

'How do you cope up here, Raine? Wouldn't you be better in the village amongst people? How do you get into bed and onto the loo?'

'I cope,' said Raine. 'And I have all my memories here. I

came to this cottage as a bride.' Her strange old face creased into a nostalgic smile. 'I have been very happy here.'

Clare turned her attention back to her cleaning as a sudden vision came to her and she saw herself as old as Raine. She would have no memories of a loved one who had gone. Only recollections of numbers she had worked on. She'd be rich and lonely and cold inside, however many crocheted blankets sat on her legs.

Chapter 43

Gladys found Edwin asleep on the library sofa wrapped up in a blanket. He had never slept out of bed in all the years she had known him. There was a bathchair outside the front door, one which usually resided in the shed at the side of the cottage where Joan was staying. It wasn't hard to work out that she had wheeled him home. Why he hadn't walked was obvious when Gladys bent over him and smelled his breath. She comforted herself by thinking that at least he was here and she hadn't found him in Joan's bed.

She poked him with her finger to wake him and he groaned as if in pain. Joan had plied him with drink and Gladys could guess at why.

She strode out of the kitchen and down to the old cottage, then rapped hard on the door. She had to knock twice more before Joan opened it, hair bedraggled, no make-up on her face, wrapped in a bright-red dressing gown and shivering.

'Hello, Gladys. I'm not feeling very well,' said Joan, her voice trembling. 'Is Lord Carlton okay? I wheeled him back home last night and thought the library sofa would be the most comfortable place for him. I made him some supper, you see, for being so kind to me, and I'm convinced the prawns were off. I haven't stopped throwing up.'

She really didn't look well at all, Gladys had to admit.

'He's hungover, that's what I think,' she said starchily. 'And he doesn't drink so how's that happened, then?'

'He had some sherry trifle,' said Joan, holding her hand to her mouth as she retched a little. 'I was quite heavy-handed with the sherry – for the taste – but he couldn't have got drunk on that. I know it was those prawns. I've a good mind to go back to Wellem market and have a word with that fishmonger.'

'Well.' Gladys swallowed, taken in completely. 'You'd better get back to bed and I'll look after Lord Carlton. Can I get you anything?'

'I just need to sleep,' replied Joan, sniffing hard.

'You do that, then.' Gladys spoke stiffly but not unkindly.

'Thank you, Gladys. Please pass on my apologies. I only wanted to say thank you to him for being so kind to me. I can't believe we're both so ill. It has to be those prawns.' And with that the door closed and Gladys took a much less charged walk back to attend to Edwin. She did not think to look in the bin outside the cottage that might have told her more of the truth than she had just been handed.

Chapter 44

Clare scrubbed and dusted and fettled until the tiny cottage shone. She took down the curtains, washed them and pegged them outside, and in the sea breeze they were dry within half an hour. They were scented with salty air when Clare hung them back up above the crystal-clear windows. As she worked, Clare told Raine more about her friends: how long they had known each other, how they didn't see each other as much as they should. The old lady was so easy to talk to. Hours flew by as quickly as a finger-click.

Raine listened with interest to everything Clare said. Maybe this is why she is here, she thought. There had to be a reason why their paths had crossed. She could feel it in her old bones.

'Aren't you tired?' asked Raine, watching Clare polish the old cabinet at the back of the room. 'You haven't stopped.'

'I love doing this,' said Clare, the truth of it shining in her eyes.

'More than your work with numbers?'

Clare laughed. 'Easily!' As her duster passed over the last fingerprint on the wood she looked at the only picture standing in a frame on the cabinet, a pencil drawing of a man's profile. He had a thin face, a long nose and a full beard and yet his features fitted well together; he was not an unhandsome man. 'Is this your husband?'

'Yes, that is my Seymour.'

'I, er . . .' Clare began. She had to ask. 'I saw a gravestone the other day, with the name Seymour on it. In the churchyard.'

'That was him. There are no more Seymours lying there.'

'Why is his grave in a line of twelve?' Clare couldn't help wincing at how nosey that sounded. Raine merely nodded, though, without looking as if she had taken any offence.

'My husband was a fisherman, part of a crew of twelve men due to go out sailing one particular day but the sea was very rough. The lord of the manor at the time, Gilbert Carlton, put pressure on the captain to take him out in the boat with the men, to amuse him, and it sank. The men all managed to make it to shore – all thirteen of them. Gilbert Carlton was buried in the church crypt with the rest of his family but the others shared a bond because of their experience and wanted to be united in death as they had been in life.'

'Why was . . .' Clare bit off the question.

'Why was Seymour buried outside the church grounds?' Raine continued for her. 'At the time of his passing, Reverend Unwin was in charge of the church. He was a horrid, sour man married to a snipey little wife and living a life of frustration. He was very envious of Seymour and myself, of our love and devotion to each other. He let him lie next to his friends but he refused to bury him on consecrated ground. He said Seymour had committed a sin against God that would not allow him to be interred on church land. This was reversed later when Unwin died and a kinder pastor took over – a cousin of my husband. But at the time Unwin was immovable. The Unwins were always a strange family, full of bitterness and malcontent. Even though an Unwin was in the fishing boat that sank and was saved.'

'Jeez,' said Clare. 'What a vile man. What on earth did Seymour do that could justify that sort of prejudice?'

'He married me.' Raine smiled.

'Jeez,' said Clare again, for the want of something better to say.

'I'm an offcumden,' Raine clarified. 'Unwin didn't like me. '

'And yet he was jealous of you and Seymour, of your relationship?'

Raine nodded. 'He was a man of many contradictions, and I have no reservations about talking ill of him, dead as he is. He told Seymour before he died that he would never be buried on church land. Seymour laughed in his face, told him that I was worth his petty censure and he had no doubt that God would disapprove of Unwin's actions. He had a strong enough faith, thank goodness, not to be cowed by Unwin's threat. Unwin said that Seymour was cursed in marrying me, and the proof of that was that we couldn't have children. Ironically – neither could he and Sarah, but that was "God's will".'

Clare whistled. 'Strong stuff. What happened to him?'

'He had a small pleasure boat,' answered Raine. 'He took it out in the bay one day with Sarah and the boat ran aground on the rocks. They both drowned. No one could understand it as the sea was as calm as a millpond on that day and Jeremiah Unwin was an excellent sailor.'

'Wow,' said Clare. She almost looked around for Scooby Doo. Mystery piled on mystery. If she had dared to, she would have asked Raine hundreds more questions about the Unwins. They sounded not unlike the Borgias.

Instead she grinned and said, 'Where did you meet Seymour, then, if you were such a pariah?'

'I was visiting the area,' said Raine, looking wistfully past Clare to the drawing of Seymour. 'As soon as I saw him, I knew.'

'You must be very lonely without him.'

'I am. Too lonely and too old.'

Clare watched Raine's smile dropping by degrees. *Well done, Clare*, said a little voice inside her. *Why not remind the lady a little bit more about her lonesome existence?*

'I'll come back in a couple of days, if you like,' she said breezily, in an attempt to jolly up Raine.

'I would not want to interrupt your holiday,' said Raine. 'But I have so enjoyed your company and would welcome it again.'

'I've disturbed a lot of dust. It will settle and need shifting. It would be a pleasure, honestly.'

'Thank you,' said Raine. 'Then it will be an equal pleasure to see you again.'

'It's good exercise for burning off calories. I might even go home a couple of pounds lighter.'

'You're a beautiful girl as you are. You should have more confidence in yourself.'

'Everyone in my family is stick thin, except for me,' Clare moaned as she picked up her bag. 'And they all have cheek-bones and normal-coloured eyes. I sometimes wonder if I'm a changeling.'

'My husband used to say that I had eyes like the jewelled waters of the sea.' Raine reached for Clare's hand and pulled her downwards so that she could kiss her cheek. 'And sometimes we find that our hearts belong in different places from where our heads would have them be.'

Clare patted Albert on the head, not that he noticed – he was fast asleep – and she closed the door behind her as she left. What a lovely old lady, she thought. And she couldn't shake off the feeling that Raine knew more of what was going on in her heart than anyone else did. Herself included.

Chapter 45

As soon as Gladys had disappeared from sight, Joan cast off her pained expression and went into the bathroom to put on some make-up and tie up her hair. She was no more ill than Gladys was, although she wouldn't like to have had Edwin's head this morning – his first hangover at seventy. What an experience. Nearly as bad an ordeal as having to go into Ren Dullem and endure the stares of all the odd-bods that lived in the village.

The manor house had felt very spooky last night, almost hostile. Joan had dumped Edwin in the first room she came to that had a sofa in it. She had only been in the library once before, on a snoop, but there was nothing there of interest. She had no liking for stuffy old books and the smell that came with them. It wasn't her favourite room in the house, drab as it was, and decorated in dull mustard colours and browns which looked even more shabby when lit by the low-wattage bulbs at night. She studied the room whilst she stood beside the snoring figure of Edwin for five minutes to make sure he was sleeping peacefully and not about to vomit and choke himself. There must have been a lot of money in all those old books, she decided. Another portrait of Gilbert Carlton in hunting pink looked down on her disdainfully. She moved her eyes away from him and onto an old tapestry hung high on a wall. It depicted the village's history: boats and the sea and fish and fields of lavender, markets – all very boring. There was nothing of interest to her in the library.

There was a path from the cottage that cut through a small copse and led out onto the road which went left to Hathersage Farm and straight on down to the harbour. She wouldn't have to pass the front of the manor house if she went that way. She left a note on the door, should nosey Gladys come back, to say that she had gone for some fresh air, then she picked up her camera, notepad and handbag and set off for the village. She didn't know what she was looking for, but she was going to find something to work on before she came back to the cottage. Joan could sniff the opportunity to make money as surely as a shark could sniff blood.

She looked up into the sky to see a puff of grey cloud, far too low to be 'real' cloud, and remembered its presence the last time she had been to this godforsaken hole. *Clouds, rain – it was rain that saved them.* Was there a connection? How the hell could rain save anyone or anything?

At the bottom of the hill Dullem was bustling, as much as it could 'bustle' anyway. There was a market in the cobbled square. Stalls were set up around the perimeter selling fresh cheeses, bread, cakes, jams, fish and things made with lavender. There was a stall selling hot pork sandwiches with apple sauce and stuffing next to the kiosk that had once shut very rudely in her face when she had approached it to buy a coffee – like she'd be offering them any more of her money. There was a flower stall beside a man selling bric-a-brac. In fact it was all men that were running the stalls and, apart from a couple of older ladies, the customers were mainly men too. Last night she'd forgotten to get 'Mary' to ask why there were no women in the community. Maybe they were all chopped up and made into the local butcher's pies and that was the real secret of Ren Dullem. Joan giggled to herself, but anything was possible in this inbred little shithole. She wondered what would happen to Carlton Hall when Edwin died. Who would inherit it? It might be worth having a look at his will if she could find it; he was bound to have a copy in the house somewhere.

She endured the stares of a man as she approached the church. He had fairish hair in unruly waves, a slick smile and very green eyes. He was handsome, if you liked the full-of-himself male who talked a good talk. That type were usually full of hot air, and rubbish in bed. She had her sights on richer pickings than men who had empty pockets and sparkling eyes, though. She recognized in the green-eyed man the male equivalent of herself: predatory, manipulative, calculating, sybaratic. Every smile was an attempt at putting a key into the lock of a heart. She had no use for him, not even as an amusing toy to outwit, and she walked on.

She took the path that snaked around the back of the church and into the graveyard. A good place to start, she thought. She began at the bottom corner by the gate: a ridiculous pet's cemetery. Beloved pets called Corky, Jess, Bill, Lassie, some dates going back to before the war. Nothing of interest. The key date she was seeking was 1928. That was when all – whatever it was – started.

She walked over dead mothers and sons, the same names being repeated: Hathersage, Hathersage, Bird, Bird, Bird, Unwin, Coffey – the old stalwarts of the village, with dates from as far back as the 1700s to as recent as three months ago. By far the grandest grave was a huge stone effigy of a praying man, his hands pressed together, his head looking dutifully upwards. This was the grave of Reverend Jeremiah Unwin and his wife, Sarah, who both died on the same day. Merely from looking at the elaborate design of the grave, she imagined that Jeremiah Unwin would have been a man right up himself whilst pretending to be humble and God-serving.

She was just about to give up when, in the top left corner, at the furthest point from the church, she found a small over-grown path. She had to part the hedges at either side to take it. It wended left then right before opening up into a circle affording a grand view of the tiny harbour with its small outlet to the sea. A small version of Cleopatra's Needle stood there, a carved stone obelisk bearing the lettering:

FRATRES A MARE

GILBERT CARLTON
SEYMOUR ELIAS ACASTER
JOSEPH BIRD
GERALD COFFEY
PETER JOHN DICKINSON
FREDERICK ARTHUR HATHERSAGE
WILLIAM WARD HUBBARD
ALBERT SHAW LANDERS
HARRISON ROBERT MOODY
BERNARD ANDREW SHAW
HAROLD ALFRED WILLIAM SMITH
JACK UNWIN
JOHN GEORGE WARD
1928

Thirteen names. Including Gilbert and that interesting date – 1928. But what the hell did it mean? Joan needed to cross-reference the names with the ledger now.

She scribbled the names down and returned to the main churchyard to find the relevant graves and see if they yielded any more information. Eleven of the graves were together in a long straight line. Gilbert's grave was not in the churchyard because obviously he would be in the family vault. Strangely, at the end, outside the original boundary of the land, was the grave bearing the twelfth name: Seymour Elias Acaster: born

1909, died 1969. Joan took the camera out of her handbag and started snapping, especially at Seymour's stone and the fence now around it. With not much else to go on, Joan wondered if the positioning was significant. Roll on Gladys buggering off home so Joan could take a long hard look at those ledgers again.

Chapter 46

'Well, if it isn't the witch. And where have you been with your big bag of spells?'

At the lip of the woods, Clare was arrested by the familiar voice.

'Val. How are you today?'

'Horny.' He smiled. 'How about you?'

'Tired,' said Clare, unable to stop a grin from pushing up the corners of her lips. He was very naughty.

'You didn't answer my question.'

'Nor do I have any intention of doing so. I've been for a walk.'

'What's in the bag?' He kicked at it with his toe.

'Victims of my spells – people who asked too many questions.'

Val Hathersage held up his hands in a gesture of surrender. 'Then I'll stop asking.'

'Good.' Clare didn't stop walking. She imagined that was what Colleen Landers would have done. Treat them mean, keep them keen.

'When are you going to let me kiss you again?' he called after her.

How about now, she wanted to shout. God, she was brazen.

'Who knows?' she said, over her shoulder.

She waited for him to call to her again but he didn't and she then cursed herself for not standing and talking to him. Colleen Landers would have walked away and not given a hoot. If he didn't come crawling after her, so what? But then Colleen knew he would because she had a confidence in herself that Clare didn't.

Clare turned to see him walking down the hill, hands in his pockets.

'Tomorrow at twelve?' she called, aware that her voice was too eager, but not caring.

'Maybe,' came the reply.

Chapter 47

As Clare opened the door to the cottage from the outside, Lara was just opening it from the inside.

'Ah, it's the scrubber,' she said.

Clare felt herself blushing slightly.

'We're going for something to eat. Coming?' asked May.

'Has all your cleaning made you hungry?' added Lara.

Clare nodded. 'Yep. I think I could eat something.'

It was market day in the village centre. They bought lavender bags and pressed them to their noses, remembering schooldays when they made them at their desks to bring home as Christmas presents. Apart from a couple of older ladies, they were the only females in the bustling square.

'It's weird, isn't it?' May said.

'The ratio of men to women, do you mean?' replied Lara.

'Maybe there's a mermaid living here,' May speculated.

'What?' the others said in unison.

'My granny was from Cornwall. She was always full of mermaid tales, if you'll excuse the pun.'

'Like what?' asked Clare.

'Like it was good luck for sailors to see one.'

'I thought it was supposed to be bad luck,' said Lara.

'My granny said they were good luck. They had a soft spot for sailors and would guide them away from the rocks. She said that if there was a run of boy births it was because a mermaid was in nearby waters – they get jealous that girl babies will be more beautiful than they are and take all the boys' attention, so girls aren't born.'

'What a load of bollocks,' Lara scoffed. 'Tell that to Carole, my aunt. She had six boys on the trot and the three of them who had kids all had boys as well. Can't remember hearing of any mermaids living in Penistone.'

A lean youth with chiselled features and a Hugh Grant-style floppy hairdo passed by. He was going to be a very handsome creature one day, May decided.

'It's raining men here. It should be a paradise for young women. There are some gods walking around,' she said.

'Aren't there just?' Clare agreed, thinking of Val Hathersage and his sexy grin.

'Oh, lookee,' said Lara with faux joy as she spotted Gene Hathersage buying a coffee at the conical kiosk. 'It's one of those handsome gods you were talking about – our helpful and kind landlord buying a coffee from the second rudest man in the world.'

As if hearing her, Gene's head swivelled and he spotted Lara pointing at him. She had no need to worry that he might come over and indulge in jolly conversation, though. 'What a Grinch,' she said with a low growl.

May nodded in faithful agreement but watched him as he bought his coffee. He had a gorgeous body: long legs and big thighs, strong arms and wide shoulders. He would be only slightly dwarfed by Frank if they stood side by side, she reckoned. With his wild hair and mean expression under that beard he looked rather like a monster from a Grimms' fairy tale having a civilized day off. Funny – and she wouldn't dare say this to Lara – but May could easily see her feisty friend with a man like Gene Hathersage. They'd spark off each other and have fun doing it. She had never met James but instinct told her that he would be too smooth, too clever and far too serious for Lara. She needed someone who would make her eyes twinkle. She hoped James appreciated Lara and that Lara wasn't forced to take second place to his achievements.

'I wish I could get my hands on this place,' said Lara, her voice bordering on lust.

May knew what she meant. This was the sort of village that would really excite her professionally too. She could easily visualize those old abandoned buildings as new businesses, serving tourists. They were too lovely to be allowed to crumble. Ren Dullem was a diamond that needed a lot of polishing – but nevertheless it was a diamond.

Lara turned in a slow circle to really take in the vista of Ren Dullem: the heart-shaped harbour, the sandy beach below, dotted with stripy deckchairs. She saw the main village with its miscellany of old cottage designs, sweet little shops and tiny intriguing roads twisting up the hillsides. She saw the pretty church with its large brass bell waiting to summon attention, to call the people to prayer on Sundays, and to weddings. And she saw the village square with an ancient maypole at its centre, bustling with market traders selling proper wares not tat. Lastly she saw Gene Hathersage's bum, and the unconscious smile dropped from her face as she found herself unwittingly appraising it. From the back he looked normal: jeans, shirt, nothing to intimate he was the most impolite, sullen creature on the planet. Artistic temperament, she supposed. She had to give him credit for the talent he obviously had with wood, not that that should excuse him for being a boorish bastard. *Stop looking at his bum, Lara.* She'd had quite enough of men's bums for a while. James had a slim bum that looked good in suit trousers. James had a slim white bum that she had last seen whilst he was lying on top of Tianne Lee.

That thought of James blindsided her and brought with it a sharp pain that struck her between the ribs. She wasn't looking forward to next week when she would have to see him again to retrieve her things from Manor Gardens. There would be a heap of anger and pain waiting to drop on her head when she was within his airspace, she knew.

May nudged her.

'Shall we go to Jenny's? I'm a bit peckish. You up for that too, Clare?'

'I'm always up for food,' Clare answered, adding to herself, *unless it's fatty beef sandwiches in a plastic package washed down with Nitromors wine.*

'Good idea,' said Lara, just hoping they didn't bump into Daisy Unwin. Seeing one village prat was enough for today.

Chapter 48

Before going over to the main house, Joan wiped off her make-up, scraped back her hair, stripped off her jewellery and reacquired her 'poorly' look. Then she wrapped herself in a shawl as if chilled to the bone and went off to enquire how Lord Carlton was faring.

Gladys was in the kitchen, her apron off and jacket on, when Joan entered, as meekly as she could.

'Hello,' she said. 'Sorry, I didn't mean to startle you, Gladys.'

Gladys noted how pale and plain Joan looked today. It brought her kind instincts to the fore and completely disarmed her.

'Sit down, Joan, before you fall. Are you still not feeling well?'

'I don't think I've ever felt this ill,' said Joan. 'I came to see how Lord Carlton was before I go back to bed. I couldn't settle. It's all my fault.'

'I'm just taking him some tea and soup. I've managed to get him into his bed. I must admit, Joan, I thought he was hungover, but seeing as you are in the same boat—'

'I would put my life on it being those prawns,' Joan interrupted eagerly, then held her head as if the effort to talk was a little too much.

'Can I get you a sandwich?' asked Gladys.

'That's very kind, Gladys, but I don't want to trouble you. I was going to go shopping today but ...' Joan cut off her sentence and rubbed her stomach.

'Look, if you've got nothing in your cupboards, there's plenty of food here to tide you over,' said Gladys, who always prided herself on keeping the kitchen well stocked. Edwin Carlton liked his food. 'Please help yourself whilst I take this upstairs before it gets cold.'

'Are you going home, Gladys?' Oh please say yes, thought Joan.

'I'm taking the afternoon off, yes. I'm going to the dentist,' replied Gladys. 'I do hope you are feeling better in the morning, Joan.'

'Thank you, Gladys.' Joan gave her sweetest smile. 'Please give him my very best regards.' She leapt to open the door for Gladys as she lifted the tray.

'You get what you want from the fridge and the cupboards and I'll help you carry it to your cottage if you like,' said Gladys.

'Don't you worry; I'll lock up on my way out.'

Gladys looked suddenly stunned. 'You have a key?' She didn't know that.

'Yes, Lord Carlton gave me a key,' replied Joan, playing it down as if it was no big deal. 'Just for emergencies. I can't say I've had occasion to use it but maybe, if you're not coming back today, I should pop in later to make sure all is well.'

'Well, Lord Carlton has his panic button,' said Gladys, her feathers slightly ruffled.

Joan stepped in quickly to smooth them. 'It's entirely up to you, Gladys. If you would rather I didn't check to see that all was well, I perfectly understand.'

Put like that, with Joan so meek she almost baaed like a lamb, Gladys could barely refuse. 'That would be very good of you,' she said, before turning and exiting through the door.

As soon as it shut on her back, Joan dropped her facade and had to stifle a giggle. God, she was good. Five more minutes and Gladys would have been handing over her life savings.

She waited impatiently for Gladys to leave, killing time by having a look in the fridge for something to eat. There were some slices of cold ham which she folded up and popped into her mouth, then she cut off a large slice of oozing Brie and washed it down with some freshly squeezed orange juice. She arranged herself limply by the kettle when she heard Gladys's footsteps outside the kitchen.

'I'll be off now,' called the housekeeper through the door. 'See you in the morning. You take care of yourself and I hope you feel better soon.'

'Thank you, Gladys. Hope the trip to the dentist goes well.'

Joan heard the mighty front door shut and waited a few minutes just in case Gladys doubled back to check on her. She didn't. Then Joan strode off in the direction of the study, her long slim legs powered with nervous energy.

Chapter 49

Despite it being market day, Jenny's café was empty except for May, Clare and Lara. They had a spicy chicken and rice dish, which was delicious, and pecan pie to follow. Clare told them all about her morning – well, the visiting-Raine part of the morning at least.

Jenny wasn't very chatty today and Lara was convinced she had been warned off from being too friendly to the off-cumdens.

God, this place was odd. But it was still preferable to what was waiting for her back home.

Clare insisted on showing them Seymour's grave in the churchyard, after they had eaten.

'*Illis quos amo deserviam*. For those I love I shall sacrifice,' Lara translated the words carved into the stone.

'Ah, that's what it means,' said Clare. 'It makes sense now. He knew that he was going to be buried on unhallowed ground and he didn't give a stuff.'

'That's quite a powerful love story, isn't it?' sighed May. 'If I were a writer, I'd use that as a plot.'

'It's like something out of the Middle Ages, though, don't you think?' said Lara, wrinkling up her nose. 'Mind you, why should that be a surprise here?'

They found the elaborate grave of Jeremiah Unwin.

'"My duties done, I shall rest in Thy house, o Lord." Sounds a bit cocky to me,' May said with disdain. 'I'm staying in Your house, God, so lump it, whether You like it or not. And notice the "I" and not the "we".'

Clare nodded. 'He probably had it designed well in advance. It wouldn't have crossed his mind that his wife would have died on the same day.'

She gave the grandiose statue a sly kick and hoped that Jeremiah felt the reverberations all the way down in his box, which she had no doubt would be very grand and black and lined in velvet. Bloody Unwins.

They took a leisurely walk back up the hill until Gene Hathersage came around the corner like Nigel Mansell on drugs and blasted his horn to make them move.

Lara extricated herself from the prickly bush which she had just had to press herself into. 'I really didn't think I could dislike that man any more, but, surprise, surprise, I've just found I can.'

May tried not to smile as she picked a twig out of her friend's blonde mop of hair. Gene Hathersage and Lara reminded her of one of those old Doris Day films in which the hero and heroine are constantly at each other's throat, not knowing they are really in love. Then she looked at Lara's thunderous expression and decided that maybe that wasn't the case here, though.

Chapter 50

Joan pored over the ledgers again looking for evidence – of what, she didn't know. The estate had begun to pay a stipend to those twelve men in 1928: *SEA & R, JB, GC, PJD, FAH, WWH, ASL, HRM, BAS, HAWS, JU, JGW* as well as into a central account marked *Village Fund*.

SEA & R? Joan checked against her notes. SEA must refer to Seymour Elias Acaster, but who or what was R? She scribbled the initial in her notepad. Joan checked forward to the first death: Jack Unwin. Payments were no longer paid directly to JU a month after his death, but the monies he would have received, had he been still alive, were paid instead into the Village Fund. That pattern was repeated in the record of the second death, Albert Landers, when the monies again joined those in the Village Fund. And so it was with them all – except for Seymour Elias Acaster. After his death his allowance or wage or whatever it could be was paid directly to R. Joan flicked forward to the 1990s to find that monies were still being paid to R. Indeed, as she heaved the great long pages over to the present-day accounts, she found R was still receiving a direct allowance from the estate.

Joan felt a prickle of excitement in her hands. She was onto something here, though she didn't know what, but she had the unshakable feeling it was going to be on a par with the Brink's-

Mat robbery. Those robbers had gone for a mere three million pounds and discovered, by chance, three tons of gold bullion instead. There was something much bigger and much more lucrative than the depleted fortunes of an old man waiting to be uncovered in Ren Dullem. But, then again, why not have both?

Now, where would he keep his will?

Joan looked around the room for a small portrait that might cover a wall safe, but there was none – the paintings on the wall were far too big to be moved for access. She took a deep breath and concentrated, trying to get into the mind of someone like Edwin Carlton. He was a trusting soul, uncomplicated and didn't have the greatest memory. Surely he wouldn't keep a copy document of something so important in an obvious place such as his desk?

Joan pulled out the top drawer and had to stifle the astonished laughter that wanted to erupt from her. At the back of it, in a long slim yellowing envelope, was the Last Will and Testament of Edwin Charles Richard Gravois Carlton. Her fingers were shaking with amused glee as she teased the papers out and straightened them.

The will was ten years old. She skipped through all the boring bits until she reached the nitty-gritty. He was leaving Gladys fifteen thousand pounds. But here was the interesting part: the rest of his estate he was bequeathing to R Acaster *To do with as is fit. And in the event of the demise of the aforesaid R Acaster, the estate will pass to the Village Fund for the future development and rejuvenation of Ren Dullem.*

R Acaster? SEA & R? Was R Acaster the wife of Seymour? Why would Edwin leave his fortune to her if she was? Joan took her camera out of her pocket and snapped the document before placing it back in the drawer. Every answer she found was dredging up more questions. But she was on a mission now – she wasn't going to stop until she knew everything.

*

Joan found an Internet café in Wellem, a grubby little place with ripped seats and keyboards dirty from hundreds of fingers. She typed *Ren Dullem*, but there wasn't even a Wikipedia entry for it, only a mention of it in a long list of place names in North Yorkshire. There was a host of non-relevant answers informing her that Ren was a computing term, that in Japanese the name Ren meant popularity, and that it was the Confucian virtue of treating each other in the right way.

Joan deleted the words in the search box with angry presses of the keys. It was unheard of in this day and age that there wasn't any information about a whole stupid village. *Precisely*, another part of her brain came back at her. There *must* be something here, and she would find it.

She typed *Lord Gilbert Carlton*. Bingo. There wasn't exactly a mother lode of information about him, merely that he lived from 1902 to 1974 in Carlton Hall, North Yorkshire, married Elizabeth Dudley in 1937 and had a son, the present Lord Carlton, in 1941. There was a picture of the old family crest and motto, and that was it. In short, there was nothing that pushed the mystery any further forward. She then typed in all of the twelve names, but there was not one single name that brought up the relevant dates or place. However, on the list of entries she noted the words: *Parish records for Glasgow*. Parish records, that's what she needed. Of course. Her next stop was the church.

Chapter 51

The rest of the day for May, Lara and Clare was quiet and lazy. Clare went for a swim, Lara read her Kindle and May did a giant crossword puzzle sitting outside in the clouded-over sunshine. They cooked the chicken fillets and steak which Frank had given them on a disposable barbecue that Lara bought at Hubbard's Cupboard. Then they settled down with big mugs of tea and watched a *Columbo* on the ancient box of a television. A gentle, easy day – and not one of them was bored or wished she had packed a laptop.

They were all in bed by ten thirty, tired out by doing nothing. The beds were the most comfortable any of them had ever slept in. Lara drifted off within minutes of her head resting on the pillow. But she snapped her eyes open a few hours later, dragged back from a deep sleep by a persistent tap-tap-tapping.

She lay perfectly still, wondering if it had followed from her dream and wasn't a real noise at all. Silence. Then, just as she closed her eyes, it began again. Tap-tap-BANG-BANG-BANG-tap-tap. Even under the weight of the quilt, she felt suddenly chilled. She wasn't imagining it; it was a real noise and something was happening outside her window.

Lara folded the quilt back and reached over to the curtain, nudging it, by degrees, to the side, but she couldn't see anything suspicious. She thought about knocking on the window to frighten whoever – or whatever – was making that noise, except she had a vision of a fist crashing in through the glass and grabbing her by the throat. She padded softly out of the room and over to the side and front doors to check they were locked, even though she knew they were because she had locked them herself before they all went to bed. She hoped whoever was on the outside didn't see the handles being pressed down.

While she was in the lounge she realized the tapping was coming from above her. Someone was on the roof. Should she wake the others? Another loud bang answered that one. She shook May awake first, her finger across her mouth warning May not to speak.

'There's someone outside,' whispered Lara. 'Banging.'

There was a loud crash as if something was falling down the roof and they both jumped. A beam of light passed by May's window and they quickly ran out of her room and into Clare's to wake her up. They had to shake Clare quite considerably because once she was asleep she was virtually comatose.

'Shall we ring the police?' asked Clare, after Lara had filled her in on why they had disturbed her. She remembered an urban myth from her schooldays about a madman bouncing a head on someone's car roof. She shivered.

BANG BANG BANG BANG BANG

'I think we'd better,' said May, heading for the phone in the corner of the lounge.

There was a rattle of metal and seven squeaks as if someone was descending a ladder. Another rattle and then quick footsteps melting into the distance. Lara leapt to the side window to see a flash of something silver disappearing down the hill.

'The phone's crackling,' May whispered, rushing back over to the others. Safety in numbers.

'Have they gone? What the hell was that?' asked Clare at Lara's shoulder.

'Whoever it was has run off,' replied Lara.

'We should go and have a look.'

'Tonight? In the pitch black?'

'I've got my torch,' said Clare.

Lara slowly turned the key in the door and opened it noiselessly. Holding onto each other and brandishing a torch, a poker and a rolling pin between them, they cautiously walked outside. Clare moved the torch to check all was safe around them before directing the beam upwards. And then they saw it.

There, bolted onto the roof, was a metal tower covered in barbed wire which definitely hadn't been there earlier on.

'What is that?' asked Lara.

'God only knows,' replied Clare. 'I'm sharing someone's room tonight, though. Or shall we drag our mattresses into the sitting room?'

Lara groaned. Not just at the ugly metal thing they were all staring at but because this meant one of them would have to pay Gene Hathersage another visit. And she so was hoping it wasn't her.

Chapter 52

Lara awoke with a horrible pain in her neck. She had been sleeping at a twisted angle on the sofa and she couldn't rub the muscles back to normal. Clare and May were still fast asleep and looking very comfortable on their mattresses on the floor of the lounge. Lara pushed the quilt back and got up to put the kettle on.

She remembered that one of them had to pay Gene Hathersage a visit today and find out why people were attaching metal structures to the roof in the middle of the night and scaring them all half to death. She bet that whatever the thing was, it would interfere with the television signal. She stepped over Clare and switched on the TV to find a mess of silver and black wavering lines. Brilliant. Someone was really out to make their holiday memorable, for all the best reasons. And when she checked the phone, that still wasn't working either.

She made herself a coffee and hoped one of the others would wake up and volunteer to go and pay the fateful visit. Clare was snoring softly and looked dead to the world; May was out for the count. Lara took two sips of coffee and knew that she couldn't just sit here doing nothing while she waited for them to rise. She poured the contents of her mug into the sink and went to get dressed. Her neck still felt as if Mike Tyson had been jabbing at it all night with his big padded gloves.

Lara set off at a march down the road, purpose thudding in every step. She knocked hard on the door of La Mer but there was no response. There was none at the back door either. Her blood started to boil as she set off for the outbuildings where last time she had found him brandishing his chainsaw. Her search was fruitless but he was here; she could sense him, like the bad smell he was. She tried knocking hard at the front door again and at the back. Then she realized there was no dog barking. He must be out after all. Then she saw him in the distance, in the field beyond his garden. He was carrying what looked like a tree trunk.

'Gene Hathersage,' she called, her voice packed with anger. 'Can you hear me?'

He turned to her voice and she saw him shake his head and puff out his cheeks. He had the nerve to look exasperated.

She stomped towards him, crossing the overgrown lawn.

'Mr Hathersage, can you please explain why there is . . . Jesus Christ!'

The ground came rushing towards her and there was a pain in her ankle that shot right up to her brain, out of her skull and headed towards outer space, making the ache in her neck feel like a tickle. She found herself writhing in agony and with a mouthful of grass.

If that wasn't bad enough, within seconds Gene Hathersage arrived to witness her creased-up face and her eyes spouting involuntary tears of pain. She felt his hands on her arms, pulling her out of the large hole she had fallen into and guiding her over to sit on one of his twisted-wood garden benches.

'How could anyone not see that?' he asked, gruff as bear. 'Are you okay?'

'No, I'm bloody not,' said Lara, the pain in her ankle forcing out hot tears of anger and embarrassment as well as pain. She could see now that she had fallen down a newly dug rectangular hole. 'What's that? Are you preparing a burial site for tenants who dare to complain?'

'It's for my dog actually,' said Gene, not meeting her eyes.

'Your dog?'

'Jock. Furry thing, four legs, tail,' replied Gene. 'Dead.'

Lara gulped back any retort on hearing the last word. 'I'm sorry to hear that,' she said, biting down hard on her lip. Her ankle felt tight and swollen.

'I'm going to have to take your shoe off,' said Gene, kneeling at her side.

'I'd rather you didn't . . .' she said as he slid off her shoe, ignoring her, and peeled down her sock. Her ankle was puffy and turning purple.

'You've sprained that. Let's get you into the house.'

To Lara's horror, he stood up, hooked one arm under her legs, the other around her back and lifted her into the air.

'You're carrying me?' she gasped.

'Only as far as the kitchen. I don't want to break my back,' said Gene Hathersage with a grunt, striding over to his house and opening the back door with a bump from his bottom. He set Lara down on a chair at the side of a huge thick-topped pine kitchen table with the command, 'Wait there.' Then he disappeared back outside.

Lara rotated her ankle and wished she hadn't. The pain shot up her leg again and brought a wave of agony. This was all she needed. What next? Was a helicopter going to land on her head?

She could see Gene leaning over in the garden, apparently picking something. She couldn't imagine what. She bet it wasn't a bouquet of flowers. She looked around her at the kitchen and found that it wasn't the sort of room she would have paired with Gene Hathersage. It wasn't pristine – there were dishes in the sink and some crumbs on the work surface – but it was a homely farmhouse kitchen with bare stone walls and wooden furniture. There was an old hairy dog bed at the side of a wood-burning stove, empty.

Gene returned to the kitchen with a handful of leaves. He put them into a stone mortar lifted from a high shelf, and started grinding them with the pestle. He added a few splashes of water from the tap, then reached down into a cupboard for some flour to add to the mixture. All this was done silently. Then, with his hand, he scooped the green paste he had made into the middle of a folded tea towel and bent down next to Lara. He carefully lifted her foot and wrapped the poultice around it. It felt very cold and slimy.

'Nothing better than knitbone for sprains,' said Gene. 'Hold that.'

'There's a plant called knitbone?' asked Lara incredulously.

'Otherwise known as comfrey.'

Lara leaned over and held the towel whilst Gene went to a drawer. He came back with a safety pin and a bandage, knelt down and began to secure the poultice to Lara's ankle.

'You won't get anything in your Harley Street that works as well as this.' Gene glowered at her as she flinched. 'It has to be tight. It'll fall off if it isn't.'

'My Harley Street? Why would I know what goes on in Harley Street?' she snapped.

'You posh London types go there, don't you?'

'Posh London types?' Lara harrumphed. 'I'm about as much of a chirpy crafty cockney as Dick Van Dyke. I'm from Barnsley.'

'You don't sound as if you are.'

Lara was cross. 'My accent might have been ironed out a bit but, trust me, I'm from Barnsley. My dad was a miner until the pits closed, then he had his own electrician business. Mum was a dinner lady. They scrimped to give me more chances in life than they had. Harley Street – ha! Posh London type, yeah, of course.'

'Anyone who paid what I asked for the cottage rental had to have more money than sense. It was an easy mistake,' Gene grumbled as he unwound a length of bandage to reapply it more tightly.

'If you were listening when I first explained, we thought we'd paid for a luxury spa – which was worth the money. Why on earth would you rent out a cottage for such a ridiculous sum?'

'I need to earn my own living,' he said. 'No one wanted me to rent out the cottage so I figured that if I charged a small fortune for it, only idiots would pay up.'

'It didn't work like that with us, did it?' Lara smiled but there was no humour in it.

'I don't know, didn't it?'

'You have to be the rudest man I've ever met, Mr Hathersage.'

'Thank you.'

'It wasn't a compliment.'

'Look.' Gene stopped wrapping and lifted his head. His eyes were so black Lara's dad could have dug them out of a mine. 'I've had a really bad week. This, I could do without.'

Lara huffed. 'You've had a bad week!' She matched his stare with her bright hazel eyes. 'You haven't a clue what a bad week entails.'

'My dog died. I think I do.'

Lara fell guiltily silent for a moment. 'Yes, maybe you do. I'm sorry. Was he old?'

'Eighteen, not that his age makes it any easier,' said Gene. 'When you came around on Wednesday morning the vet had just left. He told me that there was no hope. I wanted a few more days with him. Last night he was in too much pain to carry on and I had to let him go.'

Lara nodded. 'So that's why you've been in such a foul mood.'

Gene looked surprised. 'I was no different to how I usually am.'

'Oh.'

'Stop moving. I've got to unwrap this again; it's too slack.'

Lara shifted in the chair. 'I'm not moving deliberately. It's a reflex because you're hurting me.'

'No pain, no gain.'

'I should gain plenty, then. Ouch.'

'Do you want something to bite down on?' Gene growled.

'Yes, your head.'

He looked up; she looked down. They viewed each other's scowling countenance and burst into involuntary laughter.

'I don't know why I'm laughing,' said Lara, wiping water from her eyes. She couldn't tell if they were tears of laughter, pain or sadness. 'This time last week I was happy and both ankles were working perfectly. This week I'm homeless, single, crippled and in bits.'

Tears started plopping down her cheeks and there was no mistaking that these were big fat sad ones. Embarrassed, Lara started to wipe them away on her sleeve before she realized it was full of mud. She felt a wad of material being pushed up against her nose – another tea towel.

'Here,' said Gene. 'Have this before you flood the place.'

Lara blurted out a bubble of laughter. 'Thank you,' she said meekly.

Gene pinned the bandage and stood up.

'You should have a cup of tea or something. For the shock,' he said.

'I wouldn't mind one if you're asking.'

He turned away from her and put the kettle on. His head almost reached the ceiling beams over by the window, but Lara noticed that the beams were lower there than in the rest of the room. The cottage walls were all out of square. La Mer was probably hundreds of years old.

She studied the back of him and compared him to James but found there was not much similiarity. Gene Hathersage's shoulders were twice the width, his waist was thicker and his bum a fine chunk. Once again she thought of the last time she had seen James's bum, white, skinny and stuck up in the air. Lara's cheeks were rivers of water. The tea towel was drenched.

'Don't know how you take it, so here, help yourself.' Gene thumped a milk carton and a bag of sugar down on the table before placing a steaming-hot mug of tea in front of her. 'So, why were you looking for me?'

'Someone was on our roof in the middle of the night, bolting a big metal aerial thing to it. It scared us to death. We can't watch the TV any more. And the phone isn't working either.'

'Uncle Milton.' Gene shook his head. 'I'll sort it. Sorry about that. It's my great-uncle. On my mother's side. The Birds are all flaming loop the loop. He's over ninety and shouldn't be climbing ladders, especially in his stupid slippery pumps. He's a Bird by surname, I mean, not by species.'

'I gathered that's what you meant. What is it? Why did he do it? And why did he do it at two o'clock in the morning?' Lara poured a little milk into her cup.

'He . . . erm . . . probably thought he was improving the television reception. He invents things,' Gene explained.

'I think you mean he's trying to make our stay worse so we'll leave early.'

Gene conceded a nod. 'Yeah, most likely.' He shrugged his shoulders and quickly changed the subject. 'Not a good week for you, then, you were saying.'

'Crap, actually,' said Lara, lifting the cup to her lips. 'Pants, shit, bollocks doesn't even cover it.'

'Homeless? You said you were homeless.' He pushed a packet of chocolate fingers towards her.

Lara held up her hand to refuse and then said, 'Oh sod it,' and took one.

'I rented out my flat when I moved in with my boyfriend.

The night we drove here I found him in bed with his ex.' Lara couldn't believe the words were coming out of her mouth when she hadn't even told her best friends all this. She was sitting with her face covered in mud, her foot covered in goo, having tea with the rudest man in the world and yet it was to him she was baring her soul.

'Will you go back to him?'

'I'll have to meet him to get all my stuff. But, no, how can I? I can't get what I saw out of my head. It would always be in the way. The trust has gone. There is nothing he can say or do to put it right. But it hurts. So. Much.' She gulped, not wanting to embarrass herself any more. Although she doubted that was possible. Her dignity was in the gutter keeping her ego company.

'Sounds like you needed a holiday.'

'Damned right I did.'

'In a nice spa.'

Lara looked at him and saw a twinkle in his wild dark eyes.

'It would have been good. But Wellem Spa is fully booked now. Plus, Clare found the lagoon underneath the house and, well, there's no chance of dragging her away from that.'

'Yes, I know she found it. I saw the evidence of the torn wallpaper,' Gene grumbled.

'We will make sure it's fixed before we leave. She's not in the habit of ripping off wallpaper looking for secret doors, you know. She discovered it by accident.'

'I know. You told me before. Are your friends Yorkshire women too?' asked Gene, eating his third biscuit.

'Yep. Clare's from York, May's from Leeds.'

'Yet you live down south?'

'Plenty of women from the north live down south, you know,' huffed Lara, flicking a blonde curl out of her eye. Did he think it was tantamount to emigration?

'And what do you do? Not journalists, are you?' He topped

up her tea from a giant red teapot. Anyone would think he was enjoying her company and wanted her to stay.

'Journos?' Lara let loose a bark of laughter. Is that what the latest rumour about them was? 'No. We all work together, at a company called Cole and Craw Finance. Clare, the one with the eyes, she's an accountant. May helps to set up new businesses and gives people advice. They're both brilliant at what they do. I help ailing, more established businesses turn themselves around, or wind them down if they can't be rescued. Our jobs are quite similar really – we're all involved in trying to help people help themselves.'

'Are you any good?'

The cheek of him.

'I'd like to think so.'

'You must be bored rigid in Ren Dullem without your computers and mobile phones.'

Lara shook her head. 'I haven't been bored for a minute.' And she only realized once she had said it how much she meant it.

Then Lara noticed that a small fish had been carved into a corner on the table.

'That's pretty,' she said.

'It's my signature,' Gene replied. 'Like the Mouseman. Except I'm the Fishman.' He smiled, and Lara was reluctant to admit how much his eyes lit up when he did so.

'You made the table then?'

'Yep.'

Lara stroked the smooth back of the fish. 'You could be the Soleman. That would be cool,' she said, smiling back at him. 'You're very good. Do you sell much?'

'I'm doing okay, could do better. I'm just starting to make a name for myself, after years of trying. I was eventually able to drop the day job last year.'

'What was that?'

'Nosey, aren't you?'

'Yes.'

'The village odd-job man, if you must know.'

'So now you make a living from wood?'

Gene blew out two big cheekfuls of air.

'Ren Dullem is hardly the enterprise capital of the world. But, yes, I'm building up a nice order book. A shop in Whitby takes a lot of stuff.' Gene proffered her the packet of biscuits again, but she waved it away.

'One last question: why is such a pretty place so hostile to strangers?'

Gene stood up. 'I'd better get you back home.'

One question too far, thought Lara. She levered herself to her good foot and then gasped as Gene pushed her firmly against the wall. Without saying a word he lifted her arm and marked a place on the wall with a nearby pencil. It was like a bizarre height chart for armpits. He didn't explain and Lara didn't have a chance to ask before he bent over to pick her up.

'I can walk. I'm fine,' she said, hopping away.

'Suit yourself,' he said, holding out a crooked arm. 'You might need to lean on me, though.'

'Thank you.'

He walked at her pace out to his van and opened the door for her. It was a working van, spartan inside but surprisingly clean, though it smelled of dog. They were back at the cottage within minutes.

'I'll bring some more comfrey round later when I come to take that down,' and he flicked a finger at Milton's metal monstrosity. 'As soon as I've said goodbye to my lad.'

He helped her out of the van and she saw the shine of moisture in his eyes as he turned from her to drive back home.

Chapter 53

May and Clare were awake when Lara crashed into the cottage. They had both just dragged the mattresses back onto the beds.

'How did you get o— Bloody hell, what happened to you?' said Clare.

Lara hopped over to the sofa. 'I fell into a dog grave and sprained my ankle.'

May's hand shot to her mouth. 'Oh, Lara.'

'Don't try to pretend you don't think it's funny.'

'Let me get you a cloth. Your face is covered in mud.' May went into the bathroom and brought out a face cloth which she had rinsed in warm water. 'I won't get you a mirror; you wouldn't want to see. It's not pretty,' she said. 'So come on, then, what happened?'

'Which bit do you want first?'

'Start slowly and build up to the most exciting part.' May was almost crying with the effort of trying not to laugh.

'I went over to Gene Hathersage's place to tell him about the aerial, saw him in the distance and walked off towards him. I didn't look down, fell into a bloody hole that he'd just dug and knackered my ankle. He carried me – and I so want to die about that – into his house and put this poultice on it. He's coming back later to take off that thing on the roof, which he says was put up by his great-uncle Milton Bird. Apparently he invents things.'

'Things to ward off us offcumdens, perchance?' asked Clare, going over to put the kettle on.

'Got it in one.'

'Is Great-Uncle Milton responsible for the clouds as well? Did you ask?'

'I didn't, but I'd put money on it. Though God knows why.'

'So . . .' May raised her eyebrows. 'You've been dancing with the devil then?'

Lara shrugged. 'I'd hardly call it dancing. There was nothing remotely *Strictly* about what I've just done in front of him. Anyway, he isn't that bad when you . . .' She was going to say 'get to know him'. She amended it, though, to: 'fall down a hole and he has to come to your assistance. His dog died yesterday. He's burying him now.'

May's laughter dried up. 'Ah, that's sad.'

'Apparently when I went storming around there on the first morning, the vet had just told him that the old chap was near the end. No wonder he was half-rabid.'

'We'll forgive him, then,' Clare said with a smile. There was so much back-biting and politics in their day jobs that it was always like a gust of fresh air when things were smooth and friendly between people. 'Let's draw a line and start again.'

Lara huffed. 'I'll forgive him when he refunds us for the luxury hamper.' But secretly she felt that a little bit of her heart already had forgiven Gene Hathersage.

Chapter 54

Just before midday Clare insisted on going to the village to bring back something nice to eat, even though the fridge was well stocked. She took a slow walk down the hill, peering into Spice Wood for signs of Val. Her heart fluttered when she saw a figure moving between the trees, but when she looked more closely her spirits dropped to see that it was actually a portly lady with her hair in a high bun. She wore a black coat and was carrying a basket. Clare walked on to the shops. It was Sunday so most of them were shut. Hubbard's Cupboard was open, though. The shopkeeper, Mr Hubbard, was very pleasant to her now. She wondered if they thought she might be a relation of Raine's. If that was the case, she would let them. It was much better to be received with a smile than with a grimace.

She thought she might make a nice tasty pasta dish. Lud loved Italian food and she had made him a tiramisu cake for his birthday in March. As, once again, her thoughts touched on him, she wondered how he was getting on, if he was missing her, if he'd had sex with anyone else. That thought hurt.

She filled her basket with ingredients and took a slow stroll up the hill. When she reached the fallen tree trunk at the edge of the woods she sat and waited, anticipation tripping through her veins. At one o'clock, she admitted to herself that Val Hathersage would not be meeting her today. Her heart was a wild mixture of angry, disappointed and sad when she rose reluctantly to her feet and went back to the cottage.

'Where the heck have you been, Clare?' asked May. 'We nearly sent out a search party.'

'Sorry. Most of the shops were shut. I had to hunt around.'

'It's me who should be sorry,' said Lara. 'I know we were going to drive into Whitby today and find a nice pub for Sunday lunch. Once again I've cocked up.'

'Don't be daft,' said May. 'I'm happy staying here.'

'Anyway, it's nice to defy convention and have pasta instead of roast beef,' said Clare, putting on a big smile to cheer up poor Lara.

'You're both too nice,' said Lara.

'I know,' replied Clare. 'May, open that tin of olives for me, would you? Do you and James and the children all go out for Sunday lunch at home or do you don an apron and cook? I love doing a roast. Mind you, you've got an au pair, haven't you, Lars? You are so lucky.'

'Kristina has Sunday off. I ... er ... usually do the lunch.'

I roast it and no one eats it. The children push it around their plates pretending it's horrible. James, when he's not at work – or shagging behind my back – doesn't even acknowledge it as he chews.

'I envy you, Lars. In a nice way, I mean.' said Clare, pouring boiling water into a pan. 'Having that lovely ready-made family and that gorgeous man. He's like a film-star. I can't imagine how you must feel getting into bed with him every night. As for that house you live in! You've got it all, haven't you? I bet your mum and dad are so proud of you. Do you think you'll get married? I can just imagine you in *Hello!* or even better, one of those posh society mags.' Clare drew the headline in the air: '*Super-gorge James Galsworthy marries Blonde Bombshell and Barnsley Brainbox Lara Rickman.*'

May was the first to spot that Lara's head was bowed and she was sobbing. 'Jeez, Lars, whatever is the matter, love?'

Her sympathy made it worse. Lara could hold it back no more. They were being so sweet and she had ruined their holiday. First by booking the wrong damned place and then by falling down a hole and spoiling their planned day out. She couldn't do anything right any more. She couldn't book a holiday properly, couldn't make friends with kids, keep her man ... Feeling May's long slim arms close around her and being enclosed in her lovely floral perfume, Lara's tears continued to waterfall down her face.

'What did I say?' Clare rushed over, guilty that she had caused Lara to be so upset. 'Oh Lara, you didn't think I was being catty, did you, when I said you had it all? I think it's great that you've done so well.' She ripped off some kitchen roll and pressed it into her crying friend's hand. 'Here, Lars. I am so sorry if it was something I said. Oh my, I feel terrible.'

'It wasn't you, Clare,' sniffed Lara, taking the kitchen roll and blowing her nose on it. 'It's me. It's all a mess.'

'It isn't a mess,' May scolded her. 'Don't be daft. I'm having a lovely time. And so is Clare.'

'May, trust me, it's a mess. I'm a mess. My whole life is a bloody mess,' Lara blurted out. There – it was said.

Clare sat down at the other side of Lara on the sofa. 'What's up? It's not the holiday that's upset you, is it? It's something else.'

Lara blew her nose again before delivering the big news. 'James and I are finished. I found him in bed with his ex.'

May gasped. 'Oh, Lara, no.' History repeating itself. Poor Lara.

'His children hated me. I couldn't do anything right for them. They hated my cooking, they hated me. I felt like a hired help. Actually worse, because Kristina got three hundred hours off per week. Now I don't have anywhere to live because I've rented out my flat. And my boss is an arsehole. If he touches my bum once more I swear I'll swing for him.'

Clare squeezed Lara's arm. 'Lars, why didn't you say?'

'I didn't say because I didn't want to wreck your holiday, but I don't think I could wreck it any more than I have done.'

'You haven't wrecked it at all, silly,' May said. 'It's the oddest holiday of my life but I like it.'

'And you mustn't worry about where to live. You're very welcome to stay with me,' Clare suggested. 'You'll have to bunk up with me though and I snore.'

'We know,' said May. 'I don't snore and I've got a spare room.'

'Thank you, both.' Their kindness was humbling. 'I just can't believe that I've failed. Again. Another man goes back to his ex. I'm seeing a pattern develop.'

'Yeah, you choose shit men,' said Clare. 'I thought you were really happy.'

'I wanted to be. I thought it was just teething problems – you know, two single people learning to live together and having to adjust their boundaries and things.' Except James didn't adjust anything in her favour; with a little perspective and distance she could see how little he had actually done to help her. 'That's why I didn't say anything. I thought everything would turn out okay in the end. Then when I found him in bed with—' She shook her head in disgust.

'Do you know the woman?' asked May.

'She's called Tianne Lee. She's some sort of new hot-shot lawyer.'

Clare thought for a moment. 'Tianne Lee as in Tina Anne Lee?'

Lara snapped her head up. 'That's her. Don't tell me you know her.'

'Oh, I know her all right. And no, she is not a hot-shot lawyer,' said Clare with conviction. 'My department have had nightmare dealings with the firm she works for – Spinner and Proctor. Tianne Lee: long curly hair, chipmunk cheeks, fat legs, wonky eye.'

'She sounds lovely, Lars,' said May. 'No wonder you're upset.'

'You actually know her?' Lara asked.

'Yes, I know exactly who she is and, trust me, she isn't half as smart as she thinks she is. Bart Forbes-Philips – one of the barristers we use – ate her alive in court last month. She might very well swish her girly hair about and waggle her bum when she walks but her reputation is all smoke and mirrors. Or piss and wind, as my dad used to say.'

Lara chuckled. 'You're just saying that to make me feel better.' Then she huffed at herself. 'God, what a baby I am, revelling in the fact that you think my nemesis has fat legs, chipmunk cheeks, a wonky eye and is rubbish at her job.'

'I'm relishing it as well,' said May, 'and I don't even know her. God, I love a good bitch.'

'Oh, I could bitch well into the early hours about her. She's a horrible thing.' Clare shuddered. 'And I know at least two married men that she's been bonking. From what you've said in the past about Miriam being self-absorbed, I'd say they were from a very similar mould. Except that Miriam is very good at her job and Tianne just thinks she is. I'd also say that if he's done that to you, darling, they're very welcome to each other. What a pair of bastards. Tianne, you see, doesn't let anyone get too close to her in case they find out that she's got no substance to her. She keeps men on the edge – prick-teasing, flirting, charming them, only ever showing them her good side, playing them off against each other – power games. And you know men, they want what they can't have. She's hardly relationship material.'

'James's kids loved her.'

'I bet you anything that if Tianne moved in they'd be regaling her with tales of how crap her chicken nuggets were next to yours. And as far as the boss thing goes, you don't have to put up with any of that groping nonsense.'

'It's not just his wandering hands. He treats me like I'm an inferior species. And it isn't just me; he's like that with all the women in the department.' Lara sighed. 'And however far we think we've come in the workplace, my days would be numbered if I complained.'

May nodded. It was all true. There were ways and means of getting rid of people who kicked up inconvenient fusses. Tribunals were less about justice than about which barrister was more persuasive.

'I can't believe you kept all this to yourself without saying a word,' said May.

'We don't have time to talk, do we?' said Lara. 'We work and then go home and say, "Oh, I must ring blah–blah and catch up," but we're too tired or we've got even more work to do or men to pander to.'

'Well, that's going to change.' May raised her hand and slapped the sofa firmly, then she laughed at herself. Here she was telling off Lara when she was an even worse culprit. So it was time to come clean. *Here goes.* 'Oh, and whilst we're having a soul-purge, I'm not with Michael any more. And I wasn't brave enough to tell you before because I thought I'd lose your friendship if I did.'

'Oh, May, why would that happen?' said Lara.

'You haven't heard what I did yet . . .' And May proceeded to tell it all: meeting 'married' Michael, bonking 'married' Michael, finding out 'married' Michael was not actually married after all. Mentally, she'd had an affair with someone else's husband; physically she'd had an affair with a lying, cheating twat. When she had finished, she took a long breath and waited for her audience to tell her what a low-life she was.

And she waited.

'Say it, then,' she prompted. 'Tell me that I'm a disgrace to womenkind and you hate me.' May's eyes were brimming with tears as her friends remained silent.

'I can't believe it,' said Lara.

May waited for the onslaught.

'I can't believe men like that exist in real life. I thought *Jeremy Kyle* guests were all actors.'

'You must hate me,' said May. 'I hate myself.'

'Why the chuff would we hate you?' tutted Lara. 'I hate *him*. What a horrible, cruel thing to do to someone. You shouldn't be punishing yourself, in any case; you should be punishing him. With a big stick up the arse – one that has a burning spike on the end.' She thought of Gene Hathersage overhearing her say that and realizing that she absolutely was not a posh southerner.

'I did a terrible thing,' said May. 'Whatever you say, I believed I was sleeping with a married man.'

'Yes, but you weren't,' Clare argued furiously. She started pacing up and down as if she were the award-winning barrister Bart Forbes-Philips. 'You were manipulated and used and outmanoeuvred. He took advantage of your caring nature. What a dick. God, you two really can pick them.'

May smiled, overcome with warm relief. She felt so much lighter for confessing her secret to them.

Lara shook her head. 'At least one of us is happy. Clare, you and the lovely Lud are our beacons of light. Don't ever let us down.'

Clare smiled but stayed silent.

Chapter 55

Joan took the back path down to the church. She hated this damned village with its poky little houses and old-fashioned shops. They ought to rename the place 'God's Mistake'. Could Ren Dullem have more boring, dismal name?

She took a detour to the twelve graves to double-check that she hadn't missed any details, but she hadn't. She took more photos then decided that she would try to charm the vicar and ask him for more information, if he was inside. It was Sunday afternoon, though, and he was probably having his lunch. She crossed her fingers as she walked into the church.

Luck was on her side when she pushed open the door in the large Gothic arch and felt a rush of cool air swim towards her. A rather portly man in a voluminous cassock was sitting at the other end of the church, polishing candlesticks. He waved, then, as she approached, she saw his welcoming smile power down to fifty per cent. He's just realized I'm not a dull'un from Dullem, thought Joan with an inner smirk.

'Good afternoon, Reverend,' she said. 'We haven't met. I'm Joan Hawk. I work for Lord Carlton.'

'Ah,' said the reverend, extending a hand, welcoming but still cautious. 'Very nice to meet you. I am Reverend Acaster, if you didn't already know. Welcome to the church of St Andrew the Apostle.'

'It's a beautiful building,' said Joan, revolving a full three hundred and sixty degrees to take it all in. It was, too – very ornate with a stunning stained-glass window of a fishing boat, rays of sunshine pouring down onto it as men lifted up a net teeming with fish. The rows of pews were polished to a high shine and the old embroidered prayer cushions hanging in front of each seat replicated the boat and fishermen theme of the window. St Andrew – patron saint of fishermen, of course, thought Joan.

'I'm enquiring where the parish records for the twentieth century might be,' said Joan.

'For what reason, may I ask?' asked the reverend. His sharp grey eyes were blinking rapidly. He's rattled, thought Joan. Now what was in those records that he might not want anyone to see? *Softly, softly, Jo*, she warned herself.

'I thought I might draw a family tree for Lord Carlton's birthday in October,' said Joan. 'He's been so very kind to me and there's a space on the wall in his study where it would fit perfectly.'

She saw the reverend let go of his breath with a gust of relief that brought a trill of laughter in its wake.

'That's a very thoughtful present,' he said. 'Alas, the parish records are all kept at Carlton Hall.'

'Well, would you believe it?' Joan smiled, charming the reverend. 'I'll ask Gladys if she'll point me in the right direction. I presumed they'd be here.'

'There's no storage space. Unless you count the crypt, but the damp air down there isn't conducive to keeping valuable historical papers.'

'Of course. And am I right in thinking that the Carlton family members are down there in the church crypt? I didn't notice a family tomb when I was taking a walk around the graveyard recently. I thought I'd start collecting information for my family tree that way but it wasn't very successful.'

'Yes, the Carltons are all safe below our feet. And one day Edwin will lie at the side of his beloved Mary there too, though not soon, I hope.'

'Oh, me too.' Joan nodded vigorously. 'And it will be very sad that he is the last of his line.'

'Very,' said the reverend with a loaded sigh.

'Anyway, thank you so much for all your help,' said Joan. 'I wish I'd come to you first. I'd have saved myself a few wild-goose chases.'

'Pleasure.' The old man went back to polishing the candle-stick.

'Oh.' Joan turned round as if this was an afterthought. 'I saw a grave that looked as if it had been dug outside the church grounds. Seymour Acaster, I think the name was. Why was that? It interested me because my father's name is Seymour.'

'No, it was always part of the churchyard. The ground shifts over the years and the fence moves.'

He was lying, she knew. The question was why. She was definitely onto something here; she was absolutely sure of it. She wanted to ask if Seymour was married but she knew the reverend wouldn't tell her anything. She decided it might be best to put him totally off any scent he might have caught a whiff of.

'I'm beginning to wish I hadn't had this great idea.' She smiled, tossing her long chocolate-brown hair back over her shoulder. 'History was never my forte and I don't particularly like walking around graveyards. Maybe I'll buy him a book instead. Pretend I never asked about the Carltons.'

She saw the reverend's shoulders relax again as the tension in them eased. He believed her. 'Your secret is safe with me,' he said with a gentle chuckle.

'Reverend, thank you again.' Joan waved and walked back down the aisle.

Outside she took another long look at Seymour's grave.

Beloved husband of R. There was no R Acaster buried near, as all the other wives of the *Fratres A Mare* set were. Could R still be alive? Joan made a quick calculation in her head. She would be very old if she were.

She left the churchyard smiling to herself and wondering where those old parish records might be hiding in the house, but knowing that wherever they were, she would find them.

Chapter 56

That afternoon, just as the old clock on the wall was bonging out three mellow rings, there was a knock on the door. Clare opened it to find the bulk of Gene Hathersage standing outside holding a carrier bag and a tool box. 'There's comfrey leaves and flour in there,' he said, handing over the bag. 'Smash them up together with a little water until you have a paste and then make a poultice with them. For ...' He waved his finger at Lara in the background. 'For her ankle.'

'Would you like to come in?' said Clare, making her best effort to be friendly now that he had been kind to her friend. Thanks to Lara's ankle incident she was determined to show him that they were all on a new footing. 'I've just brewed up.'

He seemed to hum and haw for a few moments before deciding that he would. Once inside he nodded to Lara. 'All right there?'

'Alive if not kicking,' said Lara, adding softly, 'Did you manage to ... get done what you were going to do?'

'Yes. He's all tucked up now.' He coughed and turned to Clare so swiftly that she almost poured her cup of tea over him.

'There's milk and sugar on the table, Mr Hathersage,' she said.

'Thank you.'

He spooned sugar and stirred some milk into his cup and then took a long drink from it.

'You won't be getting any more nocturnal visits from my uncle,' he said. 'I've been to see him and told him off. He'll break his neck. Those silly shoes he likes have absolutely no grip on the soles.'

Lara snorted back a giggle. 'He sounds a hoot.'

'He's spent too much time on his own,' said Gene. 'He should have found himself a wife and family.'

Is that what you want too? Lara asked him in her head. Why wasn't Gene married? He was quite handsome in a wild sort of way and almost genial when he tried. She watched him drinking; his large fingers made the cup look tiny. With his mad hair and black eyes, big strong shoulders and working jeans he was the polar opposite of the highly groomed James. She had a sudden vision of the big broad chest that must lie underneath his checked shirt, and had to snap her eyes away when she realized that she was appraising him a little bit too much.

Gene took two more mouthfuls of tea and then emptied the rest into the sink.

'That was good, thanks. Anyway I'll get on now. I'll be done in five minutes.'

'Thank you,' May said, giving him her most pleasant smile, also showing that a line had been drawn and arms had been downed.

'You need a new poultice before you go to bed.' Gene threw the words at Lara, not giving her a chance to thank him before he exited the cottage.

'Ooh, Lara, I think you've pulled,' half whispered, half mimed May with a wink. 'He deffo has a soft spot for you.'

'Not even remotely funny,' said Lara, listening to Gene's heavy boots climbing up on the roof. 'Even if Mr Hathersage happened to be George Clooney under that beard and hair, I'm staying away from men. For ever. I'm going to join a convent and stop shaving my legs.'

'Book me the room next door,' said May. 'Clare, you and Lud can come and visit us.'

I won't be visiting, said Clare to herself. I'll be right there with you, ladies.

Chapter 57

Clare awoke early the next morning, disturbed by a dream in which she spotted Ludwig in the village square and, just as she waved over, delighted to see him, a beautiful thin blonde woman threw her arms around him and he reciprocated. As much as she waved and tried to attract his attention he would not be interrupted. The dream was so vivid that she woke up and found her pillow wet with tears. She knew she wouldn't drop back to sleep, so she put on her swimming costume, rolled a towel up under her arm, picked up her torch and headed for the lagoon.

The day was naturally overcast outside. For once there were real clouds in the sky weighed down with rain, as well as those strange grey puffs. But down in the cave the water was bright, clear and blue-green, and for Clare it was a world separate from the one she wasn't sure she wanted to go back to. She would have been happy as a mermaid, she thought. She wished she could hold her breath for hours. As she dived down she felt nothing of the pressures of work awaiting her return, the constant struggle to please her parents, the stress of losing Lud. It was as if nothing bad could follow her under the water; she was happy and safe there. Eventually, when she had to surface and breathe in air, her sad, sad tears joined the salty waters of the pool.

Chapter 58

In the end it was as easy to get hold of the parish records as it had been to find Edwin's will. Joan arranged herself in a pose, one to give an unambiguous impression that she was deep in thought as she drank the morning coffee which Gladys had wheeled in on her trolley. To her relief it prompted Edwin to ask her what the matter was.

'Oh, sorry.' Joan smiled and shook herself out of her fake state of preoccupation. 'I was just wondering if there were any parish records in the village. I had a conversation with my mother last night and she reckons that we had relatives living in Ren Dullem. Apparently we are related to the Moodys who lived here. Fifth cousins, I think she said.'

'Really?' Edwin said, spraying custard-cream crumbs from his mouth. 'How marvellous. That's why you gravitated to us – you're a true local.'

'Strange, isn't it?' chuckled Joan. 'That's why I must have felt at home from the first moment I came here.'

'The parish records are all here in this very house.' Edwin was animated with excitement. 'They're in the drawers in the library. There wasn't enough room in the church to keep them, so they were moved here. They used to be kept in the church crypt but the damp was destroying them. The earlier records have a great deal of foxing on them and are barely readable, alas.'

He pulled himself to his feet, though it took a couple of practice attempts. 'Come with me, Joan. I'd be delighted to show you. We can look for your relatives together.'

She followed his funny little curved back down to the dull, brown library. Edwin pulled open the long heavy curtains at the window to let in more light but it didn't make much difference, and neither did putting on the main lights – they must have totalled all of five watts.

Luckily there was a very elegant Anglepoise lamp on the desk.

'The library should have been a south-facing room, not a north-facing one,' said Edwin, switching on the lamp. 'Ridiculous design. I expect Jacob Carlton, who built the house, wasn't one of life's great readers.' He walked over to the bottom shelf. It looked full of books, but now, with the improved lighting, Joan could see it was a faux cover. Edwin slid it back to reveal a stack of heavy leather-bound tomes. Joan leapt to his aid when he tried to pick one up and almost toppled over.

'I'm not sure if they are stored in order,' said Edwin. 'What dates were you looking for?'

'I don't know,' replied Joan. 'I thought I'd start with the twentieth century, right at the beginning of it.'

She wished Edwin would bugger off and let her get on with it.

The first book was one of the very badly age-spotted volumes that had been stored in the church crypt, but luckily it contained records from far earlier than Joan was interested in. The second she picked out was in good condition but, again, too early. The third – in the words of Goldilocks – was just right: '1900 – PRESENT DAY'.

'I shouldn't really be looking at them in work time,' said Joan.

'Nonsense,' said Edwin. 'It's rather thrilling to be Hercule Poirot and Miss Marple for a while.'

'It could take ages.'

'Even better.' Edwin twinkled.

Damn, thought Joan. Still, seeing them with him was better than not seeing them at all. She opened the book to the first page and pretended to be interested in a marriage certificate dated 1904: Frederick and Anne Coffey.

'A relative of Gladys – how interesting,' trilled Joan.

'Well, by marriage. Gladys is a Shaw of course. There will be a record of her birth in the later records.'

1905, 1906, 1907 . . . There were records of deaths and marriages between familiar family names: William Arnold Bird and Florence Hathersage died, Anna Bird married Stephen Unwin, Thomas Hubbard married Maria Docherty from Wellem. Then there were the births: Martha Unwin, Catherine and Mary Smith, James Ward, Doris Dickinson, Grace Landers . . . on and on. Joan's heart was quickening with anticipation as she turned to the next page. 1909: a son born to Edith and Ebenezer Acaster Seymour. A child who ended up being buried on unconsecrated ground and was closely connected to R, Edwin Carlton's heir.

Chapter 59

At ten o'clock the others were still sleeping. They'd spent the previous evening having a cathartic bitch about Michael and James and Tianne, whilst half watching some TV, which was once again possible thanks to Gene Hathersage removing the signal-jamming aerial. But it was now eleven hours since they had all turned in for the night, and if that didn't prove their batteries were run down, nothing did. Would they ever get back into the swing of starting the day at five o'clock in the morning?

After her swim, Clare was wide awake and full of beans; it was a tense, nervous energy, though, that needed burning off. She picked up her tin of cleaning things and headed off for Raine's cottage, as she had promised to return. There was no sign of Val Hathersage near Spice Wood, not that she thought there would be at that hour. She didn't know if she was relieved or disappointed by that.

Raine was delighted to see her and greeted her warmly.

'Oh, my dear Clare,' she said, her plump, old face beaming. 'I hoped you'd come back.'

Clare smiled. 'I'm a perfectionist. I never leave a job half done. I told you I'd be back and I'm a woman of my word.'

'My lady who brings my meals in the evening thought she was in the wrong house,' said Raine. 'You're so very, very kind.'

Then she noticed Clare's wet black hair. 'Have you been for a swim today? In my lagoon?'

Clare smoothed her hand over her head. 'I didn't want to use the hair-dryer in case I woke my friends,' she explained. 'Yes, I've been for a swim. The water was beautiful.' *Just what I needed. I don't know how I'm going to be able to bear to leave it.*

'I miss it so much,' said Raine sadly. 'I haven't swum in a very long time. I wish I could see it again.'

'How did you used to get down there?' asked Clare, taking various bottles out of her tin. 'Were you able to walk when you were younger?'

'No, I've never been able to walk,' said Raine. 'My husband used to carry me.'

Clare's head was suddenly suffused with a romantic picture of that. She saw Raine, long golden hair streaming behind her, smooth and lithe as a rippled ribbon in the water; her young husband a perfect match for her. She sighed.

Her hand stilled on the bottle of bleach she'd been unscrewing. 'There must be some way of getting you back down to the lagoon.' She thought hard. It would be a feat and a half but not impossible, surely.

'If I saw it, I could never bear to leave it again.' Raine's old head shook slowly from side to side. 'No, it's best I remember it in my memories only.'

'Can I get you a drink before I start?'

'A cup of water would be nice, please.'

Clare filled up a cup and delivered it to Raine's hands. 'You're so cold,' she said, closing her warm fingers over Raine's chilled ones. 'Can I light a fire for you?'

'Thank you, but no,' said Raine. 'I don't like to be too hot. This temperature in here is fine for me. '

Clare set to work in the kitchen. Whoever came to look after Raine wasn't very good at washing down surfaces, she thought with a huff. The window in there afforded the most beautiful view over the cove. The skies were very dramatic today: grey clouds were being buffeted and bullied on their way by the wind and the sea was restless and dark.

Raine studied the young woman now climbing up on the chair to clean the inside of the kitchen window. Such a pretty girl with her neat twenties-style black bobbed hair, but too many clouds in her two-coloured eyes. She had a head that was telling her heart all the wrong things, Raine could tell. She wheeled herself nearer to the kitchen door.

'What do you think of Ren Dullem?' she asked. 'Now you've been here a few days more.'

Clare stopped working and tilted her head to the side in thought. 'I think it's the strangest place I've ever been to in my life,' she eventually concluded. 'But I like it.' Faced with delivering her opinion of the place, Clare realized that she had settled into life here more than she ever thought she would. The thought of not being able to open a door in her bedroom and tread down to an underground cavern was one she didn't want to contemplate at the moment. She was trying hard to think of the here and now and not project about what life would be like in a few days' time.

'Ren Dullem needs people like you,' said Raine. 'It is craving an injection of life and passion and care. It has become worn down by its duties. When I first came here, it was the prettiest little place I'd ever seen. I was in love with it. I was in love with the people. I know now I shouldn't have come.'

'What do you mean?'

'People say that you can't fool yourself,' said Raine, smiling sadly. 'Oh, but you can if you try. Or at least you can override the evidence that is staring you in the face. But eventually, eventually, the truth becomes too hard to ignore. I think you know what I mean.'

Clare coughed. She had become a past master at overriding her true feelings. Stamping other people's ideas of what her life should be like over her own and pretending to accept them had become a way of life to her. But her anxiety dreams every night and her bitten-down fingernails were evidence that the truth was seeping out. Clare switched her mind back into work mode and gave her full attention to the windowsill. She had brought an old toothbrush to get right into the grooves.

Through the window the clouds were tumbling over themselves as if running scared.

'There's going to be a summer storm, I think,' said Clare.

'I shall enjoy the view,' said Raine. 'There is nowhere better in the world to see a storm than at High Top.' In the distance they heard a growl of thunder. There would be a bigger storm soon in Ren Dullem. Then the skies would clear and finally the sunshine could appear once again.

Chapter 60

Lara was crushing up more comfrey leaves on the kitchen table with the end of a rolling pin, in the absence of a pestle and mortar in the kitchen of Well Cottage, when there was a heavy-handed knock on the door.

She hopped across and opened it to find the imposing figure of Gene Hathersage there, his hands behind his back.

'Oh, it's you,' she said. 'Come in. I'm just crushing mend-skin.'

'Knit-bone,' he corrected. 'How's the ankle?'

'Not bad at all,' said Lara, in all honesty. The swelling had gone down completely and the bruising had faded from black to light brown as if the healing had been accelerated. She hadn't put a lot of credence in claims of herb-magic before, but she was in severe danger of having to eat her words.

'I brought you this,' he said, and from behind his back he produced a wooden crutch. 'I measured it against the mark on the wall so it should be the right height.'

'Ah, that's why you stuck your pencil under my arm.'

His eyebrows formed a dipped arch of confusion as if he was thinking: why else would I have done that? 'Try it.'

'Oh, that's very kind of you. Thank you.' She accepted it, placed it under her arm and assumed the pose of Long John Silver. 'I didn't see a fish.'

'Fish?'

'Your signature. '

'I can whittle you one, if you insist.'

'Why not? I'll put the kettle on.'

'Then tea for me, please, if you're offering.'

There was enough milk for two cups. May had gone down to the shop for some more just before Gene arrived. It was a wonder they hadn't passed each other.

Gene took a knife out of his back pocket and reached for the crutch.

'You do realize that if I carve you a fish on here, the value of this instantly increases by ten,' he said.

'I'll remember to mention that on eBay.'

Jesus, she bet he hadn't a clue what eBay was. Was that possible in this day and age?

'It's a sort of shop,' explained Lara. 'On the Internet.'

'I know,' said Gene indignantly. 'We might not get the Internet in Ren Dullem but I am aware of what it is. I'll go into Wellem if I need to use it.'

Maybe if Great-Uncle Milton stopped fannying about with his signals you might be able to use it here, thought Lara. This really must be the only place on earth not to have the Internet and yet everyone seemed to cope quite adequately as they had done in the days before mobiles and the net and Facebook, which weren't that long ago really. She wondered what Tianne's timeline would be saying. She was glad she couldn't torture herself by checking.

'It'll only be a little one,' said Gene, his knife nibbling expertly at the wood.

'I was really only joking about the fish.' Lara felt slightly cheeky now.

'I don't mind,' he replied.

Lara swished the pot around and poured out two cups of hot brown tea.

'Not be long now until you're home,' said Gene eventually, as Lara sipped at her drink and watched him form a fish in the arm rest. 'Have you decided what you'll do?'

Lara felt her cheeks flush, remembering that she had poured out her business to him after falling into his dog's grave.

'I'm going to get my things from the house and then stay with May until I sort myself out. I'm not looking forward to it,' she said, sounding a lot braver than she felt. 'I won't let him persuade me to try again, if that is his intention, of course.'

'Easier said than done.'

'True. But it's not just that I found him with someone else, it's all the other things: the lies, the taking me for granted, the lack of thought for my feelings. I couldn't go back. I wouldn't respect myself if I did. And my mum and dad always told me that if I can't respect myself, how can I ever expect anyone else to?'

Gene nodded silently and carried on whittling.

'Did you love him?' he asked eventually.

'Yes,' said Lara. 'That's why it hurt when he invited me to share his future and encouraged my dreams and then smashed them all to frigging bits.' *Oh God, please don't cry again in front of him.* She felt the hot sharp prick of tears stabbing at the backs of her eyes. 'Plus, if that was the way he behaved, he didn't really love me, did he? Men should think with the brains God gave them instead of . . .' She shut up quickly, realizing she shouldn't be saying this to him: a man.

'Not all of them think with that,' Gene replied.

Lara flicked her hair back from her face in an unconscious gesture of someone gearing up for a possible fight.

'All the ones I've met do,' she said, as a collection of strong emotions swirled inside her. 'Anyway, I don't want to talk about it.'

'There. A fish.' He thrust his arm out to its full length and handed the crutch back to her. 'You were the one who dragged me kicking and screaming into your emotional crisis,' he reminded her, his jaw clearly rigid under his beard.

'Yes, and I made a big mistake,' snapped Lara. She felt years of fury banging on the bars and demanding to be released. 'I'm not saying all men are bastards, but there's a lot of them out there who think it's fine to treat someone like crap and then say, "Sorry, love, didn't mean to bonk my ex. It just happened. I fell into bed with her by mistake." And then they expect the heart-broken woman to be so overjoyed that they've said a few apologetic words and bought her a bunch of tulips from Asda that everything will be A-OK. Until the next time.'

'You've obviously tarred us all with the same brush,' Gene growled, putting his knife away in his back pocket.

'Yeah, well, maybe I have. Maybe that's because what I've found is that they all obviously like being black and sticky and smelling like roads.' *What on earth have you just said?* asked an exasperated voice inside her.

'And women have the monopoly on being the victim, do they?' said Gene, not even trying to make sense of that non-sense she'd just spouted about tar. 'They don't lie and manipulate and cheat at all, I suppose? They don't turn on the tears and think sex will get them out of any trouble they've put themselves in? No, they're all walking around like self-righteous radical feminists agreeing that all – sorry – *most* men are bas-tards, especially when they don't get their own way.'

Lara threw her arms up in the air. 'The sexist quote of the year.'

'I'm not a sexist. I'm a realist. Look, I think I'd better go. Take care with your crutch,' said Gene Hathersage with a sar-castic snarl as he rose to his feet. 'I'd hate for you to fall again.'

'Yeah, I bet you would,' said Lara, slamming the door on him as he went out. It missed his back by millimetres.

Chapter 61

May was just coming up the hill with a bottle of milk when she saw Gene's truck turn into La Mer. He was crunching the gears and he had a sub-zero expression on his face.. He wasn't a happy man today and she wondered who had put him in that mood.

She doubted that Frank had the capacity to be as fierce as that. She had just seen him in the village. He was delivering to the butcher. He waved across the road at her and she waved back and although her legs pulled desperately to cross over so that she could say hello, engage him in conversation, be near him, she resisted. What was the point? She would be leaving Ren Dullem in four days, never to see him again. It was best to keep away and not let him even peek inside her heart. It was no less than torment, though, walking away from him, knowing that he was as disappointed as she was that an arc of a hand in the air was all that passed between them today.

She hurried back up to Well Cottage because it was chilly and she wasn't wearing anything over her short-sleeved shirt. The sky looked as grumpy as Gene Hathersage just had, she thought: moody and full of unspent rage. She opened the door to the cottage to find Lara wearing the female equivalent of Gene Hathersage's incensed expression. Her eyes fell on the crutch propped up at the side of the table and she put two and two together and got a big fat tick for her effort.

'Oho. Do I sense another incident?'

'That man,' growled Lara, venting her fury on the comfrey leaves. 'He doesn't like women at all. He thinks we're all manipulators. But that's okay, really, because men are all twats.'

May picked up the crutch. She noticed the detail of the tiny fish, carved with all its scales.

'Did he make this for you?'

'Yes,' hissed Lara.

'Yep, that's the action of a man who hates women – making them a crutch to help them walk *and* adding a little personal touch like this.'

Lara stopped grinding. 'Yes, it was kind of him to do that. Unfortunately he used it as an excuse to say that all women are evil.'

'Is that what he said or what you heard?' Taking the time to make this for a complete stranger was not the act of someone who hated easily, thought May.

'Did you see Clare on your travels?' asked Lara, changing the subject because she didn't want to admit that May was right and she was wrong.

'Nope.' May gave a small sigh. 'Didn't see anyone at all.'

Raine's house was as shiny as a new pin. Clare's job was done and she derived such a sense of satisfaction from seeing the surfaces sparkle and the kitchen gleam.

'I wish I could come here once a week and keep on top of things for you,' said Clare. She would miss the funny old lady when she went back to London; it was a thought that dragged her mood down.

'Thank you,' said Raine. 'You haven't even stopped for a cup of tea.'

'I might have one now, if you wouldn't mind my company for a bit longer,' replied Clare. 'Can I get you one, or some more water?'

'Water would be lovely, thank you.' Raine smiled. 'Then you can sit with me and tell me about where you live.'

'It's not that interesting,' Clare called from the kitchen, over the sound of the kettle building to a boil. 'Have you ever been to London?'

'No,' said Raine. 'City life isn't for me. Is it exciting living there?'

'Very,' said Clare, pouring the water over the tea leaves and stirring them with a spoon to hasten the brewing. 'Busy, colourful, noisy, mad.' Clare walked into the sitting room with her tea and the glass of water. 'It's a thrilling whirl.'

Raine noted that whereas Clare's voice was full of gusto, her enthusiasm was not reflected in her eyes. This was not a happy girl sitting in front of her.

'You must be looking forward to getting back to it all.' As she spoke, Raine watched Clare's reaction closely.

Clare merely nodded slowly. 'Yes, well, I'll have plenty to keep me busy: new job, new flash company car, sorting out my new office.'

The girl is less excited about that than she was about scrubbing at my kitchen windows, thought Raine.

'Maybe you'll find a nice young man to bring some love into your life,' said Raine.

'Maybe,' replied Clare with a shrug of her shoulders, though she doubted it. She wouldn't have enough time for anything but work from now on. Blackwoods and Margoyles would own her every breath.

Abruptly she changed the subject. 'Raine, did you ever regret moving here to be with Seymour?'

'Never,' said Raine. 'I would have got over him eventually if I had returned home, but my life would not have been as rich. Love – real love – is a privilege, not a right. I was blessed to have a man like Seymour Acaster loving me.'

Clare nodded. 'He sounds amazing.'

'He was just a man. An ordinary decent man with a good kind heart. But we fitted together. Like this,' and she threaded her fingers together tightly.

Clare tried not to think about Lud. Decent, kind, good-hearted Lud. But she remembered how, as he had said to Clare that she and he fitted together 'like this', he had also threaded his fingers together tightly. She missed him terribly. And he had probably forgotten all about her by now.

'It doesn't look too good outside today. I don't think I'll be sunbathing when I get back to the cottage,' said Clare, over-brightly. Or rather cloud-bathing.

'Will I see you again before you leave?' asked Raine, hope in her voice.

'I'd like that, Raine,' said Clare. 'I'd like that a lot.'

Chapter 62

Clare had barely stepped out of Spice Wood when, with a roar, a motorbike came up behind her. It passed and then braked hard, blocking her path. The leather-clad rider lifted off his helmet.

'Well, fancy seeing you here,' said Val Hathersage. Head to foot in leathers and sitting astride the bike he looked breathtakingly masculine. The padded outfit lent him solid square shoulders and beefy thighs. Clare felt her heart thudding against the wall of her chest. He pointed to the tin. 'Where have you been and what have you been doing?'

Clare felt herself colour. To answer that she had been cleaning would hardly sound alluring. 'Helping someone in need,' she said. 'Is that yours?'

'Borrowed. Want a ride?' he said. 'There's a spare helmet.'

'I've never been on a motorbike before.'

'A ride for a ride,' said Val with a slow smile. 'Come on, live a little. Leave your box of spells behind a tree. No one will nick it.'

Clare wasn't sure, but Val was unlocking a helmet attached to the back. *Come on, live a little.* 'Okay, then,' she said, trying her best to appear daring and excited rather than what she really felt: scared stiff.

Chapter 63

She was here at last – at 1928. Another birth: Sarah Smith. And a death: poor old Thomas Hubbard who had only just got married. Then a marriage: Seymour Elias Acaster, Fisherman, aged nineteen, residing in High Top Cottage, married Raine de la Mer, no age, no address, no occupation. *Gotcha.* R had to be his wife.

'What an exotic name,' she said, trying not to sound as giddy as she felt.

At her shoulder, Edwin made a confirming hum but said no more.

Joan swilled the words around in her head hoping they'd make sense when placed together: *Reines de la Mer ... Ren Dullem ... Raine de la Mer ... R.*

'Why doesn't it say how old she was or where she came from?'

Tension had invaded Edwin's shoulders; she could see it.

'Parish records dated so long ago are often incomplete.'

That was a lie because, from what she had seen, the records for Ren Dullem were meticulously kept and 1928 was hardly the Dark Ages. Even in this backwards spot.

'Why do you think the village was called Reines de la Mer in the first place?'

'Oh, I don't really know.' Edwin shook his head vigorously.

'People believed that this part of the country was once attached to France, I think, and gave it an exotic name.'

That's not really answering the question, Edwin, thought Joan. She prepared to ask the big question.

'What is a queen of the sea?'

Edwin was clearly uncomfortable with this line of questioning, but out of innate politeness, he answered all the same.

'A dolphin or similar creature,' he said, trying to sound casual. 'Local sailors often mistook them for sea monsters. They believed that if they named their village after them, they would be flattered enough to give them safe passage on the sea.'

'Ah.' Joan nodded, a voice inside her saying: *That wasn't so hard, now, was it? So why all the secrecy?* No, there was more he hadn't told her. She turned over the page and felt Edwin's relief that the questions had stopped. More births, more deaths, more marriages followed. They reached the end of 1928 and moved onto subsequent years and Joan noticed how few girls were born. In fact, for the next ten years, none were born at all. She opened her mouth to ask why that was, but thought Edwin might be frightened into ending their session. *Softly, softly.*

Chapter 64

Clare was hardly dressed for a ride on a motorbike. Her thin shirt afforded her no protection against the cold wind rushing at her. Val was surprisingly sensible on the road, she was pleased to find, although she couldn't say in all honesty that she enjoyed the experience. Not that she admitted to that when they parked on a cliff top by a picnic area.

'Is there any better feeling?' Val winked. 'Apart from sex.'

'Wow, that was great,' said Clare, hoping she sounded more convinced than she felt. She was more than happy to have solid ground below her feet again. Her teeth were chattering from cold and with relief at being off the bike and safe. She was dreading the journey back.

'Colleen used to love riding with me,' he said. 'Her hair used to stream behind her.'

'Bully for Colleen,' Clare murmured to herself.

Val sat at the picnic table, his legs on the bench. 'Come here,' he said, inviting her to sit between his legs. Clare obeyed, hoping he would wrap his arms around her and warm up her bones. Instead he took a cigarette out of his pocket and lit up.

'Want a drag?'

'Thanks, but I don't smoke.'

'Neither do I. Well, I gave up.'

'Looks like it.'

'I find women like the taste of cigarettes and whisky on a man's breath. Turns you on, doesn't it?'

Clare hated whisky. The smell of it was enough to make her gag.

'I'm not sure it would turn me on that much.'

Val grabbed her hair and kissed her firmly, just as a strong, dominant hero might do in a film. Clare felt strangely detached. All she could think of was how bloody awful he tasted.

'Let's play dare,' Val said, suddenly pulling away from her. 'You first. I dare you to take your top off.'

'What? No.'

Val blew a perfect smoke ring above her head. 'It's your halo,' he said, watching it float in the air. 'Miss Goody Two-Shoes.'

Clare knew what was coming next: some comment about Colleen, no doubt. Well, she'd show him that she could be as earthy as her.

'Okay.' Clare began to slowly unbutton her shirt. Then, she tried to look much braver than she felt and eased her arms out of it, spun it around and let it fly onto the ground.

Then, out of the corner of her eye she saw an old couple carrying a picnic basket.

'Oi. You shouldn't be doing that here where children play,' called the man as Clare scrabbled on the ground for her shirt and tried to hide behind Val whilst she put it back on. 'You should be arrested. Doris, don't look. Filthy buggers.'

Clare couldn't get her arms into the sleeves. 'Help me,' she hissed at Val but he was too busy being creased up in hysterics.

'I'm phoning the police,' called the man. 'Doris. Get your mobile out of your handbag.'

'I didn't bring it, Jim,' came the reply.

'You can't remember anything, can you?'

'Let's go home, Jim. It's too cold.'

'This is a bloody disaster.'

The old couple went off chuntering to each other. Val was crying with laughter, Clare was mortified. She wondered if any satellites had picked them up and someone in a space station was sitting sniggering at her or blowing up her picture to hand over to the North Yorkshire police.

'Oh, chillax,' said Val, his green eyes ablaze with mischief. 'They've gone. Talking of picnics, as they were, I'm peckish. I wish I'd brought something to eat.'

'We could, er, find a café.'

'There's a sandwich shop down the road.'

'Oh, okay.' Clare reached for the helmet.

'I'll go and pick up something. Wait here,' he said.

'I'm not waiting here. What if that man and his wife come back?'

'There's no chance of that, is there?' Val nipped the tip of his cigarette between his fingers to kill it. 'Promise, I'll only be two minutes. Oh, haven't got any change, have you?'

'I've only got this twenty-pound note.' She pulled it from her pocket.

Val snatched it out of her hand. 'That'll do.'

'You're not going to leave me here, are you?' said Clare as he revved up the engine.

'Might do.' He grinned and roared off.

After half an hour, Clare was beginning to panic. Plus, the wind was coming across the sea now, bringing with it spots of rain. She was frozen and she had no coat or money or phone with her. How stupid was she, letting him leave without her? Her parents were right, after all: she really should learn to engage her brain more. That was their stock phrase for her when she was growing up.

To her tremendous relief she heard the mosquito-type buzz of a bike engine getting closer and into her range of vision came the black rider on the black bike. When he lifted his helmet she could smell beer on his breath.

'You've been to a pub?'

'Had to call in the Dog and Duck to get these.' He took two packs of sandwiches out of his pocket. 'The garage was shut.'

She didn't believe him but neither did she want to make a fuss.

'Cold?' he said, watching her teeth chatter.

'Very.'

Ludwig would have stripped his coat off at this point and hung it around her shoulders. Val Hathersage gave her first pick of the sandwiches. She picked the cheese and left him with the tuna.

They sat down on the bench.

'I used to come up here with Colleen,' said Val, through a mouthful of bread.

'I think you loved Colleen,' said Clare, biting back her annoyance. 'Why didn't you marry her?'

'Because she was already married,' said Val. 'To my brother.'

Chapter 65

Joan feigned puppyish delight whenever they came across the name of Moody, and she scribbled down the details on her pad. There was page after page of entries: deaths seemed to outweigh marriages, and births of boys outweighed those of girls. The pattern continued. At this rate, Ren Dullem would be a place totally populated by bachelors in ten years, thought Joan. Either that or it would be a ghost town.

In 1969 saw the death of Seymour Elias Acaster, which she noted but read without comment. She carried on turning the pages. More boys born, more marriages, more deaths of the dwindling village population but, she noticed, no expiry notice for Raine de la Mer. She *was* still living, then; that would explain why money from the estate was still being paid to her, although no other widow was afforded the same courtesy. What was so special about Raine de la Mer? And, more to the point – was there a story in it that newspapers might be interested in? Joan's mind was always on the cash.

Chapter 66

Clare stopped chewing.

'She was married to your brother?'

Val laughed. 'Yep.'

'Gene?'

'Gene.'

'Did he know you were . . . ?'

'Well, yes, seeing as he found us in Spice Wood together.'

'When did all this happen?'

'Last year. His divorce came through a few months ago. Understandably we don't talk. Frank tried to be a mediator but Gene took the stance that if he wasn't against me then he was against him. Brotherly relations are not good.' He smiled as if it were all a big joke.

So Gene Hathersage had been married to the wayward Colleen, then. *He* was the brother whose heart had been broken. That explained why he wasn't exactly in line for any Smiler of the Year award.

'Did he hit you?' Clare imagined Gene coming at him like a bull.

'I thought he was going to, but he just turned and walked away.'

'And what did Colleen do?'

'She ran after him but he wouldn't have anything to do with

her. She went half mad trying to get him back – pleading,
breaking into his house, crying, following him wherever he
went.'

'Weren't you upset?'

'That she cried about him whilst she was in bed with me? It
got annoying.'

'She slept with you afterwards?' Clare gasped.

'Yeah,' replied Val, as if it were the most normal thing in the
world. 'Colleen wanted a man who was made up from parts of
me and parts of Gene, with Frank's farm thrown in. She always
craved what she couldn't have. She was more in love with Gene
when he turned his back on her than she ever was when they
were together. Well, as much as Colleen could love.'

What a charmer, thought Clare. She couldn't wait to go
home and tell the others.

'I ought to be getting back,' she said as a large blob of rain
landed on her hand. The sky had darkened by degrees in the
last minute.

'You eating that?' Val pointed to the uneaten half of Clare's
sandwich. She handed it over to him and he stuffed it into his
mouth before picking up his helmet. Clare climbed on the bike
behind him.

'Let's see what this little beauty can do,' said Val, revving up
the engine and speeding off at a crazy pace, with Clare hanging on tightly, her eyes squeezed shut and her mouth crying
protestations.

He stopped the bike at the bottom of the hill. Clare lifted off
her helmet and was sick at the side of the road.

'Whoops. You all right there?' He sounded more amused
than concerned.

'You drove like a maniac. I asked you to slow down and you
sped up.' Her legs felt as insubstantial as marshmallows and
about as capable of holding her up.

'Lighten up, will you?'

'You could have killed us, weaving in and out of traffic like that. I have no protective clothing on, if you hadn't noticed.'

He sighed, bored. 'You can walk the rest of the way, can't you? Save me a bit of time. I've got to take the bike back.'

'And I've lost a shoe,' cried Clare crossly.

'I wasn't turning back for it on a busy A road.' Val grinned inside his helmet. That grin was starting to get on Clare's nerves. 'I'll meet you here tomorrow at twelve if you like.'

'I can't. I'm busy.' *As if I want a repeat performance of that!*

'Suit yourself.' Val treated her to another Harrison Ford lop-sided grin, but Clare wasn't in the least bit impressed by it any more. She was cold, wet, wind-blown, traumatized and, she remembered, immediately after he drove off spraying her with earth, also £20 short.

Clare arrived back at Well Cottage shivering and embarrassed. More people than ever were on the road as she'd walked back, and she'd had to pass them whilst wearing only one shoe and sporting hair like Ken Dodd's. Lara and May exchanged puzzled glances when she walked in.

'What the heck happened to you?'

'Just don't ask,' said Clare, reaching for the hand towel that was hanging on a hook by the sink. 'Don't bloody ask.'

They asked. Why was she carrying a box of cleaning stuff and walking about with one shoe on?

Clare didn't mention Val. She felt disgusted with herself, but at least the scales had been lifted from her eyes and she could see Val Hathersage for what he was: a knob. He wasn't a sexy man of mystery or a non-conformist spirit. He was Tianne Lee with designer stubble: shallow and self-serving, a tease, a game-player and, after what he had done to his brother, a total shit.

She wished she were more like May and Lara who evidently found it cathartic to unburden themselves and talk things through. She, however, would rather just forget the Val Hathersage episode ever happened. That way she might fool herself into thinking that it really hadn't.

'I've just come back from Raine's house,' she said finally.

'How come you ended up wearing one shoe, though? Did it dissolve in your bleach?' laughed May.

'I threw it over the cliff,' Clare said, reciting the story she had concocted on the walk back up the hill. 'And before you ask, no, I didn't mean to. I took my shoes off to climb up and wash the windows and didn't realize one of them had fallen in the bucket. And it's really windy up there.'

Clare couldn't believe they bought it. What they couldn't believe was that she was spending a big chunk of her holiday doing housework.

'She's a lovely old lady,' said Clare. 'I wanted to help her out a bit. It's odd but ... I feel as if I've known her a lot longer than I have. I like her company. And her cat.' Then she was distracted by the crutch at Lara's side. 'Where did this come from?'

May was standing by the window, looking across at High Top through the blur of rain on the glass.

'Why would anyone want to live up there? It looks as if the cliff might break off and take the house into the sea with it. Surely it must be risky?'

'It's the house she lived in with her husband,' replied Clare. 'She won't be moved. Anyway, I'll ask again: where did this crutch come from? Don't tell me that Gene Hathersage made it for you?'

Lara grunted by way of an answer.

'Ooh. He has the hots for you, Lars.'

'Get lost,' replied Lara.

'I heard something interesting about him ... from Raine,' Clare said and she told them what she had learned about the brothers Hathersage and Colleen Landers.

Chapter 67

The storm was like a child's tantrum. The sky stamped its feet and made a lot of noise but its energies were soon spent. The sun chased away the weakened grey clouds and the wind stilled. Within half an hour the strange, puffy, fake clouds were back spoiling things again.

'Anyone fancy a limp down to the pub?' asked Lara at teatime. 'We could have a bar meal and some very expensive drinks at offcumden prices.'

'Will you manage?' asked Clare.

'I'll find out,' replied Lara, not ruling out the possibility that Gene Hathersage had designed the crutch to fall to pieces after forty paces so she'd fall and sprain her other ankle. She immediately admonished herself for being so mean. After Clare had told them about his ex-wife, Colleen, she'd played his words back in her head and found that, as he had claimed, he'd actually been a realist, not a sexist. He was right: women could be every bit as evil as men. Take Tianne Lee, for instance. A first-class bitch if ever there was one.

She hoped they wouldn't bump into him down the hill, but a wish of this type was usually doomed, making the opposite come true. So she wasn't at all surprised when they turned the corner and there he was, walking up with a newspaper in his hand.

'Oh, just great,' said Lara.

'Play nice,' warned May.

'Evening, ladies,' said Gene, then he nodded to Lara. 'And you.'

Lara felt her lip curl back from her teeth.

'Right height for you, is it?' He flicked his finger towards the crutch.

'Yes, thank you.'

'We're going to the pub,' said Clare, as Lara and Gene stood there, glowering each other to death.

'Well, don't let me keep you. Good night,' Gene replied, bowing his head in their direction and carrying on up the hill.

'Ge— Mr Hathersage?'

Lara's sense of decency forced her to speak. He stopped walking but didn't turn around.

'Yeah?'

Lara limped up the hill and stood squarely in front of him.

'I owe you an apology. I was much too opinionated the last time we spoke. I shouldn't have said what I said. You were right. I was wrong.'

He nodded but didn't move.

'Ok-ay,' said Lara. 'Well . . . thanks for listening.' She started to walk away from him, snarling under her breath.

'I'm going to choose another dog in the morning. Would you like to come with me?'

Lara's mouth dropped open, like the mouth of one of the fishes he carved on his pieces. She turned back to him. 'Er . . . yeah, yeah. Why not?'

'I'll pick you up at ten,' he said. And was off.

'What was all that about?' asked May when Lara caught up with them.

'Gene Hathersage wants to show me some puppies,' said Lara.

'Dirty sod. That's what they all say,' Clare said with a wink.

*

The regulars were in the pub: Milton Bird puffing on his empty pipe, Shirley's Uncle Morris. Thankfully there was no Daisy Unwin; unfortunately that meant there was no Frank Hathersage either. May thought she could just about put up with abuse from the former in order to be in the same room as the latter for a while.

They ordered scampi and chips for three and noticed that their bar bill was considerably cheaper this time around.

'I think we've suddenly become locals.' Clare giggled.

'God forbid,' replied Lara. Although she didn't really mean that. She would miss Ren Dullem in a strange way. If nothing else it had taken her thoughts away from Manor Gardens and the people associated with it. Well, mostly. She shooed away a stray thought of Keely hovering with her arms folded and her overly made-up face grimacing in her evil teenage way – whilst in the background Garth picked his nose and wiped bogeys on every available surface. Lara shuddered and batted the image out of her head.

The atmosphere in the pub was certainly more accepting of them, they all noticed. Jenny and her equally portly male friend came in just after nine and smiled big hellos.

They were all quite tiddly by ten and wended a very meandering path home.

'That was a nice evening,' declared May. 'And isn't it warm? I feel as if I'm in Spain.'

'I wish,' said Clare. The gins hadn't anaesthetized her self-disgust. She hoped she never bumped into that old couple again. What must they have thought?

'I like it here,' said Lara, hobbling expertly by now. Her ankle was healing well. She would use the last of the comfrey leaves in a poultice tonight. 'I might not go home.'

May waved the word 'home' away. There wasn't enough gin in the world to dull the pain of what lay in store for her there.

'Why did we leave this holiday so long?' said Clare. 'I don't want to be one of those people who only catches up with friends at funerals.'

'Then let's promise to meet up more often,' Lara suggested.

'I promise.'

'I promise.' Clare added her voice to May's.

But they all knew, as soon as the words were out, that when they returned to their real lives, those promises would be as insubstantial as the air they were said in. Life had an annoying habit of getting in the way of living.

Chapter 68

Lara could easily have woken up with a hangover the next morning had Clare not been the sensible one and made them all drink a pint of water before retiring. The hands of the clock swam into focus: nine thirty. She sprang out of bed, cross that she hadn't remembered to set the alarm, and hobbled into the bathroom to wash and throw on some make-up. She slipped on jeans and a pink shirt she was saving for best, then gave herself a subtle spritz of perfume whilst wondering why she had agreed to go and look at puppies with Gene Hathersage.

When she emerged from the loo, May was in the kitchen putting on the kettle. She turned, saw Lara and wolf-whistled.

'Does it look as if I've made too much of an effort?' Lara panicked. 'I don't want him to think that I have. Even though I haven't, obviously.'

'I think you've got it just right,' said May.

As the clock chimed ten, a horn blasted outside.

'Go check out his puppies, then.' May smirked, her eyebrows raised.

Lara threw her the Vs, grabbed her handbag and crutch and hobbled out.

Gene was holding the passenger door open for her. She hoped he wasn't looking at her bum as he helped her in because it wasn't as small as it should be.

'The vet says there's a dog they haven't been able to home at the place I'm going to, and he wondered if I'd be interested,' said Gene, slipping the truck into first gear.

'What sort is it?'

'Greyhound.'

'Ah.' Lara smiled. 'My auntie had a retired running greyhound, Jim. He was the laziest animal I think I've ever met.' She remembered that he was constantly curled up in a ball in his fireside bed. Her auntie made him a red furry coat for winter walks which he wore with a haughty lift to his head, as if it were a Vivienne Westwood.

'This one hasn't ever run in a race,' said Gene, turning up the lane which was flanked with old mattresses and rubbish. Lara thought she heard him mutter 'Bloody Milton' under his breath.

'Where are we going?'

'Whitby. Just outside.'

They joined the A road and Lara looked out of the window. She had become too used to the slow pace of life in Ren Dullem; it was all so fast and busy here.

'You eaten?' asked Gene.

'Er ... no, not yet.' Gene indicated left and turned into a roadside café. It had a large sign above it: F annies.

'Sounds delightful,' said Lara.

'Frannies. The "r" has fallen off,' Gene explained. 'The dog people asked if I'd call at eleven instead of half-past ten. I thought we might as well pass the time by having some breakfast.'

'Oh, okay.'

He helped her out of the truck with a hand supporting her elbow, and passed her the crutch.

'You're just missing a parrot,' he said, a twinkle creeping into his eyes and warming them. He had a totally different face when he smiled, thought Lara. Almost pleasant.

A waitress led them over to a booth. The seats were bright red and bouncy and everything looked very clean. Gene handed her a menu.

'Have what you like,' he said.

Lara looked at the extensive list of offerings: everything from blueberry pancakes with cream to the Fancy Full Franny, which must have lent itself to lots of mispronunciations and made her wonder if that's what the person who created the menu had in mind.

'What can I get for you?' asked the waitress, pen poised over her pad.

'Frannie's sausage filler,' replied Lara, very carefully. 'And a filter coffee, please.'

'Same for me. With an orange juice,' added Gene, handing the waitress the menus.

'It's like a *Carry On* film in here,' whispered Lara. 'Do you think that menu is deliberately saucy?'

'As saucy as this bottle of HP,' said Gene, picking it up. Lara noticed how hairy his arms were. She turned her head to the window to stop noticing.

'So, what made you apologize, then?' said Gene. 'Local gossip machine been working overtime, has it?'

Lara puffed out her cheeks. 'I just heard that I didn't have the monopoly on mashed hearts,' she said. 'I could cringe at some of the things I said yesterday. Way over the top and not what I really think at all. I was just angry and spouting off.'

'Hmm,' he replied. 'Well, I imagine you're a bit raw. I've had longer to get over things.'

'Are you over them? Her?'

Gene shrugged. 'There's no way back, if that's what you're asking me.'

'The answer doesn't quite match the question, no.'

Gene sat back against the seat. 'With the perspective of time I've come to realize that it would never have worked. Colleen was restless. Even when we were kids she couldn't enjoy anything because her eye was always on what the next thrill would be. She had to have drama, excitement or she grew very bored very quickly. She was tired of me until I didn't want her any more and then she saw me as a challenge. It wasn't me she wanted; it was to win the game.'

She sounded like Tianne. A living, breathing grenade whose purpose was to cause as much noise and fire and destruction as possible.

'Do I still hurt? Yes, but it's getting less,' he went on. 'But I think it's more to do with my ego being battered than my heart.'

They were briefly interrupted whilst the waitress brought the coffees and orange juice.

'When I walked off after finding her with my brother I was resolute that it was over. It wasn't as easy to say no to her when she arrived at my door the next morning, crying, begging. I wanted to believe everything she said about never doing it again and how sorry she was,' said Gene, his eyes on his hands resting on the table.

'But still you didn't change your mind?'

'It wasn't the first time she'd been unfaithful. But I was determined then not to take her back. All the other times I'd fallen for her promises and lies, so when it happened again I knew I couldn't keep pinging between the pain of thinking I'd lost her and the ecstasy of having her back. Whatever she felt for me wasn't love. Not my sort of love anyway.'

He raised his eyes to hers.

'You might think you're strong now, but be prepared for a charm offensive when you go back home. Promises are easy to make and easier to break. And you'll want to hear him apologize and promise you everything will be okay.'

Lara nodded. She knew really that, however resolute she intended to be, faced with a begging, pleading James she couldn't guarantee that she wouldn't weaken. She was dreading finding out.

'Two Frannie's sausage fillers,' announced the waitress, appearing at their side, holding the edges of the plate in a folded towel. 'Watch out, the plates are furning. I mean burning.'

'She must be so used to saying "f" words they take over her whole language,' confided Lara across the table. Gene laughed. It was a nice sound, thought Lara. Genuine and from the depths of him.

'Has it put you off relationships?' asked Lara, squeezing ketchup over the sausage, muffins and eggs.

'Yes,' said Gene. 'Ren Dullem isn't exactly awash with women, as you know. That suits me fine.'

'Not all women are the same,' said Lara, hoping they weren't starting that argument again.

'Didn't say they were. I just don't want another one.' He speared a sausage as if imagining it were Colleen's neck.

'I'll take it that this isn't a date, then.' Lara laughed, then wished she hadn't made the joke, as it sounded flirty.

'No, it isn't,' said Gene Hathersage, spearing another sausage as if it were her neck this time.

Chapter 69

Clare dragged May down to the lagoon for a swim. May stayed half an hour and then left her to it. She went back up to the cottage to dry her hair before going out to the baker's. She thought that fresh cream cakes might be a nice treat for this afternoon whilst sitting outside on the small terrace.

It was a lovely day, despite those annoying pretend clouds. May put on her favourite summery dress and strappy sandals and decided to sit on the front with a coffee and a pastry from Jenny's. She found a bench and watched the seagulls squealing and circling and noseying above a fishing boat bobbing at the edge of the cove in the hope that it might offer them some pickings.

'Hi,' said a voice behind her. An unmistakable deep man's voice with a smile in it. May wiped her mouth quickly because the pastry crumbs had welded themselves onto her lip-stick.

'Hello, there,' she said, shielding her eyes from the sun.

'Breakfast?' said Frank.

'Yes.'

'Me too.' He was holding a paper bag and a coffee from the kiosk of rude Mr Unwin. 'Mind if I join you?'

I'd be absolutely chuffed to bits if you did, said May's heart. 'Of course not, no,' said May's mouth. Frank wavered. 'I mean no,

I don't mind – not no, I do mind,' explained May before bursting into a chuckle. 'Just sit down.'

As Frank opened up the bag the delicious smell of fried egg and sausage escaped from it. 'I'm just grabbing a light bite,' he said and winked.

'Doing anything special today?' asked May, hoping she didn't look like the singing detective with all the flakes of pastry on her.

'Daisy's gone to the hospital this morning with her cousin, Pauline. I always try to take her out for a nice lunch or dinner when she gets back from her appointments. She gets a bit upset with all the tests they make her do.'

'You don't go with her, then?'

'She doesn't want me to go. She doesn't want to rub it in,' said Frank. 'I'm presuming, because nothing stays quiet around here for long, you know that it was me who caused her to be paralysed.'

'I had heard.' May was thinking she obviously didn't know Daisy Unwin that well, then. May would have put money on her being a master rubber-inner.

'Your pastry looks nice,' said Frank after a few mouthfuls of his sandwich. 'Come from Jenny's shop, by any chance?'

'Yep.'

'She's a good girl, is Jenny. It's just a shame she has so few customers. The old ones don't like to spend their money eating out and there aren't many young ones left.'

'This village needs a serious kick up the butt,' May said. 'I'd love to get my hands on it. Even the name of it is ... dull.'

'You know the proper name for it?' asked Frank.

'Proper name?'

'Reines de la Mer. It's French. It got shortened over the years to Ren Dullem.'

'Reines de la Mer?' May rolled the words around in her mouth. 'Queens of the sea? Why was it called that?'

'People said that strange sea creatures used to inhabit the harbour once upon a time.'

'What, like giant squid? Sea serpents?'

'Sirens, mermaids, whatever you want to call them. Attracted by the handsome sailors.' Frank grinned. 'For good luck, the village was named in their honour so they'd be flattered enough not to cause any damage to the fishing boats.'

'How charming! And what a shame that the name was shortened. That would be the first thing I'd change back.'

'Is that what you do? Are you some sort of town planner?'

'No, I help set up new businesses,' explained May. 'I like to think of myself as a sort of financial fairy godmother.'

'Sounds a lot more fun than my job. Although I wouldn't be anything else. All I ever wanted to be was a farmer.'

'Nothing wrong with farming,' May said. 'I always wanted to keep chickens. Dad had a couple when I was a young girl: Elsie and Deirdre. I used to have a freshly laid boiled egg every morning, till an urban fox broke in and killed them.' She remembered that her dad had cried when he'd found them, for the fox hadn't eaten them, just worried them to death. He didn't get any more chickens after that.

'I've got chickens, pigs, ducks, geese and an old donkey. It's more like an animal sanctuary than a working farm.' Frank lifted the coffee to his lips.

He has a nice mouth, thought May, imagining it on her own. She swung her head away before she blushed.

'So are you going anywhere nice with Daisy when she gets back today?'

'We're going for dinner tonight. She likes this French place in Whitby. Not really my sort of thing but,' he shrugged, 'it's something I can do to make up for her having to keep going back and being prodded and poked at.'

Oh, you poor man. What a burden of guilt to carry. She only just stopped herself from putting her arms around his shoulders and hugging him. She had better go before she over-rode her safety catch.

'Well, it's been nice seeing you again, Frank,' she said, standing and picking up her litter. 'I hope you have a lovely meal later.'

'Thank you, May,' he said. She felt full of warm syrup hearing him say her name.

'Bye.'

She turned from him and began walking, knowing that he was watching her. She concentrated on trying not to trip or let the wind blow up the skirt of her floaty dress, Marilyn Monroe-style.

Chapter 70

Gene insisted on paying the bill. He wouldn't even let Lara pay as a gesture of thanks for the crutch. She could move quite fast on it now and reckoned she wouldn't need it in a couple of days. She wondered whether she should ask if he wanted it back.

They arrived at their destination at quarter past eleven: a rescue centre which had a long twisting drive flanked by huge trees that blocked out the sunlight. At the end of the drive was a large stone house with outbuildings next to it. Penny, the lady to whom Gene had spoken on the phone, was waiting for him in the doorway. She was a straight-backed no-nonsense horsey type wearing a disposable apron.

'Mr Hathersage? Welcome. I'm Penny.' She held out a meaty hand and gave Gene's a thorough shake. She threw a friendly hello at Lara too as she was getting out of the truck. 'Come in, come in and meet Gracie and Poppet. You okay there?'

'I'm fine,' replied Lara, following Penny and Gene into a sizeable kitchen dominated by a huge red Aga. At the side of it, curled into a small ball, was a light-grey dog looking up at the strangers with wary grey eyes. A shaggy little pup came bounding over from across the room, his tail wagging so much that he almost knocked himself over with it.

'This is Poppet and that over there is Gracie,' breezed Penny.

'I gave you first refusal on Poppet but if you don't want him, he's got two people on the waiting list. As for our Gracie, well, she's been in the wars a bit, poor thing. She was found very scared in the woods with her back leg in a very bad state, so God knows what she'd been through. Had to take it off but she's doing very well. The vet thinks she's no more than nine months old. Bit nervy. Doesn't like noise or plastic bags. Likes a basket by a fireside and she'll sneak up on your lap when she thinks you aren't looking. Needs some patience and love and a quiet life.'

Don't we all, thought Lara, as Poppet jumped up at her in an effort to claim her attention.

'Someone took her and then brought her back after two days because she wouldn't come to them. I want to know that whoever takes her will persevere with her. I don't want any more upsets for her, she's had more than her share,' Penny said with a stern edge in her voice.

Gene squatted down to the basket, offering the back of his hand. Penny moved away and picked up Poppet, who was trying to cut in on the action.

'Hello, girl,' Gene whispered. 'How are you doing?'

Gracie shivered to her three feet and, just when Lara thought she was going to walk away, her head came forward and she sniffed at Gene's fingers. He was talking to her gently, words that Lara couldn't make out because they were so quiet.

'He's got the touch,' said Penny. 'Lovely creature.'

Lara wasn't sure if she meant Gracie or Gene. The way he was trying to make a connection with the dog, talking to her softly, was fascinating to watch. She hadn't thought he could be so patient. Gracie didn't seem to be put off by his wild hair and black beard. In fact she settled down in her bed and let him stroke her head, even closing her eyes.

'What do you think? Are you the man for our special little girl?' asked Penny, her friendly head on a tilt. 'Or are you more of a Poppet man?'

Gene turned to Lara. 'Well, which do you think I should take?'

'Are you kidding? You have to take Gracie. Poppet's got the chance of a home, two other homes.'

Gene nodded and turned to Penny. 'Yep. I think Gracie would fit in at La Mer, if you think I'm suitable to take her.' He straightened up. 'Got a space by the fireside waiting for her. I think I must be a sucker for the wobbly-leg type.' He cast a furtive glance in Lara's direction.

'Can we say the weekend, then, for pick-up?' asked Penny, struggling to hold giddy little Poppet.

'Good for me,' replied Gene.

I won't see her settled in, thought Lara with a sad gulp. I'll be gone.

Penny saw them out.

'Pleasure to meet you, Mr Hathersage, Mrs Hathersage.'

Lara opened her mouth to say that they weren't married, but it was too much hassle to explain. For a moment, she imagined herself as Mrs Gene Hathersage. Then she imagined living at La Mer with a three-legged greyhound in a basket by the wood-burning stove in the kitchen. It wasn't a thought that had her rushing in panic to the hills, as it would have done on day one of her holiday.

Chapter 71

Gladys was frosty with her again and Joan didn't know why. She had been politeness itself to the woman and yet Gladys was throwing her enough cold looks to turn her into a snowman. That was unfortunate as Joan was hoping to engage her in conversation over a nice cup of tea and some cake, and subtly winkle information out of her.

Joan needed to go back to the Internet café in Wellem. It was such a nuisance having no access to Google in the village. There were questions that needed answering because at the moment she had crumbs of information that refused to bind together. She was missing the link that would connect all the pieces.

At the moment it wasn't much of a story to deliver to the newspapers for a mighty sum, but she suspected that it had the makings of a scoop. What she knew so far was that Gilbert Carlton, lord of the manor, was out in a boat in 1928 with twelve fishermen and the boat sank, but the rain saved them. Or a very able dolphin. For some reason Gilbert paid money to all twelve of them and the mysterious R, who was probably a woman called Raine de la Mer. And that money was still being paid to R, the wife of Seymour Acaster. R Acaster was the heir of the Carlton estate. And it looked as if she was still alive because if she wasn't, wouldn't Edwin have made a new will? Then again, Mrs Acaster had to be a hundred if she was a day. It had to be an oversight. She herself had claimed some of Stanley's benefits for a month after he died – putting it down to grief when they caught up with her. Someone in Ren Dullem had been creaming off the estate for many years, though. Joan had to applaud their brass neck.

'So why did you take me with you?' asked Lara as they drove down the ridiculously littered lane that led to Ren Dullem.

'As a guiding beacon to steer me away from sentimentality,' Gene said, and sniffed. 'I thought that as a hard-nosed business woman you would help me make a sensible decision and not automatically load me with a dog that would require extra maintenance.'

Lara snorted with laughter. 'Sorry,' she said. 'And she's female.'

'Bound to be trouble, then.'

He sounded so grumpy yet Lara knew he was play-acting with her. He was as pleased as punch that he would be adopting Gracie at the weekend. He was looking forward to seeing her wander in, sniff around and settle herself by the fire when she realized she was home.

'I was being sensible. I couldn't see you with a ball of cotton wool like Poppet. You're more of a hound man.'

'Even three-legged ones.'

'You could make her a crutch. Don't forget the fish.'

She saw Gene's eyes crinkle and his mouth smile under his beard.

They were seconds away from Well Cottage.

'Thank you,' he said, using the same gentle tone of voice he had used with Gracie.

'I enjoyed it,' said Lara. 'And the Frannie's sausage filler,' she added. 'I only wish I could see Gracie walk into your house for the first time and take up residence by the fire.'

'You'll be catching up with all your stuff on your computer by then,' said Gene, braking by the front door.

'Very probably.' She sighed, and a cold draught brushed against her heart as she visualized it.

Chapter 72

When gardeners arrived taking Lord Carlton's attention, Joan took the opportunity to nip out to Wellem to get 'some feminine things', as she put it. Gladys huffed and nodded her assent.

Joan had to ask. 'Gladys, have I offended you in any way?'

Gladys hardly knew where to start. But she remembered Edwin's warning that if she stirred up trouble it wouldn't be Joan who was out on her ear.

'Of course not,' she said with a cold smile. 'I'll tell Lord Carlton where you are, if he asks.'

Joan wasn't convinced, but she had bigger fish to fry than humouring an old woman's moods. She took the bus into Wellem which, annoyingly, was extra full of people as there was a midsummer fair on. Luckily the Internet café was quiet as everyone was outside enjoying the sunshine. Joan got out her notepad and pen, reviewed what she had written, then started to type into the Google search box.

What does Illis quos amo deserviam mean? These were the words cut into Seymour Acaster's gravestone. The answer came up immediately, under Romantic Quotes: 'For those I love I shall sacrifice.' Joan wrote it down but she was still no wiser. The translation to that quote was obviously not the magic binding agent.

Where is High Top in Ren Dullem? It was a long shot, seeing as even Google didn't know anything about the village, never mind an individual house. Google wasn't helpful. It returned search results of window-cleaners in Ipswich, shops selling sports shoes and a porn site featuring busty women smoking cannabis.

Next on Joan's list was: *Why are no girls born in an area?* That brought up lots of irrelevant results about China and India so she changed the question to: *Why are no boys born in an area?* That didn't lead to anything but wider issues of choosing the sex of a child and declining birth rates. Joan tapped her fingers on the keyboard.

Raine

She read: 'People with this name tend to be visionary, with great spiritual powers. They are inspirational and powerful and have an overwhelming desire for a stable home life and/or community.'

Apparently it was a Teutonic name meaning, not rain, but counsel or mighty army. In German it meant strong. Joan didn't even bother to write any of that claptrap down.

Reine

Lots of references to a Norwegian fishing village. Obviously it was also the French word for queen.

Joan pressed the back arrow to take her to the search bar again. To *Reine* she added *de la mer – words associated with* and wished she hadn't. Numerous entries came up, ranging from ships named as such to waltzes and hotels. Les Sirènes de la mer, Crème de la Mer, Walter de la Mare, Maris Piper potatoes ... She felt like picking up the monitor and throwing it at the wall.

She tried the only phrase she didn't recognize: *Les Sirènes de la mer.* It brought up a host of French entries. She clicked on the first and was grateful for the 'Translate this page' option. It didn't translate it very well.

**_Les Sirènes de la mer – known alsos as
reines de la mer_**

_Sirenia is an order of aquatic, herbivorous mammals
that marine waters, rivers, swamps etc. inhabit.
Including those as manatees and dugong which have
adaptations for the aquatic: steering arms and a
propulsing paddle. Hydro-dynamic with very much
muscular although appear fat. Mariners often
mistaking the presents of these animals in the waters
for mermaids, legendary creatures of the aquatic
bearing human body upper with fish tail of the lower.
Often depicted in artworks of great note as harbingers
of floods, storms, shipwrecks, drowning. Also folk
traditionally can be benevolence, saviours of humans
in need and of falling in love with sailors. An
association with Sirens of Greek mythology whose
enchantment of singing voices could not be resistable,
hences Queens of the Sea._

Joan threw down her pen in disgust. So that was it, then.
Unless old Raine was a frigging mermaid, she had reached a
dead end in her Internet searching.

The only thing she had left to do now was find out where
High Top was and introduce herself to the woman who lived
there. She'd get the story from the horse's mouth. From Raine
de la Mer herself. Or whoever was claiming monies from the
Carlton estate in her name.

Gladys asked for the afternoon off. In all the forty years she had
worked for Lord Carlton she had never asked for this and of
course he could not deny her.

'Is everything all right, Gladys?' he asked, pulling on his gardening gauntlets.

'Yes, yes, it's fine,' she lied. It wasn't fine, not at all. She needed to speak to Raine and it wouldn't wait. And no better time to do it than when Mrs Sly and Mighty was out of the house herself. Otherwise she wouldn't put it past her to follow Gladys up to High Top.

Gladys took with her a basket of food from the larder and a fresh trout from the lake. She never turned up at Raine's empty-handed. She walked as fast as her legs would take her through the village and up through Spice Wood. She knew she wouldn't sleep if she didn't see her old friend.

Raine was dozing in her chair outside in the sun when Gladys arrived. Faithful Albert was on her lap as usual. Raine's odd-coloured eyes sprang open just as Gladys was about to nudge her. Her weathered old face broke into a smile.

'Hello, my dear, how lovely to see you.' Then the smile slipped as she registered Gladys's furrowed brow and the worry in her eyes. 'Whatever's the matter?'

'Raine, I need to talk to you. Can we go inside?'

'Yes, of course. Come in.'

Gladys wheeled Raine through the door and sat down heavily on the sofa. She barely knew where to start.

Chapter 73

No one could be bothered to cook and when May suggested they go to Jenny's and have lunch made for them, there was a resounding yes by way of response.

'Are you sure Gene Hathersage didn't try to kiss you when you got out of his truck?' Clare asked Lara as they walked down the hill.

'I've told you, no. He's not interested in women. He went to great lengths to tell me that. Not that I'm bothered because I'm not interested in men.'

'Okay, we believe you.'

'Good.'

As they passed Spice Wood, Clare was relieved to see that Val Hathersage wasn't hanging around waiting for her. Not that she would have been tempted to join him. She couldn't help thinking what would have happened if the old couple had called the police and they came to arrest her whilst she was waiting 'two minutes' for Val to return with their lunch. What if she had been arrested and her name would have appeared in the national papers? What if her parents had read it? She felt sick at the thought and shuddered.

'Cold?' asked May, seeing her.

'No, someone just walked over my grave,' fibbed Clare.

'Please, please, God, make Daisy Unwin not be in here,' said

May under her breath as they approached the Front Café. She wasn't, but a few other locals were. They nodded a hello, even if they didn't actually say the word.

'Hello, ladies.' Jenny came bustling over, wearing a brightly coloured gingham apron made of the same material as the tablecloths. 'Can I get you something to drink whilst you're looking through the menu?'

They ordered three fizzy lemon juices; it was too warm for coffee today.

'There's no reason why this café couldn't be extended at the front to have an outdoor eating area,' mused May.

Lara raised her hands. 'Please don't get me started on what I'd do with Ren Dullem if I had half the chance.'

'You too?' Clare chuckled. 'I lie in bed at night planning changes. So far I've reorganized the market, redesigned the park and renovated all those derelict cottages opposite the woods.'

'Ooh, guess what I was told?' May suddenly remembered an interesting fact from her conversation with Frank. 'We aren't actually staying in Ren Dullem. We are staying in Reines de la Mer.' She sat back and let the others absorb that.

'More needed,' prompted Clare.

'Apparently the village was named after the mermaids that once lived in the sea so they wouldn't sink the fishing boats. Clare, steady on. It's a legend,' said May, seeing Clare's eyes widening.

'And who did you hear all this from?' asked Lara.

'Er, Frank. I bumped into him earlier on. We had a little chat. Don't look at me like that, you two. '

Jenny returned to take their order and they had to suspend their conversation whilst they hurriedly chose.

'Spicy chicken and rice for me, please,' said Lara.

'Baked potato with chilli and cheese, please,' May added to the order.

'All-day breakfast, please, with extra mushrooms,' said Clare, turning to Lara. 'That's your fault for talking about your breakfast this morning – you've got me craving sausages.'

'I shan't be craving any of those for a while,' replied Lara. 'Now, what has anyone got in mind for altering the harbour front?'

Chapter 74

'I'm getting old.' Gladys sighed. There was a major slump to her shoulders. She was weighed down with stress. 'I actually gave her the benefit of the doubt. I said to myself: "Gladys, maybe you've been a bit too hard on the woman. Maybe you've got things out of proportion because you like the set-up with Lord Carlton and you were too afraid of it being spoiled." So I started being a bit more friendly to Joan Hawk. Then I sneaked over and looked in her bin. I was right: she had got Edwin drunk that night. And those prawns didn't come from Wellem market, she lied. And that elder-flower cordial wasn't home-made. I'm not wrong, am I, Raine? You know I'm not. What's she up to, and can't you stop her?'

'Gladys, Gladys.' Raine closed her short stubby hand over Gladys's large and warm one. 'Look what happened the last time I interfered with fate.'

'You saved thirteen lives,' Gladys remonstrated with her.

'I condemned a whole village,' Raine replied. 'Because of my presence the village sealed itself away, girls were no longer born, people sacrificed their own happiness to protect me. That was never my intention. It was duty and honour gone mad.'

'They wanted to, though. They loved you. We all still love you. There wasn't a family in the village that wasn't related to one of those thirteen men. Everyone owed you their loyalty and allegiance.'

'What will be, will be, Gladys. I'm tired.'

Gladys's face was full of concern. 'I'm going to ask again and again until you say yes. Let us move you down to the village. None of us think you're safe up here. Cliffs are falling into the sea all the time. You're too near to the edge and there's no barrier.'

'Promise me something, Gladys. If anything happens to me, you'll make sure Albert has a good home. He hasn't long left. I'd like his last days to be happy ones.'

Gladys gasped. 'You're scaring me, Raine.'

'Promise me.'

'I'll look after Albert. You know I will.'

Raine let loose a tinkly laugh, then leaned over and gave Gladys a kiss on the cheek. 'You're a good friend. You must not worry. Now, would you do me a favour, Gladys? I have a letter to write and I can't find any paper or pencils. The day ladies sometimes put things I don't use in the top cupboards in the kitchen. Would you have a look in there for me?'

Chapter 75

Over their meal May, Clare and Lara completely overhauled Ren Dullem, carefully, though, so as not to ruin its quaintness. Any new builds would have to be made from old stone, the car park would have to be on the edge of the village, leaving the centre a pedestrian-only zone, except for authorized vehicles – they couldn't exactly deny access to lovely Frank's van. The fly-tippers' dream area on the road into Ren Dullem would be totally cleaned up and widened, the ice-cream parlour would have an upstairs café affording a view of the harbour, and Unwin's coffee kiosk would be boarded up with big nails. With all the Unwin family trapped inside.

They were just giggling about that last touch when the door opened and in walked Pauline Unwin, pulling her cousin's chair.

'Talk of the devil,' muttered Lara.

'Bloody marvellous,' said Daisy in a whisper louder than anyone else's shout.

Jenny arrived at the table with three large slices of her home-made chocolate truffle cheesecake, clotted cream on the side. They noticed that her whole demeanour changed when Daisy entered. Jenny scurried over to her table to set it with cutlery and give it an extra clean.

'That Daisy sure brings in an atmosphere with her, doesn't she?' said Lara.

'Ignore her,' replied Clare, sticking her fork into the muddy depths of the cheesecake. 'Oh, my, I've just died and gone to heaven.' Lud loved cheesecake. *Lud Lud Lud*.

'Soon be back to normal, Pauline. That funny smell will have gone.' Daisy spoke much more loudly than she needed to, since Pauline was inches away from her.

Clare giggled. 'How old is she? Ten?'

There was a clattering as Jenny dropped some cutlery.

'Oh, for God's sake, get us some more,' yelled Daisy. 'You always were a clumsy cow.'

Lara spun around in her seat; she'd heard enough. 'Don't talk to her like that.'

Daisy looked as if she had been slapped in the face and Pauline's mouth had dropped into such a large 'O' she could have stepped straight out of 'The Scream'.

'What?'

'I said don't talk to Jenny like that.'

May and Clare were silent. They didn't interfere when Lara's hackles were up.

Daisy's mouth fell into a variety of different shapes as if she were trying out some choice words before delivering them. 'What's it got to do with you?' she spat eventually. 'Can't you see how I am?' She stabbed her finger at her legs.

Lara was turning very red.

'I can see very well how you are disposed, though what that has to do with talking to someone as if they're crap is anyone's guess.'

'And what are you doing to do about it?'

Daisy's face morphed into Cassandra Wath's from Lara's schooldays. Lara had just asked her to lay off pulling a first year's hair in the toilet. *And what are you going to do about it?* Cassandra had said. *This*, Lara had replied, and she'd dragged

Cassandra over to the nearest toilet and flushed her head down it. Lara contemplated the logistics of getting Daisy into the loo. Unfortunately it was a no-goer.

'Look at you, threatening the disabled. I saw you looking at that jug of water as if you were going to throw it over me,' cried Daisy, as if she were performing to an audience.

'What jug of water?' said Lara.

'The one on the counter.'

Lara shook her head in disbelief. Daisy was joking, surely. Lara wasn't even looking in that direction.

'Let's just go,' suggested May. They couldn't finish their nice lunch in peace, and now it had been spoiled.

Clare stood and picked up her handbag. She took some notes out of her purse and handed them to Jenny.

'Keep the change, Jenny. Thanks.'

Jenny looked upset.

'And you, Scarface –' quick as a flash Daisy wheeled over and straight into May's legs – 'stop looking at my Francis. I've seen you, tart. He's mine. Piss off back down south and leave us alone.'

Lara pushed Daisy's chair away with her crutch and pushed May forwards to safety.

Before they shut the door they heard Daisy screech: 'Good riddance to bad rubbish.'

This was followed by a rather weak echo from Pauline: 'Yeah. Rubbish.' Clearly she wasn't quite brave enough to say anything in support, but even less brave about saying nothing.

'You okay?' asked Clare, bending down to look at May's legs, one of which was bleeding across the shin.

'That hurt,' replied May. There were tears in her eyes. Clare suspected they were caused as much by Daisy's reference to her scar, if not more.

'Want to borrow my crutch?' asked Lara with a soft smile, rubbing her friend's arm.

'I don't know how Frank puts up with her,' Clare said, shaking her head.

'Let's go and have an ice cream instead,' suggested Lara. 'I was really enjoying that cheesecake, as well. I shan't be sorry to be saying goodbye to her.'

May and Clare nodded their heads. The trouble was, there were too many things they really would be sorry to say goodbye to. Whilst they weren't looking, Ren Dullem had sneaked into their hearts.

The ice-cream boy-man looked just as petrified to be serving offcumdens as he had been before.

'We shall have to send him for confidence lessons when we take over the village,' decided Lara. 'He's going to waste all the profits in dropped cornets.'

They sat on the harbour front taking in the view and listening to the seagulls clamouring for attention, or fish, they weren't quite sure. There was a small boat in the distance bobbing on the gently cresting waves which were twinkling in the sunshine. Some old people were asleep on deckchairs on the small line of sand to the left. Milton Bird was one of them, a knotted handkerchief on his head and his trouser legs rolled up. His pink pumps stood side by side next to his long thin feet. He had fallen asleep mid-cornet; the ice cream was still in his hand, but it was melting onto the sand.

Lara smiled. 'Bless the mad old thing. He looks totally blissed out.'

'I'm glad you cocked up this holiday, Lars,' said Clare, her head tilted back. She felt as if the sun were holding her face in its hands.

'Yes, well done, Lars,' said May, taking a glug from a bottle of Diet Coke. 'This was your finest hour.'

'I don't want to go home,' announced Clare.

'You're okay.' Lara gave a little laugh. 'You're the only one with something to go back for.'

Clare didn't put them right. She bit down on her lip to counter the rise of emotion welling up within her. 'I'm going for a swim in the lagoon,' she said.

'I'll walk with you,' said Lara, reaching for her crutch. 'I'll sit outside and read my book. Let's get a couple of bottles of red wine from Hubbard's Cupboard and get wankered later.'

'I'll see you up there,' said May. 'I'm going to sit here and enjoy the sun whilst those stupid clouds aren't around.'

'I'm the only one without a leg injury,' said Clare as she helped Lara to her feet. 'I feel left out.'

'We could go back to Jenny's to retrieve the cheesecake and you could call Daisy a twat. I'm sure you'd get a ramming for that.'

'Cheers, Lara. On second thoughts, let me stay as the unique oddity that I am.'

Chapter 76

May stayed on the bench for another half an hour doing nothing but absorbing the quiet and the warmth. 'Busy doing nothing' was the expression that came to mind. She was always too busy to do nothing. Even when she was physically resting, her brain was usually a hive of activity, worrying about work, worrying about Michael, worrying about Susan. It was surprisingly easy not to think about Michael here. It would be harder not to think about Frank when she was back in London.

She wondered what his farm looked like from close up and thought she might have a sneak peek. She crossed the square, endured the evil eye from Mr Unwin in his coffee kiosk and walked towards the lane that led to Hathersage Farm. Frank's truck was parked so awkwardly in the first lay-by that she wasn't sure if he had crashed or not.

May looked in the window and saw Frank slumped over the driver's wheel. She rapped hard on the glass, calling his name.

'Frank, are you all right?' She opened his door and shook him gently but he hardly responded. 'Frank, what's wrong?'

She needed to get in the van with him. She ran around to the passenger door but it was wedged against a thick and prickly hedge and she really had to jerk hard to get it open far enough for her to climb inside. Her face and arms were stinging with scratches and she re-opened the wound on her leg by catching it on the step.

Once in the truck, she was in a position to push Frank backwards away from the wheel in order to see his face. He was a dead-weight. She thought he had bumped his head and knocked himself out. Then, when she saw his face, she wondered if he was drunk. His eyes were bloodshot, the lids drooping as if daylight was hurting him, and he was so very pale.

'Frank, have you crashed? Are you hurt?'

'No,' he said, his big farmer's hands reaching upwards to his head. 'Migraine.'

'Frank, I've got tablets,' said May, plunging her hand into her bag and pulling out the capsule which Lara had bought her for her birthday. It contained a pair of tights, a sewing kit, a pen, pair of scissors, nail file, emergency five-pound note and some Ibuprofen. She popped two out and put them in his hand. He swallowed them dry. Then May remembered the small bottle of Diet Coke in her bag. By now it was warm and rather flat but it was good enough for washing some tablets down. She used to get a lot of migraines and knew how debilitating they were. She still did get the odd one, but they were rare these days.

'Thanks.' Frank could talk no more. He had sunk forwards again, and his hands were cradling his head, but that was bringing him only a modicum of comfort and May knew that the best thing was to make no noise until the tablets kicked in. If his migraines were anything like hers used to be, he'd be ultra-sensitive to light and sound. She sat with him, waiting silently, not disturbing him, letting him concentrate on existing through the pain. She could imagine the thump thump thump in his temple and pitied him.

After fifteen minutes, Frank shifted position.

'Sorry,' he said.

'Nothing to be sorry for,' replied May.

'They come on so fast and I have to stop driving or I'd crash.'

'I thought you had crashed.'

Frank twisted his head slowly around to her. 'Thanks, May. I usually carry some tablets on me but I stupidly ran out and forgot to buy some more.'

'Here.' May put the packet of Ibuprofen in his glove compartment. 'Keep these. Just in case.'

He looked absolutely shocking. His face was drained of colour and his usually cheerful brown eyes were dead.

'Can I drive the truck up to the farm for you?' asked May.

'No, it's fine,' replied Frank.

'Well, it obviously isn't. Shift over here.'

May struggled out of the passenger seat again and walked around to the driver's side, this time snagging her face on a fierce bramble. She was cut to ribbons. Maybe she should have kept two of those Ibuprofen back. She bullied Frank into the passenger side and then got in where he had been sitting and adjusted the seat slightly forwards.

'And just in case you think I don't know what I'm doing, you'd be wrong. Dad was a car mechanic. I can drive anything from minis to Luton vans.'

She slipped off the handbrake, reversed out of the bush and forward up the hill. This is one way of seeing the farm, she realized. Though not the way she had originally planned.

She pulled right down the lane, as directed by the 'Hathersage Farm This Way – Slow Ducks' sign. Two ducks waddled noisily across the lane in front of them as if protesting about their presence. May pulled up in an obvious parking space at the side of a very nice classic Jaguar, presumably his 'going out in' vehicle, when he was taking Daisy to her posh French restaurant, although she doubted they'd be going tonight. The house was even prettier close up. It was painted the colour of fresh creamy butter and the heads of bright red flowers bobbed in sea-green painted boxes at the windows.

Frank stumbled out of the truck and in through the

unlocked farmhouse door, May following him into a large square kitchen and really hoping Daisy wasn't around to witness this. Not that May had any intentions of doing anything more than wringing out a cold cloth and applying it to Frank's head, as she used to do for herself.

Frank had crumpled onto a seat at a wooden table.

'Here, hold this,' said May, moving his hand and pressing the cloth against his forehead. He groaned a thank you.

What a lovely house, thought May. It was delightfully old-fashioned and simple but comfy and inviting. The broad kitchen window afforded a beautiful view of the cove. It was like looking out at a painting.

'Can I get you anything? A cup of tea or some water or something?' asked May.

'Tea would be grand, please. I always crave tea when I have one of these,' he replied, still in pain. May used to have all sorts of funny cravings when she had a migraine: lettuce sprinkled with vinegar, fruit pastilles, even the smell of Imperial Leather soap. She put the kettle on and dropped a tea bag from a tin on the work surface into each of two clean cups she found on the draining board. She remembered he took a single sugar and small splash of milk.

'Thank you, May,' he said. His face was recovering its colour, she noted. 'I might have been down there for hours. They're getting worse.'

'Have you been to see a doctor?' asked May gently.

'Yes. They're definitely migraines. I've had all the tests. Stress-heads. Not that I have a particularly stressful life, so I can't really understand it.'

Whatever he said, Frank Hathersage was a man with the world on his shoulders and the weight was breaking him.

'Frank . . .' May started. She had to bite her lip to stop herself, then found she was unable to keep her mouth shut. 'You're not okay. Any idiot can see that.'

And, to her surprise, she watched Frank's head shake slowly from side to side and heard him admit: 'No, you're right, I'm not.'

She let him talk; he knew she was listening.

'I'm not in love with Daisy. God forgive me, I don't even like her. I owe her, though, after what I did to her and I have to look after her. But the thought of marrying her ... yet I half-killed her. I've crippled her.' He was trying to cover up the fact that his eyes were wet. May's heart almost leapt with her desire to console him.

'There has to be another way of helping her rather than by sacrificing your whole life, Frank.'

'It's what we do here. We look after our own.'

'Not to the extent of making yourself ill, surely,' said May. 'You can't marry Daisy if you don't love her. It wouldn't be fair on her either.'

'She knows I don't love her,' Frank admitted. 'But her family think it's my duty to do the decent thing. She loves me. Unless I run away I have to do what is expected of me. And if I did run away I'd never live with myself for being a coward.'

'Oh, Frank. You can't carry on like this. You'll make yourself ill. Look at what the strain is doing to you.' May's hand instinctively reached for his to offer him comfort. His fingers closed around hers and she watched him lifting them, touching them, examining them.

'I really thought I could do it. I'd marry her, do my duty by her, move heaven and earth to get her walking again, and then maybe I could leave.'

'Is there a chance she could walk again?'

'It's a slight one, but yes.'

'And do you ... do you ... live together yet?'

Frank knew what she meant. 'No. We're waiting until after the wedding,' he said, closing his eyes against the thought.

God, what a joy to come, thought May.

'So, anyway, I thought I could do it. Then I saw you and you blew all my good intentions out of the water,' said Frank, so quietly and matter-of-factly that May almost missed hearing it.

'What?'

'I don't know what hit me that morning I first met you but it really did strike me like lightning. My legs actually started to shake. I knew I could never get into a bed with Daisy Unwin feeling what I did about another woman. I put it down to momentary madness, but I feel the same every time I see you.'

His fingers were threading themselves between hers. She should pull them away.

'Your head was looking for someone else to go to and save you from the situation. I was someone you didn't know—'

'Don't try to rationalize it, May. I've done that and it hasn't worked. It wasn't *someone* that brought me back to life that day, it was *you*. I've only existed in between the times I've seen you this past week – I haven't really been living. Don't tell me you don't know what I'm talking about.'

May opened her mouth but the words wouldn't come out. Yes, she had felt it; and no, it wasn't because she'd been looking for someone to repair the heart that Michael had shattered. It defied rationalization because it wasn't rational. But it was powerful and frightening and undeniable. And thrilling.

Then the sound of a car driving up to the house smashed into their perfect moment.

'That's Pauline,' said Frank.

May pointed. 'Is that the back door?'

'Yes,' said Frank, banging his head with the heel of his hand as if trying to knock something out of it.

'Tell her, Frank. Don't marry her for the wrong reasons. Don't be bullied into thinking they're the right reasons.'

Then May slipped out of the back door.

Just before it shut she heard Daisy's shrill tone: 'You'll never guess what happened to us today. One of those London bitches was going to glass me.'

Chapter 77

Only Lara slept soundly that night. May's head was too full of poor Frank to allow her brain to rest, and Clare was woken by a nightmare in which she was at work and couldn't go home until she had completed a pile of accounts, but the figures kept changing as soon as she had added up the columns. And whichever pen she used the ink turned to water and wouldn't write, however hard she pressed the nib down onto the paper. She got up at three o'clock to take some Nurofen and lay in the dark trying not to think about anything until they took effect, but that proved to be impossible, even with the thick thrumming pain in her temple.

Her mind strayed to Raine and Seymour and their story: falling in love, Seymour carrying her from the lagoon, standing up for her against the mighty Reverend Unwin, sacrificing his immortal soul for her by being buried in unconsecrated ground. She could imagine Ludwig doing those things for her. She couldn't envisage Val Hathersage putting himself out at all, even for a woman he purported to love. She wondered if he loved Colleen Landers. Probably – as much as he could. Some people could only love a little. Life must be less complicated for them, Clare thought. She didn't know if she was one of the unlucky or lucky ones, feeling everything so deeply and wanting the full fairy-story ending.

As the dull throb in her head began to lessen, Clare drifted off into a light, dreamless sleep, waking just after nine. She went down for a swim in the lagoon, diving deep into the bright water, to a world devoid of the pressures found in the life above. The lagoon would stay for ever in her memories as a magical place, symbolizing a time when she took a step out of the madness of her existence to stop and smell the roses. There weren't enough of those times in her life and she couldn't even predict when she would have the chance again.

She slipped out of the cave and into the main sea where the waters were decidedly cooler. She swam with a huge shoal of small fishes that didn't seem in the slightest bit disturbed that a big pink fish with black hair and odd-coloured eyes had decided to join them. When she looked up, she saw Raine waving down.

'I'll come up,' Clare shouted on a whim, doubting that she would be heard, but Raine nodded and wheeled herself back into the cottage.

Wrapped in a towel, Clare made the long journey up the cavern steps to High Top. Either she was getting fitter or someone had reduced the number of steps, she thought, as she took the last thirty at a run. Raine had opened the door for her and was waiting for her guest with a delighted smile on her face.

'I'm so glad you could visit me again,' said the old lady. 'Sit down. Put that blanket around your shoulders.'

Clare sat down on the sofa next to a stretched-out Albert, who was asleep, his paws twitching in a dream. In less than three days Albert and Raine and High Top would be part of her past, and who knew if she would ever see any of them again? It was a thought that she had to push back because the further it advanced to the front of her mind, the sadder she felt.

'I don't want to make your sofa wet,' said Clare.

'You smell of the sea,' said Raine, breathing in deeply. 'You love it as much as I do, don't you?'

'I don't know how I'm going to leave it behind,' said Clare. 'I wish I could fit it in my suitcase.'

'Let me make you some tea,' said Raine. 'And warm you up.'

'I'll do it,' said Clare.

But Raine insisted. 'You're my guest and after all you've done for me, it's the very least I can do for you.'

Albert sensed a knee and awoke to move his bones over to Clare's lap. He didn't seem to mind that they were chilly. He was asleep again in seconds, purring, kneading his paws on her skin. Clare could feel how thin he was as she lightly drew her fingers down his back, but at least he was content. She wished her life made her purr as much as his did.

Raine returned with the tea in a cup decorated with painted fish. Because she had to hold the cup while manoeuvring her chair, and had a slight tremor in her hands, she couldn't avoid spilling some of the tea over her blanket.

'Thank you,' said Clare, drawing warmth from the delicate china cup.

'An old friend of mine came around yesterday,' said Raine. 'She was very impressed with how the house looks.'

'Ah, that's good.' Clare smiled.

'She's the housekeeper up at Carlton Hall. You can see it from the side window there.'

'I'll have a look in a minute,' replied Clare. 'I don't think Albert would be too happy if I moved.'

'Oh, Albert,' Raine said fondly. 'He thinks the world revolves around him. The trouble is, in this house the world does. Gladys brought us some trout. He ate his share and half of mine. I don't know where he puts it; he's so skinny these days.'

'I'll miss him,' said Clare, surprising herself by bursting into tears which had been stored up inside her for so long. She rested the cup on a table to ensure she didn't cover Albert in hot tea, then pushed her towel against her face. 'I'm sorry. I don't know what's the matter with me.'

She felt Raine's hand enclose her own, and the old chilled skin gave comfort and a sympathy that made those tears flow faster.

'Yes, you do know,' said Raine. 'You know only too well what's the matter with you. You've got a wishbone where your backbone should be.'

Clare nodded. She couldn't have put it better herself. The old lady knew her too well.

'I'm in such a mess, Raine,' said Clare. 'The only time my life makes any sense is when I'm underneath the waters of the lagoon and I can leave everything behind me on the surface.'

'Oh my dear Clare.'

'I did the right thing saying goodbye to Lud. I was becoming less and less important to him and I'm fed up of being second best, so I had to let him go. But I miss him so much. I don't want to live my life without him. I won't even have a life when I get back to London. I don't know what I'm doing any more.'

'Do your friends know you feel this way? Have you talked to them?'

'I find it hard to talk. Feelings aren't "done" in my family.'

'And yet you feel very deeply. I know this,' said Raine. 'We have a connection, you and I.' She stroked Clare's wet hair.

'I'm all over the place,' said Clare, recalling her less than satisfying interlude with Val Hathersage.

'Sometimes,' said Raine, her croaky old voice smooth as she whispered, 'you have to fight your corner for your own happiness.'

'To be happy, I'd have to fight my parents, and you haven't met them.'

'You're judging yourself through their eyes. You should only judge yourself through your very own special ones. Don't you think your parents would want you to be happy?'

Clare lifted her head and her eyes engaged with Raine's. 'If I turned around to my parents and said that I wasn't taking the partnership I've been offered because it would make me unhappy, they'd be furious. I'm thirty-three years old and I'm still seeking their approval. And if that isn't pathetic enough, wait for what I'm going to say next – I finally got it, for the first time I impressed them ... And to keep impressing them I have to live a life I don't want, or fall back into the shadows again. I'm trapped.'

'My darling girl.' Raine enclosed Clare in her arms. 'If I had a daughter, I would have wished her to be just like you, but above all I would want her to be content. My happy days have carried me through the years. I have loved meeting you. Our paths have crossed for a reason. A bigger power than us has brought us together and only good can come of it.'

Clare dried her tears. She wished she could believe that some mighty force had been unleashed by her meeting with Raine and would whisk her away to Happy Land, but she was too much of a realist. It had been bred in her. She was told at a very early age that Father Christmas did not exist but she was forbidden from spoiling it for more delusional children who might. Magic was not allowed to exist in the Salter household, but she had wanted to believe in its existence so very very much.

'I wish I had your backbone. Yours and Seymour's,' said Clare. 'I don't even have a wishbone where mine should be, just a floppy, useless piece of string.'

'And yet you were brave enough to say goodbye to a man you loved,' said Raine. 'I think you're a very strong woman. But you're using that strength *against* yourself, not *for* yourself. This is your life, Clare – no one else's.'

'And I know that – deep down, I do know that,' said Clare, wiping her eyes with the towel.

'Clare, release yourself from your own prison.'

That's what it felt like. As if she were in a prison, and yet in her hand was the key to the door.

'I only wish I could.'

'You will.' Raine lifted Clare's chin with her finger. 'You are too special to be unhappy.'

Raine took the edge of the towel and gently wiped the tears from Clare's cheek.

'There. That's better.' Raine's heart creaked with pain for this beautiful girl with eyes like the jewelled waters of the sea. If only she could make her believe that everything was going to be all right. Although for that to be so, they would never have to meet again.

'I'd better get back to the others,' Clare said. She lifted Albert from her knee and gave him a kiss on his whiskery cheek. 'I'll come and see you again before I go on Friday. I want to leave you with better memories of me than sitting in a wet towel crying on your shoulder.'

Raine had thought long and hard about what she was going to say. She had sworn to herself that never again would she interfere in the affairs of Ren Dullem, but she was about to break that vow. She leaned her head near Clare's ear and whispered.

'I have a secret for you. You'll know what to do when the time is right.'

Clare listened, gasped and then couldn't remember why she had drawn in such a breath. 'I'd better get back to the others. I'll come and see you before we leave,' she said, wondering if she had said that before.

Raine opened her arms, wrapped them around Clare, and kissed her cheek. 'My lovely Clare,' she said. 'Never forget how unique you are. And never let the people around you forget it either.' As they parted, she gripped Clare's hands firmly in hers. As icy as they were, they were still many degrees warmer than her own parents' hearts.

Raine closed the door and listened to Clare's footsteps retreat into silence.

'Goodbye, my dear Clare,' she said. She wouldn't see her again. The wind was bitter to the taste now. It was almost time.

Chapter 78

Lara awoke to the smell of frying bacon and eggs and her stomach rumbled. She opened her bedroom door to find May, with a spatula in her hand, standing at the oven.

'Ah, Mr Bond. You've arrived,' said May in a Russian accent. 'Fancy some?'

'Fried bacon and eggs are very bad for you,' replied Lara sternly.

'Not to mention the mushrooms and fried bread ... You didn't answer the question.'

'Of course I do.'

'You take this one, I'll make some more.'

'No, I'll—'

But May wouldn't take no for an answer.

'Oh, May, your poor face. And your poor arms and your poor leg,' said Lara.

'I'll live,' replied May, although she was very scratched indeed.

'You look as if you've been attacked by Edward Scissorhands.'

'I feel as if I have been as well.'

'Clare swimming?' asked Lara through a mouthful of egg.

'The secret door in her room is open so I expect so.'

'This is delicious, May. I don't know how I'm going to go back to early mornings – and with nothing but an espresso before lunch.'

May sighed. There were a lot of things she wondered if she could do without after this holiday: long unhurried talks with gorgeous friends, taking time to sit and feel the sun on her face, being in the orbit of Frank Hathersage.

Clare had obviously been crying when she emerged fully dressed but wet-haired from her bedroom. She'd put on some make-up but her eyes were decidedly bloodshot.

'You all right?' asked May, putting a mug of coffee in front of her.

'Yeah, I'm okay,' replied Clare, convincing no one, not even herself. 'I'm going to miss Raine so much. I'm going to miss the lagoon, I'm going to miss being in this cottage with you two.'

'We've been having similar thoughts,' said Lara, pushing the sugar bowl towards her funny-eyed friend.

'Let's not get holiday blues whilst we're still on holiday. We've got two full days to go.' May tried to jolly them along. 'Get your drinks and let's go and sit on the terrace. It's a gorgeous morning.'

They picked up their mugs and took them outside. The daft pudgy clouds did nothing to take away the heat of the day, thank goodness, even if they did get in the way of the sun's brightness.

'Oh, your poor face,' said Clare. 'That looks so painful.'

May had told them, of course, about what had happened to Frank the previous day and why she came home looking as if she had just done four rounds with a combine harvester.

'I only hope Frank is feeling better today,' said May.

'Well, it won't be his last migraine unless he tells Daisy the wedding is off,' said Clare, dunking a shortbread finger in her drink.

'Oh. My. God. What a frigging mess,' was Lara's verdict. 'Do you think he will?'

'Probably not,' said May. 'He feels too bad about the accident.'

'Imagine feeling that trapped and not letting yourself do anything about it.' Lara blew her fringe up in a gesture of disbelief. Clare didn't say anything.

'There's something else I haven't told you about Frank,' said May suddenly. 'He said ...'

'What?'

'He said that ...' May coughed. 'He had feelings for me.'

Lara huffed. 'Well, that's no secret. And I expect that having that attraction to you made him realize that he didn't have any attraction to Daisy. Am I right? Of course I'm right.'

'Well, I suppose I have my uses. Our brief interlude has at least woken him up to some home truths.'

'Can't you just move here and marry him?' asked Lara.

'Yeah, of course I can,' replied May. 'Because life is like that. Oh, I really hope Frank finds the courage to stand up to the Unwins. He's such a gentle decent man. Probably too decent. And they don't come along very often.'

May knew that only too well. She'd never been good at relationships. Her first big love dumped her when she was in her first term at university. She was single for five years then met Trev who stole and pawned most of her jewellery. Then came Barry who played very strange and cruel head-games. She was just healing from the nasty fall-out of their break-up when she met the 'kind, sensitive' Michael and thought all her best dreams had come true at once. He had left her feeling more unvalued and lonely than she ever had before.

Lara nodded. 'I wish life were like a book sometimes. At least some people get their fairy-tale endings.' She looked pointedly at Clare.

'More coffee?' said Clare, standing up with her mug. The others shook their heads. 'I do. Back in a minute.'

'What about you and Gene? Is there a spark there, Lars?' asked May.

Lara gave a hoot of amused laughter. 'Don't be daft. He's a Yeti with a foul temper.'

'You went with him to see puppies, though. And he bought you breakfast.'

'And there the story ends,' said Lara. 'Because he hates women.'

'He liked you enough to tell you he hated them.'

'Okay, then, I'm a bit too old for holiday romances,' parried Lara.

'And yet I'm two months older than you and you're encouraging me to have one,' May threw back at her. 'Always harder to take your own advice than give it, isn't it, Lara Rickman?'

'The difference is that Frank Hathersage and you have an obvious attraction to each other. Gene Hathersage, on the other hand, is about as far away from "my type" as it is possible to get.'

'Maybe that's the point,' said May. 'The types you seem to pick have turned out to be rather crap, haven't they? You even manage to make me look like a good judge of character.'

'The answer is still no,' said Lara, decisively. As if.

Chapter 79

They had a super-lazy day. May and Lara read their books and Clare cooked them all cheese and red onion toasties for lunch before going for yet another swim in the lagoon. How could Raine bear it that this beautiful water was below her cottage and she could no longer get to it? Clare pictured Raine and Seymour, young and beautiful, kissing here, maybe even making love in the sea. How lonely she must be without him.

She swam out of the lagoon into the cooler grey waters of the sea and looked up but Raine was not outside her cottage this time. In the hazy distance was a container ship on its way to a far-flung shore. How weird it was that so much weight could float, she suddenly thought. The sea really was a thing of mystery. She had often wished she could see the bowls of every ocean, lake and loch completely drained, yielding up their secrets: the treasures, the bodies, the shipwrecks. Even the creatures that had never yet been seen by human eye – new varieties were being discovered all the time, so maybe sea serpents really did exist. And the Loch Ness monster. And mermaids. Maybe some of those sightings of manatees and dolphins were actually the real thing. Though surely even Lara with her specs off could tell the difference between a woman with a tail and a rather plump sea-lion-type animal or a fish with a long nose squirting water out of the top of its head?

You might have had sisters had it not been for me. Raine's voice slipped into her reverie. She had been talking to her friend Gladys when Clare was outside the tunnel door. A picture of the young Raine flashed again in her head. A Raine with long golden hair, the face of an angel ... and the tail of a fish. Wouldn't that just be magic if it were true?

Lara had just finished the last words of her novel when Clare arrived on the terrace.

'Good swim?'

'Lovely,' Clare replied. 'I'm going to miss the lagoon so much. If I die, will you have my ashes sprinkled there?'

'Shut up,' said Lara. 'That's morbid.'

'I'm serious. Ask Gene if he'll let you.'

'Nothing is going to happen to you, Clare Salter. You're going to go home, conquer the world and die a very old lady in the Ritz.'

Yes, one of those old dears who are rich, alone and cared for by strangers, thought Clare, swallowing hard. Not dissimilar to Raine.

She hadn't been able to get the picture of Raine out of her head since she thought of her as a half-woman. *You might have had sisters had it not been for me.* Then May's voice: *If there was a run of boy births it was because a mermaid was in nearby waters.*

Then she heard her own voice: *Clare Salter, even with your over-imaginative delusions, please get a grip.*

'Pub, anyone?' asked May. 'I know it's a bit early, but we could get some food there and—'

'Sold,' said Lara. 'I'll get my shoes.'

'Let me put some more make-up on first,' said May, going into her bedroom. She was conscious of the scratches as well as her scar now. She couldn't do much about the swelling, but at least she could make herself look a bit less like she'd had a fight with the heavyweight champion of bramble bushes. As they passed La Mer, Lara found herself looking up the path to see if Gene's truck was there. It was. She wondered what he was doing; if he was carving or eating or making things ready for Gracie the greyhound's arrival. She hadn't seen him today at all, but she had found herself thinking about him quite a lot. Her thoughts had drifted off in his direction when she was reading and she'd had to start at the top of the screen again. Going out to breakfast with a man was something she had never done before. Or picking out a puppy. And no man had ever made her a crutch. Come to think of it, no man had *made* her anything. Except cry. She was shocked to think that she might actually miss Gene Hathersage. Just as well she wasn't staying in Ren Dullem for any longer. Her heart was obviously looking to stuff up the wound it had suffered with any big old hairy rag.

The sun was still blazing on that late afternoon. The strange clouds in the air were mere wisps as if whatever machine was producing them had run out of materials. So, for once, the sky was a barely interrupted mass of blue. The lemon-coloured honeysuckle on the crumbling cottages was releasing its sweet, heady scent. Lara wished she could bottle it and uncork it whenever she felt the need to teleport her brain back to this lovely, blissful, lazy day. May inhaled it and felt a pang deep inside her, as if it had poked an old memory of playing swing-ball with her dad in their Leeds back garden whilst her mum potted plants. Clare took it in and thought of the cottage she and Lud had one day been going to buy beside the sea: covered in honeysuckle and pink roses.

They ordered three steak and ale pies, mash, gravy and peas. Three gargantuan portions arrived.

'I don't care if Daisy Unwin comes in, I am not leaving this before I have finished,' announced Clare.

'I think this is going to finish me off, not the other way around,' May said, getting ready to dive in.

Seconds later, the door to the pub opened and their three heads swung round in unison to check who it was. To Clare's horror, it was worse than seeing Daisy Unwin. In strode Val Hathersage, his green eyes sparkling.

Chapter 80

'Evening, ladies,' he said.

Lara and May returned the greeting wholeheartedly; Clare mumbled. Val stood at the bar, his bottom stuck out. It might as well have had a label on it saying, *Look at this, girls, and scream for me.* But all Clare could see were the scruffy trainers, the shapeless bottom and the leather jacket. Again she saw the image of herself in her bra being shouted at by an old man. She was no Colleen Landers, she was made for lovemaking in a nice bed with a man who cared about her pleasure, who was considerate and never kept her waiting, who brought her tea in bed and who would have gone back for her shoe had it dropped off. She liked the comfort of a nice car, not the discomfort of freezing her tits off on a bike. And she derived as much thrill from that one-hundred-mile-an-hour bike ride as she would have had from eating a kangaroo's anus on *I'm a Celebrity Get Me Out of Here.*

Oh how she missed the old attentive, respectful, sensitive Lud. More than ever.

'I'm moving on, Shirley,' Val Hathersage said to the barmaid, loudly enough to be overheard by Clare. 'I'll presume this pint is on the house, then, shall I?' He was flirting with Shirley who was curling her hair around her finger. If that was an effort to make Clare jealous, it fell on stony ground. She was worth more. Much more.

'No more trips planned with Gene, then?' May asked, chewing on the crumbly pastry of her pie.

'No, why should there be?' returned Lara.

'Because there's a spark between you and, right or wrong, if you'd had a little holiday romance it would have driven that tosser James right out of your head.'

'It wouldn't work,' said Clare.

'Universal fact. Bonking another bloke does work,' May insisted.

'Trust me, it doesn't.'

May let loose a hoot of laughter. 'And how have you become such an expert, Miss Salter?'

'Because that's what I nearly did whilst I've been here and, if anything, it's made matters worse,' said Clare, watching the jaws of her two friends drop to the floor. 'Now eat up and I'll tell you the rest when we get back to the cottage.'

Clare refused to say any more on the matter in the pub, so they gobbled down their dinners, drank up quickly, bought a couple of bottles of wine over the bar from Shirley and left her to flirt with the green-eyed man with the fair wavy hair and the sticky-out bum. Lara found she could walk faster now without the crutch than with it, and virtually took the hill at a sprint. They threw themselves into the cottage, May grabbed the corkscrew, Lara found the glasses. Once they were all sitting with a red wine in front of them, Lara gave Clare the signal.

'Shoot.'

'The guy in the pub who was flirting with Shirley is Val Hathersage,' began Clare.

'Oh.' May was surprised. 'He isn't much like his brothers, is he?'

'And the reason I didn't want to talk about it in the pub is . . . he's the one I've been seeing on and off.'

May and Lara looked dramatically at each other.

'You wouldn't do that behind Lud's back,' said Lara. 'No way.'

Clare decided the time was right to tell them the rest. 'What I also haven't told you is that Lud and I finished our relationship just before I came on holiday.'

'Oh, Clare.' Both May and Lara broke into a symphony of sympathetic noises.

'It was my choice. Lud got the chance to go to Dubai and be mega rich and important at the same time as Blackwoods and Margoyles offered me the partnership. It wasn't fair on him. He wanted me to go there with him and I couldn't turn the job down. So I thought it would be better if we ended things.'

May moaned. 'Oh, this is awful. You should have told us.'

'Well, I'm telling you now. I had to finish it with Lud. I felt second best to his work.' Clare shrugged. 'He didn't exactly fight to get me back, so I reckon I made the right call. So when we came here and this green-eyed man started paying me some attention, I suppose my damaged ego was flattered. We only kissed. Although, in my head, I did quite a bit more.' And she let loose a laugh that had nothing to do with humour.

'So when you told us you were popping out for some milk and taking an hour over it you were with him?' said Lara with a lascivious smirk. 'You dirty minx.'

'Yeah, precisely. That's exactly what it felt like. Dirty and not in a good way. It's not for me, all that risking my life on the back of a motorbike and snogging in woods.'

'You did nothing wrong, though,' said Lara. 'You were single, he was single. You weren't hurting anyone.'

'I hurt my bum on the forest floor,' grumbled Clare, making the others chuckle. 'Forget all that rubbish you read in romance novels about it feeling like a velvet cushion on your back, it doesn't. I can't get the squirrel crap out of my skirt and I'm sure I've still got an acorn up my jacksy.'

May was laughing so much she got a stitch.

'And that's how I really lost my shoe – it fell off when I was on his bike and he was taking corners like bloody Barry Sheene.'

'Stop, Clare, I'm going to wee myself,' gasped May.

'Ah, so it didn't fall off a cliff.' Lara punched her playfully on the arm. 'Liar liar, pants on fire.'

'I don't think Casanova has anything to worry about. I think Mrs Hathersage gave him the wrong name,' drawled Clare. 'Narcissus might have been more appropriate. Yep, I'm proudly on the reject shelf with you two.'

Lara filled up their glasses. 'Here's to singledom then, girls. And friendship. We might not have men but we've got each other.'

And, that, at that moment, was all any of them needed.

Chapter 81

Joan switched off the light and turned her head into her pillow. That was it, then. She needed to return to plan A: seduce Edwin Carlton, get him to marry her and leave her his fortune. There was no world-exclusive scoop that would bring her a huge wodge of easily earned wonga and save her the effort of having to whore herself with another old man.

She closed her eyes and began to drift off. The facts in her notebook swirled around in her mind, roaming freely as she started to release her hold on her consciousness. Seymour Acaster, 1928, rain and reines and Raine. Sirens and ships and thirteen men sewn into a tapestry in the library. Dolphins rescuing sailors, incompetent accountants paying out stipends to widows. R. Rain. Reine de la Mer. Queen of the Sea. The tapestry . . .

Her eyes snapped awake. The tapestry. Could that tell her anything she didn't already know?

Joan sat up in bed. Now would be an ideal time to go to the house and see. Lord Carlton didn't have a burglar alarm, just a panic button at the side of his bed, and he would be fast asleep. He went to bed at nine and it was after midnight.

Quickly Joan dressed, in black to be on the safe side. She collected the huge prehistoric torch from the kitchen shelf, picked up the key for the back door of the manor house and stuffed her camera into her pocket. She stole across the grass so her feet wouldn't crunch on the gravel, and also to avoid stumbling over any of the stone planters that were dotted around. She inserted the key into the lock and turned it as slowly as she could. Every slight sound seemed amplified by a thousand decibels. The door squeaked as she pushed it open by tiny degrees and made as much noise on the way back to the jamb. She stepped carefully over to the library and tried the door, but it was stiff and needed a firm hand. She winced as the door whined open; luckily it shut silently. Now she could switch on her torch to full beam. The tapestry was too high, though, and she needed to get up close and personal.

A ladder was fixed to a rail that ran along the wall of books to give access to the higher shelves and the tapestry above them. It was presently situated in the middle and she just knew it was going to make a noise like a banshee on heat when she pulled it across. Oh, for some WD40. The ladder was stiff and needed a hefty tug to set it rolling, resulting in an ear-grating squeal. Joan's heart leapt into her mouth. But then it glided smoothly to the end and she climbed up, the torch stuffed down her top.

The images in the tapestry were crudely drawn. She pulled herself along, shining the torch on the picture. The 'action' started in 1850 – Anne and Henry Carlton married. What a pair of mingers. It had to be an arranged marriage. In the next frame a baby was born but it was sewn into an angel's arms. Not good news, then. There was another date, which she couldn't make out, and a woman with her arms crossed and looking a bit dead. Joan pulled herself along past a tapestry semblance of Carlton Hall and some men with large skinny dogs, obviously hunters. More married people, another baby . . . blah blah. And now we come to the headline act, she thought. She smiled, seeing the half-submerged boat. Fish were leaping out of the sea between thirteen male figures – some in the air having just leapt off the boat, others in the sea. The words *Reine de la Mer* could just be made out but only because they were picked out in holes. Someone had removed the stitching.

Joan pulled herself along to find a large blue dolphin emerging from the sea. She pulled further on. Thirteen men were standing in a line, a golden light behind them. And there the tapestry ended.

She rolled herself back to the boat part again. There was something not right about that dolphin. She put her fingers on it and found that it stood too proud and was sewn with a thicker, wool-type thread that wasn't as faded as the rest of the tapestry. This was added later, she surmised, poking at it. Then she nipped it to see if it could be pulled off, but it was sewn firmly. She felt about herself for anything sharp; the only thing she could find was her hair slide. She used it to saw the middle of the threads but they weren't giving. Then one thread broke. This was taking some time, but it was working. With renewed vigour she sawed again and more threads snapped. There were hundreds of them so no wonder the dolphin bulged. Someone had gone to a lot of effort to cover whatever lay beneath the dolphin.

Back and forth the edge of the hairclip sliced into the threads until they were all severed. Joan pulled out as many as she could then she lifted the torch to see what was there.

Reine de la mer.

Under the dolphin was a neat needlepoint figure: the top half of a woman with long golden hair emerging from the waves.

Chapter 82

Lara walked past the warning sign, with its dire threats to trespassers, thinking that Gene Hathersage was no more capable of shooting them than she was capable of joining the Bolshoi Ballet. She knocked on the door and it was snatched open. It was his natural heavy-handedness rather than an indication of how the visitor would be received, she knew.

'I brought your crutch back,' she said. 'I didn't know whether you meant me to keep it or not.'

'Well, obviously I didn't,' said Gene. 'I have such a procession of short women falling down holes here that it's bound to come in handy again.'

He moved aside to let her in. He had a bag of well-loved dog toys on the table and also the old chewed bed which had been at the side of the wood-burning stove.

'I thought I'd have a clear-out for Gracie's arrival on Sunday,' he said, with a cheerless laugh. 'But I don't think I can let them go.'

'Why don't you take his favourite toy and bury it with him?' suggested Lara. 'Burn the rest. I always used to burn my letters to Santa because my dad told me that smoke finds its way to where it's meant to be going.'

Gene nodded slowly. 'That's a nice idea. Thank you.'

'So, should I keep this?' She held up the crutch.

'That's up to you. Are you likely to fall down any more holes?'

'God knows what's in store for me.' Lara shrugged. 'I'd better keep it, then. As a souvenir.'

She turned to go.

'Do you want a coffee?' asked Gene. 'I could do with one myself.'

Lara looked at the toys and understood that he might need some company. 'Yeah, okay, why not?'

He had a very broad back, she noted. Big shoulders and strong arms. He made rotten coffee, though. Weak as witch pee, as her nan used to say. She asked for another spoonful of granules.

'So, have you any more tenants for Well Cottage?' said Lara, nodding with approval at his second effort.

'Are you joking? At those prices? I'll leave it on until the end of the season, but I'm not holding out any hope. I have to go into Wellem to reply to those emails, and quite honestly it's a big faff. It takes me ages. Plus the first lot of tenants have put me off for life.'

Lara covered up the smile that was tugging at the edges of her lips.

'I shall miss this place,' she said. 'I'm not looking forward to going home tomorrow at all. I've got holiday blues.'

'You'll be back at work on Monday and not remember any of it,' said Gene, picking up the dog ball and rolling it around in his hand.

'I don't think I can forget this week and a half. It's been . . .' She searched for the word and couldn't find it. 'I don't know what it's been.'

'Boring, tedious, painful?' he suggested.

He had got the wrong end of the stick entirely. 'Not at all. No way. Crazy, funny, bizarre, but in a lovely way. I'll be taking a bag full of warm memories with me. As well as a crutch.'

He dropped the ball and it rolled under Lara's chair. She bent to pick it up and handed it to him. Her hands looked tiny compared to his. She imagined them cupping her face, stroking her cheek.

'I've got something to show you,' said Gene, taking a long swig of coffee and then putting his cup down on the table. 'Come with me.'

He led her out of the door and across into the outbuilding where he worked. One of his projects had a sheet over it. He pulled it off and revealed a dog lying down, paws straight out in front, head resting on them, asleep.

'It's Jock,' he said. 'If you haven't guessed. It's not quite finished. '

Lara bent down to it. She knew what a labour of love this must have been for him and, though she had never seen old Jock, she had no doubt that this must be a brilliant likeness of him.

'Oh, Gene,' she said, her voice flooded with sympathy.

'Don't start me off,' he said, pressing a thumb and forefinger into his eyes.

Lara couldn't remember closing the step that separated them but suddenly she was there, her arms around his waist, and his moved to circle hers and then he was bending and his lips were on hers. His kiss was gentle and sweet. His big hands were in her hair, then stroking her neck, then cupping her face, holding her cheek, and it was every bit as nice as she had imagined. Then he was pulling away, those hands now on her arms. He didn't need to say anything. They both knew that neither of them was ready to open up and let someone take even a cursory look inside. There was no need for apology or analysis, it was simply a kiss between kind, decent people whom life had pushed together for a brief spell. In another time, another place, there might have been more. They merely carried on as if what had happened had been a little diversionary arc from the main path and the main path had now been rejoined.

'I'll drop the keys off tomorrow before we leave,' said Lara.

'No need. Just leave them under the mat at the side of the door where you found them.'

Gene replaced the cover over the dog as gently as if he were covering the real Jock with it. Then they fell into step as they left the outbuilding.

'Well.' Lara turned to face him at his door. 'Thanks for the crutch and all the patchweed.'

'Knitbone.'

'That's the stuff.'

'Take care and drive safely tomorrow.'

'We shall.'

'Bye.'

'Bye.'

She heard his door open and creak shut, so there was no need to turn and wave; she knew he had gone inside.

But he was still there, watching her as she walked off, aware that she was pressing her finger to her lips and tracing the place where his had touched hers.

Chapter 83

Joan had hardly slept. Her brain was awash with electrical activity, ideas sparking, trying to turn an impossible suspicion into a real situation. What she had deduced was nonsense. It was a woman who had saved the thirteen men's lives in 1928. What sort of woman could do that? A mermaid? Every sensible bone in her body was telling her that it was a loony story.

But what if it weren't.

It was right up there with the Loch Ness Monster and the Yeti. Then again, how much money had sightings of them fetched? Fake as they were.

At nine o'clock exactly, Joan started ringing newspapers: the *Mail*, the *Sun*, the *Telegraph*, the *Mirror*.

'I think I've got a story,' she told the switchboard operators. 'And I want to know how much you'd pay me for it.'

She was careful not to give away her location or too many details, but she had always been very good at teasing.

'Have you got cast-iron evidence and photographic proof?' each of them asked.

'I've got a lot of photographs to show and I'll have everything else you need by tonight.'

Annoyingly, they didn't sound as interested as she had thought they would be. They clearly thought she was one of many nutters who rang and claimed to have seen the ghost of

Anne Boleyn in their cellar or Elvis in a chip shop. In a hissy fit of pique she rang the *Sunday Enquirer*, a sensationalist publication, and was delighted to find that they were more than keen.

'You think a *what* is living in your village?' asked the reporter to whom the switchboard transferred her call. He was obviously writing notes as they were talking. She could imagine manic Teeline squiggles.

'A mermaid,' said Joan. 'I know what that sounds like. But I'll be able to prove it by the end of today.'

'Where are you?'

'Down south, that's all I'm telling you.' She'd withheld her number. They wouldn't be able to tell.

'Cornwall, by any chance?'

The mermaid capital of the UK. Nice try.

'Near,' lied Joan. 'What would you pay if I gave you the story?'

'Two thousand.'

'You're insulting me. I'm putting the phone down n—'

'Wait . . . wait . . . Look, if you're willing to give us a world exclusive . . .'

'I am.' Joan enjoyed hearing the panic in the reporter's voice. World exclusive. That sounded very big and very thrilling. And very full of money.

'And you can definitely get photos?'

'Yes. And they'll pass any scientific test you care to run them through.'

'Well . . . *if* it all checks out . . . and let's face it, love, you'd need some serious proof, but if you had it – well . . . you could more or less write your own cheque.'

'Then I'll be back in touch with you first thing in the morning,' she said, and as she was putting down the phone she could hear the reporter once again pleading with her to wait.

Twenty-four hours would make him even keener.

*

Joan didn't turn up for work that morning nor did she bother explaining where she was. If need be she would make up some excuse about feeling ill and having to go to the doctor. She didn't want Gladys alerting anyone to where she might be going, pre-warning R – whoever or whatever R was. She took the back road into the village and wondered what on earth to do next.

She tried to get a coffee from the man in the kiosk by the square but the old bastard waved her away again, refusing to serve her. Fuming, Joan walked down to the harbour front. This damned place – she couldn't wait to stamp it and all its stupid inbred people into the ground. She hoped that whatever scandal it was covering up was big and dirty and splattered them all with shit.

She followed the course of a seagull which seemed interested in her and she shooed it away, just as the coffee man had shooed her away, in case it crapped on her hair. And as she was look-ing up, she saw it: the cottage on the headland. On *top* of the headland. *High* up. It couldn't have been more obvious. It was the only house she hadn't looked at so it had to be that one.

How did one get to it, though? She decided to head up the hill first, then take any turning to the left and see where it took her.

Chapter 84

You might have had sisters had it not been for me.

If there was a run of boy births it was because a mermaid was in nearby waters.

Raine.

Apparently the village was named after the mermaids that once lived in the sea so they wouldn't sink the fishing boats.

Reines de la Mer.

Queens of the sea.

Raine.

He said Seymour had committed a sin against God that would not allow him to be included on church land.

Seymour was cursed in marrying me.

Clare awoke with a start, feeling that she was drowning in the lagoon. She could feel her body floating downwards and in her dream she had long hair that swirled around her face in the water. She sat bolt upright and thought about the mad dream she had just emerged from. She would go and visit Raine today and they would laugh when Clare said that she'd had a dream about her, about Raine being cursed by Reverend Unwin because she was a creature of the sea and not a real woman.

Clare walked down the hill in order to get fresh milk. When she turned the corner Val Hathersage was leaning against one of the trees in Spice Wood, smoking. He looked very handsome, as always, but her pupils weren't dilating.

'Ah, it's the witch,' he said, his green eyes glinting, no doubt hoping to excite her.

'Good morning, Mr Hathersage,' she said. 'How are you today?'

He caught her arm as she was about to pass.

'Whoa, whoa, there. Why didn't you say hello to me last night in front of your friends? Am I your dirty secret?'

Got it in one. 'No, I was busy talking; you were busy chatting up Shirley.' She instantly regretted saying that because it made her sound needy and jealous, and she was neither where he was concerned.

'Did you hear me say that I'm moving on?'

'I did. Where are you going?'

'Ireland. To try my fortune.' He grinned and tried his knicker-melting smile again, to no effect.

'Want to go into the woods, lady?' he asked, with an Irish accent.

'Erm . . .' Clare scratched her head. 'I think I'll pass.'

'Sure now? I'll have you screaming my name out so loud they'll hear you in Whitby.'

'Thanks, but I'm going for milk. The others are waiting for me,' said Clare, although she doubted that Val Hathersage would cut the mustard in the bedroom. He wasn't considerate out of bed, he was hardly going to be a love god in it.

'Good luck, Val. Enjoy Ireland.'

He rubbed his hands together and grinned. 'With all those colleens waiting for me, I just might.'

Clare didn't know if the word was deliberate or not, but, then again, she didn't care.

When she came back up the hill, he had gone. She noticed a slim woman with long brown hair and a handbag over her shoulder walking into the wood. A visitor for Raine, thought Clare, unless it was one of Val's conquests who was off for her rendezvous in the woods. She tittered to herself and carried on, wondering why, when she opened her mouth, she could suddenly taste something bitter in the air.

Clare had a coffee and a big fluffy omelette with the others and then went down for a swim in her lagoon. She was crying by the time she reached the bottom of the steps, but down there she was well away from the earshot of the others. They would have been devastated to know she was so depressed. She could only admit to herself that she knew how Frank Hathersage felt: snared in razor wire. Remaining trapped in it would kill them both; yet breaking free would cut them to ribbons. And, worst of all, they had coiled every strand of it around themselves.

Raine left Albert safely in the house. She kissed his old head and patted a throw around him. He didn't wake up to return the goodbye.

Raine opened the door and the wind rushed at her, eager with its welcome. She reached behind and unfastened her long snow-white hair so it flowed around her like a wedding veil. She lifted her head to the sun and smiled.

'I am going home,' she said to herself.

Slowly she wheeled herself to the front of the house and she swept her old jewelled eyes across the vast expanse of sea. The waters were wild today, rising and foaming in jagged peaks, the waves pushing and jostling with each other. Just as they had been on that day all those years ago when she looked up and saw the massive dark shadow of the boat, heard the creak and snap of its mast, felt the vibrations as its great body plunged down. Splashes, cries, flailing arms, thrashing legs – their hair floating around their heads like angels as they descended to her. *It's raining men*, she had thought. *It's raining men*.

She breathed in deeply, and the bitterness stuck to her tongue like nettles to the skin. She felt a movement behind her. Raine did not turn as she spoke.

'I've been expecting you, Joanna. How clever of you to find me.'

Clare didn't want to go back up the steps, knowing that packing to go home awaited her. Home. She let loose a mirthless laugh and it echoed around her in the cave as if taunting her. Home was where the heart was and her heart wasn't there in the trendy flat with the expensive furniture and luxury kitchen. It was lost, floating around, looking for a nest to settle in and be warm and looked after.

The blue-green waters of the lagoon beckoned her back. *Don't go yet. Stay, just for a little while. Enjoy. Think of nothing but the water.*

Clare slipped back into the pool and, for the last time, let the waters take away the heavy load that threatened to weigh her down and crush her.

Chapter 85

So this was R, then. Raine? Raine de la Mer? A shrivelled old woman in a chair. That rhymes, Joan snickered to herself. She hadn't a clue what was going on here but something was. How did she know her name for a start? Big-gob Gladys, no doubt.

'Hello,' said Joan. 'How very nice to meet you at last, Mrs Acaster, or can I call you Raine?'

Raine did not reply. She sat with her short, stubby hands clasped in her lap, her long, fine white hair loose and blowing around her, her old crocheted blanket covering her legs. She studied Joan with her clouded blue eye and her emerald-green one. She was not afraid of this woman. But this woman should be afraid of her.

'Raine? Raine de la Mer?' asked Joan. 'That is who you are, isn't it?'

'That is my name.'

'Surely not a *reine de la mer*?' Joan put on an exaggerated French accent. 'A *sirène*. A queen of the sea.'

Raine studied her, this dark-haired woman whose features were twisted into a cruel but fascinated smile. She had always wondered how the final act would begin. She found herself slightly amused that this woman thought she had the upper hand. Raine knew how this scene was going to play out. Joan Hawk did not.

'What do you want?' Raine asked.

Joan scrutinized the old lady with blatant interest. Her skin was like leather, her lips full and pale – and those eyes. Joan's hands, holding her camera, were trembling with the anticipation of what one single photo of this woman could mean to her life.

'I want to know what you are,' she answered eventually. 'I want to know why, because of you, Ren Dullem seems to be such a screwed-up place? Why are no girls born here? Why does everyone freak out if I ask questions about anything connected with you? Why do you live up here like a queen bee? It's because of you that the village has closed in on itself, isn't it? Why would it do that? Why was your husband buried outside the churchyard? Is it because he married a *thing*?'

Raine was composed and calm. Her old hands lay in her lap, one over the other. 'And then what will you do when you know all the answers to the questions you have asked?'

'I'll go. I just want to know.' Joan smiled.

'No. You'd turn Ren Dullem into a circus. You'd make a mockery of all those people who closed ranks around me. You'd kill the village more than I ever did.'

'I need to see.'

Quick as a flash, Joan reached down and yanked off Raine's blanket – then she stepped back in astonishment.

'What the fucking hell are you?'

'You know what I am. You worked it out and now you want to parade me in front of everyone, don't you? For money, of course for money. That's what has always driven you, isn't it, Joanna? And this would be the big one for you, wouldn't it?'

'Of course for money,' Joan agreed. There was no point in denying it. She lifted her camera, pointed it at Raine and said, 'Smile.' *Click.*

Joan was heady with euphoria. Ren Dullem hid itself away to protect this? Jesus Christ, she was going to be rich and famous beyond her wildest dreams. *Click.* TV appearances, books, maybe even a film. They could devote a whole section in Ripley's Believe It or Not to Raine de la Mer. *Click.* There would be merchandise. *Click.* Worldwide tours. *Click.*

Joan was almost drunk with joy now. Her hands were becoming sweaty. The stupid old woman was just sitting there, looking deformed, letting Joan snap away with abandon, as if all the fight in her had gone.

As Joan wiped her right hand on her trousers the camera left her slippery hand. She bent down to catch it and missed. Before her fingers could gain hold of it she felt the ground rumble as Raine wheeled towards her. It was too late to step aside. Raine carried Joan forward with her, until there was no more ground for the chair to wheel upon.

I am going home.

This can't be happening, Joan thought, struggling uselessly against the grip of the old lady's vice-like hands. Down they plunged through the air, as if someone had slowed down time. Joan's scream was lost under the salty waters of the sea.

Clare could see Raine sitting in her chair. She waved, but Raine was looking straight out to sea. She opened her mouth to shout, then the visitor she had seen in the wood appeared at Raine's back so she didn't. They looked too close to the edge for comfort.

The wind was building today. The waters were spiky and unfriendly. Clare turned back to the cave entrance and took one last look behind her to see Raine and her visitor gone.

Chapter 86

The afternoon was a glum one. Packing didn't take long, but it was a weighted symbol of the end of their holiday. A holiday which hadn't turned out at all as expected, but was better for that.

'Let's go to Jenny's and have something to eat. And if Daisy Unwin is in there, sod her. I'm not leaving my cheesecake for anyone,' said Lara, zipping up her case with a flourish.

'I'm in,' replied May. 'Jesus, I feel pathetic. I didn't think you got holiday blues once you grew up.'

'We don't take enough holidays to know,' said Clare, unhooking her bag from the kitchen chair. 'Come on.'

Down the hill Lara tried not to look at La Mer to see if the truck was there, but failed. It was. He was in. In another time and place maybe she and the hairy Hathersage brother might have just got it together, she thought, remembering his kiss. It made her head go light and both legs weaken. *Que sera sera.*

Clare didn't even look aside at Spice Wood. In her head it had already been demoted from its status as possible location for passion to a place merely full of trees.

Jenny buzzed around them like a portly bee when they entered.

'I'm so glad to see you again,' she said, heaping apologies

their way. 'I'm so sorry about yesterday. Whatever you have today is on the house.'

'Don't be daft,' May replied. 'You'll never run a business that way.'

'What is it with Daisy Unwin that makes everyone so damned scared of her?' Lara wanted to know.

'I think it's a hangover from schooldays,' Jenny explained. 'There weren't many girls there and they tried to keep in with her so that she wouldn't bully them. She used to poke fun at me because I was fat. She won't soon. I've been dieting. Three stone off so far.'

'Well done, Jenny,' cheered Lara. Jenny was such a lovely person with a real bonny, smiley face. Daisy really was a horrible cow. She was hardly Twiggy herself.

'Well, I don't need to see a menu,' said May. 'I want exactly the same as I had yesterday.'

'What's going on out there?' Clare pointed her finger at the window. People were running around, knocking on each other's doors, a stream of them racing past the café and up the hill.

Jenny was on her way to the door when the ice-cream man-boy crashed through it.

'It's Raine,' he said. 'She's missing.'

Chapter 87

Infected by the panic, Clare rose to her feet, all thoughts of food forgotten. The others followed her up the hill and through the wood to High Top, where a mass of villagers had gathered.

There was a large lady standing on the cliff edge, her hair escaping her tight bun in the strengthening wind.

'Her chair has gone,' she was saying through her tears.

Clare came forward. 'I saw her earlier.' People turned to her. 'I was swimming. She was up here. She had a visitor and then, maybe a minute later, they weren't there any more. I presumed they'd gone back into the house because it was breezy.'

The lady with the bun strode forward and her hand fell on Clare's arm. 'What did he look like? This visitor?'

'It was a she. I saw her earlier as she was going through the wood. She was slim and wearing dark-blue trousers and a red top, I think. She had long brown hair. Very slim.'

Clare felt the woman squeeze her arm more and more tightly as she spoke. Her body became rigid with tension.

'Joan Hawk,' said the woman, releasing Clare and dropping her head into her hands. 'What has she done with Raine?'

'They've gone for the boats,' came a shout from behind.

One of the crowd had picked up the camera and now he beckoned at the sad lady with the bun to come over.

'Dear God,' she said, viewing the collection of photos which the camera held. 'She unpicked the tapestry ... Oh, my ... Gravestones, ledger entries, my goodness, that's the will ... She even took the blanket from Raine. There's no doubt, no doubt at all what she was up to.' She was shaking her head, crying. 'I knew she was evil. Pure evil.'

'We need to destroy those pictures,' said Mr Hubbard at her shoulder. 'They must never fall into the wrong hands.'

Someone showed him how to take out the memory card and Mr Hubbard crushed it under his foot. Then they threw it, and the camera, into the sea.

'I need to take Albert,' said the lady with the bun, picking up Raine's blanket from the ground and inhaling the dear scent it carried. 'Someone find me something to carry him in, please.' Then she turned to the quietly sobbing Clare and took her hand. 'Raine thought very highly of you,' she said. 'Thank you.'

May, Lara and Clare joined a slow procession back to the village. A sadness had descended on the place like a pall of grief. The harbour was full of small boats, all out looking for Raine. She could only be in the sea. They went back to Jenny's café.

'I'm so sorry about your friend, Clare,' said Lara, giving her a squeeze. 'I'm not quite sure what's just gone on, though. Who's Joan Hawk?'

'I honestly don't know.'

'I hope they find her,' said May. 'Poor old lady.'

Clare wiped her eyes. Then she leapt up from her seat.

'Oh my God, I think I might know where she is. Get the boats to come around the cove to the lagoon.' And she ran up the hill as fast as her legs would take her.

Chapter 88

She was there. Clare saw her curled up, as if sleeping, at the bottom of the lagoon. Through Clare's blurred vision, Raine's hair looked golden, shifting gently in the water as if nudged by a gentle breeze. The years had been stripped from her, her skin was plaster-white, her hands long and smooth. Fully clothed except for her shoes, Clare dived into the blue-green pool, swam to the bottom and wrapped her arms around her lovely friend, until she needed to surface and breathe.

The boats sounded their approach. Clare brought Raine reverently towards the lip of the lagoon. First on the scene were two small boats, one steered by Gene Hathersage, the other by Frank.

'I can't lift her,' said Clare.

Frank instinctively held Gene's boat still whilst he leaned over to take her from Clare's arms. Above the water the image was gone and Raine was a lifeless old lady, deformed, gnarled and so very, very precious to them all.

'I've found her chair,' shouted someone from a nearby boat. 'No sign of any other person, though.'

'The coastguard is on his way,' was called in reply.

Frank helped Gene lift Raine into the boat. He handed over

a blanket and Gene placed it respectfully around her, holding her tenderly.

'Hang onto the rope, I'll row you in,' said Frank.

'If you want to stay on in the cottage, just do,' Gene said to Clare. 'Long as you want.'

'Thank you,' she said. 'Thank you, Gene.'

Chapter 89

The rest of the day passed in a blur. Clare and May and Lara went over things a million times as they sat in Jenny's cafe at the nice table overlooking the sea. Clare told them all that she knew about her lovely friend Raine and they let her talk.

'I know what I saw.' Clare was adamant. 'I wouldn't have believed it but I saw her with my own eyes in her lagoon.'

It was harder for Lara and May to accept what Clare was telling them: that the old lady called Raine was a mermaid. The villagers of Ren Dullem obviously wanted to believe it, whether it was true or not. Then again, people liked to believe in mysterious things and beings. They wanted the Loch Ness Monster to be real, along with spirits and UFOs. They wanted to trust that magic existed. But people were also gullible – didn't Anna Anderson fool hundreds of important people that she was Anastasia Romanov?

'I'm staying for a couple more days,' Clare announced. 'I'll get a train back.'

'We'll stay with you,' Lara insisted. 'We wouldn't leave you. How could we – after what we've all been through today?'

'Gene said we could stay in Well Cottage,' said Clare, still very tearful. 'You won't say anything to anyone, will you? The village has come to trust us.'

'As if you need to ask!' exclaimed May. 'And even if I did

want to say anything, who'd believe me?' She didn't add that she didn't understand any of it. How could she? It was ludicrous. It would make more sense that Raine was a self-deluded old lady who had built up a myth around herself for no other reason that she wanted to be a creature of the deep. After all, only Milton Bird was alive to witness and remember first-hand what had really happened in 1928 – and he was two nuts short of a fruitcake.

Jenny brought over some fresh coffees for them. She was very red-eyed.

'She was a lovely old thing. I suppose if she had to leave us, then going back to the sea was the way to do it.' Jenny coughed and looked at Clare. 'We thought you might be the same as her, you know, with your eyes.'

Clare smiled. 'I wish.' Something flashed in her brain, a thought brushing past. But it quickly hurried off when she tried to catch it. Something Raine had told her. But it was gone.

Jenny made them something to eat. Clare picked at hers; it was delicious but she wasn't hungry. Not even the cheesecake could tempt her.

'How can we go back to normal life?' asked Lara, as they eventually left.

'I don't know what normal is any more,' replied Clare.

Chapter 90

Ren Dullem was a solemn place the next morning. Even with the absence of those stupid clouds and the sun bright in the sky, the gloom was almost tangible. May, Clare and Lara didn't really know what to do with themselves. Lara drove them all into Whitby in an attempt to cheer Clare up. It didn't work very well, especially when they decided they ought to shop for something to wear at the funeral as their holiday wardrobes consisted of jeans, T-shirts and a few floaty summer dresses. May forced Clare to eat fish and chips at a harbour café because she hadn't had anything for almost twenty-four hours. When they got back to Well Cottage Clare didn't even want to go down to the lagoon. She had been trying not to cry all day but her eyes had been leaking continuously.

'Do you think we should go to the Crab and Bucket and see what's happening?' suggested Lara.

Clare nodded. She put on some make-up but it couldn't disguise her red, puffy eyes. And, really, she didn't care.

The Crab and Bucket was fuller than usual. Only two tables weren't taken. Shirley greeted them with a sympathetic smile.

'Hi,' she said. 'Sad day for us all. Poor old Milton is inconsolable.' She tilted her head towards the old man in the corner. He was wiping his eyes with his sleeve. Today he was sporting a black armband and a red rose in his lapel, and his hat was off, sitting like a pet at the side of him.

'Please send a pint over to him,' said Lara. 'And put it on my bill.'

'Has he eaten? Send him a pie over as well,' added May.

'He's been fed, don't you worry. But I'll send him that pint and let him know it's from you,' said Shirley. 'That's kind of you to think about him.' She looked at Clare. 'Raine thought a lot about you, miss. And anyone who was all right for Raine, is all right for us.'

Clare turned away to wipe her eyes and May gave her a squeeze.

'The funeral is tomorrow at ten,' said Shirley. 'Everyone would like it if you were to join us. Someone was going to call up to Well Cottage to ask you.'

'We'll be there,' replied Lara.

'Usual?' asked Shirley, pointing to the gin optic.

'The usual,' Lara said and she smiled. Lord, they really were honorary locals. She was touched.

She fished in her pocket and handed Clare a tissue. 'It's clean,' she said.

'Thanks,' said Clare. Her eyes looked even more different in colour when they were glassy with tears.

They sat at a vacant table. 'To your lovely friend Raine,' said May, raising her glass. Clare and Lara clinked their glasses against it.

'I'm still in shock,' said Lara. She didn't say to Clare though that she was less in shock that the oldest inhabitant of the village had died and more in shock that a whole community could believe the old dear was a mermaid they'd been protecting in their midst since she landed on their shores in 1928.

'Do you believe in Raine, Clare?' asked May softly.

Clare had no doubt now. Nor would she ever have. The vision of Raine under the water was something she would never forget. And even though the sensible part of her brain was telling her she had been hysterical and imagining things, she didn't want to listen to it. 'Yes, I do.'

They stayed for two drinks each but were tired as none of them had slept particularly well the previous night. They waved goodbye to Shirley and were just going through the door when Milton appeared behind them. Silently, he held out his hand to Lara and she shook it and smiled. He did the same to May. But when it was Clare's turn and she took his hand, he lifted it to his lips and kissed the back of it. That brought a fresh load of tears rolling down her face.

'Goodnight, Milton,' she said. 'We shall be there tomorrow. To say goodbye with you.'

He turned and went back to his seat, his shoulders weighted, his gait a little unsteady after all the pints of beer which people had been sending over. Whatever she was, Raine de la Mer had been queen of his heart for many years and his loss was huge.

Chapter 91

'I'll catch you up,' said Lara to the others, as they were about to pass La Mer. 'I'm going to take Gene Hathersage some money for staying this extra day.'

His truck was in the drive and she felt her spirits lifting at the sight of it. She knocked lightly and he opened it with his usual unconsciously aggressive snatch.

'Hi,' she began. 'I came to pay you—'.

'There's no need,' he replied. He did not stand aside to let her enter.

'I insist,' said Lara, wishing he would invite her inside, close the door and kiss her again.

But Gene stood his ground. 'I was going to give you some money back anyway. I just haven't got it organized what with . . . you know. I'll send a cheque on to the holiday agency.'

'Don't be silly. It was worth every penny. And we never managed to replace the wallpaper.'

'Don't worry about it.'

'I should at least compensate you for that.'

He looked at her without saying a word and she didn't know what to say either. The silence between them was palpable.

'Well, if that's all . . . Will you be at the funeral tomorrow?' he said eventually.

'Yes, and then we'll be going.'

'Right.'

'Well, thank you. Just in case we don't get the chance to say goodbye tomorrow.'

'Yes, goodbye.' Then he closed the door and Lara felt her eyes cloud. Her footsteps back down the path were heavy and slow and she was cross with her heart for feeling disappointed.

'Lara.'

She turned, hearing him say her name. He was running towards her at crash speed. When he reached her, he lifted her high then buried his head in her neck. She felt his warm breath on his skin and wished he would not let her go for a long, long time.

'I shall miss you,' he said. 'I shall really miss you. I shall think of you in your very different world and wish you lived in the same one that I did.'

Then he set her down and returned to his house as fast as his long legs would take him.

Chapter 92

The church bells began to toll at half-past nine in the morning; it was a terribly sad doleful sound. The girls headed down the hill, joining the stream of people who were filtering into the church. Everyone was in black, without exception. Milton had on a black suit, a black dicky bow at his throat and he was carrying a bowler hat. His trousers ended a good few inches short of his shoes – also black, but the effort he had made was evident. May's heart gave an excited leap to see Frank; he was looking very handsome in his black suit. Daisy was sporting a black fascinator with a blackbird on it, a net dropping over her face. She glowered at May but even she had to be on her best behaviour today.

They filed into the church. Lara saw Gene standing at the back with the younger men of the village. He too was wearing a black suit, a black tie. He looked cultured and smooth, rough and wild at the same time, with his hair flowing behind his shoulders and his thick beard, which looked more trimmed than it had done the previous night. He nodded at Lara and she returned his greeting with a smile.

The church was crammed. There were flowers everywhere. Then six men brought in Raine's coffin on their shoulders. It was white, covered in a froth of white Yorkshire roses. They set her down reverently at the foot of the altar.

Behind Lara the heavy church doors thudded shut and a
locking bar was dropped. Reverend Acaster, fully gowned, laid
his hand on Raine's coffin affectionately before speaking.

'The sea is important to us in Ren Dullem. It has fed us and
nurtured us, it has given our families a living and we have been
privileged and honoured to have in our midst one of the sea's
greatest treasures.

'We are gathered today to say goodbye to our Raine, our
friend, our *reine de la mer*. Not only did she save thirteen of our
menfolk, but she sacrificed everything she knew to stay with
the man she loved. *Illis quos amo deserviam*: For those I love I
shall sacrifice. The words carved into the headstone of her
beloved husband, Seymour. The words became just as relevant
for him when Jeremiah Unwin refused to bury him in consecrated ground because of what she was, despite the fact that
Jeremiah's life would never have occurred but for Raine.'

A grumble rippled around the church. Clearly Jeremiah
Unwin wasn't thought of with any affection.

'Raine was a humble woman, a simple woman. She had few
wants, few needs and today we are taking her home. To the sea.
Her wedding band will lie with Seymour and her ashes will be
taken to her beautiful lagoon in the Hathersage cave.'

There was a lot of sniffling in the church. Clare was crying
silently, and even the Reverend Acaster was wiping his eyes on
a white handkerchief as he spoke. May and Lara stayed quiet in
their assumptions that they were caught up in a situation of
mass hysteria. The power of suggestion was a strong and curious thing. Besides, what other explanation could there be –
except that Raine was the genuine article?

'Raine saved a man from every one of our families when she
brought all thirteen back to shore on that day in 1928,' the
Reverend Acaster went on. 'Her greatest wish was that her selfless act should not be outweighed by adverse long-term effects.
She wanted to see Ren Dullem thrive again, rise and prosper.

With her passing to the next life the debt we owed her, which she never wanted to hold us to, has been discharged. Ren Dullem is safe. Her last act was carried out to protect us, as much as her first act was.'

The reverend blew his nose loudly and had to take a few moments to compose himself.

'Now we can openly celebrate her. There is no proof she was anything other than an old lady who lived and died amongst us. Her kind are safe. If any of them still exist. We have not betrayed them.

'Remember Raine de la Mer with affection and love. As she loved us. And I urge you all to pray for the lost soul of Joan Hawk.'

Gladys's 'huh' reverberated around the church.

'Someone's daughter,' said the vicar pointedly. 'The coast guard have not been able to recover her body. Find it in your Christian hearts to wish her well on her way.

'Now let us pray. Our Father . . .'

At the end of the service, as each pew emptied, there was a general move towards the coffin. Not one person left without laying their hand on it and wishing Raine some personal, private message of affection.

'You must stay for something to eat,' said the lady with her hair pulled into a tight grey bun; the woman who had taken Albert. Apparently her name was Gladys, and Clare recognized the name. She was accompanied by an old stooped man in a black morning suit with a line of medals on his chest.

'Thank you,' said Clare. 'We'll be glad to.'

The three friends joined the stream of people who headed for the village hall from the church. The tables were heaving with refreshments. It appeared that many people had brought food and wine in honour of Raine's wake.

A waitress appeared at Lara's elbow with plates of nibbly

food: quiches and pastries, sandwiches and tiny stuffed potatoes. These had the hallmark of Jenny.

The mayor had donated crates of champagne to toast the old lady's memory. Lara allowed herself the one glass but wished she could have had a few. She didn't want to go back and sort out the mess with James. She had barely thought about him for days and now he was looming on her horizon again.

Suddenly a wheelchair barged a path through the crowd and Daisy Unwin sat, cross-armed and furious, in front of them.

'Isn't it funny that everything was okay until you three came? Suddenly Raine is dead.'

'Daisy, be quiet,' said Frank, arriving behind her.

'No, I *will not* be quiet.' She smirked, knowing she had the whole of the hall's attention. 'How dare you shout at me, a disabled woman . . .'

Then Clare remembered.

It happened almost in slow motion. Lara and May watched Clare put her plate down on a nearby table. She took three strides so that she was standing beside Daisy, then she pushed cousin Pauline out of the way, grabbed hold of the handles of Daisy's chair and tipped her right out of it onto the floor.

Daisy screamed.

'What the heck, Clare?' Lara made to grab Clare and drag her to a position of safety before she got lynched.

'She can walk,' cried Clare. 'Can't you, Daisy? There's nothing wrong with your legs. I know.'

'You can't know,' shouted Pauline. 'Only we know.'

'Pauline, shut your mouth,' shrieked Daisy.

Pauline began to stutter in a panic: 'I meant that . . .'

'Shut up, shut up, Pauline.'

'Is it true, Daisy? Can you walk?' Frank cut through to the front of the gathered crowd. His usually gentle voice was tight.

'Don't be stupid. Of course I can't. Help me back into the chair.'

'Can she walk, Pauline?' Frank bent to stare into Pauline's face.

Behind her glasses her eyes were blinking madly and her head was shaking protests. 'Of course she can't. The doctors have said she won't walk again.'

'No they haven't, you idiot,' yelled Daisy. 'They've said I might.'

'Yes, that's what I mean.' Pauline was really flustered now. 'You might walk after the wedding.'

Daisy dropped her head into her hands.

'You might walk after the wedding? When you've got Frank safely down the aisle?' Now Gene had come forward and he really did have the power to intimidate the truth out of people. He turned. 'Is that the case, Pauline?'

'I don't know,' said Pauline, on the verge of tears. She was looking at her cousin on the floor for guidance.

'If you can walk, Daisy, you'd better get up. Today isn't about you.' This was from Gladys.

'I've got a bit of movement in my leg. I was saving it as a surprise,' mumbled Daisy, her face colouring. She wiggled her foot and pretended to be in pain after doing so.

'You should be ashamed of yourself, Daisy Unwin,' said Gladys. 'I think you had better get up and leave.'

'Help me up, for God's sake,' Daisy called. Pauline bent down and tried to lift her.

'Not you, YOU.' She stabbed her finger at Frank. He didn't move. 'Francis, did you hear me?'

'I've heard nothing but your voice for a long time,' said Frank. 'You've put me through hell.'

There was a grumble of disgust as people moved away from the woman sitting on the floor and starting to sob now. They were gathered here out of respect for Raine, not to witness such a stomach-turning spectacle of self-ridicule.

May began to panic. 'Are you sure she can walk? I wouldn't like to . . .'

Lara nudged her. 'Watch.'

Ignored, the snuffling Daisy, her fascinator now over her face like a visor, made a very dramatic, puff-filled struggle to stagger to her feet. With her arm around Pauline she had to make a stiff-legged zombie limp through the townsfolk to get to the outside door. It was a walk of shame to end all walks of shame.

'How the bloody hell did you know she could walk, Clare?'

'I don't know, Lars,' she said. 'Raine knew.' A wisp of a memory came to her: Raine talking low into her ear. 'I think she told me. She said that I'd know what to do when the time was right.'

May and Lara turned to each other and raised their eyebrows. Mass hysteria? Maybe it wasn't that simple to explain after all.

Whilst Clare was talking to Gladys, May saw Frank standing alone and rubbing his neck as if his collar was chafing his skin. She walked over to him almost sick with sadness that this was the last time she would ever talk to him.

'We're going to make a move,' she said. 'Leaving with a bang. Are you all right, Frank?'

He repeated the question back to her. 'Am I all right? May, I feel as if I've been carrying a millstone around my neck and someone's just lifted it from me. Oh, yes, I'm all right. Are you? You're covered in scratches. Was that from the other day when you helped me?'

'Ah, they'll heal.' May waved her hand dismissively. 'You won't be making an honest woman of Daisy Unwin, then?'

'I don't think anyone will make an honest woman out of her,' replied Frank, shaking his head. 'Thank you.' He reached for her hand, lifted it and pressed it to his lips.

'Goodbye, Frank. Be happy.'

He let her hand go, slowly, but not slowly enough, then he walked over to his brother.

Clare finished off her glass of wine and popped it on a passing waitress's tray. In her other hand she held a brooch which Gladys had given to her. It had been Raine's, she explained, and thought Clare might want it. It was in the shape of a key.

There was such a feeling of warmth and affection in the room that Clare didn't want to leave it and return to the cold of her lonely life. As May came towards her, Clare took hold of her arm. 'Ready?' she asked.

'No,' May smiled, watery-eyed.

Lara took a last look at the dear people of Ren Dullem. Jenny was smiling, relieved of as much of a burden as Frank was. Daisy Unwin would never have the upper hand of her again. Frank was laughing and talking to Gene. Gladys was loading Edwin Carlton's plate with bite-sized chocolate cakes. Lara wanted to bound across the room and say another good-bye to Gene, to feel his cheek against hers.

'Let's go,' said May, placing a hand on her shoulder. 'Please. Let's go now whilst I can.'

Lara knew what she meant.

'Goodbye,' they chorused silently as they slipped out through the door. 'Goodbye, lovely Ren Dullem.'

Chapter 93

They dropped Clare off first, outside her flat in Queens Park.

'Good luck with the promotion,' said May, giving her a big squashy hug. 'Let us know how the first day goes.'

'You'll be brilliant. Have lunch with us soon.' Lara threw her arms around Clare. 'It's been wonderful, hasn't it?'

'Yes, yes, it has. It's been . . .' She couldn't think of the word. She didn't even know if there was one.

'You take care. And we *will* see each other outside of work soon. I promise,' added May.

Clare waved them off, managing to hold back the tears, but they flowed from her as soon as Lara's car had turned the corner. She wondered if they would ever stop.

'I'll be back at yours in less than two hours, if that's okay with you, May,' said Lara.

'Do you want me to come with you? I don't mind,' May asked, touching her arm.

'Nope. I'm a big girl. I need to do this myself. But thanks.'

They turned into May's street and when they saw the number of bouquets littering her path they thought there must have been a crash.

*

Lara pulled up outside Manor Gardens and could barely press down the brake with her foot because her leg was shaking so much.

Come on, Miss Rickman. You can do this. Think of that skinny bum. One – two – three. She got out of the car, opened the boot and dropped the two back seats to make space for her luggage, then strode across the pavement, down the path and in through the front door.

It was as familiar if she were coming in from a day at the office. It would be so easy to slip back into this life full of luxury trappings. James appeared at the lounge door.

'Darling, I've been trying to get hold of you. I've rung your phone and I rang the spa and no one knew where you were.' His arms were round her before she could put up any resistance. They didn't feel anything like as nice as Gene Hathersage's big crushing arms around her. She found it shockingly easy to keep her arms stiffly at her sides.

'I've just come for my things and then I'll be gone,' she said, enjoying the sound of strength in her voice.

'You mustn't go. I made a dreadful mistake. I have never missed anyone the way I've missed you. I love you. What can I do?'

'You can let me go and get my things.'

She walked out of his arms and into the kitchen to retrieve her coffee percolator which she placed by the front door. Then she stomped up the stairs. He followed like a hungry Labrador suspecting his master had a pocketful of biscuits.

She pulled her clothes out of the wardrobe and stuffed them into the black bin bags she had purchased from the garage on the way over. She revisited the memory of trussed-up Tianne for a second and hoped James had washed the sheets. Then again, did it matter? She wouldn't be sharing them again. Behind her, James's voice dissolved into white noise. 'I love you. I was stupid. We have something special. We'll have a holiday. Just you and me, no children.'

On cue, Keely arrived in the bedroom doorway.

'Well, look what the cat dragged back in,' she said.

'Keely, go away,' said her father. 'I'm talking to Lara.'

'No, you're talking *at* Lara,' said Lara. 'Lara isn't listening.'

'I used to clean Garth's toilet with your toothbrush,' Keely said with a smirk.

Lara froze. 'The pink one?'

'Spot on.'

'That's unfortunate, Keely, because, one: mine's black' *and placed right away from your grasp at all times* 'and your father uses the pink one.'

'Jesus Christ,' said James. 'You did what?'

'And two: I knew that you did, so I swapped it for yours.' Lara smiled.

Keely paled before her eyes. 'You didn't.'

'Trust me, I did.'

Keely ran off, retching. Lara couldn't believe she was doing this. She felt absolutely nothing for James, no ghost feelings, no worries that she was ensnared in temporary madness and would flip over any minute now into pleading with him to let her stay.

'Please, listen to me, darling. I don't just want you back, I need you back.'

'Where's Kristina?' Lara asked, spotting the overflowing laundry basket in the corner. .

'She ... er ... walked out,' said James. 'Never mind about her, I'm talking about us.'

'Ah.'

'Another au pair will be arriving soon. I promise you there won't be any extra duties.'

'Extra duties?' Lara laughed at the very thought of it. Never again would she have to wipe a bogey from her bedside cabinet or make meals that no one ate.

'Darling, please stop and think. Don't throw it all away.'

Lara whirled round. 'Throw what away, James? What would

I be throwing away? Being taken for granted? Having to look after your children, who hate me – and it's mutual, by the way, they're vile little brats. The infidelity? Oh, and the crap sex, of course. How could I forget?'

'I'll try harder. I'll spice things up. I haven't seen Tianne since that night and I never will again.'

'I, however, have been snogging someone's face off,' said Lara with a grin that would have the Cheshire Cat asking for tips. 'A nice, hunky, gorgeous wild man. Goodbye, James.' Lara dropped his house keys into his hand, picked up her bin bags and headed for the stairs. 'If I've missed anything, just throw it away. It won't be important.'

She strode out of Manor Gardens, laden like a donkey with all her possessions. She only wished Gene Hathersage had been there to witness it all. She thought he might have been proud of her.

Chapter 94

The bouquets were all in various stages of decomposition, indicating that they'd started arriving a good week ago. Worryingly, there was a fresh one by the door. Michael hadn't given up, then.

May had to push the door hard to move the weight of post behind it. Most of the items had the same handwriting – letters, cards, presents. She ripped one open – an 'I'm Sorry' card. Inside were lots of drawn hearts and I love yous. It was like a five year old's effort for Valentine's Day.

She wished Lara would hurry up; her company would be nice. The house felt cold and stale. She spotted Michael's comb on the worktop and threw it in the bin.

Then the doorbell rang three times, insistently, and she really didn't need a clue to work out who it could be. She hoped she was ready for him.

She stalled as she went down the hallway, seeing his face pressed against the glass. Her heart leapt in conditioned recognition; it was a hark back to all those times when his presence brought a flood of warm feelings to it. May took the biggest breath that her lungs would allow and opened the locked door.

'May, I've missed you.' His arms were open, ready, waiting. 'I forgot you were going on holiday. I've been out of my head. I even drove up to the spa to see you but they said that you were having a treatment. Did they pass on the message?'

May wanted to laugh. The lies just kept on coming.

'I think you should go,' she said.

'I can't. I love you. I want to marry you.'

Two weeks ago May would have married this man in a minute and yet now he was nothing to her.

'I don't love you. I don't want to marry you. Please go away.'

'I'm not giving up on you.'

She shut the door in his face, hoping he would leave. His proposal wasn't romantic or flattering. He was like an annoying mosquito and she wished she had a big enough fly swatter handy.

She had just lugged her suitcase upstairs when she heard a strange noise from outside. Someone was singing. Or rather attempting to.

You are joking, thought May, crossing to the window. There in the middle of the street, arms open wide, Michael was murdering a romantic song with his strangled falsetto voice. A couple of the neighbours opposite were standing on their doorsteps to watch, highly amused. Another had stopped washing his car to listen.

May opened the window. 'Michael, go away,' she shouted. He was holding a red rose towards her.

'Give him a chance.' This was from old Mr Wilkinson next door. He was standing beside Michael, his stick in one hand, the lead restraining his pet Labrador in the other.

'No, Mr Wilkinson, I won't,' replied May.

'A man serenading you? What's he done that's so bad you can resist that?' called the car-cleaner from across the street.

'Invent a dying wife so he can get me into bed,' screeched May. She closed the window just as Mr Wilkinson started hitting Michael with his stick and the big black Labrador started ravaging his trousers. Then she heard Michael shriek as a bucket load of dirty car-washing water completely saturated him and his rose.

Chapter 95

Clare switched on her phone and immediately columns of emails started to appear. Work, work, work, another congratulations from her father telling her that her siblings were delighted. Yeah, of course they were. She'd just raised the bar and set a new challenge for them – and they would rise to it and exceed her success, she had no doubt. She didn't scroll down any more. She threw her phone on the worktop and opened the fridge for the half bottle of white wine she knew was in there. Another email pinged its arrival. Clare sank a glass in one. Her hands were shaking.

The intercom buzzed. She hoped it wasn't a courier bringing her something to do for tomorrow.

She picked up the handset. 'Hello.'

'Hello, it's Lud. Where the bloody hell have you been?'

She threw herself on him when he walked into her flat.

'I've been looking for you. I drove up to the spa, and they said you weren't booked in. I've tried emailing you, ringing you . . .'

'It's a long story. We ended up in the wrong place and we didn't have any phone signal. Oh, it's so wonderful to see you.' Clare couldn't let him go. She breathed in the wonderful clean scent of him, held onto his familiar shape.

Lud held her at arm's length. 'Clare, I have to talk to you.'

She looked into his dear, dear face with dread. *I've met some-one and am going to marry them. I wanted you to know first.*

'I've got something to tell you.'

Clare closed her eyes against the words she knew were coming.

'I've neglected you, *Liebling*. I've been a fool. I lost sight of my priorities and I'm ashamed of that. I can't tell you how fabulous Dubai is. But I'm as miserable as hell without you. I would rather stay in London and see you. I don't want to be without you. I love you. I'm going to reject the job in Dubai so I'm back in London with you. And I *promise* that I won't even look at my phone when we are together.'

Clare burst into tears. Big, splashy, happy tears.

Lud kissed her face. 'I couldn't get you out of my head. I thought, *What are you doing, Ludwig Wolke?* You should be whisking Clare away to beautiful places, laughing, having fun. I've forgotten how to have fun, Clare. Help me remember.' And he gave her the biggest most passionate snog that she had ever had in her life.

'I've been miserable without you too,' she said when she came up for breath. 'But I don't want you to give anything up for me.'

'I'd give anything up if it means we are together again . . .'

'Lud,' she began.

Release yourself from your own prison. It was as if Raine were beside her, whispering the words in her ear, pushing a key into her hand.

'Lud.' She took a huge breath. 'I don't want to be a partner at Blackwoods and Margoyles.'

There, it was out. And it was like purging something vile and nasty that had been poisoning her.

'But you've worked for it for years . . .'

'I haven't worked for it for years for me.'

Lud understood her. He always had. He held her face in his safe, square hands. Then his phone rang in his pocket but he didn't even acknowledge it.

'What do you want, Clare? You – sexy, beautiful, darling, amazing Clare Salter. What do *you* want?'

'I want to never go back to Blackwoods and Margoyles. And I want to go to Dubai. But most of all I want you, Ludwig Wolke.'

'Then that is exactly what you shall have. Now, which do you want to do first, put the kettle on or pack your case?'

Only the rain has the right to rain on your parade.

ANON

September

Chapter 96

It was eight o'clock and Lara still hadn't finished work. She yawned as she stood at the photocopier and dictated notes into her phone while she waited for the document to be duplicated. She reckoned she would be through by nine.

'You're working late, Lara.' She saw Giles Billingley approaching. He had a very strange walk, as if he were gliding, or sliming, over to her.

'That's right, Giles,' she said, now in the orbit of his overpowering cologne. Something very expensive, no doubt, yet it smelled cheap and too sweet, like floral disinfectant on him.

'Good girl,' he said. 'That's what I like to see.' He was stroking her bottom and Lara, without thinking, whirled around and cracked his face. She felt her palm sink into his wobbly cheek, and hoped there was enough soap left in the Ladies to make her hand feel clean again.

Giles Billingley staggered to the side in shock. 'You'll pay for that,' he said. 'Don't ever waste your time applying for promotion.'

Lara was in more shock than he was. God, why did she do that? What had she done?

Why did he have to go and touch her? Who the hell did he think he was?

She was angry for all sorts of reasons and felt stupidly and suddenly tearful. Then she noticed her voice recorder was still switched on.

May was at home. She had just got in.

'Sorry, I know I promised I'd cook but that little git sprang a meeting on me.'

'May, stop that a minute and listen to this, will you?' Lara played her the recording.

'You slapped him? What for?'

'He grabbed my arse.'

'I thought so.'

'So that's my career ended.'

'You could fight him,' said May, throwing some chicken breasts in the oven.

'You know what they're like. Old boys' club.'

'Okay, then threaten them with outside exposure. Leave the damned job, get the biggest payout you can and march out.'

'And do what?' asked Lara.

'Ask Lud for a job in Dubai. Then take me with you,' May suggested. 'I need a holiday. I feel as if I haven't had one for years.'

Lara switched on her laptop. 'Taking time out made me realize how much more there is to life than work. I half wish I'd never gone, to be honest.'

'You know that's a lie,' said May She would never wish she hadn't gone, because in that place she had met a man who was her benchmark for the future. Never again would May give herself to anyone who wasn't up to the decent, kind, honest, lovely standard of Frank Hathersage. He had shown her what a real man was. Michael had given up after being beaten up by Mr Wilkinson, bitten by his dog and drenched by the bloke across the road. She hadn't seen him since and never wanted to again.

'I know,' replied Lara. 'I didn't mean it. What I do mean is that Ren Dullem changed the shape of me. When I came home I no longer fitted into my life any more. Do you know what—'

She didn't even finish the sentence before May interrupted her.

'I know exactly what you mean, love.' She knew because she felt the same.

Lara thought about Ren Dullem more than she dared to admit, even to May. She thought about Gene Hathersage thundering towards her down his path. Even more than that she thought about him picking her up and holding her. Timing really was a bummer sometimes.

There was a jingling noise heralding a message that Clare wanted to connect on Skype.

'Incoming, incoming,' Lara squealed, flapping excitedly and moving over so May could sit next to her.

Clare's merry face appeared; even her swinging black bob looked happy

'Hellooo, hellooo,' she said, waving. The others waved back.

'How are you? You look great,' said May.

'I am great. It's fabulous here. The weather is wonderful, the sea is gorgeous, Lud's fabulous . . .'

Lara grinned. 'And we are very happy for you, darling.'

'Look, I've got some very important news.'

'You're pregnant? I knew you were glowing.'

'Shut up, Lars, and let me talk, please. I've had a letter,' she said, and paused for dramatic effect. 'From Raine's solicitor.'

'Ah, and has she left you something nice?' asked May, imagining a necklace or a lovely pearl ring.

'Yes, she has actually. She's sort of left me Ren Dullem.'

Chapter 97

My dearest Clare,

I have been thinking about the conversation we had when you told me what you and your friends did for a living. I can think of no better people to restore Ren Dullem to its former glory, bringing in the new and yet keeping the old loveliness.

I have put a lot of money away over the years. The Carlton estate was very generous but I never needed to spend any of it. I saved it for my beloved village. And if you are reading this, then I am gone and with me has died the need to contain our beautiful Ren Dullem.

Will you and your friends consider the possibility of turning Ren Dullem into the flower it should be? The monies from my savings have gathered interest and should, I hope, be enough to pay you all a generous salary for at least three years, by my calculations. The Village Fund will, as I understand it, also be at your disposal.

I knew there was a reason why our paths had crossed and I die happier for knowing you whether you take up the challenge or not.

My fondest wishes to you always.

Be happy, my lovely girl.

Raine de la Mer

*

'Dear God,' said Lara. 'That's a mighty ask.'

'I've been thinking,' said Clare. 'I don't need to be there; you're the business experts. We can Skype and I can look over the figures. We could do this.'

'Whoa, whoa, whoa,' said Lara, rubbing her forehead as if that would help put all the jigsaw pieces currently floating around inside her head into some semblance of order. 'There's a lot to think about here.'

'No, there isn't,' argued May. 'You're unhappy. I am certainly unhappy. We work for other people who cream off the best of everything we do. We know what we're doing, we're very good at it and, as Clare said, we could do this. If she can leap and land safely, I'm bloody well sure we can. And first thing tomorrow, Lars, you are going to walk straight into Giles Billingley's office with your recording and tell him that if he doesn't make you redundant with a massive pay-off, you're going directly to the police and the press.'

Lara opened her mouth to bring some reason to the proceedings but found that she really didn't want to.

'Oh, bugger it, let's do it,' she said.

Don't sit inside and pray for the rain to pass when you could be out walking in it, dancing in it, kissing in it.

LINDA FLOWERS

October

Chapter 98

There was a notice pinned to the door of Well Cottage:

RISE - key under mat.

'Nice to see that nothing much has changed.' Lara grinned. 'Wonder if he's left us a luxury hamper?'

'It's a full moon again, have you noticed?' May pointed upwards. 'Just like the last time we arrived here.'

Lara looked up and smiled. Just like last time, she repeated to herself. She hoped it was a sign that not too much had changed in Ren Dullem. She couldn't bear it if it had.

She opened the door quickly to escape the falling rain and walked into the dear familiar room with its thick walls and nipple light switches. She remembered the first time she had done so, but on this occasion she didn't huff and want to swap it for a luxury log cabin in Wellem Spa. She dumped her case on the floor and went to put on the kettle.

'Same room? Or do you want the one with the secret lagoon?' asked May, shaking raindrops from her hair. She was laden with bags, like a packhorse.

'I couldn't possibly have Clare's room. She'll need it for when she comes next month. Coffee? There's no sign of a luxury hamper. We'll have to complain to the management.'

'I bet you can't wait,' May said, winking at her. 'Does he know you're here?'

'No. I didn't want to put him under any pressure.' This was a ridiculous gamble that might not pay off. Lara couldn't be sure that the gruff, handsome, big, sensitive, sexy Gene Hathersage, whom she hadn't been able to get out of her mind, would even remember her. He may have been seduced back to Colleen Landers for all she knew. So she could end up with her heart smashed into pieces. Again. She should be getting used to it by now: all her men running back to their exes. She had loved her years in London, but there was nothing for her in the Big Smoke any more. She had thought about Ren Dullem too much since she left it to ignore. Coming back to it was like a part of her was coming home.

'So they're expecting a company called RISE, personally recommended by Ms Clare Salter, to be sorting them all out, then,' said May.

'Yep. Which bag is the milk and coffee in, May?'

'Sod the coffee. Go and announce your arrival first,' replied May.

Lara didn't wait to be told a second time.

Chapter 99

The sign to warn trespassers off the property was still hanging on the gate to La Mer, but it had been joined by a new one:

Beware of the dog

Painted at the bottom of the sign was the silhouette of a three-legged whippet.

Gene's truck was in the drive. He was in. Lara's heart began to bounce around inside her. Despite the heavily falling rain, she could only walk slowly towards the house, worried now that she might not find him alone. Or what if he opened the door, saw her and looked horrified?

When she reached the door her hand came out to knock, then pulled back before it made contact. Her jaw was tight with anxiety. Oh God, oh God. She stretched out her hand again and knocked quickly.

The door was yanked open with his customary heavy hand and Gene Hathersage appeared in the doorway wielding a lump hammer. His eyes rounded to the size of crop circles.

'You,' he said.

'Yes, it's me,' replied Lara. 'I've come to ask where the welcoming luxury hamper is. We have no bread, no cheese, no milk awaiting our arrival in your cottage.'

'We? Who? I wasn't expecting you.'

'You're expecting people from the company RISE. Rickman, Salter and Earnshaw. Salter is in Dubai at the moment, though, but she's coming over for a fortnight next month, and Earnshaw is presently standing by a boiling kettle.'

'Wait.'

The door slammed in Lara's face, leaving her standing in the rain. She was confused – was that the end of the exchange? Then again, this was Gene Hathersage; what had she been expecting? Bouquets?

The door was snatched open again, just as she was wondering whether she should go.

'Had to ring someone,' he said. 'So you took up Raine's offer, then?'

'How could we not? We spent over a week redesigning the place when we were here before. It would be a shame to waste what we'd thought of.'

He nodded slowly. His hand was curled so tightly around the huge hammer that his knuckles were white. Anyone who didn't know Gene Hathersage properly wouldn't have wanted to meet him down a dark alley when he looked like this.

'You, er . . . you didn't go back, then?' he asked eventually. 'To him.'

'It was surprisingly easy not to.'

'I know. Been there. I'm glad. For you. That you didn't.'

'I couldn't have done.' *Not after you kissed me, Gene. Not after you held me. Once was enough to tell me that.*

The rain was dripping off her fringe, down her face. She knew that her nicely applied make-up would be a total mess by now.

Behind her a speeding van vroomed up the hill.

'I had to tell Frank that May was back. He was building up courage to go and find her in London,' said Gene. 'He doesn't have a lot of confidence. He didn't know if it was the right thing to do, but he was going to give it a go.'

Lara smiled. 'That's nice to hear — that he missed her. She really missed him.'

She waited for Gene to say that he had missed her. He didn't. She stood feeling awkward now outside his door. Had she called this wrong?

'It was me that recommended we honour Raine's request,' he said quietly, almost bashfully. 'I reckoned that if you didn't come back then you were happy with ... him and if you did come back then maybe that meant you might have wanted to come ... er, to come back and ... well, see me.'

'I did,' she said, her autumn-tinted hazel eyes fixing his dark dark-brown ones. 'And I wanted to see how Gracie had settled in.'

'My God, is it raining?' said Gene suddenly.

'You just noticed?'

'Yes. I only noticed you.'

'Nice line,' Lara acknowledged, her hair now totally plastered to her face.

'You'd better come in,' said Gene, at last putting the hammer down and moving aside.

'I thought you'd never ask,' replied Lara, shaking the wet drops off herself before crossing his threshold.

She walked through the kitchen to see Gracie dozing in a furry pink bed at the side of the wood-burning stove.

'She looks comfortable,' said Lara.

'She's settled in well. She's found a new home that fits her better than the other one.'

Lara raised her head to him. Like me, she thought. Oh God, why didn't he just grab her and kiss her? She was aching for him to do so. To be this close to him and not have him want to hold her was torture. She should go. If he had been pleased to see her, he would have let her know by now.

'As you might have gathered, she is the world's most rubbish guard dog,' said Gene, making polite conversation. 'She never barks when anyone comes to the door. Only when they leave, funnily enough.'

Lara swallowed hard to push down the tears rising inside her. She could fall in love with Gene Hathersage. She was halfway there already. Dammit. He was pleased to see her, but not *that* sort of pleased.

'Well, I'll witness that for myself now, then. Nice to see you again, Gene,' she said, her voice wobbly. 'I'll be away.'

'Oh, no, you won't,' said Gene Hathersage, taking her hand and pulling her into his big woodman's arms. 'You're not going anywhere.'

Two Years Later

Whitby Examiner

MAJOR AWARD FOR SEASIDE VILLAGE

North Yorkshire seaside village Reines de la Mer has been granted the national award for best rejuvenated seaside village. Reines de la Mer was known locally as Ren Dullem for many years, but has reverted back to its original name as it appears in the Domesday Book.

Lord Edwin Carlton told the *Examiner* that the success was all down to RISE, a company the village employed from its own personal budget to oversee the major changes needed to bring the village up to spec.

The founder members of RISE, Mrs Lara Hathersage, Mrs May Hathersage and Frau Clare Wolke, are equally generous in their praise. 'The village is full of wonderful people, beautiful buildings and amazing scenery. All we are doing is polishing a jewel,' said Lara. 'We have a long way to go, but the award makes us all proud that our achievements have been recognized.'

'Everyone is delighted,' May commented. 'Business is booming.'

'Our next project will have to be the school,' said Clare.

'There has been a baby boom in the village with ten girls being born in the last six months alone. Our nursery needs an extension.'

Frau Wolke, wife of international German banker Ludwig Wolke, has herself just given birth to her first child, a daughter called Regen, which is the German word for rain. The Wolkes are based in Dubai.

According to local folklore the bay was once inhabited by mermaids and today's villagers continue to uphold the claims.

'Early French inhabitants of the village named it in honour of the creatures so that they would not sink their fishing vessels,' said Milton Bird, a local inventor. 'Mermaids don't just live in Cornwall, you know. We've had them up north as well.'

Miss Jenny Dickinson, owner of the Mermaid Café, said, 'For many years no one even knew that Reines de la Mer existed so it is completely unspoiled and holidaymakers can be assured that we shall never let it lose its charm.'

'The area was renowned for smugglers but we shall never know if the myths about mermaids are true or not,' said Lord Carlton with a twinkle in his eye. 'But isn't it wonderful to believe in a little magic in life?'

Acknowledgements

Just a few million essential thank-yous I need to distribute, if you'll bear with me.

Thanks to the fabulous team behind me: my agent Lizzy Kremer at David Higham Associates, Harriet and Anne and everyone else there who sorts me out, and at Simon and Schuster: my editors Suzanne Baboneau and Clare Hey, my buddy and PR guru Nigel Stoneman, Ally Grant, Alice Murphy, S-J Virtue, Maxine Hitchcock, Dawn Burnett, Rumana Haider, Dominic Brendon, Gill Richardson, Kerr MacRae, Ian 'God' Chapman ... simply everyone. You're all a joy to work for and with – I'm lucky to have you.

Thanks to my wonderful copy-editor Clare Parkinson who reduces me to rubble with her cleverness. She's written this book so if you're not happy with it – I'll forward on her email.

Thanks to Jill Craven at my local library for her passion and devotion to the job of getting people into libraries. Jill, you've been there selflessly helping me from the beginning and I wish you a big hit of karma.

Thanks to all my readers who write the loveliest kindest emails to me. You've put many a smile on my face and made me feel that I was right to pack in the accountancy job. The world of numbers is a much safer place without me.

Thanks to P & O Cruises, and my dear friend there Michele

Andjel, for all their fantastic support and sharing their ships with me. One day heaven, for me, will be an eternal ride upon the waves with a glass of ice wine in my hand on one of your 'girls'.

Thanks to wonderful people who support my charities and supply beautiful gifts at my launches so we can raise a bundle for www.yorkshirecatrescue.org and The Well, a complementary therapy centre for cancer patients in Barnsley: Slurp.co.uk, stmoriz.co.uk, callulaglass.co.uk, Douwe Egberts coffee, Walkers of Scotland, Andy at beatsonhouse.co.uk, Jason at the Holiday Inn, Gillian at costumehistorian.co.uk, Rob Royd farm shop... and many more – you're all just brill.

Thanks to Stu at nm4s.com who looks after my gorgeous website. Thanks for making it idiot-proof which, with me in charge, it needed to be.

Thanks to my lovely friends and family for their unconditional love and support: Mum, Dad, Maggie, Traz, Cath, Tracey, Spam, Hels, Kaz, Paul, Alec, Fraz, Peter, Chris and Jude and my two lads for putting up with my bad tempers when I'm near a deadline and not hating me too much.

And last but not least, thanks to Pete – for giving me my very own happy story ending.

Welcome to Yorkshire

yorkshire.com

Win a Luxury Break at The Raithwaite Estate in Whitby, North Yorkshire

Nestled in a green valley beside the beautiful North Yorkshire coast is The Raithwaite Estate. The picturesque country retreat is set within 100 acres of breathtaking countryside and sweeping gardens, and is reached from York by an extraordinary drive through the rolling heather-covered North York Moors.

The recently renovated retreat, which opened as a hotel in October 2011, has been brought back to its glorious prime and now comprises the 45 bedroom Raithwaite Hall and a stunning six bedroom Lakehouse. The Keep, with 28 guestrooms, opened in summer 2013 as an extension of the accommodation on the Estate, while 60 individual charming cottages, tearooms and spa pods will be built in stages over the coming two years. A beautiful spa, gymnasium, sauna, swimming pool, restaurant and stylish bar complete the luxurious refurbishment in the Main Hall, establishing the property as one of the finest luxury country retreats in the North of England.

The lucky winner and a guest will be treated to a two-night stay in one of the Estate's luxurious guestrooms with an award-winning full English breakfast on both mornings. A decadent afternoon tea for two is also included in the prize, with homemade pastries, finger sandwiches, scones with clotted cream and exquisite teas from around the world.

The Raithwaite Estate, Sandsend Road, Whitby, North Yorkshire, Y021 3ST
Telephone: 01947 661661 Website: www.raithwaiteestate.com

When planning your break to Yorkshire visit www.yorkshire.com, and you can enter the competition at the address below - good luck!

RAITHWAITE ESTATE

YORKSHIRE COUNTRY RETREAT

http://pages.simonandschuster.co.uk/millyjohnson

CBS⦿drama

Whether you love the glamour of Dallas, the feisty exploits of Bad Girls, the courtroom drama of Boston Legal or the forensic challenges of the world's most watched drama CSI: Crime Scene Investigation, CBS Drama is bursting with colourful characters, compelling cliff-hangers, love stories, break-ups and happy endings.

Autumn's line-up includes Patricia Arquette in supernatural series Medium, big hair and bitch fights in Dallas and new Happy Hour strand daily from 6pm with a doublemeasure from everyone's favourite Boston bar Cheers.

Also at CBS Drama you're just one 'like' closer to your on screen heroes. Regular exclusive celebrity interviews and behind the scenes news is hosted on Facebook and Twitter page. Recent contributors include Dallas' Bobby Ewing (Patrick Duffy), CSI's Catherine Willows (Marg Helgenberger) and Cheers' Sam Malone (Ted Danson).

www.cbsdrama.co.uk

 facebook.com/cbsdrama

 twitter.com/cbsdrama

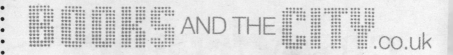